"In one character *The Bonnet Book* truly portrays the realistic and accurate experiences of America's 350,000 orphan train riders. Author Nancy Menees Hardesty perfectly captures the independent spirit of a young American woman who, like all orphan train riders, began life with seemingly insurmountable disadvantages, but who turned those disadvantages into opportunities and prevails through hard work and unabashed persistence. A delightful read that speaks to the indomitable American spirit!"

John Shontz, Project Coordinator
National Making a Difference Project
The Orphan Train Saga

"A wonderful story about fourteen-year-old Blanche Spencer and her experience traveling to St. Louis, Illinois, and Oklahoma between 1902 and 1911. Blanche's pioneer spirit, determination, and perseverance helped her become an independent, self-taught young lady. The book brilliantly illustrates the rugged life in the Midwest and Blanche's drive to be successful. The first chapter captured me with life in rural Illinois in 1902, and I hated to see the book end. I wanted to learn more about Blanche's life. It is a good read for all ages!"

Norma Lee Hackney, PhD
Director, Shawnee Hills Arts Center

"*The Bonnet Book* is a time-travel trip that takes you on a compelling read back into American history. You will experience the 1904 St. Louis World's Fair, Temperance camps, and orphan trains; meet Annie Oakley and the folks of early American small towns—all seen through the adolescent eyes of the author's grandmother, a strong Midwestern American woman. Meticulously researched and based on the original "Bonnet Book," the author's grandmother's actual diary, this book is rich with intriguing storytelling, as well as a personal journey into our fast-moving history."

Diane LeBow, PhD
President emerita Bay Area Travel Writers
Professor emerita

"Nancy Menees Hardesty shares her family history and brings us a delectable read, *The Bonnet Book*, about the trials of a young woman in the early 20th century. An exciting and compelling story, *The Bonnet Book* is an adventure tale of the author's paternal grandmother. Hardesty's attention to detail is meticulous as the story unfolds about a bustling St. Louis, Missouri, rural southern Illinois, and finding love and marriage in Oklahoma."

Cheryl Ranchino Trench, Columnist
Swinford Publications

THE BONNET BOOK

Nancy Menees Hardesty

The Bonnet Book
by Nancy Menees Hardesty

Published by Solificatio
2020 Trade Paperback Edition
Copyright © 2020 Nancy Hardesty

Cover art: Cutout from *Silhouettes: A Pictorial Archive of Varied Illustrations*, Dover Pictorial Archive Series published by Dover Publications, 1979
Cover photo: Detail of Bonnet Book diary of Blanche Spencer, Blanche Spencer Menees Family Archives
Chapter heading art by Nancy Hardesty

ISBN-10: 0-9977619-4-6
ISBN-13: 978-0-9977619-4-8

To Charles Menees,
my father and a newspaper journalist,
who loved music and taught me to write

To Mary Kay Menees,
my mother and a school teacher, who recognized the young
adult enterprise of Bonnie, saved and organized her estate
papers, and nudged me to write this book

Contents

Preface

From my early childhood until she died at ninety-six, when I was thirty-nine years old, my paternal grandmother Blanche (Bonnie) Estelle Spencer Menees was a strong and colorful presence in my life. She lived from 1888 to 1984. We corresponded almost until she died.

I never thought I would write about Grandma Bonnie. In an adult education writing program, I received an assignment that changed the course of my life. I chose to write about Blanche being a Temperance speaker as a child, wearing her signature white dress and white shoes. In that assignment, I instinctively put Blanche on the stage to present a poem she was famous for reciting, "The Drunkard," an anonymous Temperance poem, because my family knew she had done this. Blanche came to life under my pen! There she was—I saw her on the stage getting ready to recite her poem, and I felt her thoughts. It was so compelling to bring young Blanche to life that I knew I must continue writing her story.

Mary Kay Menees, my mother, had saved all significant heirlooms from Blanche's estate and written Elder Hostel reports (1991-2001) about Blanche, her mother-in-law. I soon realized I needed to do field research to broaden my knowledge of her early life. Off and on for about a year, I traveled with ninety-four-year-old Mary Kay to St. Louis and locations in Illinois, Texas, and Oklahoma.

I consider this book a work of historical fiction since there were some periods and events that could not be fleshed out by my research, and I had to rely on my instincts to fill in the details. However, I want to emphasize the care with which I assembled the historical aspects of the story:

1. The timelines and locations in the book are for the most part accurate.

2. The family names are all correct. I did, however, change the names of all others.

3. Blanche was an "orphan train child" at fourteen years of age in 1902. About 150,000 orphan children were transported across the United States on trains between 1859 and 1929 under the program of a Methodist minister named Charles Loring Brace. These children were given to families on farms and small towns in the Midwest. History later named this group "orphan train children." For further historical and current information about orphan train children see www.nancymeneeshardesty.com for several pages devoted to the subject.

4. The tiny Bonnet Book does exist and is under lock and key in my files. This 118-year-old booklet contains forty pages of hat sketches and notes, supply lists for the pony cart that are central to the story, and also other famous quotations and cooking notes. It appears to be the recipe book for Blanche's young adult life, one of her self-education tools.

5. The historic wooden hat-supply trunk exists and has been restored.

6. The January 22, 1911 letter from Austin Spencer is the only letter in the estate from this early period of Blanche's life.

7. The St. Louis 1904 World's Fair, Union Station, and other St. Louis events and places are lifted straight out of history or were part of my own St. Louis childhood.

8. The October 1910 Oklahoma State Fair chapter, "Opening Night," is pieced together from many newspaper articles and postcards of the event. One of the sketched hats in the Bonnet Book exactly matches a hat from one of the newspaper articles!

The Author's Notes at the back of the book give a more complete story of book development and historical references. The following website features much more information about the six years of research and writing of *The Bonnet Book*, including a blog: www.nancymeneeshardesty.com.

There are twenty-one blog chapters, each containing a photo. Many significant items in the story are included in the photos in the blog posts, including the following: the tiny Bonnet Book itself, the wooden trunk, the wedding dress, the Meadowbrook cart, the wedding ring, the train stations, the redbud trees, the marriage license, and the wedding park.

In addition to historical research, I relied heavily on personal recollection for the intimate details of Blanche's everyday life at the dawn of the twentieth century. My mother Mary Kay Menees, whose sharp mind is still recalling details at age 96 in 2018, and Vivian Modglin Parrish, Blanche's niece, who wrote journal entries in the 1970s, together provided the rich tapestry upon which I reconstructed Blanche's journey. In summary, the story includes factual input spanning 130 years and four generations of strong Midwestern women.

It has been an honor and a great pleasure to give voice to Blanche's story of self-education at the dawn of the second industrial revolution and her gumption and survival in the last colorful days of the Wild West of rugged Oklahoma. Blanche is a resilient Midwestern woman who rose above her childhood misfortunes and became an inspiration for my family and for the community in which she lived for the rest of her life.

Young adult Blanche Estelle Spencer

Brush Arbor
Oraville, Illinois • August 1902

Blanche could not catch her breath! Whew! She could do this, yes, she could. Her heart was pounding, *pounding* in her lean young body, as she sat on the edge of a stump, trying to gulp the hot humid air into her lungs without moving the raised flowers on her white dress. She gulped air again as she looked out across the sea of stern, tanned faces below the crude plank stage. The large crowd wilted by the oppressive heat moved paper fans back and forth in lazy arcs and listened to Reverend Larsen's droning words about God's wrath. Blanche was about to speak about alcohol. She didn't actually know much about alcohol, but somehow she understood that her words were very powerful. She knew she had a message for these folks, and it was important that her delivery reach each one of them.

On this sunny, sultry August afternoon, the dense leaves of the brush arbor overhead gave green shelter, which was very pleasant after the hot dusty road from town and far better than the nearby cornfields buzzing with insects. Sud-

1

denly, a fat yellow and black caterpillar dropped to the floor from the leafy bower near Blanche's seat and started an awkward crawl. It lumped along on an unpredictable path across the stage. She, on the other hand, as the only child speaker at the Temperance Camp, continued to sit as she had been instructed by her pa and Reverend Larsen, wearing her white lacy dress enlivened with a light blue sash and white shoes with stockings, ready to recite a poem ripe with Temperance wisdom.

She took a deep breath and focused herself, as she let the air out very slowly; she was about to begin. A fiercely competitive student, Blanche had loved memorizing this poem, and she now reveled in its recitation. From her previous performances, she knew she could roust these people out of their Saturday afternoon stupor.

Reverend Larsen turned and caught Blanche's eye. He stepped to the side. Blanche rose, smoothed her dress front and back, straightened the blue sash, and walked across the rough planks to the center of the stage. She cleared her throat as she looked at her pa, Austin Spencer, standing at the back of the shady arbor.

"My name is Blanche Estelle Spencer. I am fourteen years old." She spoke clearly and forcefully to reach the people in the back rows. "I am going to recite for you 'The Drunkard,' a poem about a farmer and his wife. Please listen closely," she said, as she tilted her head, her golden curls cascading forward off her left shoulder.

Dressed in farm coveralls and calico dresses, the country folk were hot and exhausted. Many could not read. They had no radios. There were no movie theaters. These inexpensive camping vacations, social and cultural gatherings of local families, provided welcome exposure to new ideas, new music, and new faces. For a few days they could forget their hard lives.

Whereas they would otherwise be wary of a guest speaker, the adults relaxed upon the appearance of the talented local child speaker. Blanche was a pretty girl, with high cheekbones and a lovely oval face. Up on the stage, she was a bright light, a fresh flower, a spark at the end of the last day of a long week of the Temperance Camp.

All eyes and ears were now focused on Blanche.

She began:

"The Drunkard"

Tom JONES was a drunkard
There was NO DOUBT about it.
You could tell by his nose, his coat and his hat,

From the first words, Blanche's voice went up on a minor musical note, a dissonant tone suggesting alarm. She raised her right hand with the index finger pointed up. No longer childlike, she stood tall and leaned forward with a furrowed brow, for she was about to give a warning to these weary spectators. The entire crowd snapped to attention. The paper fans stopped.

Blanche pointed to her nose, and her eyes widened. Several men in clean coveralls lowered their heads and brushed their noses.

And his ragged 'ole trousers,
Where could you match 'em
Or where find a woman to PATCH 'EM?

Women in faded everyday dresses nodded.

But the reason was this:
The poor woman couldn't
For that pair of trousers was Tom's only ONE,
So what could he do while the patchen' was done!

One ragged man, sitting in the front row, stealthily put his hands on his knees to cover the holes in his very worn only pair of pants.

One evening, cold sober, he came home to tea.
And, after a pause, "Good Wife," said he.
"There's somethin' I've missed,
And I've missed it for weeks,
Say, what has become of the ROSE on your cheeks?"

"Become of the roses, Tom,
You know where they goes.
You stole 'em to redden
The end of your NOSE!"
Tom thought for a moment, then said to his wife,
"It's wrong, and I know it to have lived such a life.

And now, my dear wife, I'll do as I oughter,
I'll go on the good temperance and drink ONLY cold water."
And now he upholds the great temperance call.
Keeps to his pledge beer, cider, and all,
And now a good temperance man he'll always

remain,
And on his wife's cheeks bloom the ROSES
AGAIN!

As Blanche recited the poem, she had every head arching forward. She widened her eyes, she spoke clearly, and caught up in her delivery, she lost all sense of being on the stage.

By the last lines of the recitation, she had soothed her voice into loving sweet tones about abstinence, clasped her hands in front of her heart, and stood, beaming, at the front of the stage. The crowd smiled with her as Blanche's message about Tom Jones sank in. Then they laughed. Some farmers threw caps and broke into loud applause. Blanche's whole face smiled, she curtsied, then bowed once again to more applause. She looked past the crowd and caught her pa's smiling eyes. Her successful performance made her feel very grown up.

"And that ends today's meeting! Thank you, Miss Blanche Spencer!" said the corpulent Reverend Larsen, as he stood, mopped his beaded brow, and continued clapping for Blanche. There was much lively chatter as the crowd stood up. Late-week attendees, who had heard of her talent from tent neighbors, rushed forward to see Blanche up close.

Blanche bent down from the stage and shook a few hands, smiling and thanking the crowd.

Her father, Austin Spencer, slim with wavy red hair, stood below the stage in front of Blanche. He now reached for her hand and swept her down onto the grass. They walked hand in hand out of the brush arbor as the crowd dispersed.

Blanche and her father headed for the campgrounds further up Rattlesnake Creek, stopping for a drink at the well of an adjacent farm as they headed to Reverend Larsen's tent. They wandered past primitive family tents, sited near the creek, which ran near the small town of Oraville, Illinois. Local families cooking dinners at campfires smiled at Blanche as she walked by.

Many families attended the Temperance Camp for a week, as a local summer vacation after grueling planting chores were done, and before crop harvest. There was lots of visiting to do, which entailed everything from swapping recipes, quilt pieces, and baby clothes to meeting new babies and finding potential mates.

The sun was low in the sky as Austin Spencer and Blanche arrived at Reverend Larsen's tent. Mrs. Larsen was setting up a crude stump table in front and pulling up three lower stump seats. The reverend had an allowance from his Temperance committee for speakers and entertainment, and in this remote location he chose to spend some of this money on getting local meals brought to his tent, as a thank-you for Blanche. Austin backed up and stood by the side of the tent, barely visible in the tree shadows. He had not been invited to these suppers but wanted to stay close by.

"Sit here," Reverend Larsen motioned to Blanche. He sat on a stump with his back to Austin. Blanche took the seat he offered, from which she could not see her pa. Reverend Larsen's cheek had an orange glow from a nearby fire, and when he turned to Blanche his dark eyes also glowed. He grinned, showing a mouth full of crooked teeth, and grasped Blanche's wrist with his sweaty fingers.

"Once again, a perfect performance, my sweet cherub," he said softly, as he tightened his grip on her wrist.

Blanche swayed back on her log seat and caught her breath. As the hairs stood up on the back of her neck, she smiled nervously. Sitting back up, she fastened her gaze on flushed Mrs. Larsen, at the stump table taking food out of a straw hamper. Blanche clenched her teeth in disgust, while at the same time her stomach growled loudly from hunger. Her wrist ached from the pressure.

At that moment, Mrs. Larsen walked up with brown paper napkins, and Reverend Larsen released his grip. Mrs. Larsen commented on how nice Blanche's white dress looked from the back of the arbor. Blanche shivered, let out her breath, and smiled.

Blanche relaxed and concentrated only on the delicious food, which was far better than her family's regular diet of porridge and frog-leg stew. The meals with Reverend Larsen, sometimes two a day, were a mixed blessing for Blanche. Her body was desperate for nutrition—for meat—and she only tolerated this unpleasant man so she could eat. Consequently, as hungry as she was, she ate only one of her two pieces of chicken, carefully wrapping the other in her napkin.

As the threesome finished, children began to scamper and catch the night's first fireflies. The heat of the day was finally slow dancing with the breeze off the creek. Austin stepped out of the shadows.

"You've become quite the public speaker this summer," he said, proudly patting her shoulder, "with all of your afternoons memorizing and our practice sessions at school. Today you had the crowd following every word! Well *done*, Blanche." He clasped both hands across his chest.

Blanche stood up and bowed her head to her hosts.

"Goodbye Mr. Larsen, and thank you for dinner Mrs. Larsen," she said and turned, tightly holding her pa's hand. She smiled as they began the walk home, which would take them out from the creek-side grove and away from the shimmering orange sun, between the two cornfields, down Ripley Road, and back to quiet Oraville. The open dirt road still radiated heat from the day. Blanche's white shoes and stockings picked up a dusting of the brown powder spraying from their footsteps, the dust sparkling like hot ashes.

"You know, Pa, I am beginning to feel confident on the stage. I'm not so afraid of the crowds anymore!" Blanche said.

Blanche was energized. Maybe it was the food. Maybe it was completing the assignment. No! She thought of the sandhill crane she occasionally saw in the cornfields. The majestic gray shadows glided over from the Mississippi River to look for grasshoppers and frogs. With great poise, they stood between the corn rows with their heads high, necks straight, looking for movement and supper.

Blanche straightened her back and neck like the cranes. She could talk to adults—she could make them applaud. She could stand in front of people and tell them a story! How lovely and exciting it was. She and her pa were becoming a team on the Temperance Camp work. Pa, the schoolteacher, worked behind the stage to find poems and teach her word inflection, and Blanche worked onstage. It was exciting to be doing something bigger than just living in Oraville—and doing it very well. She wondered if it would lead them to bigger camps with bigger stages, far from Oraville. Why, the train tracks ran right in front of their house. She and Pa could just hop on and travel to the bigger camps and learn about the bigger world. *This could be quite thrilling*, she thought. She breathed deeply with her sense of accomplishment. The textured dress shimmered, its threads catching the last light of the setting sun.

Blanche handed the wrapped chicken to her pa. Austin

stopped, leaned forward at the side of the road and hungrily ate the dripping piece of chicken, licking his fingers as he finished. He cast the paper and the chicken bones into the roadside ditch and wiped his hands on his dark threadbare trousers.

As they walked between the cornfields, Blanche heard the familiar rustle of the cornstalks. It seemed like music to her.

She and Pa walked silently past the warehouse and water tower next to the GM&O railroad tracks and toward their small white house in Oraville, just beyond the tracks. As they reached the corner leading to their house, Austin took Blanche's arm and motioned her forward toward his school.

Blanche sat on the school steps, carefully folding under her dress. Austin sat next to her and jumped right into his speech. Though he had not rehearsed, the arguments had been churning around in his head for months. He had learned some new and interesting information from a neighbor at last December's school Christmas party.

"Blanche, there is a group called the Children's Aid Society, started by a Methodist minister. This group sends children by train to get better schooling, learn job skills and new languages. Your mother and I are sending you away with this group to St. Louis. Your train leaves on Thursday, five days from now." There were telltale wrinkles on his brow as he spoke.

"But Pa," gasped a stunned Blanche. "I thought I would go to school *here* in a few weeks!"

Pa leaned forward with a firm tone. "No, I am sending you to St. Louis. You are already a fine student, but it is time for you to go to a bigger city to get more education and to learn to be a proper young lady."

"But, Pa!" Blanche could think of nothing else to say. Until now, life had seemed perfect!

"Early Thursday morning I will take you by horse and buggy to Murphysboro, where you will board a train to St. Louis. There you will be met by members of the Children's Aid Society. According to Mrs. Larsen, you should wear the same outfit you are wearing tonight," he said. "And she has left a new blue sash and hair bow, as well as a blue knitted shawl for you to take on the trip. You and I will spend the next few days packing. I want what is best for you, and I believe this is the next step in your education." Austin pointed a cautious finger in the air in front of Blanche. "I do not want to hear any complaints." He was unsure about his decision, but to her he must appear unswerving.

Blanche suddenly stood up in front of the school steps. She inhaled deeply. Austin sat next to her. He clasped his hands together in his lap to keep them from shaking. "I know this is very sudden," Austin pressed on as he stood up. "Reverend Larsen agreed to help me with all of the arrangements, as long as you finished the Temperance Camp recitations. Your obligations there ended today."

"Oh my," was all Blanche could get out of her mouth.

"You must trust me on this, Blanche. We are Methodists and this is a Methodist organization. You will be offered a bright future. And we will write to you."

A quiet sob escaped Blanche. She felt confused about being torn from her family, unable to see that any good would come from it. Austin put an arm around his daughter and fiercely pulled her to his chest. They stood quietly for a few minutes.

Austin continued, "I spoke to someone at the camp today, and they will get a message to your friend Lucy to come and say goodbye to you tomorrow after church."

Another quiet sob, as Blanche's arm encircled her pa's waist.

"This *will* happen Thursday, Blanche. You must trust me on this. Now, we must get home. Tomorrow I will explain everything to the family while you are visiting with Lucy. Can you follow my instructions?" he said, as he pulled her away from his chest and took her chin into his hand.

Blanche's mind was spinning. She closed her eyes. Her pa was her emotional support, her teacher, the person she most loved and respected in the world. He had never mistreated her, let her down, or violated her trust.

She held her breath, eyes still closed.

She had to do as he said because she trusted him. She let the air out of her lungs.

She let the directive sink in.

Then she opened her eyes and looked straight into her pa's. Clear face, no fear.

"Yes, Pa. I will be strong, and I will do it," she said.

A chill ran up her spine.

Is this what growing up feels like? she wondered.

Shoelaces

Oraville, Illinois • Late August 1902

T he mule was disturbed by bees. It reared up and knocked over the rickety cart to which it was attached, spilling sweet corn onto Wheeler Street. As the mule continued to bray and kick the broken cart, Lucy held her pony tightly and tried to catch the bridle of the mule with her free hand. One of the mule's reins wrapped around Lucy's leg, and she frantically stepped high to loosen it.

"Help! I need help!" she cried.

A farmer dashed down the church steps and past the Spencer family, running to his mule and broken cart. He untangled Lucy and her pony, then proceeded to calm the mule and pick up the corn.

The Spencer family waved and smiled at Lucy as she approached Blanche. They continued down Wheeler Street, avoiding the pile of corn.

"Lucy, I'm going away!" wailed Blanche, as she ran toward her friend.

Blanche and Lucy, just a few months apart in age, had

become close friends the previous school year. Lucy had taught Blanche how to ride and handle Willow, the gray pony with the black mane. Lucy had received the message to come say goodbye to Blanche.

"Me, too! Oh, no!" cried Lucy. "My pa is staying in Chicago and wants me to come live there. He thinks the schools are bigger and better and that I could get a better education in Chicago. What is happening to you?"

"Oh, Lucy!" Blanche had tears in her eyes, as she forced a smile. "My pa is sending me to St. Louis on Thursday. He says the same thing—bigger city, bigger schools, better education."

The girls walked arm in arm across the churchyard, settling on two stumps in the shade, their hands clasped, their pastel sunbonnets touching at the brims.

"Goodness. Everything is changing so fast!" said Blanche.

"I know. I've wanted to talk to you so badly! Now, what is going on?" Lucy asked earnestly.

"Well, Pa feels the Temperance Camp made me grow up, and it is time for me to travel. He thinks going to St. Louis will be good for me. I feel I did very well in the performances and could possibly perform at a bigger camp next year. Since you are leaving, too, I will not be sad about leaving friends behind," said Blanche. "You are the friend who understands me best and knows my feelings."

The girls talked for almost two hours. The pastel shades of their sunbonnets went dark then light as the elm trees swayed over their heads. With sudden laughter, both faces would swing up to the sky, the sunbonnets rocking back like an opening clamshell. Then the clamshell would close as the hats came together again. The girls wondered how their lives would be different, if faraway travel would be exciting, how it would feel to sit in a class of students all their own age.

Eventually the girls walked over to Willow, seeking comfort from the pony. Both girls climbed on, and Lucy led them slowly to the Spencer house at the end of Childers Road. The house, at the edge of town, was a cramped white clapboard, with two small bedrooms barely big enough for beds. The parents shared one bedroom with baby Grace, and Blanche and her two older sisters squeezed into the other. There was a root cellar below the kitchen, accessed by an indoor stairway. Pa and a neighbor had blocked off the space above the stairway and created a tiny bedroom for Blanche's two younger brothers, big enough for a single bed the two boys shared. The room was too cold in winter, so they slept on the floor in front of the fireplace.

Lucretia Spencer, Blanche's mother, came out the front door of the house and brought Lucy and Blanche each a jelly biscuit and half a cob of sweet corn. Lou had the bony frame of a woman with a meager diet. She had soft brown hair and deep-set eyes framed by dark circles. She was exhausted from long years of carrying eight children, losing two of them, and cooking for and clothing her family under primitive conditions. Lou gave Lucy a restrained smile as she handed her the lunch but did not speak. The girls ate their late lunch sharing smiles and giggles.

"I will never forget you and your sweet pony Willow," Blanche remarked, after they finished eating. She hugged her friend with one arm and put her other around the pony.

"You know," Blanche continued, "we could write to each other! I may need someone to write to about scary older men and handsome boys. When you get to Chicago please send a letter to Pa at the school, and he can send it to me."

"Well, maybe it could work," said Lucy. "Anyway, I will sure miss you when school starts. You will be at the big city school by that time."

The girls shared one last hug, their sunbonnets touching, their tears flowing.

"Yes, goodbye. And remember to write," said Blanche.

Lucy hopped on the pony and slowly rode Willow down Childers Road, past the water tower. Blanche watched until Lucy disappeared.

Blanche walked home, her sunbonnet facing down. *I wonder if Lucy will write*, she thought. Will I send letters to Pa and Ma? Will I be afraid of the big city? Of strange men? Will I be happy with another family?

Lost in contemplation, she was unaware of her location until she heard a clatter of footsteps in the gravel behind her. She turned as her two younger brothers—Merwin, ten, and Lamont, seven—rushed into her arms. She gave each a kiss on the forehead.

Blanche smiled as she ran home holding hands with her brothers. It was now late afternoon. Blanche thought she would just go rest on her bed until supper. *When does that train leave?* she wondered, as she stretched out. *This is all so sudden, it makes me so tired.*

She didn't make it to the evening meal. She slept twelve hours, without stirring.

On Monday, Blanche spent the entire morning washing undergarments and stockings and hanging out her dress. She had a stain on the dress, and she had thought of a clever way to erase the dark spot. She turned over the hem at the back of the dress and, at a lower side seam allowance, found a full-size white flower that could be cut. Blanche snipped the flower with extra fabric, turned the dress over, folded the fabric, and stitched the flower over the stain. She finished the patch, rubbed the new flower, and sighed contentedly as she held up the dress.

At the evening meal, the whole family talked about her trip. Everyone seemed excited for Blanche, for Pa had described the trip as an opportunity, not a banishment. The other siblings all expressed a strong fear about traveling alone. Austin announced that he had borrowed a horse and buggy from a church elder for the Thursday ride.

After dinner, Ma and Pa lingered at the table while Blanche's older sisters Lelia, twenty-two, and Bertha, twenty, each gave Blanche a hug before they went to wash dishes. The boys stopped to give Blanche a group hug before they took baby Grace to the front porch.

"Blanche, bring your sewing bag to the table," requested Pa. "Ma wants to show you something."

Blanche kept the flour sack under her bed, lined up with her shoes. She retrieved it and came back to the table.

"I think this will work!" said Pa, turning the bag over in his hands. It was made of a gray-colored cloth with a coarse weave, many imperfections, and some red-stamped patches on one side.

"Blanche, your pa wants you to use this as a sort of purse for the trip," said Ma. "Tomorrow, in the morning light, you will need to turn the top down two inches to the inside and stitch a very tight seam."

"What will I carry in it?" asked a bewildered Blanche.

"Well, you should take your sewing supplies and some lunch," said Pa. "And I will see if I think of anything else.

Since the trip is just one day, it will not be necessary to take extra clothes." Pa and Ma did not want Blanche to take any of her other tattered clothes with her.

"Yes," said Blanche slowly, as she envisioned putting things into the purse.

Reality was setting in.

Pa rose early on Tuesday. He remembered a very old pair of shoelaces that he had saved and stashed in a drawer of his desk. He washed, dressed in his only suit, and headed for the school. He was the principal and sole teacher of the school, which was located in the Methodist church. Four religious denominations shared the church building, and each group held services there once a month. During the week, the Oraville school classroom was at the back of the sanctuary.

When he got to school, Pa sat at his desk, which fronted a long blackboard and pull-down maps rolled up tight. He pulled several books from the shelf past the McGuffey readers and leafed through each, looking for what he wanted. He had decided to copy "The Drunkard" and "Maud Muller" onto small sheets of white school paper. Doing so took all morning because "Maud Muller" had fifty-four stanzas. Once he was finished, Pa wrote his name and address on the back of the poem.

When he went home for lunch, Pa took with him the folded papers and the shoelaces tucked in his coat pocket. After lunch he washed the shoelaces and laid them to dry on the windowsill in his bedroom—out of sight of the boys, for whom he felt they would be a temptation.

Blanche spent the morning hemming the flour-sack

bag, wrapping up her sewing threads in paper scraps and talking Bertha out of a small chip of her beeswax knob, so she could use it to store her three needles. Ma came to Blanche's bed where she was working and offered her a decorative hair comb missing a few teeth.

"This is my old one, but you can have it for the trip. Remember to try to comb your hair before you meet new people," Lou said softly, with a tense expression on her face. This was Lou's only comment about the trip.

Later in the afternoon, Pa brought Blanche the dry shoelaces and showed her how to double-thread them into the flour-sack bag to give her purse a drawstring with two handles. The purse was square when finished but did not look quite so large when gathered with the drawstring. The cloth was very coarse, and the red painted markings were quite visible, making it a very odd purse. But since Blanche had no knowledge of how a purse was supposed to be, she was pleased with the bag's practicality.

On Wednesday, Ma baked a blackberry pie with berries Blanche picked from nearby railroad track easements. That afternoon they walked over to a friend's house on Holliday Lane. In return for the pie, they got a large bag of shelled walnuts. By evening, Blanche's trip lunch was packed, everything wrapped in paper scraps: a handful of precious dry-apple crescents, a large handful of walnuts, two hardboiled eggs, and two biscuits. The food was carefully placed in the purse before bedtime, with the sewing supplies and the comb, since Blanche and Pa would be leaving the next day.

That night, Lamont appeared at the foot of his parents' bed screaming in terror. Pa took him to the living room. Since Lamont was clutching his stomach and complaining of cramps, Pa first thought Lamont must have eaten too much cake at a neighbor boy's birthday party. But soon Lamont was flushed and feverish. Pa prepared water-soaked rags and gave Lamont a cool bath, but they didn't seem to bring him any relief. Even before dawn, Austin knew that his travel plans now must include taking Lamont to a doctor.

At daybreak, Pa bathed, dressed in his suit, and woke Blanche. They would be going to Murphysboro to drop off Blanche early, then he would take Lamont to a doctor.

Blanche dressed in her white outfit, with the new blue sash and hair bow. She put her sunbonnet and shawl and the bulging purse on a chair by the front door. Ma woke up, started a fire in the stove, and prepared a quick breakfast. Pa pushed to leave immediately—he wanted to travel before the heat of the day became too intense. The older girls, Merwin, and Grace were still sleeping.

The borrowed buggy seated two people and had a folding top, which was open. Pa fastened the horse into the bridle and tugs and was checking the reins when Blanche hurried outside, followed by Ma. Blanche turned and gave her mother a hug and a hesitant smile and climbed into the buggy. As she sat down, Blanche took out the hair bow and put on her sunbonnet, thinking she might need the sun protection during the buggy ride. Pa dashed inside, grabbed Lamont without waking him, and brought him to the buggy, putting his head in Blanche's lap.

"I'll try to be back by supper, but don't wait for me. Feed the others at the regular time," said Austin to Lou as he turned the buggy around. "We could be delayed at the doctor's office."

Lou watched them leave, her left hand on her forehead, almost over her eyes. With a limp wave of her right hand, she turned back and wiped her hands on her apron. She was rather relieved to have one less mouth to feed.

In the morning sun, the buggy headed past the school and out of town. The journey to Murphysboro was about three hours. Lamont had not awakened. Curled up into a tight ball, he faced the back of the carriage, his head in Blanche's lap and one arm sprawled over his reddish and swollen face. When the buggy came to the first descent of Beaucoup Creek, the horse stopped to drink out of the tiny stream.

"Blanche, Reverend Larsen says you may be asked to sing or recite a poem at the St. Louis train depot. Do not recite 'The Drunkard.' Only do 'Maud Muller'—the first six stanzas would be enough. To assist you, I have copied these two poems for you to keep. You can study 'Maud Muller' on your wait in Murphysboro." Pa handed her the folded sheets of paper.

"Say, what are your thoughts about the Mark Twain books we read during the winter months?" asked Pa, as he got the buggy out of the creek bed and back onto the flat road.

The Spencer family had not had much school in January and February 1902, due to very bad snow and ice storms. Austin Spencer had read *Tom Sawyer, Huckleberry Finn,* and *Robinson Crusoe* out loud to his family during many snowbound days.

"Is this schoolwork?" asked Blanche. "Well, I liked the adventures of Huck Finn and Injun Joe, in the second book, but they were hard to understand with the funny words."

"Well, Blanche. Both Huck Finn and Injun Joe used different dialects, so there were many odd-sounding words in the book."

"Yes, after a few chapters, I was able to understand what was going on. Will the people in St. Louis have a different dialect?"

"There might be some unusual words here and there, but I think you will understand everyone," Pa replied.

"I hope St. Louis will be interesting, not frightening," said Blanche.

Blanche and Pa talked on and on about Tom Sawyer and Huck Finn, hardly noticing the miles and miles of cornfields, the gently rolling hills, or the descent into the valley of the Big Muddy River, where Murphysboro was located.

Pa came to the junction near the river, then turned right on Walnut Street, heading uphill toward the Murphysboro train depot. The depot was very distinct, the only two-story brick building. All of the houses on the street were single-story white clapboard. The depot was tall and stately, much more decorated than buildings in Oraville.

Lamont began to stir and whine, and Blanche worked to keep him on the seat as she exited the carriage.

"You have about a four-hour wait," said Pa. "I had planned to wait with you for a while, but now we must get across town to a doctor. We have to see what we can do for Lamont's rash and fever. Here is your ticket from Murphysboro to St. Louis, compliments of Reverend Larsen. I suggest you put it in your purse."

Lamont stirred, suddenly missing his soft, warm pillow, and began to cry.

"Remember, I love you very much," said Pa, as he bent to kiss Blanche's cheek. "Walk directly across to the station, and do not leave before your train departure. I am sure you can make your afternoon productive—you are good at that. I will not be back after the doctor visit, for I want to get Lamont home before the late-afternoon heat, if possible. Goodbye, and have a safe trip."

Pa sat tall in the buggy, with Lamont propped against his leg. Pa was an excellent horseman from his young adult days as a farmer near his hometown of Vergennes, about three hours from Oraville. Today he had worn his Panama hat with his suit, making him look very important as Blanche watched him drive away. Blanche saw his worried and determined look as he lifted the reins and hurried back downhill and on to the east end of town.

Blanche looked down, put the ticket into the purse, then glanced across the street. She had been to this town before, but never to the train depot—and never alone. *I must explore the depot.* She headed into the tall red-brick building.

Blanche opened the depot door and walked inside. The room was very fancy. Oak seats, oak walls, polished wood floor, brass doorknobs, and high windows with colored glass. Blanche was alone in the room, but there was a ticket person at the far end. She sat in a back corner.

Blanche took a deep breath and bit her lower lip, as her eyes welled up with tears. She clenched both fists and her back stiffened. Blinking back the tears in both eyes, she sighed deeply.

Oraville was gone. Her family was gone.

Her world was gone.

She clenched her fists tighter, put them together, and shook them back and forth in front of her chest. Why had she come? Because Pa gave her no choice.

She unclenched her fists and shook her golden curls. Yes, everything would be fine. Pa said the train would be exciting and fun and full of adventure. Last fall, he had conducted a school field trip to study the steam locomotive on the local Mobile and Ohio Railroad coming through Oraville. He showed locomotive diagrams and assigned train poems, then marched the students two blocks to see the Wabash No. 573, a huge, hissing black locomotive that traveled up and down the state of Illinois. The size and power and practical use of this giant engine made a lasting impression on Blanche. Now she was about to take her first train ride. She was curious about the ride, eager to see the Mississippi River and the big city of St. Louis for herself.

But her travel curiosity was not as intense as her loneliness in the empty waiting room. She stopped the tears as she pulled her purse to her and her shawl close. Leaning her head against the wall, she cried silently, thinking of lost Oraville, her lost family.

She sat for half an hour, eyes closed, breathing deeply, trying not to cry again, not to think. The ticket master watched her over the top of his rimless glasses but remained at his counter.

Across town, the buggy pulled up out of the valley of the Big Muddy River. Having visited the doctor, whimpering Lamont curled up on the shaded seat and put his head on his pa's lap. As they headed home, Pa turned right without going uphill past the depot. He wanted to think about anything but the departure of his daughter from downtown Murphysboro. Instead, he spent a long time thinking about his upcoming fall teaching schedule, which was very limited due to Oraville's hard times. He had only taught half of the last year, so his salary had been frighteningly low. Could he find a creative solution to keep his family together?

Lamont woke occasionally, drinking some water and sniffling. Otherwise, mercifully he slept most of the way home.

Austin arrived home midafternoon. He dropped Lamont into Lou's waiting arms, then returned the buggy to the side of the elder's house. He got out quickly and looked in the buggy to make sure nothing was left behind. Blanche's hair bow, still fluffy, sat where she had taken it off at the start of the trip. Absentmindedly, he stuffed the bow into his suit pocket.

Austin knocked on the house door, graciously shook hands with the elder, and turned to walk home, passing the church.

Pa suddenly stopped, then went quickly into the cool, quiet school. He walked to the water bucket for a dipper of water and sat down at his school desk. He felt the light-blue hair ribbon in his pocket and pulled it out. For a long minute he stared at the bow. Then he lifted it to his nose.

With a scream, he jumped up and dashed around the desk to the bench in front of it. He threw himself violently down and brought both hands to the sides of his head, thrashing his feet about.

What had he done!

He pounded his head and moaned.

This child!

The only one who carried his spark, his love of learning, his deep passion for words, his love of nature. The one who made his heartbeat quicken and his spirit sing.

How could he have sent her off by herself?

He shivered and shook his head. He had imagined a glamorous urban life for Blanche, his daughter on a wide boulevard with a parasol and an armful of books. Had he let his dreams overcome his good judgment? Would she be safe? Would she be successful? Without him, would she grow to sense her own worth?

"Oh dear Lord, guide and protect her," he cried, as he turned his head into the high-backed bench.

Pa turned, eyes closed, and lay on his back for a while.

Surely good people would help Blanche and give her a home. Austin lived among people who took care of each other's well-being and safety. He must trust the same would be true for Blanche. He had told Blanche it would be so.

He still clutched the light-blue hair bow. He had crumpled it. Tears flooded his eyes anew, as he smelled the bow again. He nosed it gently and breathed deeply, as if the bow were a bouquet of tender, sweet-smelling roses. Then he delicately rested the bow on his lapel and—with his last tears—moved it over his heart. Finally, he covered it with his hand.

Hand Ballet
Murphysboro, Illinois • Late August 1902

Blanche awoke with a strange sensation. What was it? Her right shoulder was warm and yellowish sunlight glowed on her hands. She looked up to the window above her, skewing her sunbonnet. The top half of each first-floor window was bordered with six-inch squares of wavy glass in colors of yellow gold, sky blue and bright white, which were set apart by pieces of white-painted wood. The early afternoon sun was shining through the colored glass panels and touching her folded hands. As she turned away from the window, the color on her hands flowed from yellow into bright blue.

She put her hands together, thumbs crossed, and formed a butterfly shape, fluttering in one color, then another. Her dancing hands moved back and forth in the shifting colors, making butterflies, birds, graceful sweeping swirls right in front of her eyes. She lost herself in the poetry of her moving hands. She had no sense of the rest of the world, of anyone watching her. She had no sense of tears falling down her cheeks.

The ticket master looked over, saw the hand ballet, and smiled. She was not the first child to discover the magic windows. He was happy to see her in a lighter mood.

Slowly, the color changes slid off Blanche's lap and onto the floor, gliding across the room. She caught the eye of the ticket master and gave him one of her hesitant smiles.

I am alone, she thought. *I have maybe two more hours. I will review Pa's notes.*

Blanche got up and walked to the ticket master at the far end of the waiting room.

"Good afternoon, young lady," he said. "Are you traveling alone? Do you need a ticket?"

"Hello, my name is Blanche Spencer, and I am from Oraville. I have a ticket, and I am going to St. Louis. Do you have a quill I could borrow?" Blanche looked the ticket master squarely in the eyes.

"Well, let's see. I have an extra pencil. Would that work?" he said, holding up a short yellow pencil.

"Yes, that will be fine. Will you please let me know when the afternoon St. Louis train is coming?" Blanche asked, reaching for the pencil.

"Yes, miss. And, you can keep that pencil," the ticket master said with another smile.

"Thank you very much."

Blanche went back to her corner seat and settled in. *Oh my,* she thought. She did not see the blue hair bow in the purse. *Oh.* Small tears sprang to her eyes but were quickly gone. Lamont must have been holding it. Maybe it was a comfort to him.

Blanche watched the last of the stained-glass window patterns creep up the front of the ticket counter and slowly disappear. She sat up, looked around, and realized she was very hungry for a hard-boiled egg and a biscuit.

Blanche took out her travel food. She peeled the two eggs into the wrapping paper. Her fourteen-year-old appetite overcame her, and she ate the eggs in two bites each, followed by the biscuit. Sucking on an apple slice, she then walked outside to look for the water pump.

She helped herself to a long drink of cool, fresh well water, then headed back into the depot for two more apple slices and a few walnuts.

Blanche was an industrious child and loved learning new things at school. It was not uncommon for her to make lists for her schoolwork. She wrote down a list of things that made her happy today: her dress, the colored windows, her poems. Then she practiced "Maud Muller," the entire fifty-four stanzas. Speaking the memorized stanzas in a hardly audible voice, Blanche worked her way through the poem two times.

On her second review of the poem, near the end Blanche came upon a line she did not remember from before: *Ah, well, for us all some sweet hope lies deeply buried from human eyes.*

She stopped and frowned, until a curious look spread across her face. *Maybe—just maybe—*she thought, *there is sweet hope for me in this trip ahead, sweet things which have not yet come to pass.* She lowered her chin and looked up with a determined expression. *I am alone, but I must look after myself.*

Suddenly, Blanche heard the distant sound of the train. She hurriedly put her papers and pencil and lunch remains into her purse.

Wooo, wooo.

Chuga, chuga, chuga, chuga, chuga, chuga.

She cocked her ear, listening closely.

Could it be? The sound was so familiar!

Blanche jumped up and looked out the window.

My goodness! Her old friend, Wabash Locomotive No. 573, was coming to a stop. The black barrel of the giant locomotive was clicking and dripping water, and the wide skirt of steam had a yellowish cast. Her favorite iron giant would be taking her to St. Louis! She was thrilled.

Blanche turned, extended a wave and a smile to the ticket master, and, with a tall, straight back, marched out the door, her sunbonnet still askew on the back of her neck.

Orphan Train
Belleville, Illinois • Late August 1902

Blanche saw the uniformed conductor with a brimmed hat about four cars back. Blanche, the only passenger boarding the train at Murphysboro, walked over to him, pulled out the ticket, and handed it to the conductor. He punched it and waved her on up the steps.

Blanche looked in awe at the train car's domed ceiling with tiny glass-shaded lights and windows trimmed in wood. The bench seats were made of honey-colored strips of oak, which spanned the backrest then curved down to form a flat seat. The train car was relatively empty. A small group of neatly dressed children and one adult sat near the back, and a few other seats were filled with ordinary travelers dressed in street clothes. Blanche chose a seat on the west side of the car, near the front. This was her first train ride. The train whistle and movement of her giant friend were all very exciting.

"Oh, my," sighed Blanche. "On to St. Louis!"

Blanche settled into her journey, content to watch Murphysboro's white houses slide away and miles of tall, billowing green cornstalks come into view.

She heard a scuffle behind her. Glancing over her right shoulder, down the aisle she saw nothing unusual.

Suddenly she felt a poke in her back.

Tiny little hands, about the size of Lamont's, were poking at Blanche's shoulder blade. Sixteen little fingers were squirming and rising at the edge of her seat, like some sort of busy-bug invasion. She heard little giggles and snorts.

Blanche smiled at the hands then looked out the window, pretending to ignore them. But the smile continued to play at the corners of her mouth.

More snorts and giggles.

Little boys, I think!

Blanche turned toward the aisle, reached over the back of her seat, and caught hold of a wrist.

Up jumped a disheveled and darling three-year-old boy with blue eyes, rosy cheeks, and a mischievous grin. Then up jumped a smiling duplicate of the first boy.

"Hi! We're riding the train wiff Mrs. Cabbage. Who is riding wiff you?"

Blanche let go. The boys stood together in the aisle, arms locked.

"Hello," interjected a stern-faced woman who had walked up behind the boys. "I am Mrs. Isabel Savage. By any chance are you Miss Blanche Estelle Spencer?" Mrs. Savage had her gray hair in a bun. She wore rimless glasses and a nondescript gray dress.

"Yes, that is me. Where did you get my name?" asked Blanche.

"Hello, Blanche. I have your name here on a note from a Reverend R. Larsen. It says that you would join our group. I am the placing-out agent for the orphan program of Illinois. I am taking six orphans over to St. Louis, Missouri and, for some reason, Reverend Larsen assigned you to travel with our group. I see you have just met the busy twins. Come back and meet the other children," she said, placing one firm hand on each of the twins' shoulders.

"I will come and sit with you."

"Good, you can follow our noisy trio to the back of the car," Mrs. Savage said, as she marched the towheads down the aisle.

As Blanche walked to the back of the railroad car, she wondered about Reverend Larsen's directions, about her pa's understanding of the trip, and what would come next. Pa had given her no further information, so she followed this unknown woman with some uncertainty.

The little group had taken over the back seats of the passenger car, which had oak tables between the last two seats. The other children seemed clean and polite, but they also looked bewildered, with blank faces and wide eyes. The twins climbed into a seat facing the rear. Mrs. Savage directed Blanche to sit with her on the seat facing the twins. In the corner next to the twins' window Blanche saw a large, bulging canvas bag.

"So you have met the twins, Teddy and Tully. They are three-and-a-half years old. Across the aisle are Sarah, five, Dora, eight, Will, six, and Riley, nine years old. We've been on the train since noon, and everyone has been pretty well behaved. We have a fairly late arrival into St. Louis, and I am not at all sure how this will work out."

Blanche smiled politely, trying to understand her association with this group, while Mrs. Savage continued.

"Blanche, do you understand the program you have

joined? The original Children's Aid Society was started in New York City in 1859 by a Methodist minister named Charles Loring Brace. He had an idea, first, to house and feed the many orphans in New York City. Then he extended the program to bring the orphans to areas of the American frontier where new farms and towns were being built and where labor was needed. So now the program mostly brings orphan children from the East Coast to states like Wisconsin, Kansas, and Missouri for adoption. Our Illinois program is a smaller local effort with the same goals, although our placements will hopefully be in St. Louis, not rural areas, as an experiment."

"But I am not an orphan!" said Blanche in a high-pitched tone.

"Well, occasionally these programs also assist children whose parents are very sick and are unable to care for their children, or children from families with few opportunities."

"My father told me there was not much more to learn in Oraville and that he was sending me to St. Louis to get more education and to learn to be a proper young lady," said Blanche, tears brimming in her eyes. She did not remember the word "orphan." What did orphans have to do with her? She was certainly not an *orphan*!

"Yes, it seems he has sent you, with the help of Reverend Larsen, to do just that, to have more opportunities in the big city." Mrs. Savage gently rested her hand on Blanche's clenched fists. "And I think Reverend Larsen placed you on this particular train so that you could be an assistant to me. Are you old enough to help me for the rest of the journey?"

"Why, yes. I have two younger brothers and a baby sister. I can certainly help you." The fear was gone from Blanche's voice.

Mrs. Savage pulled two moist towels out of her canvas bag and sent one across the aisle.

"Everyone, please wash your hands so we can have supper," she said cheerfully. "I will not pass out food until all hands are clean. Blanche, can you take this second cloth and wipe the faces and hands of the twins? Then please double-check the others across the aisle."

"Yes ma'am." Blanche got out of her seat and quickly got both faces and four hands clean.

Mrs. Savage sat back, smiled, and congratulated herself on fitting the last lovely piece into her travel plans. *Self-confident girl, smart, a good assistant. Someone sent this capable girl to St. Louis, out of the stifling poverty of a tiny town among the cornfields. Maybe St. Louis could give her polish!*

"Time for supper," said Mrs. Savage. "Our new assistant, Blanche, will be passing out cheese sandwiches and carrots and apples."

Most of the children were well-behaved and hungrily gobbled the sandwiches. The twins were another matter. They made fists with bread chunks and moved about. Blanche reached across the table and made sure that most of the food got into the eager little mouths.

Mrs. Savage polished the apples. She then looked for another towel while Blanche passed out apples to each child. After everyone had eaten their apples, Blanche made the rounds with damp towels. Mrs. Savage held off on supper for herself and Blanche. They ate when the others were finished.

Their stomachs full, the children got sleepy. Soon they were leaning on each other and the tables. At eight thirty, when all the children except Blanche were dozing, the conductor came to the front of the car to make an announcement. There was a fire under Eads Bridge, going into St.

Louis. Two barges were burning, and all bridge traffic had been stopped. The train was being diverted to Belleville, Illinois for the night.

Mrs. Savage and Blanche looked at each other in surprise.

"Well, that ends the problem of the St. Louis night arrival," said Mrs. Savage. "But I wonder where we will go for tonight?"

The conductor came back a few minutes later with more details. Belleville had a small second depot, owned by the Illinois Central Railroad, which had little traffic. The train would stop to let off the group to spend the night in the depot. They would catch another train into St. Louis tomorrow morning.

While the iron giant spent a weary hour changing tracks several times and threading its way towards the Belleville rail yard, the children slept. Blanche dozed but occasionally looked up, intrigued by the blinking lights at the street crossings. She'd never seen a night train before. Mrs. Savage rested with her hands in her lap, praying for a safe and uneventful arrival in Belleville.

The Wabash No. 573 stopped with a jolt at ten o'clock in Belleville, Illinois. Mrs. Savage descended with the children and her bulging bag. As she got off, Blanche turned and faced the locomotive. It was nighttime, and the black giant had a silvery cast from the station lights and steam. Blanche clasped her hands together in the dark, choked on a deep breath, and said one last time, "Goodbye, my friend. Goodbye Oraville. Goodbye Pa." Almost blinded by tears, she then turned and walked slowly toward the depot door. A kindly night watchman was holding the door open for her.

While Mrs. Savage assisted with bathroom chores, Blanche showed the children how to lie down under the bench armrests and use their outstretched arms as pillows.

Blanche tucked the twins onto a bench, their heads touching. They fell asleep quickly. Blanche herself found an empty bench and, with effort, wedged herself under an armrest. She quickly dozed off. In the eerie night glow of the depot, Mrs. Savage rested upright, grateful that her little flock was safe and dry and together.

Union Station
St. Louis, Missouri • Late August 1902

The westbound passenger train carrying Mrs. Savage and her group of children crossed the Eads Bridge a little after nine o'clock. Blanche's eyes grew wide at how high the train was above the Mississippi River. She saw riverboats, small boats, barges, floating trees, swirls of water, the St. Louis waterfront bustle, a world of river life so much larger than what she had learned from Huckleberry Finn. On the shore, she saw a hundred carriages and wagons. Tiny people bustled about as if on an anthill—more people than in all of Oraville.

In no time at all, the train crossed the bridge and passed into the underbelly of St. Louis, into the web of riverside warehouses and train tracks that led to Union Station.

The train followed a long, slow curve and crawled into a yawning four-story arching structure of steel and glass. It was like a feeding station for cattle on a farm, thought Blanche, with trains hunched to the front. In reality, it was the terminal for many St. Louis passenger trains.

Blanche's train came to a stop just in front of a huge

sandstone building, ending its journey with a bellow of steam that clouded around the river of disembarking passengers.

Mrs. Savage issued firm directions: "I want the girls to hold hands and get on one side of me, and the boys, the same, on the other side. Blanche will follow me, holding the hand of each of the twins. Union Station is as big as a small city, and it would be very frightening for any of you to get separated from our group. Please stay with me!"

Holding hands, the little party headed past the hissing, steaming locomotive and toward the building. Mrs. Savage led them through a door and up a wide stairway. The children ascended the steps carefully, holding onto the brass banister. The twins, of course, were the slowest with their stubby legs.

As Blanche held both of the twins' hands, she looked up. Above her, on the Grand Stairway, she saw her second stained-glass window in two days. This one had three panels, each of them very artistic and elaborate, all yellows and blues. The images seemed to be of three angels sitting on benches in a garden. Blanche continued to look back at the angels as she headed up a second flight of stairs.

Once Blanche got the twins up the last step of the second stairway, she looked up.

Her mouth and eyes opened in speechless wonder.

Blanche could hardly comprehend the size of the space. This was the Great Hall, the main passenger waiting room of Union Station. White angels on a high, green wall held lights in their outstretched arms, and gold angels jumped out of a dark wall. Green snakes circled rows of pink arches and white columns. In front of them Blanche saw swirls of tile and gold medallions, as well as treelike structures with rows of lights. And chairs—hundreds of chairs! There were balconies as high as barn tops and a curved ceiling as high as heaven!

Hundreds of people bustled about. Blanche stood still, transfixed. The magnitude and grandeur of the space was beyond her comprehension. The twins, also overwhelmed by the big space, wrapped their arms around Blanche's legs. The three of them just stared as they were jostled by other ascending passengers.

Mrs. Savage moved everyone through the crowds to an information desk.

Presently a woman in a black uniform with gold buttons came to meet the orphan group. Blanche stared at the guard's waist, where she wore a chain with maybe thirty keys attached. The woman led the group through the masses of people to another corner of the vast room, then down two flights of a narrow stairway to a dimly lit hallway. The woman opened a door and motioned for the group to go inside. The room, covered in white tiles, was a seldom-used public restroom. The woman instructed Mrs. Savage to make use of the facilities. She would come back in an hour to get them.

This was the children's first experience in an enormous train-station restroom with modern plumbing. The room had two benches just inside the door. The children stared at the row of ten closed doors. On the opposite wall, they saw a mirror thirty feet long, below which there were ten or twelve porcelain sinks.

"Now, boys and girls, we have a serious hour here to clean up before we meet new families. Anyone who must use the toilet, go do that first, behind those doors. Then, each of you find a sink. Blanche, please take this towel and comb. I want you to go down the row and attend to each child. First wash the stains off their clothes, so the wet patches can begin to dry. You should also have each child clean their face and hands as well as possible. Then comb their hair. When a child is finished, they should come and sit on this bench—and sit still. Does everyone understand?"

The children nodded vaguely, with solemn expressions.

Blanche started to get the twins out of their dirty clothes and into clean ones. She scrubbed the little arms and faces till they were shiny, then did her best to comb their hair.

Mrs. Savage started at the other end of the line of children. She quickly transformed Will, Riley, and Dora, which left Sarah for Blanche. As Blanche was finishing up, Mrs. Savage bent over her canvas bag and rustled about inside it.

"Blanche, now it is time to attend to your own clean-up."

Blanche had forgotten about herself. She hurriedly

washed her face and hands and got out her own comb to smooth her straggly curls. Leaning over the sink in the bright lights, she did not notice her dress.

"Now little ladies," said Mrs. Savage, "I have a present to make you feel special. Sarah and Dora, I will help each of you with a pretty, new white hair bow. They go very nicely with your white dresses. And, Blanche, this light-blue bow is for you, since it matches your sash."

"Oh," was all Blanche could say. She was still on duty as a helper, not thinking of herself as a participant in the upcoming orphan presentation.

She fastened her new bow with a hairpin at her left temple to hold the curls back.

"My, young ladies!" Mrs. Savage said, as she clasped her hands below her smile, "you all look quite clean and lovely. And, gentlemen, you all look like future train conductors." The children all smiled.

The guard reappeared.

"We are as ready as we can ever be," said Mrs. Savage, running a comb through her own hair. "Let's go upstairs."

The group retraced their steps up the stairway and back into the large bustling room. They followed the guard along the east wall of the Great Hall, through an arch that said "Market Place" in tiles. Walking past the open market, a few of the children—none of whom had had breakfast—stopped in their tracks to stare longingly at the food. Mrs. Savage pushed them further down a long hallway, toward a tall black curtain with many folds. Overhead was another mosaic that read "Theater."

The theater had muted light and a wide, fan-shaped set of windows opening onto the train platforms. Below the windows were two pale-green benches with armrests.

"Everyone, please take a seat. Blanche, please sit at the front end of the bench and see that no one leaves." Blanche collapsed into her seat. She was hungry and tired from the travel, as well as her first exposure to city buildings and masses of people.

"Now, let's all sit still for a few minutes. Put your hands in your lap and relax."

Blanche sat at the front end of the theater, closest to the exit. As she straightened her skirt, she was upset to notice an apple-juice stain down the front of it. In her haste, she had not seen the stain while she was in the bathroom. Now she was helpless to do anything about it.

Blanche tipped her head back, closed her eyes, and breathed deeply. Her stomach growled. Her hair was combed, and she had a new hair bow. It was both exciting and exhausting, her first morning in St. Louis. She wondered what came next. Most likely the Methodist people would come to welcome the group.

～

The Robeys stood in a crowd of thirty or forty people, mostly shop owners, butchers, and masons, all in their work clothes, waiting for the program to begin. Mrs. Robey, altogether unfamiliar with this orphan-viewing process, had dressed in an expensive but conservative dark-green dress and matching hat. As the children filed out to the platform, Mrs. Robey thought they seemed a bit unkempt. They looked bewildered, like animals caught in night lights. Maybe they were more suited for working on farms than city life.

～

Mrs. Savage guided the seven children onto the wood platform to the left of the curtain. The three-year-old twins and the five- and six-year-olds stood in the front row. Blanche, the tallest, most healthy-looking child, stood in the middle of the back row. The eight- and nine-year-olds stood on either side of her.

Mrs. Savage primly walked to the front of the group and gave a ten-minute introductory speech, explaining the orphan program of Illinois. Then she introduced the twins by name, Teddy and Tully, and asked them to step forward. They awkwardly stumbled forward, holding hands and practically making faces with their smiles. Some of the audience chuckled.

Three other children stepped forward and gave their names. Then, nine-year-old Riley stepped to the front, said his name, and turned to Mrs. Savage. She nodded for him to go ahead. Riley began to sing:

> Row, row, row your boat,
> Gently down the stream.
> Merrily, merrily, merrily, merrily,
> Life is but a dream.

The freckled lad vigorously moved his arms as if paddling in a canoe. Once he finished his off-key performance, he returned to his place on the platform.

Now Blanche stepped around Riley and went front and center. She quickly adjusted her blue waist sash to cover the apple-juice stain, cleared her throat, and straightened her back, looking over the crowd. This was like the Temperance Camp stage, she thought, but not as many people.

Her white dress with raised flowers had acquired a

sprinkling of coal dust from the two train trips. It was now more gray than white. Blanche was not aware of this.

"My name is Blanche Estelle Spencer. I am fourteen years old. I will recite for you six stanzas of a poem called 'Maud Muller.' This poem is about a farm girl who meets a judge." Blanche spoke precisely and slowly, with confidence.

She began:

"Maud Muller," by John Greenleaf Whittier

Maud Muller, on a summer day,
Raked the meadow sweet with hay.

Beneath her torn hat glowed the wealth
Of simple beauty and rustic health.

Singing, she wrought, and her merry glee,
The mock-bird echoed from his tree.

But when she glanced to the far-off town,
White from its hill-slope looking down,

The sweet song died, and a vague unrest
And a nameless longing filled her breast,—

A wish, that she hardly dared to own,
For something better than she had known.

Blanche spoke in a sweet tone. Her limp curls swung gently on her shoulders as she looked at the faces in the audience.

As Blanche recited the middle stanza, Mrs. Robey felt a

chill run up her spine. She grabbed her husband's hand and squeezed hard. Mr. Robey's chest puffed out, and his pocket-watch swung back and forth from the vest pocket of his expensive suit.

"Thank you very much," Blanche said. She made a slight bow and went back to her place.

She thought her poem delivery was fine! All the same, she certainly did like reciting "The Drunkard" much more.

Mrs. Savage went to the front again.

"If anyone wants to come up to meet a particular child, I invite you to do so. Come right up!" She smiled brightly.

The crowd stirred and divided into those who were interested in the children and those who turned to go.

The couple behind the Robeys hurried forward to talk to Riley. Two couples were already jockeying for the front spot, right in front of the twins, pushing elbows and trying to talk to Mrs. Savage.

Blanche held her breath and wondered what would happen next. She was slightly light-headed from hunger, not at all sure what was going on.

The Robeys put their heads together and talked briefly. Then they walked over to the corner of the platform. Blanche watched them come forward from the crowd. Mr. Robey signaled to Blanche to step off the platform and come over to where they stood. He was a very portly man, with sagging jowls, a balding head, and dark bushy eyebrows. He seemed scary, almost overwhelming to Blanche, and she stepped forward cautiously.

"Hello, my dear," he said. "I am Mr. Robey, and this is my wife, Mrs. Robey." He moved even closer to Blanche, his confident gaze on her face. "You did a lovely job on that poem. Where did you learn this poem, and who taught you to speak so clearly?"

"Hello, I'm Blanche Spencer. My pa is the schoolteacher in Oraville, Illinois, and he had me learn the poem, all fifty-four stanzas. He helps me learn to pronounce words and to make a poem sound nice when I speak." She spoke as if she were talking to a Temperance Camp person who had come to congratulate her after a performance. She wasn't trying to impress him.

"And did your pa send you to St. Louis?" asked Mr. Robey, raising his eyebrows.

"Yes, he wanted me to come to the big city to get a better education and to learn to be a young lady. He said there was not much more to learn in Oraville."

While Mr. Robey conversed with Blanche, Mrs. Robey sized up the young lady. About twelve years old, clean, but with limp hair, the girl was articulate and able to converse with an adult. Despite her soot-covered dress, she certainly looked healthy, and she was mature and polite.

"Well, perhaps you could learn to be a young lady if you came to live with us," said Mr. Robey. "We wonder if you would like to help take care of our two young daughters and learn about St. Louis?" He smiled, both palms up and beckoning.

"Why, yes. Would I also get food at your house?" asked Blanche.

"Of course," said Mrs. Robey. "We have a cook who comes every day."

Blanche found the offer enticing. "Would there be lunch for me today?"

"Yes, very soon," said Mr. Robey, turning to his wife. "First, though, we must talk to Mrs. Savage."

Mrs. Savage was handing papers to a couple standing

with Riley. They bent over the desk to sign a half-page document. The couple shook hands with Mrs. Savage, and the woman smiled at Riley and put an arm around his shoulder. Riley gave Blanche a fleeting glance, before walking away with his new mother.

Mr. Robey moved forward and assumed a commanding stance. After a few words with Mrs. Savage, she pulled out more papers. Mr. Robey signed one of them, then motioned for his wife to do the same. This half-page document placed Blanche with the Robey family until age eighteen. It stated she must be treated as a member of the family, comfortably clothed, and taught a trade for adult life.

"Blanche," said Mrs. Savage, "you have been a wonderful assistant to me, and I know you will also be a helpful member of your new family. Take care, my dear." She bent and rested her thin lips on Blanche's forehead. Then Mrs. Savage turned to the four adults still fighting over the twins.

"Come with us young lady," said Mr. Robey. Blanche tugged at the purse strings coiled around her wrist, suddenly fearful of leaving with strangers and venturing into a strange city. But, trusting Mrs. Savage's calm demeanor and forehead kiss, she did as told.

Mrs. Robey followed, blue shawl draped over her arm.

The three walked down one flight of the Grand Staircase, passing the stained-glass angels, out the front door of Union Station, and past a slender stone chimney with a large clock. Mr. Robey had two firm fingers on Blanche's shoulder as he steered her forward.

The whole city opened up in front of Blanche: clanging green streetcars across from the station; strolling families on gravel paths; wide boulevards with carriages of fancy-costumed ladies; and, rows of four- and five-story red-brick buildings. She watched it all with small-town wonder.

Mr. Robey signaled to his driver, who was waiting nearby. Their horses and carriage approached. The group quickly climbed in. Blanche sat on the wide leather seat between Mr. and Mrs. Robey, marveling at the many buildings as she rode west on Market Street on the way to her new life.

Vinegar Dreams

Robey Household • St. Louis, Missouri
September 1902

A uniformed driver with a top hat steered the stylish carriage up Market Street, en route to the Robey household on West Bell Place.

Blanche watched her first city unfold before her blue eyes—tightly spaced buildings with unusual details; advertising services; a store with a carved fish over the entrance; a red-white-and-blue-striped pole at a barber shop; a ten-foot-high beer mug at a tavern. Their swift carriage followed other horse-drawn ones up the wide and busy boulevard. Sometimes they passed a double train car on a track in the center of the street. *A city train,* Blanche thought. None of what she saw seemed intimidating to her. It was just the first colorful page of her big-city adventure.

After twenty minutes, the carriage stopped at a three-story red-brick building with a glass vestibule. The building was much larger than a house, and it was in a cluster of eight similar buildings.

"Come inside," said Mr. Robey, after he helped his wife out of the carriage. He offered his hand to Blanche.

"I will see that you have food," said Mrs. Robey.

The Robeys entered the building and turned to a solid wood door on the left.

"This building has two flats per floor," said Mr. Robey, as he put his key in the lock.

They entered a spacious room with dark mahogany furniture and a plush pale-green-striped sofa below the front bay window, which was screened with velvet drapes over sheer curtains. On either side of the sofa Blanche saw brown leather chairs and side tables covered with crocheted doilies. Next to one chair was a muted-gold floor lamp with a beaded-fringe shade. There was a large, colorful rug on the floor.

"Oh Greta!" called Mrs. Robey.

A plump, rosy-cheeked woman in a gingham dress and long white apron appeared in a doorway.

"This is Blanche Spencer. She is going to join our family to help take care of Beth and Alma. But just now, she needs food."

The maid nodded and turned to go to the kitchen.

"Blanche, let me show you the water closet, where you can wash up," said Mrs. Robey.

Blanche followed Mrs. Robey to the room and closed the door. Just a few hours ago, she had seen a flush toilet and porcelain sinks for the first time. It was amazing how quickly one got used to these things! She came out feeling much refreshed.

"Here we are," said Greta. She set down plates of biscuits, cheese, and fresh peaches on the dining room table, as well as a glass and water pitcher.

The two parents sat politely at the table. Mr. Robey was

head of Jewish Charities of St. Louis and had a commemorative gold pocket watch engraved with an award from his temple. He pulled the watch out of his vest pocket.

"Blanche, I want you to take a bath. Then you may take a nap on Alma's bed. While you rest, Mr. Robey and I will discuss the future arrangements," said Mrs. Robey.

Blanche ate quickly but without forgetting her manners. She suddenly realized she was exhausted.

Once she was done eating, Blanche followed Mrs. Robey down the hall.

"Greta has drawn a warm bath for you. After, while you nap, I will see if I can find other clothes for you."

Mrs. Robey closed the door, and Blanche climbed into a large tub, sinking into the warm water.

My, she thought, *my first bathtub bath! How lovely compared to an Oraville summer bath in Rattlesnake Creek! I wonder what else is new in this home?*

Blanche lingered, washing with a white bar of soap. Eventually she crawled out of the tub, practically asleep. She put on her slip. When she opened the door, she found Mrs. Robey waiting.

"Follow me," said Mrs. Robey. "You will soon get to know these hallway doors by memory. This is the girls' room. I think you will just about have time for a two-hour nap before the girls are home from an outing with friends."

Blanche stumbled onto a single bed covered with a fancy chenille bedspread adorned with fluffy pink flowers. She reclined on top of the spread as Mrs. Robey put down a towel on the pillow for her wet hair.

Blanche exhaled as she adjusted the towel-covered pillow. She wanted to think about everything that had happened, but she drifted into a deep and dreamless sleep.

Blanche awakened to talking outside the bedroom door. Mrs. Robey knocked on the door, peeked in, and then brought the girls in with her.

"Blanche, I want you to meet Beth, who is nine years old, and Alma, who is six. Your job will be to help take care of these girls. You will dress them, get them to meals, clean their room, and help them with homework."

Both girls clung to their mother, sizing up this strange girl in their bedroom.

"Hello, my name is Blanche Estelle Spencer. You can call me Blanche. Do you girls have long names like me?"

"My name is Beth Robey," said the first girl, with a very serious expression on her plain face. She was turned slightly away from Blanche.

"I am Alma," said the dark-haired, pretty six-year-old, who had a friendly expression and wore a very large hair bow. She was not hiding, but firmly held her mother's hand.

"Blanche, I have gotten a dress from Lara Doyle, the Irish maid who takes care of my mother. Perhaps it will almost fit you."

Blanche stood and took the green gingham dress, put it over her head, and shimmied to slide it down over her shoulders. It was soft and smelled clean. It quickly molded to her body.

"Why look, it is just slightly big, but somewhat too long at the bottom," said Mrs. Robey, measuring with her hand.

"Oh, that is not a problem. I have my sewing kit with me. Can you tell me how much to take up?" asked Blanche.

"About the width of my hand," said Mrs. Robey. "Measure your hand against mine."

Blanche put her hand to Mrs. Robey's and was struck by how icy it was. Then she brought her hand down and looked in her purse.

"Just fold the old hem inside, Blanche, so that you can finish quickly and wear it to dinner. Girls, let's go wash up and let Blanche finish her sewing."

Mrs. Robey took both girls' hands and turned them out of the room.

Blanche drew out her needles and thread from her flour-sack purse, very happy to have a chore that postponed thinking about those *big* unanswered questions. Using her two extra needles to pin in the new hem, she then stitched quickly. In twenty minutes she had the skirt completely hemmed. She carefully put away her sewing supplies in her purse.

Blanche slipped on the dress and walked to a mirror on the closet door. The bodice had a scooped ruffle and side darts to accommodate a woman's figure, a design slightly more mature than the dress of a girl. Blanche, at fourteen, still had an almost flat chest, but somehow the scooped ruffle felt feminine and flattering. Yes, she felt, well, different. Tall. Curly golden hair. More like Lelia, her older sister, she thought. Not so much like the little girls in this house. The dress was quite worn, but the dark-green color was practical. She turned and glanced in the mirror at the hem. The length was just right and, because of her careful stitching and the flower pattern on the gingham, she could not see any of the new hem stitches.

"Blanche?" Beth said quietly, as she knocked on the door.

"Yes. Come in!" Blanche twirled around from the mirror.

"Oh!" said Beth, putting her hand to her mouth. "That used to be Lara's dress, and now you have made it *your* dress. You are so clever. Can you teach me to sew?"

53

"Well, yes. We could learn together," said Blanche. "Did your mother send you here?"

"Yes, it is time to come to dinner," said Beth, with a friendly glance at Blanche's face.

"Then, let's go!" Blanche turned with a radiant smile, taking Beth's hand.

There was a large group at the rectangular table, eight people. Mr. and Mrs. Robey were still in their best clothes, each sitting at one end of the table. Mr. and Mrs. Lang, Mrs. Robey's parents, who both had short, gray hair and wore dark tailored outfits, sat on the far side, near their daughter. Lara Doyle, with her rounded shoulders and downcast eyes, sat next to Mr. Robey and closest to the kitchen, so she could assist the cook. The three Robey children, including seventeen-year-old brother Wallace, who was much taller than his father, sat across from their grandparents. There was an empty chair for Blanche between the two girls.

Introductions were made around the table. Blanche looked each person directly in the eyes, as an adult would do—not a shy child. Her Temperance Camp work had taught her confidence in a crowd, and she was not intimidated by this new situation.

Greta and Lara Doyle carried in large bowls of steaming food, which were passed around the table. Sliced chicken and gravy. Potatoes and carrots. Green beans and pickles. Next, a basket of fresh dinner rolls came around the table. Blanche thought the rolls were nice, like fresh bread, but separate for each person. *How lovely!* She carefully watched others split their roll and put butter inside with their knives.

When she tasted her roll, the rest of the meal floated into the background. Blanche ate her entire roll first, slowly, loving the warmth of the bread and the light texture of each buttered bite. She remembered only biscuits from Oraville; this roll with its delicate scent hinted at a new life.

There was friendly chatter at the table. Tomorrow was Labor Day, and there was an afternoon parade. The entire family would be dressing up and spending the whole day at the lively, citywide social event. Blanche ate slowly, listening with curiosity to the conversation.

After dinner, the family moved to the parlor and settled onto the refined furniture, the beaded-shade floor lamp lighting everyone's face with a theater-like glow. Blanche glanced over with each load of dishes she carried to the kitchen under the direction of Greta. There was brief murmuring, then quiet, as if a stage curtain had just risen. Mrs. Lang lifted her hands at the piano, nodded to her husband, and began to play a few songs with Mr. Lang, who accompanied her on the harmonica. The couple had played Austrian folk songs together their entire marriage, and they communicated through eye movements and leaning into certain musical phrases.

Blanche had never heard a concert in a home. The instruments sounded beautiful up close, even though she watched from the dining room. She stopped, carrying another armload of dishes, and tilted her head at the sounds of the unusual music, which was unlike the Methodist hymns or Christmas carols that she knew so well.

As Blanche finished in the kitchen, Mr. Robey, sitting erect in his chair, glanced at his pocket watch in the light of the floor lamp. He called Blanche into the room.

"Blanche, Greta is cleaning the pantry for you. You can sleep there. You will have your own room for privacy, with a door and a light." Mr. Robey closed the pocket watch and returned it to his vest pocket.

Mrs. Robey rose from between her daughters on the

sofa, patting Alma affectionately on the head.

"Come, Blanche," she said. "Greta will walk you to the girls' room to get your belongings. I have put your white dress in their closet. You can use your shawl as a bed cover." The two walked down the dark hallway, Blanche a few feet behind Greta.

As they returned to the kitchen, Blanche smelled the strong odor of vinegar coming from the pantry. Greta stepped aside as Mrs. Robey approached.

The pantry was only six feet wide, with floor-to-ceiling shelves and cupboards on both sides. It had no window and seemed airless. Opposite the pantry door was a built-in cabinet with a pull-out enamel surface for mixing dough. Below that were bins for flour and onions. Beyond the tall cabinet were two more cupboards containing baking supplies and bins of potatoes. The wall that backed the kitchen contained narrow shelves and was generously stacked with jars of jam, preserved vegetables, nuts, coffee, and spices. At the back wall were cleaning supplies, all stored neatly on old newspapers. This left a mere thirty-inch by six-foot space, with a floor drain in the middle. A single gas light hung by a bare cord from the ceiling.

"Well, here we are," said Mrs. Robey.

Blanche saw a folded tarp with an old feather mattress over it. There was also a ragged pillow covered in purple floral fabric at the far end of the pallet, next to damp mops.

"You will be warm and dry here—much better than at the train depot. Greta will walk you to the bathroom, and then you can find your way back here on your own."

"Yes, ma'am," said a very tired Blanche.

Blanche finished her bathroom chores and found her way back to her bedroom, which she knew was really a kitchen pantry, not a bedroom. But on this first night, she was grateful for any safe place to sleep. She turned on the single dim light, closed the door, and took off her gingham dress, hanging it over the aprons. She got the pillow next to the wet mops and brought it over to the pantry door. The smell of vinegar and onions filled her nostrils. She turned out the light, leaned against the pantry door, and wiped a single tear from her cheek.

She thought about the day. She thought about the two sweet girls to whom she was assigned and their very reserved parents. She was in a home with nice furniture, lovely music, and good food. Maybe this was the beginning of "sweet hope" and new things to learn. But then here she was, about to sleep in an airless pantry.

It was not a happy space, but it was safe.

A sob came out as a choke.

It was not a home, but it was a home place.

More choking.

It was not pleasant smelling, not like Oraville. But it was warm.

Tonight I will have vinegar dreams, she thought. *Sour and scary dreams.*

She tumbled over and wrapped herself in the blue shawl.

Star
Labor Day, September 1902
St. Louis, Missouri

"Mornin' to ya," said a woman, as she opened the pantry door and reached in for an apron.

Blanche slowly came to her senses, returning from a faraway place. She looked up and was frightened to see the large stranger looming over her.

"We're set to share the same space, lass," the woman said cheerfully. "My name is Greta O'Malley, and I am the cook. We met yesterday. In the daytime, I will need this space for me cookin' supplies. In the night, you will have a snug little sleep space. Tell me yer name again, lass."

"I am Blanche Estelle Spencer. Please call me Blanche." She rubbed her eyes, wondering if the woman was speaking a dialect. "Where are you from?"

"Me home was in bonnie Ireland, bless me stars. I live with me son in a section of St. Louis called Kerry Patch. I loves to cook, and the Robey family loves to eat and can pay me. So, I take the early trolley across town and spend my day here. You and I, we will be a team!" Greta said cheerfully, as she turned and walked into the kitchen. Blanche noticed a slight limp.

"Oh yes, I guess we will," said Blanche, folding her blue shawl.

"Hurry up lass, get yer dress on. I brought you a few things from me relatives—underwear, socks," Greta said, tossing down a small bundle of clean hand-me-downs. "These things should help till we figure out the rest. Hurry down to the bathroom before the others are up, then come help me in the kitchen."

Blanche washed and dressed quickly, then hurried back to the kitchen. Since she had never been a servant, she looked about with wild and confused eyes, unsure of what to do.

"Let's see. Here, you can set the table like this. Nine places, including you and Lara Doyle. Do this quick, as everyone but me and Lara Doyle is goin' to the parade. I'll get to cookin'."

Not long after, Greta handed Blanche serving plates of steaming food, which she carefully carried to the table. Another heavenly meal of fried eggs, bacon, and biscuits. Blanche was able to sit down and eat her own plate of food after helping serve the meal.

"Well, everyone, we will leave in half an hour," said Mr. Robey, as the meal concluded. "Please get your hats and parasols."

The children jumped up to gather their belongings.

Mr. Robey assigned places in the carriage: the daughters with the parents; Blanche with the grandparents; and Wallace, in a suit like his father, riding with the driver.

The Labor Day parade would march down Fourth Street, which was mostly six-story, brick office buildings, windowless warehouses, and a few corner smoke shops. Unlike most of the parade goers who were crammed at the curb, the Robey family would be sitting in a roped-off section of the courthouse steps, along with some of Mr. Robey's business associates.

The carriage dropped off the Robey family, and they climbed to an upper row of steps, so they could see over a curbside fence. Mrs. Robey nervously glanced down to the bottom of the steps, where people were crowded several rows deep—pushing, shoving, calling out to others, quite unruly before the start of the parade.

The parade began as Blanche and the family settled into their places. First, a group of stern-faced, bulky iron workers passed by, banging on large drums and marching in quick rhythmic strides with a precision Blanche had never seen in her life. Then came stomping railroad workers wearing striped caps and white gloves, followed by quick-stepping brick masons with wooden hods on their shoulders and flags showing bricks. Finally, tanners strolled past wearing leather aprons and waving black hands. This was big-city labor, with noisy workers, so different from the quiet farmers and townspeople of Oraville.

A German marching band, dressed in dark-green and bright-gold uniforms, followed the labor groups. As the trumpeting band surged forward, the Sousa march sent a vibrating shock wave through the St. Louis crowd. People jumped to their feet and enthusiastically waved small flags. Blanche furiously tapped her foot in time to the music, tears of joy springing to her eyes, as she experienced for the first time in her life the collective exhilaration of a big-city crowd. All of the Robeys, including Beth and Alma, grinned and cheered with the music.

After the sounds of the band faded down the block, Beth and Alma began to squirm and squint in the bright sun, despite the protection of their straw hats. Blanche turned to Mrs. Robey.

"Might I take the girls to look around below the steps, but not leave this section? Maybe we could get a bit of shade?"

"Yes, fine. Stay very close. The crowds are boisterous, and you girls could get lost! We will send Wallace to check on you every few minutes," said Mrs. Robey, as she nervously looked over the pulsing crowds below their step seats.

All three girls descended the steps, hooked arms, and turned right. They watched a vendor in a pirate hat hawking paper parasols, caps, and small flags. Blanche stared at the lovely ladies buying parasols, totally unaware of how plain she appeared in her green gingham dress and her Oraville sunbonnet. Beth and Alma clung to the fence and watched another band march by.

Hand in hand, the three girls proceeded to the shade of a tent beyond the flag vendor. In the tent, a couple had set up a three-sided cardboard theater with a cut-out stage opening. With their puppets they were performing a comical story, which Blanche recognized from *Tom Sawyer*. She squatted, put an arm around each of the girls' waists, and explained the story to them.

The puppeteers were good, their voices theatrical and humorous, and the lively puppets danced back and forth across the stage as the small crowd cheered them on. Wallace came by, laughed at the show, then left.

After his climb up the steps, Wallace gave his puppet report. Mr. and Mrs. Robey looked at each other, their eyebrows going up.

The three girls walked a little farther, to where two mounted policemen in black uniforms had stopped to give buckets of water to their horses. The large animals tossed their manes and bridles, sending streams of water flying in every direction. Beth and Alma looked on with wide-eyed shyness. They had never been close to unhitched horses, and to them the horses were more exciting than the parade.

Blanche knew horses, so she knew to keep the girls at a safe distance, holding on tightly to both of their hands. The policemen laughed at the shy girls, shook their hands, and picked them up to pet the horses' noses. Blanche watched proudly, with a big smile. Wallace found the group, then reported to his parents that his sisters were in the arms of policemen, petting horses.

Blanche took Beth and Alma back to the edge of the fence. A troupe of ponies was marching by with one white pony in front. Two boys followed in green jackets and lederhosen and with feathers in their caps, carrying a beer-company banner. Behind the boys, six matching black ponies with sparkling silver and green crowns passed by.

"Look girls, these are ponies, not horses!" exclaimed Blanche. "They are half the size of the policemen's horses. The ponies must be trained to march in a parade like this. Notice the feet of the white pony and her high prancing step."

Beth and Alma had their eager eyes glued to the white pony. Its mane flowing, it stopped occasionally, turned sideways, reared up, and did several steps on its rear legs, before continuing its proud march. Neither excited girl could take her eyes off the white pony until it was gone from view. The final band of the parade followed.

The Robey family had come down from the steps and was standing behind the girls. Blanche had one hand firmly on each girl's shoulder and was stooped over talking to them about pony tricks. As she talked, Blanche turned and smiled at the Robey parents. Mr. and Mrs. Robey looked at each other again with raised eyebrows. Beth turned and saw her mother.

"Oh, Mother, we saw the most beautiful white pony! She was the best in the whole parade! Blanche is teaching us about horses and ponies. She knows these animals, and it's all very exciting! Can we see the white pony again?" Beth asked, her light-brown hair bouncing up and down.

"Well, not today. We must all stay together in this crowd as we walk to our carriage," said Mr. Robey. He glanced over his shoulder at the throngs of strangers piling up behind them.

"I have more surprises about ponies when we get home," Blanche said. "Let's see if we can prance like the ponies in the parade." The three girls giggled, locked hands high in the air, and marched down the block ahead of the adults, their hats bobbing in the afternoon sun like fishing corks in rough water. Blanche held their hands tightly and kept calling, "Step higher, like the white pony in the parade!" The little girls valiantly tried to bring their knees up as high as their shoulders. The adults who followed shook their heads and laughed.

Suddenly a large crowd moved onto the road from a side street, surrounding Blanche and the girls and blotting out the view of the Robey parents. Rowdy figures pushed forward and Blanche lost Alma's hand. She tightened her grip on Beth and lunged forward, frantically looking for the small girl in the pale-yellow dress.

"Alma, where are you?" Blanche screamed.

"Oh no, oh Alma!" cried Beth, running next to Blanche

and holding on tightly.

Blanche pushed forward as other people crowded in. She lowered her chin and clenched her teeth. She would find her charge somehow! The two girls were swept ahead by the crowd, unable to see in any direction.

The crowd abruptly slowed at a wide intersection. Blanche could see a policeman up ahead. Just in front, Alma was running to the policeman with outstretched arms. She was sobbing, disheveled and terrified.

Blanche and Beth got to Alma just as the policeman reached down to scoop her up.

"Alma is my charge. We were separated by the wild crowds. This is her sister, they are in matching dresses," blurted Blanche, somewhat breathless.

"What happened, officer?" Wallace ran up, his parents close behind.

"Now folks, is everyone together again? The parade crowds can be quite unruly. I suggest your group stay close together now. Don't separate."

"Officer, we have a new nursemaid. She's from a farm and does not know big-city crowds. She did not protect my daughter," said Mr. Robey, as he glared at Blanche.

Mrs. Robey picked up Alma and cradled her head. Blanche looked on, dumbfounded, her face white and dazed, still clutching Beth's hand. Mr. Robey reached over and yanked Beth's hand into his own, leaving Blanche face-to-face with the policeman.

"Watch your step, young lady," warned the policeman, before turning back to the crowd.

Blanche raced to keep up with the Robeys, who had now bunched together in a protective group. Her eyes stung with tears of shock. Everyone walked without speaking for half a block. Blanche could hear Alma whimpering, her head buried in her mother's neck.

As Blanche lifted one leg to get into the carriage, Mr. Robey spoke gruffly.

"How could you be such a careless girl! We must watch your every move!"

Blanche cowered in the carriage on the way home, looking at her folded hands, trying hard not to cry.

I thought I was doing my very best, she thought, scared of being punished.

Back at the flat the family silently ate a cold supper left by Greta. Wallace was curious about the policeman on horseback and wanted the girls to talk about the horses. The girls were tired and didn't talk. Blanche ate little, still fearful of being punished. She just looked at her plate.

"Blanche has pony secrets to tell us, Mother," whispered Beth. "She has to come into our bedroom to show us. Please?" she pleaded, a large furrow in the brow of her plain face.

"Yes," brightened Alma. "Pony secrets. Please?"

"Now, both girls, first wash up quickly!" said Mrs. Robey.

"Come with me, Beth and Alma, one at the sink and one at the bathtub." Blanche rallied to an easy chore as she ushered the girls to the back bathroom. "Now, first, we will take off your dresses, then your socks and shoes. Stand still while I work with each of you."

She grabbed a towel, wet one end with warm water, and confidently gave a quick cleanup to each girl, who remained still in her firm grip.

"There, ready for pony secrets?" She smiled as she spoke.

Mrs. Robey was surprised at the fast and thorough cleanup of the girls. She dressed the girls in nightgowns as Blanche, herself, washed up.

"Now, please, pony secrets!" said Beth, smoothing down her nightgown, as she stood in her bedroom door.

"Yes. But first get into bed and pull your covers up," said Blanche, as she settled onto the floor in her slip. Her curls fanned back above her head in a golden halo that contrasted with the dark floor.

"Here are the secrets! You must watch my hands!"

The girls twisted to face Blanche. She began to wave both hands slowly in the air.

"Secret number one. The nose of a pony is softer than the nose of the horse you petted today. The pony's nose is as soft as the fluff on your bedspread. This is how you rub the pony's nose."

Blanche held her arm high and did a rocking motion with her right hand, as she had done with her friend's beloved Willow. Both girls raised their right hand and mimicked Blanche's motion.

"Secret number two. When you stroke the pony on the neck, she likes it. She is very happy and flutters her eyelashes."

With lovely downward strokes, Blanche pretended to stroke the neck of a pony.

Both girls raised their hands high to stroke the neck of the pony, swooning as they did so.

"Secret number three. We have to name our new friend, the white pony. What shall we call her? Snow? Whitey? Star?"

"Star," the girls said in unison. "Her name is Star!"

"And," Beth continued, "she is white like the stars in the night sky."

"Yes, star-white pony," said Alma, cocking her head from side to side.

"Oh my, wonderful pony secrets!" said Beth, as both girls giggled and rolled in their beds, cuddling their pillows.

"And," whispered Blanche in a soothing tone, "when you remember being lost and want to feel better, you can rub the fluff on your bedspread and pretend it is the nose of the pony named Star."

Mr. and Mrs. Robey stood at the door, watching closely. They could hardly believe this day of surprises and calamities. Policemen holding their daughters. Girls prancing as the crowds rushed in. Policeman saving their daughter. Puppet tricks in the bedroom. Star, the new family pony. This was the family's first nursemaid. She was kind but naïve. She might be reckless with their daughters, so they, as parents, must be vigilant.

Blanche looked up. As the parents parted, Mr. Robey sternly motioned her out of the room. Blanche's hands shook slightly, and she looked at the floor as she moved quickly down the dim hallway to her pantry-room.

The pungent refuge enveloped Blanche in a warm cocoon. She sank down and burrowed into the blue shawl.

Pantry Hug
St. Louis, Missouri • September 1902

"Morning, Blanche," greeted Greta, as she opened the pantry door to retrieve her apron.

Blanche donned her dress and hurried to the bathroom to wash and comb her hair. When she returned, Greta was busy with pots and pans and directed her to set the table and carry out food.

Blanche took her seat after everyone else had started breakfast. A plate came around, piled high with strange food. Blanche sat still, passed the plate, and observed what everyone else did. Family members took two slices of thick yellow bread, then put butter and a thick golden liquid on it. They also had sausage and slices of cantaloupe.

"Blanche, try this! It is so delicious!" said Beth, holding a dripping bread piece on her fork.

Blanche, who was learning new foods and new customs each day, smiled. She took two slices of the yellow bread and prepared her plate as she had seen the others do.

"My," she said, "this is very lovely! Rich and sweet and

so nice!"

"It's a family favorite called French toast," offered Greta, setting down a fresh plate.

"While everyone eats, I want to explain the schedule for today," said Mr. Robey, after checking his pocket watch. "First, the carriage will take Wallace across town to school. Then, in about an hour, Mrs. Robey, Blanche, Beth, and Alma will take the carriage to Eugene Field School to register the girls." He spoke firmly, looking at Blanche. But her eyes were down, looking at her food.

"Blanche, after the school visit, you must carefully observe the route between the school and our flat. Starting tomorrow, it will be your job to walk the girls to school each day, rather than ride in the carriage, which I need each morning for my business. Do you understand?" Mr. Robey's question was loud and stern.

Blanche looked up, startled. She nodded, her mouth full of breakfast delight.

Later, the girls and Mrs. Robey got in the carriage and rode the eight short blocks to school, past red-brick apartment buildings and row houses. Blanche carefully recorded the route, but it was just down one street. The destination landmark was the school itself, sitting back from the corner. The building was four stories high with large windows. It had fancy curved-stone details and clover-shaped windows near the roof. There were four-story castle-like bell towers in two corners.

As they went inside, Blanche noticed that she was older than all the other children. A creeping fear seeped into her mind. She saw students, well-dressed school officials directing traffic, large stairways, and huge rooms with wooden desks. She did not speak, just firmly held the two girls' hands for the two-hour tour, straining to stay focused and not lose the girls again.

Presently Mrs. Robey turned with hands full of papers. She directed everyone back outside to their carriage.

"I see the school is for younger children. Where will I attend school?" asked Blanche, her eyebrows arched in a question as she caught up with Mrs. Robey going into the flat.

"You will discuss this tonight with Mr. Robey," Mrs. Robey said in an even tone, turning to let everyone in the front door.

Busy setting the table, bringing out the food, and taking out the garbage, Blanche did not have time to sit with the others for lunch. As Greta was cleaning up the kitchen, Blanche took her saved plate and sat down to eat.

Lara Doyle slid into a chair next to Blanche.

"We 'aven't had time to meet proper, yet. I am Lara Doyle. I work for Mr. and Mrs. Lang and also clean this flat for me room and board." A thin, pale girl, she spoke quietly.

"Yes," said Blanche, with an easy smile, "it has been very busy here!"

"Yes, you 'ave busy little charges to keep you movin'," said Lara. "I wanted to give another dress to you. I hear that ye can sew, and probably ye kin take up the hem of this 'un." Lara patted the dark-blue gingham dress draped over her arm and handed it to Blanche.

"Thank you," said Blanche, "I will work on this after lunch."

Blanche was touched by Lara's kindness and wanted to alter the dress quickly as a show of her appreciation. Also, working with a needle and thread would mean Blanche would not have time to think about the future.

70

"Well, I must be off. I get my cleanin' done when the house is a bit empty. We will talk later. I am glad to have a friend in the household," Lara said with a weak smile, squeezing Blanche's shoulder.

In the afternoon light, Blanche sat on a chair in the living room and hemmed the second dress, guessing the measurement would be the same as for the first dress.

After dinner and helping Greta, Blanche finished her chore of putting away the many cooking items in the pantry, then walked into the parlor to talk to Mr. Robey. His large frame almost overflowed the leather chair.

"Mr. Robey, I want to ask you about a school for me," said Blanche. Her hands were clutched, and she had a forced brightness in her voice.

"Yes, Blanche, let's walk down to my study to talk," said Mr. Robey, standing and straightening with effort.

They went along the hallway into a dark-paneled room that Blanche had not seen before. There was a window, and two walls were lined with dozens of books, more than Blanche had ever seen in one place.

"Have a seat there," Mr. Robey said, pointing to a large, black leather chair.

He sat at his desk, across from Blanche. His back to the window, he practically seemed to block the evening light. She was dwarfed by the size of the chair. Her golden head rested only about halfway up the back.

Mr. Robey straightened both sleeves of his jacket and coughed lightly before speaking.

"Blanche, we will not be sending you to school. Your job will be to get Beth and Alma safely to and from school, keep their room clean, do their mending, and help them with homework. We will be watching you closely after the parade mishap. You will also occasionally help Greta as she requests. She has a bad right knee, as you may have noticed." Mr. Robey's tone was void of warmth.

Blanche had both hands on the wide armrests. Her grip tightened and her eyes widened, but no words came out of her mouth. She was speechless. She did not have a close relationship with this large man with the stern face and menacing eyebrows, and she was afraid to speak. With tears welling in her eyes, she turned to look at the books in the room, wondering about *his* education.

"Is this a library?" she asked quietly. "I have read about a library, but I have never been in one."

"Yes," he said, "this is my business library. There are no books here for children. Blanche, I know you are disappointed not to go to school. We get a newspaper every day, called the *St. Louis Post-Dispatch*. Maybe you can find articles in the newspaper to teach yourself to read. I will show you where I stack them. Now please run along. I must work."

Blanche lurched out of the chair, still looking at the wall of books. She was unable to look at Mr. Robey because tears were running down her face. Almost blinded, she walked quickly out of the room and turned down the hallway. She stumbled into the kitchen, let herself into the pantry, and closed the door. Then she slumped against it, sliding onto the floor.

Tears freely flowed down Blanche's face. She grabbed a white apron sash, dangling near her face, to dab her eyes. She cried quietly for twenty minutes, so unhappy and feeling so abandoned. More education was the main reason her father had sent her away. It was the reason for coming to St. Louis, to grow up in a big city, go to a big school, learn more poems, and learn to be a lady. What had happened now? She was living with a cold family that was completely foreign to her, with no one to show her love. She was utterly alone, sleeping with potatoes and onions and the vinegar smell! She wished she had her pa to talk to. He did not even know where she was.

What had happened? All of those big questions she could not answer over the last few days tumbled forward into her consciousness. The orphan children on the train. Her father sent her with the orphans to St. Louis, for a program for orphans. And she was being treated like an orphan! Maybe Pa did not know where the orphans went. Maybe no one—not even Reverend Larsen—knew what they ended up doing.

That was the program, a way to give orphans to families who wanted them. But there was no work plan. Pa had a *work plan* to teach about trains; she saw the plan unfold each year—maps, diagrams, field trip, spelling words, poems. Pa did not mention a work plan for the orphans, and Mrs. Savage did not talk about one either. There was no plan, no list of job assignments. Her back quivered with chills of crystal-clear realization.

Now here she was. Taken in by a wealthy family with a work plan of their own—to get nursemaid help for their two young daughters. What Mr. Robey had just told her—that was their only plan! No help for the orphan. Food and shelter, yes, but no other help. Clothes from the maid, maybe education from the newspapers. No family love, no hugs. Bare-minimum kindness, old feather mattress on the pantry floor. Nothing else.

Blanche took a few deep breaths, her eyes closed. She felt like she had in the Murphysboro train station, alone and helpless. She fell asleep with these troubling thoughts in the airless pantry, at fourteen years old overwhelmed about how to handle her life, how to change anything.

Sometime later, there was a soft knock at the pantry door. Lara Doyle had seen Blanche stumble into the pantry, crying. Lara did not know what was wrong, but she knew distress. She knew sadness.

"Blanche, it's me, Lara Doyle. May I come in?" she whispered.

Blanche scooted over, reached up, and turned the pantry door handle. Lara squeezed in and shut the door. Then she knelt down, took Blanche into her arms, and held her in the dark.

"Oh, Lara," Blanche cried softly, wrapping her arms tightly around Lara's warm neck. "I thought I was coming to St. Louis to get more education and to become a young lady. Now I know I am just a servant. The Robeys will not send me to school. My heart is broken. My mind is confused. I am just so disappointed."

"Do ya have a real family?" asked Lara.

"Yes, my pa and ma and five sisters and brothers in Oraville, Illinois. My pa said he was sending me to St. Louis to have a better life. Not this!" Blanche sobbed anew into Lara's shoulder.

"Well, here is how ya start to get out of yer sadness." Lara, who was thirty-three, propped Blanche at the back of the door. "I know, I am an orphan with no family. I say prayers a lot. And I try to think about the good things in me life, not the bad things. Here, I 'ave people who are kind to me and give me food. This is a safe family to live with, not like some. Can ya remember any good things in yer life, Blanche?"

"Why yes, I wrote down things on the day I left!" Blanche said. She sat up, just a glimmer of hope in her voice.

"Then save time every day to write down good things. Do work chores quickly and save time for yaself. Maybe early afternoon after yer chores are done and before ye go to get the girls. I do it and it helps. Would that cheer you up?"

"Oh yes, I am thinking about what I will write now. Thank you so much," Blanche said, giving Lara another hug.

"Well, I best get out of here, back to me own room. We can come here for secret meetings when we need to." Lara squeezed Blanche's hand.

"Yes, thank you," Blanche sighed deeply, stood up, and opened the pantry door.

The flat seemed quiet. It was several hours since dinner, and Mr. Robey and the Langs were all sitting in the living room, reading books and newspapers.

Lara departed on tiptoes. The adults, who could see the pantry door from the parlor when the sliding doors were open—as they were now—knew exactly where she had been. But no one bothered her as she went to her bedroom.

Blanche washed up and went to bed on her pallet in the pantry. The pantry was her retreat, her crying place. She fell back exhausted. A faint vinegar haze permeated the room, though it no longer bothered her.

Lara was kind, gentle, hugging Blanche, the only person who treated her with love. The family wanted nursemaid services and saw no need to send Blanche to school. She was bitterly disappointed and heartsick, but she knew nothing of St. Louis, had no money, and could not leave. Still, she must have hope. She tucked her chin, took a deep breath, and put her hand on her forehead.

The next day was busy with school errands and papers to fill out. Blanche had little time to relax. As Greta started to cook dinner, the girls approached Blanche to go over the pony secrets, still totally entranced with their new friend, Star. The three of them talked ponies until dinner.

After, Mrs. Robey decided to bathe the girls and said she wouldn't need Blanche.

Blanche approached Mr. Robey again, as he was reading his newspaper in the parlor.

"Mr. Robey," she said matter-of-factly, "it is time to write to my family about my arrival in St. Louis. May I have a sheet of paper and an envelope to do this, please?"

Surprised, Mr. Robey looked up with a scowl and piercing eyes.

"That will not be necessary!" he said loudly.

"Oh, I can write the letter. You do not need to trouble yourself with it. We had letter-writing lessons at school," she said proudly, with a smile.

Mr. Robey jumped up, his neck bulging and his face red. He loomed over Blanche.

"No one is writing letters! Do you understand!" he said, as he threw down the newspaper.

Tears again sprang to Blanche's eyes. She stared at the fluttering papers, then at Mr. Robey's face. She, too, had a scowl.

"I just want to let them know I am alive and safe and living with a family," Blanche said firmly.

"Don't ask again, Blanche," he said, glaring at her.

Blanche bowed her head and walked to the pantry. She opened the door, slipped inside, and crumpled onto the pallet, burying her head in the pillow. She forgot to close the door. She felt utterly powerless and overwhelmed by a deep longing for her own family.

Mr. Robey knocked loudly on the pantry door molding.

"Blanche," he said, an earnest expression on his face, "tomorrow I will send a telegram to your father to tell him you are living here with my family and that you are fine. Please give me the name of your father and the town." He stood very erect, but his demeanor was not as menacing as it had been in the living room.

"Austin Spencer, School Principal, Oraville, Illinois," Blanche said, with her head turned sideways on the pillow. "And, thank you very much," she said softly, as she pulled the blue shawl around her shoulders. She was lost in the cold currents of this family.

That night, the pantry was very much a cold, lonely cave in a dark wilderness.

The next day Mr. Robey sent the following telegram to Oraville:

AUSTIN SPENCER   SEPT 1902
SCHOOL PRINCIPAL   ORAVILLE ILL

YOUR DAUGHTER LIVES IN ST LOUIS CARES FOR OUR TWO DAUGHTERS STOP SHE IS FINE STOP DO NOT TRY TO CONTACT US IN ANY WAY STOP
AR   ST LOUIS MO

Of course, Blanche did not know the content of the telegram—or even what a telegram was—but she trusted that a message had been sent to her pa.

That week there were daily school-escort trips and bedroom-cleanup and meal chores for Blanche. She performed these dutifully. Soon the weekend arrived. On Saturday the girls went off to a friend's house. Blanche finally had several hours alone to think.

After Greta left, Blanche lay on her pallet in the pantry all afternoon. This was her only home. She thought about her beloved poems, the train lesson, Tom Sawyer, Huck Finn, and Robinson Crusoe. She fondly remembered her pa reading through all of last winter's storms. Well, at least things were not as bad for her as they were for Robinson Crusoe!

Blanche thought about her friends in Oraville—though Lucy had gone to Chicago. What else did she love about Oraville?

And what about St. Louis? Was it getting more interesting? There was a little pull making her want to stay in St. Louis and not go back to Oraville. In her mind it was as if there were a tiny blinking light, and she was being drawn to it. She could not describe what it was. The girls? The white pony? The food? The bathtub? No. All of these were lovely, but…what was it?

She thought and thought but could not figure it out. What was it? Lara Doyle had said to think of the good things. Well, in Murphysboro, the good things were her white dress, the colored-glass windows, and her poems. She only had some of these now. What was good here in St. Louis? She had seen her second stained-glass window. She had seen her first parade, her first huge school, and her first puppet show. She had even seen her first white pony. What were all of these? Her heart quickened. These were things that pleased her mind and made her smile. These were things that excited her! That was it! There were new things in St. Louis that Oraville did not have, and they excited her.

Was that enough? Blanche sat up and leaned against the

pantry door, the aprons crowning her head. Yes, new things did excite her. Could she do this here, see new things every day? How? In Mr. Robey's newspaper? On the walk to Beth's school? What about on a walk to her school?

Her school!

She sat straight up, as a chill rippled from her shoulders to her waist.

Her school? Her own school, just like her pa had a school? Yes! She would design her own school right here and now.

First, the name would be the "Blanche Estelle Spencer St. Louis School of Self-Education." She, herself, would be the principal and head teacher! She would put together hard assignments for her most demanding student: herself!

What would my assignments be? Let me think.

Little Assignment: One vocabulary word or one math problem every day.

Medium Assignment: One school assignment with Beth or work ahead in Beth's school books. One assignment each day.

Big Assignment: Read one book or memorize one poem per month. But how?

Blanche flopped back down onto her pallet, lost in thought. Where could she possibly get books to read? There seemed to be no children's books in the house, and she had no money to buy books if she found them. Undeterred, she continued trying to find a solution.

Her own school? When would she attend? Well, Lara

said do chores quickly to save time for herself. She could use this time for schoolwork.

My goodness! What a secret this is! The little girls have pony secrets, and I have big-girl Blanche secrets! Can I do this? I must do this myself, secretly. It will be a lovely puzzle to try to run this school—and also to be the best student!

Blanche lay in the dark pantry, determined. Her self-education program had lifted her out of self-pity and into an exciting new chapter. She took a deep breath and gave herself a big pantry hug, crossing both arms and glowing at her new plan.

Soulard Market
St. Louis, Missouri • September 1902

Monday was the first full day of school. Everyone was up and getting ready for the busy day. Blanche ate scrambled eggs and toast with the girls, who talked excitedly about going to the brand-new school.

The three girls left half an hour before school started and walked the eight blocks to Eugene Field Elementary. Blanche held both girls' hands as they crossed the street. Through a large crowd of parents and students, the three rushed up a wide stairway filled with excited voices and clomping feet. Blanche escorted her charges to their classrooms, patting each on the shoulder as they entered. Alma would only be attending half a day, then she would go to a private after-school program with other girls. She would get a ride home with other parents.

Blanche headed back down the school steps in the west bell tower and out the front door. She walked with purpose to the Olive Street corner, crossed between carriages, and started the eight blocks north to the Robey flat.

For my school, three types of assignments, she mused. Vocabulary words would be first. She would find Mr. Robey's newspaper, look for new words, and write them down. Then she would have to find a dictionary. Once homework began, she would begin to look at Beth's classwork for the medium assignments. Third, she would need to find books. This seemed impossible. Well, she would think about ways to get books, maybe from Wallace. Good!

By the time she reached the flat, she had a small plan for each category of assignment. *I seem to be off to a good start as a teacher,* she thought. *Now let's see if I can also be a good student!*

"Blanche, is that you?" called Greta, as she walked out of the kitchen, wiping her hands on her apron. "I thought we would use this fine September Monday to deep-clean the pantry. Come with me, and I will get you started."

Blanche crossed the living room, walked into the kitchen, and smiled weakly at Greta. Robey chores first, Lara had said—and try to do these quickly.

Greta instructed Blanche to get a chair, empty the pantry shelves, wash them with vinegar, dry each with a rag, and, finally, restock the food supplies.

Blanche walked to the dining room to get a chair, where she saw the stack of newspapers under the table next to Mr. Robey's chair. *Fine,* she thought, with clear resolve. *Clean first, then tackle the newspapers.*

Blanche unpacked, washed, and repacked shelves for three hours, finishing about two thirds of the pantry. As she strained on tiptoes to reach the highest row of shelves, Greta told her to stop, fixed her deviled eggs for lunch, and suggested Blanche finish the shelves and mopping the next day.

"Eat your lunch, then rest a bit before your school errand," said Greta cheerfully. She was grateful for Blanche's help, since she was used to handling all such chores alone.

Good, thought Blanche, tucking down her chin and taking a deep breath. *Maybe I can work this hard each day and still have study time to myself.*

Blanche picked up the top newspaper on the pile under the side table and brought it to the dining room table. She stared at headlines and a cartoon while she ate her lunch. The newspaper, the *St. Louis Post-Dispatch,* was the first large newspaper she had ever seen. It had a very large title in ornate script, and she did not understand what the title meant. There was a scramble of big and small headlines across the top, as well as a cartoon of a fat man in a suit with a confusing caption about politics. Then there were also photographs and a map.

After her attentive scan of the front page, Blanche began to focus on words she did not know. Meanwhile, she finished her eggs and tomato wedges and ran to get her poem pages and yellow pencil from her flour-sack purse.

Blanche turned over the last page of "Maud Muller" to use the back side for her homework. In the top-right corner, she neatly wrote *V* for "vocabulary words." Then she copied several words down, leaving space for definitions:

> vestibule
> diploma
> electrocution
> casualties
> disturbance
> cardinal

Well, these took half a page. Now, where will I get a dictionary?
Mrs. Robey came into the dining room to remind

Blanche that it was almost time to leave for the school.

"I see you are looking at the newspaper. Can you read?" asked Mrs. Robey, her mouth straightening into a tense horizontal line.

"Oh yes, I can read," Blanche said. "Mr. Robey said I could borrow his newspapers to teach myself new things, and that is what I am doing!" Folding her newspaper, she smiled at Mrs. Robey.

Mrs. Robey stared at Blanche, quite shocked that the girl could read.

"Well, return the paper to its proper place, and be certain you are not late to pick up Beth," Mrs. Robey said sternly.

"Yes, ma'am," said Blanche, grabbing her sunbonnet.

A spring in her step, Blanche walked out the door and headed for the school. *I can do this,* she thought. *Just work hard and fast on my chores, then fit in a bit of newspaper time to look for new words. My goodness, the teacher has a good lesson plan, and the student is trying to catch up!* She grinned to herself, almost lightheaded. She was going to get her St. Louis education after all. Sweet hope!

∼

On Friday after school, Blanche found a chance to approach Wallace. He was walking out of the kitchen with a glass of water and an apple.

"Wallace, I know that you go to a different school than your sisters. Does your school give you spelling words? And do you use a dictionary at home to look up new words?" inquired Blanche politely.

"I am much more interested in math problems than in words. If you want to use my dictionary, you can keep it in the girls' room, and I will just borrow it when I need to." Wallace was open and friendly. He immediately went to get his copy of *Webster's Collegiate Dictionary* and handed it to Blanche.

"Thank you very much!" exclaimed Blanche.

With both hands, she carried the thick book to the girls' room. The book had a tan leather cover and a black band with gold lettering on the side. At the foot of Beth's bed, there was a small nightstand with a lower shelf. Blanche smiled broadly as she put the very first book onto the very first shelf of the Robey children's library. She sat for a moment, savoring her accomplishment.

In addition to Saturday meals, Greta prepared a roast-chicken dinner to be reheated on Sunday and also on Monday.

On Sunday, as Greta walked home from church with her son and his wife, she tripped on a step and badly twisted her left ankle. She soaked the black and swollen ankle, but by that evening she felt she would not be able to get across town on Monday to help the Robeys. Before dark, she sent her son on horseback to inform them of her injury and her need for several days of rest.

The Robeys had a fine chicken dinner feast on Sunday. On Monday, they had fruit for breakfast, bread and cheese for lunch, and meager chicken and vegetables for supper. On Tuesday, Lara Doyle cooked pancakes for breakfast. They filled everyone's stomachs, but they were lumpy and burned. Greta's absence really began to be felt.

When Tuesday dinner consisted of more lumpy pancakes, Mr. and Mrs. Robey frowned over another unsatisfactory meal. After dinner, Mr. Robey stomped around, slamming doors as he moved about the apartment. He kept walking past the kitchen and mumbling. Blanche retired to the pantry and sat nervously on her pallet. The family crisis made her feel very insecure. She had never experienced such anger from her own pa. And if she was asked to step in and help, she did not know how to cook at all! Her mother had never taught her because she already had two able older daughters cooking with her. Blanche waited for a knock on the pantry door, until she fell asleep.

On Wednesday, after Blanche got the girls to school, she walked out to find Mrs. Robey waiting for her with the horses and carriage.

"Blanche, I am taking you with me to Soulard Market. First, we will go pick up Greta, who will stay in the carriage but direct us as we shop for food for the family."

The carriage traveled east on Page Boulevard to get Greta in Kerry Patch, then proceeded south on Broadway through blocks of red-brick warehouses. As the women approached the market, Blanche saw many wagons and dozens of vendors carrying loads on their heads.

This was the best market in the city, since it had both river and rail access. Cattle was shipped in by train and butchered daily in a warehouse at Second Street and Sydney, southeast of the market. Fishing barges sometimes docked just below the market and sold river fish to waiting butcher wagons packed with blocks of ice and burlap tarps. The market was where Greta shopped for the Robey family on Mondays and Fridays.

The Soulard Market buildings had been devastated in the Great Tornado of 1896. So, the market currently operated in a large field owned by the Cerre family. The center of the field was green with grass, surrounded by two rows of wagons with a pedestrian path between them. Shoppers walked the square buying from the open wagons and tents. There were meat wagons displaying racks of ribs, roasts, and pigs' feet, as well as shiny, fat catfish, carp, and buffalo fish from the Mississippi River, all displayed neatly on blocks of ice. Butchers continually cleaned fish as they arrived, and below the back of their wagons were stinking and fly-infested piles of fish entrails. There were also bins of beef fat for tallow and bins of bones. The vegetable and fruit merchants offered colorful displays, normally without unpleasant odors. Horses and donkeys, with blinders on, stood patiently at their wagons, the smell of horse manure hanging like a cloud of smoke above the market. Secondary businesses had sprung up across the street, including small taverns set up by German beer makers.

Greta, who had brought her two huge straw baskets, directed the driver to park on the corner closest to her favorite vendors. She had written out her crude list on the way to the market. She pointed out certain wagons and tarps to Mrs. Robey.

Mrs. Robey, carrying one basket, descended from the carriage twitching her nose and fluttering her eyes, followed by Blanche with the second basket.

Farmer Jones, with the white horse, sold very fine meats. Mrs. Robey approached him and purchased a large precooked corned-beef roast and eggs. Another wide wagon near the carriage had a colorful spread of fresh vegetables and fruits, and Mrs. Robey and Blanche purchased onions, potatoes, and carrots there. Then they marched their purchases back to the carriage, stepping delicately through dusty patches, mud from dripping ice, and piles of horse manure.

Mrs. Robey remained at the carriage with Greta, who directed Blanche to do the final shopping. Greta had cleverly thought of pickled vegetables to minimize the need to cook and sent Blanche to find the vendor halfway around the square.

Blanche headed out by herself with the huge basket and four dollars. Colorful displays of fruits on white tarps caught her eye, as did artistic displays of bushel baskets of corn and root vegetables.

Every minute of this solo trip was exciting for her! She must not tarry, but she so loved learning about new places, new things, and new people. She located the pickled vegetables vendor by his two pinto ponies. He and his wife had white hair and spotless white aprons. They seemed to take great pride in their wares. Blanche asked a few questions, and they told her which bottles were the freshest and would thus keep the longest. Blanche purchased sauerkraut, pickled beets, pickled cucumbers, and beans, as she had been instructed to do. Then she carefully counted her change. Aha! She burst into a wide smile. She had just done math homework today with these purchases!

As Blanche threaded her way back through the wagons, she saw a sign for Farmer Eckert's peaches. She had had peaches on her first day in the Robey flat and remembered their taste. Just the thought of them made her mouth water. She made a mental note but kept walking. The freedom of shopping by herself was exhilarating. The hazards of manure piles, moving loads, and pedestrian crowds were just part of the colorful market.

"Mrs. Robey, I just saw a sign for Farmer Eckert's peaches. Would you like me to go back for a few?" Blanche inquired when she arrived back at the carriage. She handed up the basket of bottled preserved vegetables.

"Oh my, yes," said Greta. "Those are the best peaches. Please go get a dozen if you have enough money." Mrs. Robey nodded with a tight smile, anxious to leave the market.

Blanche walked back among the wagons, proud of her keen observation and her initiative. She bought a dozen huge peaches. As she turned to leave, something caught her eye.

Ahead of her was a wagon with a small man sitting on the rear step smoking a pipe. His sign said "Books, New and Used." His cart was filled with rows and rows of books, separated by wooden slats. Some were fat, some thin. The bindings and book-cover titles were in all colors of ink. Blanche's face lit up at the carpet of color in the wagon, and the vendor beckoned her over with a friendly wave.

"Are you a book lover?" he asked, with arched bushy eyebrows and a kind smile. He removed his pipe, emptied it, and put it in the pocket of his tattered wool jacket.

"Oh yes!" The words escaped Blanche's mouth in a rush. "I do not have any money to buy books, but I have a question. Do you have any books I could read to younger children?"

"Why, yes, I have a few. I am here most days of the week. If you could come back next week with money, I could show you the children's books."

"Oh, thank you very much! I take care of two small girls and want to read books to them. I will try to come back next week. I must hurry now. Goodbye, and it is very nice to meet you!"

Blanche hurried off back to the carriage, across the mud holes and the manure, so distracted she didn't realize they were ruining her white shoes. She had just found a source for books at Soulard Market, and she was delighted! She was already mulling over how she might be allowed to help Greta on future shopping trips.

As Blanche arrived at the carriage, she smiled at Greta and Mrs. Robey, handed up her fruit and the change, and climbed up. Greta questioned Blanche and assured Mrs. Robey that Blanche had done careful and honest shopping on her own.

All three women rode back to Kerry Patch lost in their thoughts. Greta smiled to herself, already planning to ask for further shopping help from Blanche. Mrs. Robey stared at Blanche's smelly and ruined white shoes, wondering how they would find other shoes for this girl. Blanche tingled with excitement about the book vendor, already imagining an armload of exciting books to read to Beth and Alma.

Before she got down from the carriage, Greta gave Mrs. Robey instructions about serving the corned beef with boiled potatoes and pickled vegetables for the rest of the week. She also asked for the use of the carriage and driver and Blanche for the next two Mondays and Fridays of Soulard Market shopping. Mrs. Robey agreed, grateful she herself would not need to return to the dirty, smelly market. Blanche listened intently and, when her name was mentioned, she nodded and smiled in agreement.

It was getting late when they returned to the flat, so Mrs. Robey instructed the driver to go directly to the school to pick up Beth. After they had picked up Beth and arrived home, Mrs. Robey spoke.

"Blanche, please put down your parcels, and take off your shoes and stockings. I am afraid your muddy shoes are beyond hope and will ruin the carpet. After you deliver the parcels to the kitchen, find Lara and see if she has any shoes to fit you. Also, send Lara to find me for instructions on how to clean my boots."

Blanche obeyed, taking off the wet shoes and stockings, which were now brown up to the knees. In her bare feet, she carried the parcels into the kitchen.

Blanche found Lara beating rugs outside the back door. Lara quickly stopped what she was doing and headed for her small closet. Blanche sat on the rear step and waited, noticing for the first time the seven adjacent buildings lined up along the block. Eight buildings times six families. This corner of red-brick buildings was home to forty-eight families, probably more families than all of Oraville!

Lara returned with a pair of old, dark-brown, hard-soled moccasins and a pair of black stockings. Blanche tried them on, but the moccasins were quite large on her feet, her toes leaving more than an inch of space at the top of the moccasin. Lara again disappeared, returning with a ball of coarse twine. She showed Blanche how to loop the twine around the front of each moccasin to make it stay on her foot.

Blanche waddled back into the kitchen, her gait uneven in the large slippers. Mrs. Robey had just entered the room. She watched Blanche's funny walk and looked at the top of the moccasins. She rolled her eyes as she left the kitchen.

The following Monday, the driver dropped off the two girls at school, then drove Blanche into the city. They picked up Greta and her baskets and headed for Soulard Market. The driver handed Greta an envelope and spoke softly to her about shoes for Blanche.

The cook directed the driver to a street two blocks from Soulard Market. They stopped in front of an old two-story brick building with a large sign, "SHOES." A bell rang as Greta and Blanche pushed open the front door. The store manager looked up in response to Greta's inquiry and pointed to a large bin in a corner, piled high with old and dusty pairs of shoes.

"Let's see what we can do for those feet of yours!" said Greta, limping slightly, as usual. "Sit on that plank bench fer me."

Blanche had never been in a shoe store. As she looked around at shelves and shoe boxes, her nose twitched with the smell of leather and chemicals. New shoes with shiny leather and gold trim were on display throughout the store. Greta pulled shoes out of the bin labeled "Used Shoes, $1/pair."

"Here are three pairs, Blanche. Let's see if any of these fit your feet." Blanche pulled off the large moccasins fastened with twine.

"*Tsk, tsk, tsk,*" Greta reacted.

The first pair of dusty, scuffed boots was too small, but the second pair seemed just right.

"Sir, could we have a bit of assistance, please? Is this a good fit shoe for this lass?"

"Let me look," said the manager, kneeling in front of Blanche. His dark-stained hands picked up each foot, felt the big toe, and turned the boot from side to side.

"Yes, this pair is a perfect fit, with some room to grow. And you found yourself a well-made pair which should last until this young lady outgrows them! That will be one dollar even, and I can also throw in a pair of black stockings for this price."

"Thank you very much! Now, let's leave the new shoes on, carry the old moccasins back to the carriage, and get over to Soulard Market. We are off to a good start!" said Greta.

Blanche stood up and walked a bit in the high-top black leather boots, admiring their good fit and sturdiness. She had never had new shoes, except the white ones; she always wore outgrown shoes from her sisters. She smiled her thanks and followed Greta out of the store.

For the rest of the afternoon, Blanche didn't give the shoes another thought. The colorful wagons, the loud calls of the vendors, and the acrid smells of decaying meat smothered her senses, as Greta directed the driver to the most practical parking location. The cook picked up one basket, gave another to Blanche, and they headed into the sea of wagons. They shopped quickly and returned to the carriage with their first purchases of meat, eggs, and vegetables.

Suddenly, Greta spotted an aproned woman with her hair tied in a bandanna, carrying heavy trays of bread. Greta called to her, and they chatted for a minute.

"Blanche, I will take a coffee break with me friend, to rest me bad ankle. Here is money. Please get another dozen peaches, and just enjoy the market for half an hour. Can you do that?"

"Yes ma'am, with pleasure!" grinned Blanche.

Greta and her friend headed to a tavern adjacent to the open-air market, their heads leaning into one another.

Blanche adjusted her sunbonnet and headed in the direction of Farmer Eckert. First though, she stopped at the book vendor for her first official visit.

Angus McGregor, in his tweed jacket, was contentedly working his pipe and watching the crowds.

"Why, hello, young lady!" he said, slapping his knee. He stood up, removed his straw hat with a flourish, and shook Blanche's hand. To Blanche he seemed like a merry elf about to share a secret.

"Good, you are here! I want to quickly tell you what I am looking for," said Blanche, rising onto her tiptoes and clasping her hands together.

"Now, you stand square in front of me," Angus interrupted. He gently put both hands on her shoulders, bent down to eye level, and looked into her blue eyes with his own twinkling brown ones. "First tell me *your* story, then your *book* story."

Blanche felt a wave of relief. Her eyes filled with tears, one rolling down her cheek. She had not experienced a nice man yet in St. Louis, and his warm greeting touched her heart.

"Oh, you are so kind," was all she could say, as she grabbed one of his outstretched arms, her small fingers digging into the tweed sleeve.

"There, there. I already sense you are a strong lass. My name is Angus McGregor. I am a retired English literature professor from Washington University here in St. Louis, and I come to this market to sell my books and to meet new people. Now, tell me your story," he said. "You have a stage; I will be your audience." Angus focused only on her face.

Blanche steadied her feet, smoothed her dark dress, and looked straight into Angus' friendly face. In ten minutes or so, she had told him everything: about her home town, the Spencer family names and history, the Temperance presentations, her pa's travel ideas, the train ride with the orphans, Union Station, the Robey family situation and her job with them, her self-education school, and her quest to find books.

"I have decided I don't actually want to go back to Oraville," she concluded. "I am learning so much in St. Louis, even here at Soulard Market. I just miss being able to talk to my pa, and it is hard being a servant. And I miss my family."

Angus had a daughter and grandchildren in Scotland, but no local family. He was a widower. His books were now his family. As he listened, his heart opened to this lovely, bright fourteen-year-old. He understood that she needed a friend. He also understood, as an adult, that he needed to develop this friendship with care and propriety.

"Blanche, I can help you with books. But you cannot tell your host family, and I can never meet you anywhere except at this market. Do you understand?"

"Yes," she said softly, as she looked into his clear, brown eyes. After other men she had met, his rules made her feel safe. "Can you write to my pa and tell him details about my situation, and tell him how I feel? I do not think Mr. Robey said much in his letter."

"Sure, Blanche, but all correspondence has to go to my address, so that you do not anger your St. Louis family." Angus stood, patting his chest. "And all letters must stay with me. You will not be able to take them to the Robey house."

"Yes, I understand," she said, with a catch in her throat. "It would be such a relief to contact them. I will be back here on Friday. Could you send my pa a letter by then?"

"Yes, I can send a letter by Friday. On Friday I will also bring you a book or two for your children's library."

"Yes. Oh, dear. I must get to the peaches," said Blanche, as she glanced over her shoulder.

"Go. We will speak on Friday." Angus raised a hand in farewell. He realized Blanche was rising above her servitude, using books for mental freedom and inspiration. He was deeply impressed with her request and vowed to work hard to find the correct books for her.

Blanche got Farmer Eckert's peaches and hurried back to the other end of the busy market. She spotted Greta stepping back into the crowd.

"There you are," said Greta with a smile. "I've rested me ankle, and I see you have the peaches. We will just get a few more things before we depart."

They shopped another twenty minutes, then returned to

the carriage and headed to West Belle Place. Greta hummed, mulling over all of the family and neighborhood news she had just gotten from her friend.

Blanche leaned back in the opposite corner of the carriage, lost in book dreams. She reviewed the kind words of her new friend and felt at peace. The Robey household was her workplace. This kind man, his wagon, his books, it all felt like a welcome shelter for her in the big city.

Greta and Blanche visited the market again on Friday, and the cook again took a coffee break with her friend. With quickened steps, Blanche walked to the book wagon.

"Hello, young lady," said Angus, removing his pipe and his hat. "I have written to your pa, but it might be some time before I receive a letter back. But here is the really good news!"

Angus pulled out two books, putting the first one into Blanche's waiting outstretched hands.

"The first book is called *Black Beauty*. At some point this book was dropped into a mud puddle. Some of the pages are stained, but all of the lettering is readable. This is the lovely story about the life of a horse. Since you told me about your pony tales and pony secrets, this was the closest book I could find. Your girls should love this one. It has many illustrations.

"The second book is longer," said Angus, as he handed her the thick book. "It is the story of Heidi, a five-year-old orphan in Switzerland who has many adventures. I remember reading it to my own girl when she was young."

Blanche held the book carefully in her hands. The cover was gray, with *Heidi* in large black letters, and there was a scratched, colored oval picture of a dark-haired girl standing on a mountain path, waving one hand. It seemed that a dog had chewed at the binding on the lower-left corner of the book.

"Once again," said Angus, "this book is damaged, but still readable. I am starting a box on my wagon for free damaged children's books. Today, you just found these books in my box. Do you understand?"

"Yes. I am so grateful to you," said Blanche, clutching the books to her breast. "These are the very first books of my own I have ever had! This is the very best day of my new life in St. Louis!"

"Books can be very special," said Angus raising his bushy eyebrows. "Now, run get your peaches, and get back to the carriage!"

Blanche got the peaches, then carried the fruit and her precious books back to the carriage. She climbed into the carriage and started looking at the *Black Beauty* book, with illustrations of a beautiful black horse with expressive eyes. From across the street Greta saw her in the carriage, delighted to see Blanche reading a book. She smiled as she got into the carriage.

After arriving home and carrying in all of the groceries, Blanche had a quiet hour before her school errand. She settled down on a living-room chair with her books. She began *Black Beauty* and was thrilled with the thinking horse. Then she began to look at the illustrations in the *Heidi* book.

That night after the girls went to sleep, Blanche spent several hours in her pantry bedroom thinking about building her book library. She did not take these first two books for granted. Blanche feared the Robeys might put restrictions on the books she acquired, so she would be clever and watchful with these new ones. She must immediately cultivate the reading interest of the two young girls, so that reading would soon become a source of entertainment for them and perhaps a strong factor in their education.

Blanche was deeply grateful to her new friend, Mr. McGregor, for finding two fine books that would captivate the girls. She would read to them every night, reading the stories over and over. Surely the Robeys would not take away books that brought joy to their children!

Blanche struggled that night to understand how she could best help Beth and Alma with the new books. She remembered her father coaching her on "The Drunkard" poem, explaining word meanings and phrases and intonations until she had a firm grip on the meaning of the poem and how to present it. Her pa's coaching in the empty schoolroom made Blanche a successful public speaker on the Temperance Camp stage.

That's it, she thought, *the work behind the stage creates success on the stage.* This would be the challenge with Beth and Alma. Blanche's reading at home would be the work *behind* the stage. And school readings and recitations for Beth and Alma would be the work *on* the stage. As a servant, now she could only operate *behind* the stage. But Pa had done this coaching with love and joy. Surely she could follow in his footsteps!

I will do this very carefully. I must get that first evening of reading done without interference from the parents. Self-education will be my path, and books are stepping-stones on the path. I must work through the girls.

Black Beauty
Robey Household • October-December 1902

On Sunday evening, after many weekend kitchen chores, Blanche finally found time to begin her reading program with Beth and Alma. She sat on Alma's bed, and the girls snuggled up on either side of her in their bedclothes.

"Just look at this horse's eyes. He seems to be full of spirit!" Blanche said, as she rubbed the horse picture on the cover of *Black Beauty*. She also let each of the girls rub the picture. Then, using all of her coaching skills from Pa and her performance skills from the Temperance Camp, she began to read several chapters of the book. Beth and Alma were spellbound by the happy and sad tales of the talking black horse and by Blanche's theatrical reading of the story. They had never experienced being read to and were immediately drawn into this intimate but educational experience. They snuggled closer, and both girls entwined their warm arms with Blanche's. They wanted more.

"What a beautiful black horse he is, and his life is sad but also happy. Can you please read more?" asked Beth, with a serious face. She was trying so hard to understand the personality of the horse and the meaning of the chapters.

"Black Beauty," said Alma, gently rubbing the horse on the book cover. Only six years old, she absorbed the story on a different level than Beth but still had strong affection for Black Beauty.

Blanche read more chapters with an animated voice.

"Black Beauty, White Star," said Beth. "I wonder what kind of life our Star pony would have living on a farm."

The girls excitedly talked about this comparison. They looked at book illustrations page by page, this time talking about what their pony would do in each situation. They spent the entire evening in horse and pony heaven.

The next night included further reading of *Black Beauty*. The bright and inquisitive girls challenged Blanche with their questions, and Blanche immediately developed new skills to use *Black Beauty* as a teaching book.

"You see, Black Beauty stumbled because his shoe fell off. What lesson do you learn from this?" prodded Blanche, propping the book on her knees.

"Well, you should take good care of horses, if you want them to work for you," said Beth, with a solemn frown on her face.

"I fall in big shoes," giggled Alma.

"Yes, you both are correct!" said Blanche lovingly, smiling from face to face. All three of them tickled their toes together.

Mr. Robey walked in, frowning.

"What is the commotion? What are you doing?" He walked to the bed and grabbed *Black Beauty* from Blanche's hand.

"Where did you get this?" he demanded.

"From a box of free damaged children's books at Soulard Market," said Blanche.

"Did you steal it?" He waved the book in front of the three girls, the blood vessels bulging on his neck.

"No." Blanche spoke calmly. "I did not steal this book. Look at the condition it is in. Who could even sell this book?"

"*Hrumph*," he scowled, leafing through the mud-spattered book. "Well, enough of this," he yelled. "Blanche, go to your bedroom. No more books!"

Blanche scurried down the hall and into the pantry. Beth and Alma sobbed behind her. She shut the door and collapsed in a heap below the aprons. Wrapping herself in the blue shawl, she tried to calm down. She was not crying, but she was very upset. This scary older man had just threatened her. She tried to think.

Books are *important. And* Black Beauty *is quite a fine book.* "I will not give up on books," she said, as she shivered and wrapped her shawl more tightly around her shoulders. She reached over and picked up *Heidi*, now her only St. Louis book.

A tense two weeks followed. The adults did not appear when the girls ate breakfast and left for school. In the evening, Greta held Blanche back and sent her to the pantry with her supper, as directed by Mr. Robey. Blanche stretched out on her pallet and ate with the plate near her face. She read *Heidi* while she ate, detaching herself from the sense of punishment pervading the flat. *I will not be punished for books and reading,* she thought. *In my family, reading was a sacred activity! I will read alone if I cannot share the books. Thank goodness my tiny home has a light and a door! And a book!*

She began to relish her time alone in the pantry where—even if only briefly—she was not anyone's servant, but an eager student with an eager mind.

Blanche conducted her daily chores for the girls but avoided eye contact with the parents. She spent every evening in the pantry. She watched Heidi adapt to new circumstances, and she felt a kinship with her, since she was doing exactly the same thing.

Reading occupied her mind. But her heart and soul were lonesome for the evening company of her charges. The family was cold and strict, but the two girls treated Blanche with love and respect. She longed for that on the pantry evenings, which occasionally felt lonely.

After two weeks, Mr. Robey asked Blanche to join them at the dinner table. Almost immediately the girls started talking books. Beth had a homework assignment to do—a book report. She had a list of acceptable books for the report, and *Black Beauty* was on the list.

"I want to work with Blanche on this book, Father," said Beth. "She is the one who found the book and helped me understand it. I need her help to write the report. Please?"

"Well, Blanche, I guess we will bring *Black Beauty* back into the family. I will bring you the book after dinner. Would you be willing to help Beth with her report?" He looked at Blanche squarely, over his glasses, speaking in an even tone, but not smiling.

"Yes, of course," Blanche said, turning to Beth. "We can get started after dinner, as soon as I finish helping Greta."

"Father, may I listen, too?" pleaded Alma. "I can help figure out the pieces for the report."

The parents' eyes met down the length of the table. Both nodded solemnly.

After dinner the three girls hurried to the bedroom.

They talked of horse faces and people's expressions, people who were mean or kind to animals, the differences between farm life and city life, loyalty, family love, and hard work. The three girls studied and talked until they all understood the lessons in the story to the best of their abilities. They never even noticed the mud-stained pages.

Beth spent the two evenings that followed writing a simple but insightful book report.

The girls' bedroom, with its white walls and pink and white chenille bedspreads, was the only room in the flat with warm colors. The other rooms had dark walls and dark furniture. When the nightly book-reading hour began, all three girls would laugh and squeal with delight, and the room would come to life. Blanche was beginning to feel like their older sister, spending the evening curled up on the bed, their arms and feet entwined. Secretly she was also reveling in the success of her program.

Blanche soon began to read *Heidi* to them. Heidi was a five-year-old orphan living in a small mountain village in Switzerland. An unpleasant aunt took Heidi to her grandfather's mountain cabin, high in the Alps, where she spent a summer and learned about mountain goats and goat herders, mountain food, sunrises and sunsets, and wildflowers. The three girls' imaginations soared with this book, especially with the four or five lively sketches in each chapter. The girls became secret Heidi sisters, following every intrigue of her mountain adventure.

When they got to the very last sketch, which showed two girls, both Beth and Alma were almost in tears. They so wanted the story to go on that they were quite bereft when it ended.

With the end of the year approaching, the Robey household began to change. On December first, as the result of an end-of-year sale, new beds arrived for Beth and Alma. The old beds were removed, and the chenille bedspreads were moved to the new beds. These were spindle beds, painted shell pink. Beth's bed had a shell-pink trundle bed below, which could be rolled out. Mr. and Mrs. Robey said Blanche would move onto the trundle bed, which would be pushed under the bay window each night.

A new dog-eared book came from Mr. McGregor: *Alice's Adventures in Wonderland and Through the Looking Glass,* by Lewis Carroll. This book seemed strange and fanciful, but since it centered on a girl named Alice, Blanche felt the girls would enjoy the magical adventure. Blanche decided to delay starting the book until after the holidays, so that she would have a chance to study up for her students.

In mid-December, the Robey family began a celebration for their winter festival, which Blanche later learned was called Hanukkah. This festival, based on a lunar calendar, lasted for eight nights. Each night one helper candle was lit on a nine-candle menorah. Then one other candle, starting on the far right, was lit with the helper candle. After the candle ceremony, hymns and joyful songs were sung. These songs were sometimes rounds, and they were about the mystery of light, a spinning top called a *dreidel*, and ancient tales. Later the girls played a game with a small dreidel and chocolate coins, called Hanukkah gelt. After, the family shared a festival dinner that included beef brisket, latkes (potato pancakes) with apple-sauce, beets, and noodle pudding.

The Robeys did not force their religion on Lara, who was Catholic, or on Blanche, who was Methodist. Nonetheless, the home had its own holiday spirit with evening prayers, candles, and joyful songs. Learning about a new religion was another big-city experience for Blanche. She enjoyed making comparisons and contrasts with her own religion. The blessings and candles were symbols similar to those of her own church, but she found the ceremonial foods such as latkes a bit unusual.

On Monday, December 15, Greta and Blanche made a grocery trip to Soulard Market. Greta was still being asked to prepare the festival foods of beef brisket, latkes, and special bread. The market had glimpses of traditional December holiday color: wares displayed on red blankets, wagon frames festooned with children's paper garlands, and bits of tinsel here and there moving in the cold breeze and catching the winter sun. Greta took her coffee break, as usual, which gave Blanche a chance to visit Mr. McGregor.

As Blanche approached, she saw that he had a strange expression on his face, a furrowed brow and an indecipherable look in his eyes. Mr. McGregor walked Blanche to the side of his wagon, where it was more private. He withdrew a small envelope from the breast pocket of his tweed coat, all the while holding Blanche's blue eyes with his brown ones. Blanche looked down, saw her pa's handwriting, and an open envelope. Shaking, she clumsily withdrew the blue-lined paper. The message was short, bittersweet.

Dec 1, 1902

Dear Kind Angus McGregor and My Dear Blanche,

My heart sings to hear of your good fortune and safe home in St. Louis. Blanche, please continue your private studies. I will not write often, to ensure your safety. All of us send you love and good wishes for the Christmas holidays.

Lovingly, Pa

She scanned the letter quickly, familiar with Pa's script. She read the letter over and over, choking and starting to cry. Her watery eyes glanced up at Mr. McGregor, then back to the letter. She read it again, looking for more family news, more love, more comfort. What was everyone doing in the late fall? How was school going? Did they miss her? Her hands continued shaking as she held the small white page. She fell forward onto Mr. McGregor's shoulder and sobbed violently, wanting so much more from the letter.

Mr. McGregor let her cry, then held her up, looking into her sad eyes.

"Blanche, you must be strong. You do not know what Mr. Robey said to your pa. I suspect that he forbade correspondence with you, and your pa is protecting you with this short letter. I did inform him that I would hold all correspondence at my house and not let you take any letters to the Robey home. He knows you are safe. He knows of your home school. He knows of my books to you. This is what he chose to send you."

Mr. McGregor took her chin into his hand. "You must look upon this letter as a Christmas blessing and a short message of love. He said his 'heart sings' and he signs the letter 'lovingly.' You must make these words large in your heart and soul. You can be thankful for your educated, eloquent, and restrained pa. Blanche, although this may not comfort you, I must tell you that many rural parents have had to send their children away because they could not feed them. You are not alone. Now, in a very few minutes, you will give me the letter. Walk behind the wagon and cross the street. Then turn around and come back through the same way you went out. Tell Greta that you had a stomachache, and you went to look for a bathroom. Tell her you do not feel well and want to get home quickly. Go into your room and lie down and put the pillow over your head. Stay there as long as you can. You must keep your emotions, your overwhelming sorrow and small amount of joy, to yourself, so the Robeys don't find out you are corresponding with your pa. Can you do this?"

Blanche looked at him solemnly, nodded, and looked down at the letter, her golden curls falling forward. With one last gulp of a sob, she delicately folded the letter and handed it to him. Mr. McGregor then led her to the pedestrian path and hooked her straw basket onto her arm. She blinked, with blurred vision, and turned without saying goodbye, walking past the Eckert wagon and taking a cut-through to the street. She walked hypnotically past Mr. McGregor again, stepping slowly through the big messy puddles of the December market.

When Greta returned to the carriage, she found Blanche waiting with a tear-stained face and a painful expression. Blanche moaned something vague about a stomachache and no bathrooms, then slumped against the carriage. The driver helped her into the carriage, and they departed for the Robey flat immediately.

Blanche staggered in the front door and stumbled down the hall to the girls' bedroom. She fell across her extended bed and put the pillow over her head. She was overcome by disbelief and sadness. Mrs. Robey was quite concerned that normally robust Blanche was suddenly so unhealthy, and she herself took the carriage to get Beth.

Later, the Robey family prepared for their in-house Hanukkah festival. Without speaking, the girls dressed in the bedroom. Mrs. Robey looked in on Blanche before they began the night's celebration, making sure she saw a shoulder rise and fall, then gently closed the door.

When Blanche heard the piano and singing in the parlor, she began to choke and sob into her pillow. She hugged the pillow over her head, curled up her knees, and cried until she was out of tears. The loss of her family was such a very painful hardship. Her mind kept going back to three words "singing heart" and "lovingly." She adjusted the pillow, pulled up her covers, and swooned into a restless sleep. When Beth and Alma came to bed, she was fast asleep.

The next morning, Mrs. Robey let her sleep in, thinking the young girl might have a sickness of some sort, probably from that smelly market. Everyone whispered in the flat, with sickness in their midst. Mrs. Robey took the girls to school herself.

Blanche awakened midmorning and walked with blurry eyes to the bathroom. She was slightly nauseated and thought perhaps she had a touch of flu, perhaps something she picked up at the market. A visit to the bathroom told her otherwise, and she looked for Lara Doyle to help her with this new "problem." She tumbled back into bed after getting supplies and help from Lara.

Later, Greta came in with a big tray and a big smile on her face.

"Now lass, this is nothing to be sad about. Cheer up and eat hot tea and biscuits with jam. Yer just growin' up, gettin' to be a young lady. Didn't you say yer pa wanted St. Louis to make a young lady out of you? Well, it sure is happenin'!"

Blanche looked up through fresh tears, unable to speak. She touched the tray, nodded, and fell back onto her bed. She well understood what was happening. She had lived in a farm town; these female events were part of nature.

"Well, rest now. Mrs. Robey said to give you the day off. Eat your biscuits and tea, and go back to sleep if you want. You'll feel much better tomorrow!"

Blanche ate, then slept again. She spent the afternoon thinking about her pa and her Oraville family sitting in front of a roaring fire, sharing the *Robinson Crusoe* book. She hardly noticed the minor cramps and discomfort.

For the next several nights, the Robey family repeated the Hanukkah rituals, lighting one more candle each night. Blanche stayed in the bedroom, even through dinner. Finally, she came out to watch the rituals and eat with the family.

For the next week, Blanche went through the motions of her job. She was physically present but felt weak and out of touch. The Robey family was very involved in their holiday celebrations and left Blanche alone. The parents assumed she still felt bad; the little girls just thought she was sad. They always watched Blanche's face closely and were beginning to recognize her moods.

By late December Blanche again had clear eyes and a calm heart. She had skipped three visits to Soulard Market, as well as two weeks of reading to Beth and Alma. As she resumed the night reading, Blanche went back to *Black Beauty* and *Heidi*, the old familiar book friends who provided warmth and companionship. She was not ready to tackle a new book.

Blanche finally returned to Soulard Market with Greta on Christmas Eve. Greta would prepare food on Christmas, then not work again until December 29.

Soulard Market was cold and slushy, the ground covered in melted snow. There were only a few vendors. Everywhere down the row, horses snorted steam. Blanche saw vendors with neck wraps slapping their hands together. The December cold dampened the market smells and swarms of flies, but it increased the danger of slippery, icy puddles in the pedestrian path. Greta secured a beef roast, more pickled vegetables, and a few other staples. As usual, she took her coffee break, which freed Blanche to visit Mr. McGregor.

Blanche could see him up ahead, a heavy wool overcoat covering his tweed jacket. He also wore a dark beaver-fur hat, and pipe smoke curled around his collar.

Mr. McGregor removed the pipe when he saw Blanche, knocking it against his palm to remove the tobacco and putting the pipe in his coat pocket. He gave Blanche a wide grin and a big hug. Blanche smiled back cheerfully, with no tears.

"I want to thank you for so many things. I—," she began.

"Your friendly face is all the thanks I need," Mr. McGregor said, as he took off the fur hat and slapped it against the side of his coat. "I trust you are getting ready for the holidays?"

"Well, actually, no. The Robeys are Jewish and celebrated Hanukkah the week I got the letter from Pa. I was sad and lost in my thoughts. I had a difficult two weeks, but I did keep my promise to you and my pa. I kept the secret, and I am much better now."

"I am sorry I do not have another book for you because my recent searches have been unsuccessful. I promise to keep looking after the holidays." Mr. McGregor's words came out with frosty breath. "Let's see, maybe I can direct you to a bit of Christmas cheer. Take that shortcut beyond the Eckert wagon and cross the street. A store over there has Christmas lights and a display in the window. Go now to see the display, then come back to the market. Around noon I think you will catch a Christmas carols concert down near your carriage."

Blanche walked uphill and across the street. The window display was simple, but to her it was magical. Around the large windowpane, a few lights made everything glow. A small artificial Christmas tree was decorated with simple ornaments and colored chains. Next to the tree sat a puppet Santa with a jolly face and a sack of presents. On the floor next to the sled, Blanche saw a full-size lighted street lantern sitting in sparkling artificial snow.

Blanche had never seen a Christmas display window. She stood there for ten minutes with her hands clasped below her chin and a sweet smile on her face, which was lit up by the display lights. She took a deep breath and let out a cloud of vapor into the cold air. She felt warm inside, happy again after a long and very sad month.

Realizing that she had been away for some time, Blanche reluctantly left the Christmas window and headed for the Robey carriage. Sure enough, on a corner near the carriage, a small group of carolers was singing holiday songs. First "Away in a Manger," then "O Tannenbaum," then "Deck the Halls." The songs were all familiar to Blanche from church and school events, and she quietly hummed along with the singers.

Greta arrived, happy to see Blanche smiling. The singers moved on after the three songs. Greta signaled the driver and the carriage headed west. Blanche hummed "Deck the Halls" all the way home, while fondly remembering last December's Oraville school concert. She recalled the cedar smell and the happy faces of family and friends.

That night Mr. and Mrs. Robey dressed elegantly and left before dinner. Blanche reread the girls a favorite chapter of *Heidi*, and they went quickly to sleep.

Greta had assigned a kitchen pantry shelf for Blanche to store her underwear, blue shawl, purse, and other belongings. Blanche had gotten her shawl and was coming out of the kitchen when the Robeys came in the door, their shoulders frosted with snowflakes and their cheeks rosy. They took off their coats and turned toward the bedroom.

"Happy holidays to you!" said Mr. Robey cordially, momentarily turning back. "I was just at a business dinner, and these were given to me as a party favor. These little blank books are too small for my large hands, and I thought you might like to have them."

Mr. Robey handed Blanche two small booklets, each about two-and-a-half inches wide by five inches high. Blanche sat at the dining room table to receive them.

"Thank you very much. This is a lovely gift, and they're not too small for my hands!"

Blanche held the booklets and looked up at Mr. Robey.

"Well, good night. Please turn off the floor lamp when you go to bed."

As Mr. Robey turned to go, he took out his pocket watch to check the time. The watch case sparkled and sent a reflection across the room to the piano.

Blanche studied the two booklets, one black, one soft brown. Each cover had a rough texture like leather, but Blanche thought they were probably paper. Down the right side were the letters of the alphabet, in square black letters. The edges of the pages in each booklet were shiny gold, except for the edge in the binding.

Blanche held the booklets delicately, as if they were prayer books. With so few possessions of her own, these immediately felt special and important.

What will I use these for? she thought. *I know. I will use the shiny black book as my vocabulary word book! This will become an official place for the vocabulary word lists. The brown one, who knows? I can just put both books on my shelf for now. I will wait for inspiration for how to use the second booklet.*

Blanche turned off the floor lamp and headed to the girls' bedroom. Christmas windows, Christmas carols, and now these two special Christmas presents. She crawled into her trundle bed feeling very much at peace.

1904 World's Fair

St. Louis, Missouri • June 1904

There was a new normal in the Robey household with all of the children growing up. Blanche, now sixteen, had grown into a lovely, thoughtful young woman. Sometimes there was a sad look in her eyes, but around Beth and Alma she was all smiles. She still saw Mr. McGregor about twice a month to get new children's books for the nighttime reading program. Bland, short letters from Oraville still arrived about twice a year.

Blanche had become more self-confident about how to conduct herself, but in a quiet way. She did not have people her own age to relate to. In the fall of the preceding year, Wallace had left for college to study engineering. Lara Doyle's painful shyness and lack of education meant that with her Blanche seldom had meaningful conversations. Since Blanche rarely talked to other young people, she was uninformed about social graces or current fashion trends. Intellectually, however, she was increasing her vocabulary, reading many books, and feeling very satisfied with her self-education program.

Beth was now a very serious eleven-year-old, her light-brown hair parted in the middle and pulled into a knot at the base of her neck. Alma, saucy as ever at eight, still had dark, curly hair and always wanted to wear very large hair bows. As both girls had gotten older and more educated, they had begun to emulate Blanche's good posture, reserved mannerisms, and way of speaking with careful diction.

The evening reading program continued almost every night. The three girls still sat together on Alma's bed, with Blanche in the center. Partly due to this stimulation, the girls progressed rapidly in school. They learned to do their homework efficiently, albeit carefully, to make time for Blanche's book readings.

Whereas initially Mr. Robey tolerated the damaged books from Soulard Market, after the first year he suggested trips to the public library. He took the three girls to the Central Library in the downtown Board of Education building at Locust and Ninth Street and registered for library cards for each of them. He then walked his children and Blanche to the youth section. The dimly lit children's room had bare bulbs hanging from the ceiling, tall, crowded stacks of shelves, and a cluster of dingy tables. Nonetheless, it did contain hundreds of books.

After the first visit, about once a month Mr. Robey summoned his carriage from Keyes & Marshall Brothers Livery to take the three girls to the library to search out books. Beth and Alma chose more horse and farm-animal books, while Blanche began to read young-adult adventure stories.

Due to the Eads Bridge and the development of new city

parks, St. Louis was experiencing a period of rapid growth with great industrial expansion. Because of this growth and prosperity, in 1901 thirteen-hundred-acre Forest Park was selected to be the site not only of the 1904 World's Fair, but also of the 1904 games of the III Olympiad. Some sixty foreign countries would have exhibits, as would most U.S. states.

The Robey family lived just north of Forest Park. They often traveled on Kingshighway, which bordered it. Since her 1902 arrival, Blanche had observed earth moving and tree removal where the fairgrounds were being constructed. She watched construction of "embassy homes" at the edge of the park. They would house dignitaries from all over the world.

"They are building more than a thousand buildings at the fair, and I want to visit all of them," Beth said, looking at a crude map of Forest Park she had brought home from school to show her family. "Next fall, our school will take field trips to visit one country exhibit from each of the earth's continents. What an interesting way to learn about foreign people—including pygmies!—and foreign lands!"

At the beginning of 1904, Blanche had been really excited for her first visit to the fair, which would open in April. Unfortunately, Mr. Robey decided to schedule the family visit for after school was out in late June, thus avoiding the overwhelming crowds of the first two months of the fair. The Robeys' anniversary was in late June, so the excursion would also be in honor of that.

Two days before the visit to the fair, Mrs. Robey sprained her knee. She was barely able to walk and felt the visit should be postponed. Mr. Robey did some quick research and found he could rent a large horse-drawn carriage for the day. This would be the transportation for their celebratory visit.

Blanche now had an adult figure with straight shoulders and a slim waist. She took great pleasure in altering her clothes for her feminine figure. She had a new flowery gingham dress, compliments of Lara Doyle, and she worked for a week to alter the fabric to give it a formal and womanly bodice, making it look more like a party dress. Doubling the front-scooped ruffle with material from the bottom of the skirt and gathering fabric at the top of the sleeve to create a blousy effect, she gave the dress a more womanly style.

The morning of the day of the fair visit, Blanche excitedly put the dress on. She was tall now and looked admiringly at her curves in the mirror. She then headed to the breakfast table.

My! she thought. *With this dress, I will be a lady, riding in the carriage, watching our city welcome the world to the fair.*

Blanche floated down the hall in her lovely dress, humming under her breath, and joined the family. Beth and Alma were eagerly talking about animal exhibits and whether there would be exciting rides at the fair. Wallace, home from college, talked about engineering feats he wanted to see, particularly the 265-foot-tall Observation Wheel.

The ride to the fair was delayed by streams of traffic. The whole family broke into laughter and clapping when they finally made it to the Wabash entry gate. But with thousands of people crowding the gate, laughter quickly gave way to concern.

Mr. Robey assisted his wife out of the carriage, since personal vehicles were not allowed in the fair. She limped slightly but said she could manage. The family stood together, in their good clothes, quietly watching the expanding crowds and waiting for their rented carriage.

Blanche could hardly contain her excitement. She tightly held Beth and Alma's hands as the crowds expanded in their direction. The three of them looked up at the elaborate gold-painted Wabash gate, where train passengers arrived from downtown. Blanche already felt she was in another world, someplace even bigger than St. Louis. The air was filled with exotic scents from around the globe.

Their rental horse carriage arrived. It was open-air with a shaded top, painted dark green, and had benches facing inward on two sides. Their group, including the Langs and Lara Doyle, spread out on wood-plank benches. The children and Lara sat on one side, the four adults on the other.

The carriage went first to the Grand Basin to view its magnificent water features. The Des Peres River, which had once meandered through Forest Park in shallow pools, had been rerouted, channeled, and filtered for the fair. Its waters became the Grand Basin, a large, rectangular lake several acres in size and fed by a hillside display of artificial waterfalls. These waterfalls and fountains became the design axis of the St. Louis World's Fair, and the large palaces of Machinery, Industry, Manufacturing, and Education were grouped around the base of the Grand Basin. Wallace jumped off the carriage, taking a deep breath of the freshwater smell, and urged his father and Mr. Lang to follow. They excitedly discussed the white cascades of tumbling water from the many fountains.

While the men looked at the fountains, the women stayed in the carriage and studied the fashions of the crowds promenading around the Grand Basin. There were women in long black skirts, white blouses, and sensible wide-brimmed hats. Others wore long, pastel summer gowns with elaborately decorated hats stretching to the tips of their shoulders. All of the men wore dark suits and formal hats, and many held parasols for the ladies. Foreign fair workers in embroidered aprons and floor-length robes crossed the boulevards and cut through the crowds. The Robey women wore well-made but conservative clothes. They seemed underdressed in comparison to the fashion statements being made in the crowd. Blanche studied the dresses and hats in awe. She still felt happy with her altered gingham dress.

When the men returned, the carriage drove to the Observation Wheel, which looked like a giant bicycle wheel. Mr. Robey handed money to Wallace, and the four young people paid and entered one of the swinging compartments attached to the giant wheel. As, one-by-one, the compartments filled, Wallace and the girls ascended 265 feet to the top of the wheel. The wheel made several slow turns once all of the compartments were full, and the Robey group spent the turns in giddy aerial exploration of the vast fair.

"What a structure, and what a thrill!" said Wallace, taking off his cap at the top of the wheel and waving to his parents out a side window of the compartment, carefully holding onto a guardrail with one hand.

The three girls clasped hands, giggled, and looked across the panorama of the fair. They saw the glint of sunlight off the Grand Basin, wide boulevards lined with rows of newly planted trees, and the group of ornate palaces around the Grand Basin.

"My!" said Beth, "This must be the most magnificent fair in the world!"

"I'm scared but excited!" said Alma, as she clutched Blanche's warm hand. The compartment was swaying slightly.

Blanche glanced across the colorful layout of buildings below, thrilled at the aerial view from the moving wheel. The wheel began its slow final descent.

Still excited and laughing, the young people exited and piled back into the carriage, which headed past the Palace of Agriculture toward a huge floral clock built into a hillside. The arms of the clock were fifty and seventy-five feet long, respectively, and the face was composed of thousands of pink and red flowers. The entire family lifted their noses like hunting dogs, inhaling the lovely scent of the flowers. Even Mrs. Robey took her husband's hand, lovingly smiled at him, and turned to take in the magnificence of the clock. Their driver mentioned that it was the largest clock in the world.

The carriage horses bowed their heads, straining up Art Hill, which overlooked the Grand Basin. The family got out of the carriage to take in the view of two buildings: Festival Hall, at the top of the central water cascades, and a permanent sandstone structure called the Palace of Art.

Alma, who had seen enough of buildings, pulled Beth and Blanche toward a crowd at the bottom of the Palace of Art steps. She noticed camera bulbs flashing and wanted to investigate.

A woman stood two steps up from a crowd of reporters, who were writing frantically in their notebooks. She was calm and smiled, wearing a white-collared tan dress that had two dozen medals pinned to the front of the bodice. In response to a comment from one of the reporters, she threw her head back in a hearty laugh, sending her long brown curls flaring out across her shoulders. Her cowgirl hat tipped back on her head.

The three girls watched, spellbound. They had never seen a woman laugh with such self-confident abandon.

The woman raised both arms, smiled charismatically, and shouted "As I always say, keep on aiming and keep on shooting, for only practice will make you perfect!"

"Annie Oakley, what is your advice to women?" shouted another reporter.

"When learning the use of a firearm, a woman learns at the same time confidence and self-possession. Every lady who has the chance should learn the use of firearms, so that she may protect herself in times of danger."

Annie Oakley stared at the reporter to make her point. Then she lifted her trick-shot rifle above her head and punched the air with the gun, as if she had just won a shooting match. Flashbulbs recording every step, a man in western clothes took her arm and led her off the steps to a small waiting carriage.

The girls watched the departure with surprised silence. They were all smiling and a bit awed by this famous woman, whose name they recognized. Beth and Alma had never heard a woman speak to a crowd, and Annie Oakley made a lasting impression, since she was clearly a skilled woman with strong opinions who was not afraid to speak in public.

The girls hurried back to the family carriage, chattering about the famous woman they had just observed. The driver took them to the Flight Cage. As they approached it, Wallace stood up, unable to contain himself.

"I think this is the largest bird cage in the world!" he laughed. "Can we walk around it?"

Mr. and Mrs. Robey were happy to remain seated while the young people got out. The steel-beam and wire-mesh Flight Cage was over two hundred feet long and fifty feet high. It was landscaped with exotic trees, shrubs, and even a flowing stream. Wallace saw a sign for a pedestrian tunnel under the cage. He led the girls inside the shadowy passage, where they could watch from behind screened openings.

"Look at those flying birds with white feathers—and ones with pink feathers, too!" Alma exclaimed. At the same time, she rubbed her nose because of an acrid smell of birds that had settled in the tunnel.

"The birds with greenish feathers are peacocks, from India. We learned about them in school," explained Wallace. "They're like watchdogs, and they're screaming because we are strangers coming into their cage."

Nearby a large peacock, his feathers in a magnificent fan, pointed his black and white head up to the sky and uttered a piercing series of closely spaced wails. The younger girls shrieked and jumped back as the calls erupted.

After the peacock calls everyone grew anxious in the cold and damp concrete tunnel, which echoed the loud bird sounds. Beth tugged at Wallace's coat to leave, and they were all glad to exit. They emerged from the tunnel and rushed back to the carriage.

At the request of Mr. Robey, the carriage traveled down the east end of the fair to the Manufacturing Palace. This beaux arts palace was one of several large buildings facing formal gardens, like those of French castles. Mr. Robey had several business friends with booths in the building, and he wanted to make courtesy stops with his family to see them. They went inside, all following Mr. Robey.

Allowed to explore on her own, Blanche wandered down a hallway, drawn to an elaborate corner exhibit consisting of twenty-foot-tall columns and an overhead trellis interwoven with lovely artificial vines and flowers. Above the trellis was a translucent ceiling, lighted by some sort of skylight. Blanche was amazed to see an enormous textured map of the United States mounted on the back wall of the exhibit. Each state was formed with artificial flowers in different colors, and a sign next to the map read: "Rosenthal-Sloan Co.: Flowers and Feathers."

After carefully studying the extraordinary map, Blanche directed her attention to the booth itself. At the base of the pillars were wood-and-glass display cases, which extended from waist level to the floor. Inside one, she saw elaborate Victorian ladies hats decorated with the "Flowers and Feathers" of the Rosenthal-Sloan Millinery Company. An ornately decorated bright-red hat that seemed to have the wings of the cardinal, famous in St. Louis, drew Blanche's eyes to another display case. She sat on the floor to study the red hat closely.

The hat was a combination of red felt and deep-red velvet. It had bright-red feathers with gray tips—like the cardinal itself—which were placed at an unusual angle, giving the entire hat a sense of flight. Blanche gasped, amazed by its birdlike quality! She moved her hands toward the hat, imagining holding it and adding an accent red ribbon bow below the feathers.

The passing crowds became a colored swirl behind her, and the noise of the pavilion dropped to a whisper. Blanche had never seen anything in her life like these exquisite hats. Each one seemed to float above its stand like a work of three-dimensional art. As her eyes moved from one hat to another, she noted a tall, white hat wrapped in layers of black and gray chiffon that was particularly striking. She scooted—not very gracefully—across the hallway floor from one display case to the next. Over and over her hands moved outside the glass, wanting to hold the hats. She spent almost an hour lost in imaginary hat construction.

When Mr. Robey found her, she was still sitting on the floor, oblivious to the world, making unusual hand motions in front of the elaborate hats. She did not even notice him as he came up behind her. He wondered what her hand motions meant.

Out of the back of the booth strolled Benjamin Moritz, the booth manager, and a member of Mr. Robey's temple. Noticing Mr. Robey, he beckoned him over. In hushed voices they discussed the young woman sitting on the floor, doing hand ballet in front of the display hats. As the conversation came to a close, Mr. Robey rubbed his chin thoughtfully, bowed slightly, and gave a firm handshake to his friend. Then he walked over to Blanche.

"Miss Blanche Spencer, we have finally found you. Will you come now to share dinner with the family?"

Blanche reluctantly turned her eyes from the beckoning hats, then stumbled to her feet.

On Mr. Moritz's recommendation, Mr. Robey took his family to Beaud's Restaurant for dinner, in the Palace of Manufacturing. The restaurant had plush red-velvet seating and murals on the walls. The friendly aromas of fried meat and freshly baked bread filled the air. It was a moderately priced establishment with excellent food. The party of nine sat at a corner table in front of a wide window framed by red-velvet curtains. Blanche had never in her life heard of whitefish or Waldorf salad—or chicken in a pie! The group ordered some of everything on the menu then began to discuss their day. Beth wanted everyone to share their favorite exhibit.

"Well, my favorite exhibit by far was the Observation Wheel," said Wallace, speaking very much like a young engineer.

"I loved the bird cage with the hundreds of birds and

the secret tunnel," said Alma, spreading her arms in mock flight.

"I thought the interview with Annie Oakley was very interesting," said Blanche, who wanted to keep the hat display her own private secret.

"We loved the Palace of Art and views of the Grand Canal," said Mr. Lang.

"Me, too," said Lara Doyle.

"Oh my," smiled Mrs. Robey, "the most special treat for me was not having to walk all day. And I fell in love with the floral clock. Thank you so much for this lovely anniversary excursion." She fondly touched her husband's shoulder, in an unusual display of affection.

"I think I am very hungry, and I think I will love the dinner the best!" said a prim and happy Beth.

The Sweet Sisters
Rosenthal-Sloan Millinery Company • St. Louis, Missouri
January 1908

Blanche continued to think lingering thoughts about the World's Fair. She had noticed the many fancy dresses at the fair and dared to hope that someday she might have fancy clothes, too, although she had no way of making money to buy them. And whereas she had worn her lovely curls down on her shoulders, she saw many women at the fair wearing a swept-up hairdo, which Greta told her was called the "pompadour." In the bathroom, secretly she had tried pinning her hair up with hairpins, but her attempts only ended in jumbled haystacks on her head.

World's Fair memories lingered in the minds of all of the Robey family for the next few years. Alma developed a strong interest in birds and wanted to read books about the comical, big-billed pelicans. Mr. Robey loved to buy jewelry for his wife, and he found for her a small brooch of colored stones and gold clock hands depicting the fair's floral clock.

In the summer of 1907, Mr. Robey announced that the

last week of July the family—not including Lara Doyle or Blanche—would take a train trip to Chicago to visit relatives. Mrs. Robey left thread and a five-yard piece of gingham with Blanche and suggested she design and make a new dress for herself while they were away.

Before their departure, Mr. Robey firmly emphasized their policy that Blanche, now nineteen, should *only* leave the house with Greta for shopping. She was not to go out of the flat for any other reason. Blanche yearned to explore St. Louis but, with a heavy heart, accepted this Victorian restraint. Blanche was the Robey's ward, not a free woman.

The family had moved to 5259A McPherson Street. This summer, 1907, Blanche had the girls' bedroom to herself, but it got minimal sunlight. Blanche found that she preferred reading in the sunny new living room, with no one around to interrupt her.

On Monday, after the family departed for Chicago, Greta and Blanche took an afternoon trip to Soulard Market. After initial shopping, Greta declared she would take a long coffee break with her friend. Blanche was free to buy peaches and explore.

Blanche wandered to Farmer Eckert's wagon, knowing she would probably see Mr. McGregor first. The relationship between Blanche and Mr. McGregor had evolved over the six years of their friendship, and they now discussed other subjects besides books. He had become a big help, giving her sound advice on which literature and poetry books to read. He also gave her emotional support when her disappointing and infrequent Oraville letters arrived, as well as ongoing encouragement for her small triumphs, such as her sewing projects.

As Blanche walked toward Mr. McGregor now, she

realized that she was almost as tall as he was. He greeted Blanche, directed her to the back corner between the two wagons, and pulled a letter out of his pocket. Blanche had been receiving about two letters a year from her father. Now, though, she had not gotten one since her birthday the previous year, in May 1906. The previous letters were all almost the same—short, inadequate, void of intimacy or family news. Mr. McGregor had opened this letter, as usual, and handed the envelope to Blanche with an unclouded face. She pulled the familiar white sheet from the envelope, not expecting any extraordinary news.

July 31, 1907

Dear Kind Angus McGregor and My Dear Blanche,

My letter is tardy this summer, but the family and I send you belated good wishes for your 19th birthday. Your sister Lelia died on Jan 27, 1907. We all miss her. I am sorry to send you sad news.

Lovingly, Pa

Blanche held the letter with two hands, bowed her head slowly, then raised it, her eyes filled with tears. As usual, Mr. McGregor was there to help. He leaned forward, took hold of both her elbows, and looked straight into her eyes.

"Blanche, each of these letters becomes a milestone in your life. Somehow you grow up with or in spite of the news in the letter. You must mourn your sister's passing but not blame yourself or your family in any way." His tone was soft and loving.

Blanche sighed, as a few tears rolled down her cheek. "We were not close, because she was so much older, but she was my sister."

"Your sister Lelia is now peacefully in Heaven. You must give her a loving farewell and move on. Can you do this?"

"Yes, Mr. McGregor. I will go home today and weep quietly. But without details, it is hard to imagine their lives and feel my sister's loss."

"Well, please continue to keep this correspondence a secret, as always. Oh, and by the way, I have a late present for your birthday," he said.

Mr. McGregor handed Blanche a small book with a plain white cover and modest black lettering. It was *Poems* by Currer, Ellis, and Acton Bell.

Blanche adjusted the basket and slid the book in among the peaches. Smiling weakly, she thanked Mr. McGregor and headed back to the carriage.

Later at the flat, Blanche read several of the poems in the small book. She was always interested in word use in poems, which was so different from word use in novels. She came to a poem called "Presentiment" and lingered on it for a long time, because it reminded her of the death of her sister in the winter snows of Illinois.

> She's thinking of one winter's day
> A few short months ago,
> When Emma's bier was borne away
> O'er wastes of frozen snow.

She did not want to memorize the poem, but she spent a sorrowful evening reading it over and over, in memory of Lelia. Only later did Blanche realize that her mentor had probably given her this book specifically so that she would find the poem.

With the Robeys away, Blanche had a somewhat lazy week, sleeping in and working on the new dress a few hours each day. She was increasingly proud of her womanly curves. Fitting a dress for herself required careful darts in the bodice and precisely measured gathers at the waist and shoulders.

She had begun to look out the windows with restless longing, wondering what was beyond the next block. She was old enough to be independent, though she did not know this, and felt a vague notion of discontent at not being allowed out of the flat. Despite these stirrings, she did not defy the Robeys' orders, spending her evenings indoors rereading books from the children's library. Blanche felt that all books were a window onto the wider world.

The school routine began in September, and Blanche again became busy with errands, as well as homework tutoring and night reading to the girls. Beth was now attending Central High School on Grand Boulevard. Since her father dropped her off each morning, Blanche only had to walk Alma to and from school. Meanwhile, Blanche felt an overwhelming sadness, maybe for the loss of Lelia or maybe for the lack of opportunity to do more with her life.

That all changed one evening in early November 1907, when Mr. Robey gruffly called to Blanche during her dinner-cleanup chores.

"Blanche, when you finish your chores, please come find me. I have something important to tell you."

Blanche hurried through her cleanup work and went to Mr. Robey, seated in the living room.

"Let's go into my office," he said, upon seeing her. He rose, putting the pocket watch in his vest pocket and looking at Blanche with a face she could not interpret.

Blanche followed Mr. Robey into the office and sat in the black leather chair. She sat high now, filling it up, her golden head near the top of the chair's back, her feet almost touching the floor. She looked at Mr. Robey and waited.

"Blanche, you have done a wonderful job with our daughters. As part of our original obligation to bring you into our family, we promised to provide you with skills for your adult life. I have made arrangements to send you to a school where you can learn a trade. At the World's Fair, I noticed your interest in the hats at the Rosenthal-Sloan booth. Benjamin Moritz is a friend of mine, and we talked about you that day, while you were absorbed in the hat display. Mr. Moritz is willing to admit you to his spring hat-making workshop at Rosenthal-Sloan."

Blanche felt an immediate surge of energy course through her body. She gripped the black leather armrests and took a deep breath.

"I don't understand, I have no money for such a school," she whispered, confused.

"I have made arrangements for you with Mr. Moritz. He has some discretion with scholarship funds. The program begins on January 9, 1908. You would still live with us and still read to Beth and Alma. I feel the girls are old enough to do schoolwork on their own. You would attend workshops full-time each week. Would this interest you?"

"Why yes. It would be... I have an interest in... I—"

"I think Mr. Moritz and I both saw this interest of yours that day at the booth. I know you left your own family to seek better opportunities in St. Louis."

Mr. Robey stood up, smiling, his rotund form filling out his suit vest. He pulled out his pocket watch and glanced at the gold disk.

"It is about time for book reading with the girls."

Blanche could hardly contain her excitement as she left.

The following week Mr. Robey and Blanche set out in the carriage toward 1700 Washington Avenue, where Rosenthal-Sloan was located. Mr. Robey was dressed in his customary business suit and top hat, Blanche in a clean gingham dress. She tapped one foot nervously. When they arrived midafternoon, Blanche looked at the unusual seven-story limestone building with curiosity. The building was decorated with circular carvings. The circles were not in the form of hats exactly, but Blanche felt they symbolized them. Hats on a hat school. How lovely!

They entered a well-lit, two-story lobby. Blanche recognized the huge flower map from the World's Fair. She stood smiling up at the map, while Mr. Robey walked to the reception desk. The receptionist directed them to sit in the enclosed waiting area, where there were many well-dressed ladies in large hats. Blanche stood next to Mr. Robey, as she continued to study the fanciful flower map.

Mr. Moritz soon arrived, a large man with silver hair and eyebrows, rimless glasses, and a silver mustache. He wore a dark three-piece suit with a bow tie. He was accompanied by a prim assistant, a middle-aged woman in a black skirt and tailored white blouse. Blanche was introduced to Mr. Moritz and Miss Gertrude Adams, who then offered to take her to the office to register for the program. The men went off on their own to talk business.

FLOWER MAP AND WRITING ROOM.—ROSENTHAL-SLOAN MILLINERY CO., SAINT LOUIS.

Miss Adams and Blanche climbed up one flight of stairs to a glassed-in office. Blanche carefully filled out several sheets of registration forms and was given a map of St. Louis streetcar routes. Miss Adams then took her back downstairs to the lobby. She would see Blanche again in January, on the first day of classes.

When Mr. Robey returned, he and Blanche departed for his carriage. Mr. Robey directed the driver three blocks north, past tall, imposing office buildings, and up Seventeenth Street to Delmar Boulevard. He helped Blanche off the carriage, asked her for the streetcar map, and showed her the location of the Delmar streetcar stop at Kingshighway. He then handed her two silver streetcar tokens.

"I must head to my office and do not have time to take you home. As it shows here on the map, you will only need one token to ride out to the stop at Kingshighway," he said.

"Get off at this corner and walk four short blocks to our flat. This will be a familiar corner in our new neighborhood. Do not look at or talk to strange men. Good luck!" With that, he got back into the carriage, signaled the driver, and departed.

Just as the streetcar arrived, a bulky man hurried past Blanche, knocking the tokens out of her hand and under the streetcar. Stunned, Blanche looked at her empty palm, people rushing past her to get on the streetcar. Her mind raced. She had no money!

The streetcar pulled forward, clanging as it departed. Blanche rushed to the tracks and bent over to search for the tokens. In the dim light of dusk, she saw only a few paper scraps, gravel, and grime. She saw no dull silver objects. She looked up and down the tracks and carefully scanned back and forth, both on the tracks and on each side of them, looking for silver among the gravel. Nothing.

The rush-hour streetcars will not give me a free ride, she thought. *They would just make me get off the car!*

Blanche buttoned her wrap and quickly walked the three blocks back to Rosenthal-Sloan. She banged on the heavy door of the building, but there was no answer. Shaking in the freezing weather, Blanche turned to the street, wishing she had gloves. The five- and six-story buildings on Washington Avenue were empty and unlit, extending down the street for two blocks in the growing darkness. At the end of the second block she saw a faint light. She bent her chin down, clutched the wrap, and held her flour-sack purse tight to her chest, setting off for the light. She was determined to get home to the Robey flat.

On the second block she heard loud singing. She hid in a dark doorway and remained perfectly still until two drunken men across the street passed. Her heart pounding, she now felt helpless and alone in the city darkness.

Stepping out of the doorway, she looked in both directions, then continued her march toward the dim lights, which turned out to be coming from a small tavern. She knew proper women did not enter taverns, but she had lunched in several small taverns near Soulard Market. So, she knew almost all were family run—and she hoped this one was, too. She gathered her courage and went in. She sat on an empty stool at the end of the bar and watched for the barkeep to notice her.

"What will you have, miss?" He spoke with a smile.

"Good evening, sir," said Blanche, teeth chattering from the cold night air. "I've lost my streetcar tokens and cannot get home. Do you have any such tokens here? I work at a hat company on the next block and could bring you money tomorrow for the tokens. I give you my word," she said, hoping he would believe her.

"Where you headed, miss?" asked the barkeep.

"McPherson at Kingshighway, near Forest Park."

"Hey, fellas, we have a pretty lass here looking for streetcar tokens!" A large, burly patron walked up and raised a beer mug above Blanche's head. "Maybe we can get her to dance on the bar counter for tokens!"

Blanche ducked under the beer mug and pushed away the man's arm. She was more annoyed than scared.

"Leave her alone," said the barkeep.

"Say, miss," began a slim, dark-haired, and clean-cut patron on her left. "I work for Keyes Marshall Livery, and I'm just heading up to the Keyes station near your home. You could ride with me."

"Miss, this is Todd Marshall, brother of one of the owners of Keyes Marshall Livery. You can trust him," said the barkeep.

"How do I know you will take me safely to McPherson Street?" Blanche asked, as she looked at the patron with a cautious glance, her stomach in knots.

"Because I have two daughters about your age, and I would want someone to befriend them in a jam. I would like to help. I should be getting home anyway," he said.

"Sure, Todd," called a man, while others whistled and snorted.

"Come, miss," said Todd Marshall, as he got up. "This is no place for a nice lady like yourself."

"He'll get you home safely," insisted the barkeep.

Blanche rose, shivered, and looked closely into Todd Marshall's eyes. She decided going with him was her best option.

"What is your name, miss?" asked Todd Marshall, opening the front door.

"Miss Spencer."

"Proper name for a proper and lovely young lady. Here is my carriage," he said proudly.

Blanche climbed up to the carriage seat, behind two dark-colored, snorting horses whose backs appeared silvery in the tavern's lights.

"Off we go," Todd Marshall said, cracking the whip.

Blanche closed her wrap at the neck and held tightly to her purse. She gulped in a breath of the cold air and narrowed her eyes. She was frightened by the rushing speed, the unfamiliar dark streets, and this dangerous night journey with a complete stranger.

The driver began to sing Irish folk songs. He turned to put an arm around Blanche and squeezed her shoulder. She stiffened, trying not to let her teeth chatter, and looked straight ahead. *Please let me get home safely!* she thought.

Todd Marshall withdrew his arm, continued to sing, and guided the horses west on Olive, which turned into Lindell. Then he veered right onto McPherson.

"Will you recognize the house, miss?" he inquired politely.

"Yes, the house is at the corner of McPherson and Kingshighway," she said.

"Ah yes, a busy intersection. A few more blocks. Goodness, you got no gloves, miss." He reached towards her, and she again stiffened.

"Relax, miss, I mean no harm, just wantin' to keep you warm," Todd Marshall said softly.

As they arrived at the corner of McPherson and Kingshighway, Blanche saw horses and two policemen on the front steps of the house. They were talking to Mr. Robey.

Todd Marshall stopped his carriage at the curb, jumped down, and ran to the steps.

"Mr. Robey, nice to see you sir! Does this young lady belong at your house?" he asked.

Mr. Robey and the two policemen had turned at the sound of the carriage and came lumbering down the stairs.

"Oh Mr. Robey, I am so relieved to see you!" Blanche exclaimed.

"You certainly have some explaining to do," Mr. Robey said harshly.

He reached into his suit coat, took out a wallet, and withdrew a few bills to pay Todd Marshall. The policemen, tipping their hats, turned to go.

"Thank you, Mr. Robey. As always, we appreciate your business. Young lady, better get inside out of the cold," Todd Marshall said, bowing slightly.

Mr. Robey scowled, grabbed Blanche's arm, and pushed her toward the steps.

"You have put yourself in great danger," he growled. "We need an explanation for this late arrival."

Blanche trembled as she hastened up the steps.

~

December 1907 came and went. The holiday routines remained about the same each year. Blanche continued to observe and partially participate in the Hanukkah celebration, almost able to hum along with the songs. And each year there were a few more Christmas display windows.

Blanche performed her family chores each day with a feeling of giddy excitement pulsing in the back of her throat. She was about to get both education and a degree of freedom. Meanwhile, she worked with resolve through each day, willing the next one to pass even quicker.

On a dark January day, Blanche rose very early, washed, and dressed in her new, handmade gingham dress. She neatly combed her shoulder-length hair. She placed her old, dark-blue wool cape from Greta on the parlor sofa. Then she made a bread and cheese sandwich, wrapped it in newspaper, and placed it with an apple in her flour-sack purse. Today was her first day of school, and she could hardly contain herself.

Mr. Robey had given her ten silver tokens, and she had made a small gingham drawstring bag in which to carry them in her purse. After having lost the first tokens, she knew she had to be very careful with these. Blanche hurried the girls through their morning chores, knowing she would have to take Alma to school early in order to catch her streetcar.

After Alma waved a warm goodbye to her at the steps

of the school, Blanche turned and hurried four blocks to the streetcar stop. She stepped onto the eastbound Delmar car for a twenty-minute ride. The car was very crowded, so she moved halfway back and caught a strap to hold on. As she swayed with the movement of the streetcar, she studied her surroundings. Men read the morning *Globe Democrat* newspaper, and women speaking softly in Italian carried canvas bags. After glancing about briefly, Blanche mostly kept her eyes down. She made sure she had her purse, lunch, map, and tokens. She had to get off at Seventeenth Street, so she carefully listened for the name of that street.

Blanche alighted at her corner and quickly walked three blocks south to Washington Street, her heartbeat quickening with every step. She turned left and saw the hat factory. Working girls, almost all wearing black skirts, black leather boots, and winter coats, streamed into the building.

In the foyer, Blanche spotted Miss Adams holding a sign: "Beginning Hat Making, third floor, take left stairway to room number three." Miss Adams smiled as Blanche raced up the iron stairway.

In the classroom, Blanche perched on a second-row stool, removed the purse from her wrist, and took a deep breath, looking around the large, dull-white studio. There were six rows of stools, long workbenches, and very tall windows along one wall. Most of the young women were in black skirts and white blouses, and a few greeted each other. Blanche felt a bit left out and wished she had some friends to greet.

She also felt plain and old-fashioned in her gingham dress, realizing for the first time the totality of her six-year isolation from other young women. In spite of her excitement to learn new skills, she wondered if she would even fit into the school.

Miss Adams and another woman came into the room and stood behind the demonstration table, which was piled high with fabric samples, ribbons, feathers, and artificial flowers. Blanche's eyes darted from one pile of supplies to the next. She tapped one foot against the stool, listening closely to every word.

The two women introduced themselves. The woman with Miss Adams was named Miss McGuire. They took turns giving a two-hour introductory lecture.

At the lunch break, the girls were instructed to eat at their stools. They could go out to get water and go to the bathroom, but they had to return in time for the afternoon lecture.

The young women gathered together, everyone speaking at once. Blanche watched from the edge of the group as they introduced themselves to each other. Tongue-tied, she wondered if she could fit in.

A girl with auburn hair motioned for Blanche to join them.

"I'm Pauline!" smiled the perky gal, as she patted the back of her cropped hair.

"I'm Emma!" exclaimed a tall, dark-haired girl with rimless glasses and a lovely smile.

"I'm Lily!" purred a petite brunette with porcelain skin and an elaborate hairdo.

Blanche introduced herself, too, smiling at each of the girls.

"I am excited to finally be here. My aunt got me into this program. She already works here and loves it!" said Pauline, her smile wrinkling her pug nose.

"I have a friend here, and she gave me a tour of the

building," said Lily. "What about you, Blanche?"

"Well, I got interested in this program after seeing the Rosenthal-Sloan exhibit at the World's Fair. I registered last fall, and here I am!" Blanche was still sitting on her stool. "Lily, I love the way your hair sweeps up. What do you call this hair style?"

"This is a sort of pompadour hairdo, very popular right now. I can show you how to do it. I even have extra hairpins in my purse!" Lily patted her carefully arranged hair.

"Oh, I would love that!" glowed Blanche.

"Listen, Blanche, we need to dress you in working-girl clothes, not a gingham dress," Emma said frankly. "You are about my size. Tomorrow I can bring you my extra skirt to see if it fits."

"But I just made this dress. It is new and clean!" said Blanche defensively.

"Yes, obviously it is well-made," Emma replied calmly. "But it's the dress of a country schoolgirl. You are now at a hat company in a big city, and you might feel more comfortable dressing like the rest of us."

"I suppose you are right," Blanche said softly, blushing.

"Blanche, we want you to fit in, not stick out like a hayseed!" giggled Pauline. "I have all of my aunt's old blouses because she is buying new ones, now that she makes a salary. I will bring you two of them tomorrow, and you can try them on with Emma's skirt."

"That would be nice," said Blanche tentatively. "I work as a live-in nursemaid and do not get out much. And I have very little money. I am proud of my dressmaking skills, but I agree it would be best to dress like the rest of you. I hope the clothes will fit tomorrow. Thank you both."

The classmates, all in the second row, returned to their

stools. Each one eagerly faced Miss McGuire. The afternoon lecture, again shared by the two teachers, was about the history of fashion design, current trends, and the current interest in very large hats for women.

The teachers, who obviously loved their work, began to pick up and comment on pieces of fabric and ribbons. The way they handled fabric and rolled ribbon through their fingers made the schooling very real to Blanche. She tuned out the rest of the room and focused only on the hands holding rich velvet and shimmering silk. The fabrics displayed their own individual characteristics, such as weight, fold, and radiance. Blanche, so excited she was almost holding her breath, began to see the differences.

All too soon, the lecture ended, and the girls were dismissed.

Lily turned to Blanche with a bright smile. "Let's get to the coatroom and fix your lovely hair!"

"Yes, we will all help," giggled Pauline, raising her eyebrows and smiling with expectation.

The classmates scurried to the coatroom.

"See Blanche, I always carry extra hairpins," explained Lily, holding out her palm. It was full of long, black, open-U shaped pins. "Let's see what we can do!"

Lily produced a large comb and set to work on Blanche's fair hair. The others crowded around, giggled, and gave friendly suggestions. Lily moved the comb through Blanche's natural waves with confidence. In a matter of minutes, Blanche's hair was sweeping up, with a descending wave on one side. The rest rolled on the sides and was neatly pinned in place. A few curls trailed at the back of her neck.

"My goodness!" exclaimed Emma. "You look ten years older! And so lovely! Come look in the bathroom mirror."

The girls rushed into the bathroom and placed Blanche before a mirror above a sink.

Blanche stared at her reflection. She was stunned, her eyes and mouth wide open, all of the other girls giggling behind her. Blanche saw a striking young woman with swept up hair, a long neck, sparkling blue eyes, and straight shoulders. She was more lovely than she ever could have imagined. A young working woman, not a child!

A wide grin spread across Blanche's face, as she turned to embrace her new, sweet hat sisters.

"My goodness, indeed! That little girl is now gone forever! Thank you so much, Lily. Thanks to you all! Oh, I must go to catch the trolley."

Blanche raced three blocks up Seventeenth Street to Delmar, where she crossed to stand at the streetcar stop. She tightly clutched her tokens as she got an aisle seat on the car. Settling in for the twenty-minute ride, Blanche thought over all that happened.

At Kingshighway, she disembarked and walked to McPherson Street. Since she didn't have a key, she knocked on the front door.

The door opened.

"I'm sorry, we don't want—goodness! Blanche, is that you!" said a startled Mrs. Robey, jerking her head up and stepping back. "Oh my, one day of classes and you come home looking like a working girl!" The girls ran to the door.

"You already look like a hatmaker!" said Beth, wide-eyed.

"You look beautiful," Alma said, rushing up to Blanche and throwing her arms around her waist. Her mother looked at her with a glare.

"No, she does not!" Mrs. Robey said loudly. "She looks

like a salesclerk in a downtown store—uneducated and wearing a fancy hairdo to attract men!"

Mrs. Robey threw her hands into the air and turned to walk into the flat. Stopping herself, she pointed a finger at Blanche. "Mark my words, this hairdo will lead to trouble!"

After she went inside, Blanche sat on the sofa. She was stunned, unable to say anything to Mrs. Robey. How disappointing, how crushing these comments were.

I wonder, thought Blanche, *did Mrs. Robey miss this chapter of her own life? Did she have Wallace at my age? Did she miss being a young adult with a career just up ahead? I love this hairdo because it makes me feel like an attractive woman for the very first time!*

Before dinner, Mrs. Robey insisted her husband meet in their bedroom to discuss Blanche. Mrs. Robey was concerned about Blanche's exposure to the business world. She felt maybe it was too soon to let Blanche go to hat school. Mr. Robey smiled.

"These are the same concerns you will have for Beth and Alma. Your concerns are valid, but they must be balanced with letting these girls become trustworthy and sensible young women. It has to happen sometime. We will see if Blanche can properly handle the challenges ahead. She is simply moving into the social world of her new peers, and that is to be expected. Beyond that, she is growing up!"

Blanche was serene at dinner, glowing after her first day of hat school. Keenly observant, Greta had not asked her to help. Each family member had greeted Blanche with a startled face and genuine disbelief. Blanche smiled as she passed a bowl of mashed potatoes, leaned sideways to help Alma cut her meat, and calmly answered questions from the Robeys about the hat workshop. She was changing into a lady, right before their eyes.

The Bonnet Book
Rosenthal-Sloan Millinery Company • St. Louis, Missouri
1908-09

O*h yes!*

Blanche's eyes flew open at dawn the next morning. She lay on her trundle bed, as the first morning light cast a soft pearly glow on the window shade.

That little brown booklet from Mr. Robey. I can take it to school to take notes on hat making. I can record the hat-making steps until I master them. It will be called the "Bonnet Book"!

Blanche rose quietly and got to the bathroom early. With hairpins she had stashed in her streetcar-token pouch and a comb in her right hand, she began to organize her long hair. Having watched closely yesterday, she coaxed the front into the soft wave cascading down the left side, then rolled sections into a twist on each side and pinned them in place. Finally, she gathered the remaining hair, formed a loose knot at the back, pinned it in place at the base of her neck, and left a few loose curls.

Blanche smiled proudly into the mirror, as she turned

her face from side to side. How utterly simple and lovely and flattering!

Blanche quickly put on her new gingham dress and laughed softly to herself. This might be the last day *ever* to dress in gingham. She had been very nervous about fitting in at the school, but the Sweet Sisters had warmly brought her into their lunch group. Today they were bringing her working-girl clothes. After seven years, she had only two friends, Mr. McGregor and Lara Doyle. The new friendship with the Sweet Sisters brought much-needed comfort and companionship to her lonesome life.

With a flutter of excitement, Blanche stretched forward on tiptoes to reach her kitchen shelf. From the very back, she took out the little brown booklet with its soft, leather-like cover.

It is *small,* she thought, *so I must write only the most important facts in here.*

She put the booklet in her purse, along with her yellow pencil, a sandwich, an apple, and the token bag.

As the family began their morning rituals, Blanche effortlessly got Beth and Alma dressed for school and sat down to breakfast. Then, dressed in heavy coats, Alma and Blanche rushed out the door and walked to Alma's school. The weather was bitter cold.

Blanche caught the streetcar. Today she got a window seat, where she could think.

I have an idea, she thought. *Tomorrow I must bring the black booklet also and add one new vocabulary word to study each day.*

The streetcar jolted and the brakes screeched. As the car came to a sudden stop, Blanche was thrown forward in her seat. She could see two other streetcars ahead. She also saw a group of men in black coats carrying shovels and heading to the streetcar tracks.

"Ladies and gentlemen," announced the streetcar conductor. "There is heavy ice on the tracks, which can cause the cars to derail. A crew is coming to chip the ice off the rails. This will cause a delay, but we will be on our way as soon as possible."

Oh dear, I will be late for school, Blanche worried, biting her lip. Because she had a window seat, she could see some of the crew shoveling silvery chips of ice into wheelbarrows. Mounds of chipped ice were already piled on the curb.

After about fifteen minutes, the tracks were cleared, and the streetcar began to creep forward. Blanche alighted at Delmar and carefully and quickly walked the three blocks to Rosenthal-Sloan Millinery Company, noticing other girls running in from every direction. She raced up the steps and hastened to the workshop room.

A canvas bag was draped across her second-row stool. Emma was the only other person in the deserted room. She smiled at Blanche and pointed to the bag.

"I guess everyone is delayed," said Blanche, catching her breath from running up the stairs. "And this is for my afternoon fitting?" she giggled, looking at the canvas bag. "What a sweet friend you are to bring me a skirt!"

"I can't wait to see if it fits!" smiled Emma. "If it does, it's yours, because I have two others!"

Blanche sat on her stool, her chest still heaving. *Let's see. Bonnet Book out, with pencil,* she thought. Then she began to study in detail the colored fabrics and textured ribbons on the demonstration table.

A few minutes later, some other girls hurried into the studio, their hair windblown and their cheeks rosy. Once all of Blanche's Sweet Sisters had arrived, the lecture began.

The first hour was a discussion about current types and shapes of hats, such as pompadour frames, which provided a ledge for support for large hats; felt hats with large brims, almost out to the shoulders; tall riding hats; and straw hats and bonnets. All of the information came at Blanche so fast. She was only able to jot down names—there was no time for writing descriptions.

After lunch, the teachers began explaining how to make the first hat, a popular model called "Pretty Miss." Two prototype felt hats were perched on eighteen-inch-high metal stands, and the teachers simultaneously began demonstrating how the fabrics and accessories were used to create a Pretty Miss hat.

The students learned about velvet, including how folds of it present a deeper hue of the velvet's color. They learned about silk, how the weave of the silk threads glows with a rainbow of shimmering variations of color, and how these shimmering colors behave like a cluster of fireworks when crushed into a rosette. The teachers showed that silk moiré has a wavy appearance, and how silk-moiré ribbon can be used on a hat to present an effect like cascading water. The teachers passed around materials so the girls could see the differences. Blanche was on the edge of her stool the whole time, touching each fabric with reverence.

The sample hats began to take shape, each teacher creating her own version. When finished, the Pretty Miss hat had a large crown and drooped slightly in front. The front featured a wreath of pink silk roses, rosebuds, and foliage, framed on either side with deep-pink velvet ribbon in a succession of flat loops. A wide velvet ribbon circled the hat crown around the back.

Although it was a rather simple design, there were

subtle tricks to anchoring the flowers and matching or contrasting the velvet-ribbon loops. Blanche felt as though she already knew how to construct this hat.

By the end of the afternoon, Blanche and the Sweet Sisters were mentally exhausted, their brains whirling with details. They walked to the coatroom, where Blanche opened the canvas bag and took out the skirt. She tried it on with the blouse from Pauline, which had a high ruffled neck, front tucks, and modified mutton sleeves.

Before everyone's eyes, Blanche's second transformation occurred. Her slim body was a perfect fit for both the skirt and the blouse. The Sweet Sisters smiled and purred like kittens as they twirled Blanche around. They pushed her to the bathroom mirror, where once again she was thunderstruck. In the mirror she saw a working girl with a lovely pompadour, clothed in the tailored black and white style of the day—a stunning young woman, a calendar girl for a 1908 trade magazine. She smiled and thanked Pauline and Emma for the clothes. Then they all hurried down the stairs, exhausted, to catch the streetcars.

Lost in the mastery of hat construction, fabric variation, and fabric responses to folding, to light, to other fabrics, Blanche rode home on the Delmar streetcar. She tried to imagine the light and color response to a crushed fold. It was a new language for her, and she embraced it. The hat work had tapped into a passion in her being, and she seized it with a singleness of mind, forgetting all thoughts of family abandonment and servitude. The streetcar clanging, the buildings, the passengers, all disappeared.

At the flat, Blanche barely paid any mind to the food, the dinner chatter, the Robeys. Blanche felt so well suited to hat making that she was excited beyond words. Her new skill would be her ticket to the outside world, to personal and financial freedom. This work was at the back of the stage, helping others who would display their hats in public. Blanche could hardly wait to make real hats for real ladies. She excused herself from dinner and quickly retired to the bedroom. She fell asleep with shimmering folds of fabric billowing before her eyes.

Hat-construction demonstrations continued all week. Blanche brought her Bonnet Book and sketched each hat with design notes. Her hat sketches were adequate enough to stimulate her memory, but she did not consider them excellent diagrams.

The following week the students were paired with experienced hatmakers and began making their own hats. In her Bonnet Book, Blanche studiously wrote down notes and assembly instructions for each hat.

After Blanche had constructed about thirty hats—working much faster than the other students—she began to pick up even more speed, coming up with creative twists and turns and fabric combinations beyond the actual lessons. The demonstration hats might have one bow; Blanche's hat would use three. One model hat had feathers pointing down, with a bow on top; Blanche's hat had feathers pointing in two directions, wrapped in a twisted, wide ribbon with a rosette instead of a bow. Her hats quickly became the talk of her class, the ones to be copied.

When she was at home, Blanche still carefully performed her usual chores, but with a growing detachment. The only closeness Blanche felt at the Robey household was for Beth and Alma. At night on Alma's bed, she hugged the girls and continued to read to them. Tied up in their own schoolwork, the girls no longer pestered Blanche for other play time. They understood her need to concentrate on her own schooling, and they accepted this with admiration and respect.

By the end of 1908, thanks to her exceptional talent, Blanche had earned her own trays of supplies and a corner table with natural light at the back of the trimmers' workshop. She was now officially called a trimmer's apprentice. All newly created hats were reviewed by a teacher, and most were then added to the sales room inventory for purchase. Blanche's Sweet Sisters sat nearby, and they always shared lunch. Blanche had never had women friends before, and this group of four had become very close, encouraging each other in their hat assignments and also sharing their private lives, their hopes and dreams.

Pauline, who was very fashion-conscious, hoped to travel. Lily was more conservative and wanted to get married. Emma wanted to make money to help support her family. However, each girl's ambitions grew larger as her hat-making skills improved. They started thinking about working in a small or large hat shop or even traveling to a work assignment beyond St. Louis.

Blanche's learning continued another year. She had begun creating hats that were unique. The sales force always wanted her exceptional hats, since they were so distinctive in style and color and texture. Wealthy customers noticed and remembered Blanche's creations, returning again and again for them.

Hat making challenged Blanche's creative mind and fulfilled her soul. She knew she had found her calling. She had been placed in a fairy wonderland of kaleidoscopic fabrics in different colors, textures, and shapes. Each night, she dreamed of new designs. Each day, she implemented these with speed and creativity.

Wealthy customers wanted "stand-alone" hats with high feathers. They wanted hats that would be the reigning swans at the women's tea. Other customers wanted streamlined hats with no feathers at all, hats that would hug their heads on rides in their enterprising husbands' newfangled automobiles. On and on went the requests. On and on went

Blanche's nimble fingers and lightning-quick creativity.

Rosenthal-Sloan had a small lending library that Blanche used to further her self-education during her busy hat-making year. She checked out books on fabric manufacture to study the origins of silk, felt, wool, moiré, and other fabrics. Blanche felt that learning how fabrics were made increased her understanding of how to creatively bend and fold and twist each of them.

After about a year, on an ordinary workday, Mr. M. Brenner, a Rosenthal-Sloan vice-president, sent a written request to Blanche for a special meeting. Blanche walked to his second-floor office puzzled but not fearful, for she knew she was performing well.

Mr. Brenner was an energetic, confident businessman. He had an Illinois map spread out on his desk. When Blanche walked in, he was tracing a route with his index finger. She sat in a brown leather chair opposite his large desk.

"Miss Spencer, you have greatly excelled in our hat-making program. I hear of many compliments on your hats, and I want to congratulate you on the fine work. It is because of your skill that I want to talk to you. We have a very loyal client, a Miss Candace Moraine in Cobden, Illinois, who buys hats and supplies from us, and who has asked us for a temporary hatmaker to work with her for eight months. I think you would be a good fit for this assignment, and I would like to send you to Cobden. As part of this move, we would transfer you from apprentice status to full hatmaker with your own weekly salary. I have already spoken to Mr. Robey, and he has given his blessing to your promotion and transfer. You would need to be ready to leave in two weeks. We would, of course, pay your train and lodging expenses. I am hoping you can make a decision right away."

As Mr. Brenner talked, Blanche was distracted by flashes from her Illinois past. The Spencer family might have been blurry in her mind, but it was October, and she still recalled that meant it was time for the cornstalks to turn dry and for the family to finish canning. Then her mind was flooded with St. Louis images, the streetcars, the World's Fair, the hat factory itself—and her Sweet Sisters! Her mind jumped back and forth as Mr. Brenner talked.

In spite of her memories and the good things that had happened, her curiosity about new things and new places won out. Blanche smiled graciously at Mr. Brenner. She knew he wanted success for her, and she agreed to his plan. Her life was about to change again, from the St. Louis chapter to an unknown one. The new job would mean complete freedom, living and working on her own.

St. Louis Farewells
St. Louis, Missouri • October 1909

A *promotion and a new city! Am I ready for this?*

Blanche was riding the streetcar to Rosenthal-Sloan, bracing herself for a very busy last week. Last Friday she had met with Mr. Brenner to sign the contract for an eight-month job in Cobden, Illinois. Her salary would now be a bit more than she had been making as a full-time milliner for Rosenthal-Sloan the past few months. Before she could start her new job at the new salary, though, first she had to finish her current assignment.

Blanche still had to put finishing touches on a few hats that were in progress. She spent her last two days at Rosenthal-Sloan visiting the hat forms department, as well as the flower, feather, ribbon, and notions ones, exploring the newest products. Until then, she had never been to those various departments to see the breadth of their supplies. She didn't realize, for example, how many different sizes and types and colors of feathers were available.

For Blanche's departure, Pauline had made a Rosenthal-Sloan reservation for a small windowless back room and had brought lunch. Lily brought flowers from her yard, and Emma came strolling in with their gift for Blanche.

During the last lunch, the young women talked excitedly and shared with Blanche their hopes for her success. The four girls felt a special bond that had grown alongside their hat-making skills and confidence in their abilities. Blanche was overwhelmed when the Sisters presented their farewell gift. She had never received a wrapped present in her life! As she opened the large cardboard box, she gasped with delight. She picked up the present: a women's purse in golden-brown leather, with a lovely tooled design of open lilies on one side. The purse was about twelve inches square, with rounded corners and a brass clip on top, which was also etched with scrollwork. There was dramatic black stitching on both the purse and the strap.

"Oh, ladies! I love this purse! So practical and so lovely!" Blanche ran her fingers over the tooled-leather vase and flowers, looking at her friends with a glowing smile.

"We got so tired of your flour-sack purse. This seemed the perfect gift for your travel and new job," said Emma.

"And, Blanche, with the long strap you can put the purse over your head and hold it close if you need to run—or dance!" giggled Pauline.

Blanche transferred her word book, the Bonnet Book, and the flour-sack purse to her new purse, the Sisters lovingly looking on.

When it came time to part, each girl gave a warm good-bye to Blanche.

"Always keep your hair this way. It flatters your face," said Lily, with a delicate hug.

"Put lunch in your purse for the trip, my sweet friend,"

advised Emma, placing both hands on Blanche's shoulders.

"I meant it about dancing, Blanche. Have a good trip full of beautiful hats, handsome men, and dancing!" Pauline giggled again, grabbing Blanche by the waist.

Aglow from the warm gathering with the Sweet Sisters, Blanche headed home with new hats she had made for the Robey ladies. It was the first time she had made presents for her second family, and she felt proud to bring home fancy new hats for all the women.

She put her new purse strap over her head for the trip home. She wanted to catch an early-afternoon streetcar, which would be less crowded, so she could safely get the new hats home to the Robey flat. As she walked through the Rosenthal-Sloan lobby on her way out, she passed three very handsome men in elegant suits and top hats.

On the streetcar ride home, she thought about the men, their expressions as they lifted their top hats and smiled as she passed. *Hmmm,* she thought. *I guess now I can make heads turn! Perhaps I'll meet handsome men in Cobden!*

To say goodbye to Blanche, one week before her departure Mr. Robey arranged a Saturday lunch on a Mississippi River excursion boat named the *Sidney.* The entire family would attend the cruise, even Lara Doyle.

Full of Robey and Lang women in fancy new hats, holding their heads high, the open carriage bound for the river made its way down Olive Street to Market Street. It was a sunny Saturday morning.

Blanche wore a white straw boater, banded with velvet ribbons and an elevated chiffon bow in back, with elongated end ribbons facing up, like the wings of a flying dove. Mrs. Robey and Mrs. Lang both had versions of the Pretty Miss hat, one gray with pale-pink roses, the other brown with white roses, both stylish but not overly elaborate. Mrs. Robey had been unable to hide her disappointment, probably hoping for something more dramatic. Blanche saw her disappointment, smiled anyway, and ignored Mrs. Robey's lack of gratitude.

My hats are made with heartfelt creativity and good workmanship. I must never feel offended if someone does not like a hat, Blanche told herself.

She looked across the carriage at the straw bonnets on Beth, Alma, and Lara. The bonnets were lovely and jaunty, each with a broad brim turned up on one side and embellished with a large silk cabbage rose of white, pink, or yellow. The young women were delighted with their hats and smiled with pride. They were quite a bouquet of fancy ladies, riding high in the expensive carriage, eliciting lots of glances and waves from the sidewalks. Mr. Robey, dressed in his best suit and hat, was secretly pleased to be making a fashion statement on Olive Street.

The group disembarked on the riverbank and walked the short distance to the *Sidney,* which sat like a floating white palace on the brown waters of the Mississippi.

By 1909, riverboat cruises out of St. Louis were advertised every day in the newspapers. The Robey family had never taken one. The *Sidney,* a four-deck vessel, was about forty feet wide and 120 feet long, painted white with red trim. Its bow and stern were draped in red and white bunting, and the promenade deck was wrapped with snapping flags. The boat's lower deck contained sitting rooms and storage space for shipped goods, while the main deck featured a large lounge and dining room. The promenade deck had two large black smokestacks, as well as many rows of benches for sightseeing passengers. Finally, the small fourth deck contained the wheelhouse.

The Robey family walked up the wide gangplank at the bow of the boat. The riverboat was always crowded on weekends, and the crowd was smartly dressed. Ladies wore wide sun bonnets and floor-length pastel gowns, and they carried parasols. The men wore business suits and hats. The Robey women felt especially stylish, since they were all in the latest-fashion hats, made by Blanche. The family chose a corner table on the main deck at the bow of the boat, and Blanche and the young girls went to the promenade deck to watch the boat cast off.

As their excursion got underway, Blanche walked with the girls on the deck. She felt truly grown up for the first time, like a St. Louis matron on an elegant outing. She walked slowly to savor the impression she made with her elegant hat, lovely face, and new hairdo and clothes. She felt pride as an attractive young woman with a special assignment and a promising career ahead of her.

Blanche and the girls leaned against the promenade deck rail, holding onto their lovely hats, as they looked down at the rolling ribbons of water. They all jumped as the departure whistle—one long, screaming, raspy trill—pierced the air. The whistle shocked them into even greater excitement. They waved at folks on the shore and watched frothy waves roll off the bow of the boat as they headed upstream.

The Robey group converged in the dining room for a lunch of fried chicken legs and potato salad. From their corner table, they watched the scenery pass by as the riverboat steamed upstream: the Eads Bridge, the castle-like Union Electric Power Plant, and various barren horizontal sandstone buttresses. They noticed how the captain changed course slightly to steer the boat between "snags," the term used to describe floating or lodged horizontal tree trunks.

"Look, Father," said Beth, "the boat is swinging out around that tree in the water. What is a tree doing in the water?"

"A tree trunk in the water comes from a storm somewhere upstream," said Mr. Robey, "when a dead tree at the river's edge is swept away by high waves. The captain does not want to get his engines entangled with the big log. Notice that he is also avoiding the mounds of dirt in the river, where it is probably very shallow. I think these are called sandbars. The course of the river changes every day, and the captain must always be on the alert for anything that could cause damage to his boat."

After a leisurely lunch, the boat turned around and headed back past the St. Louis wharf, farther downstream. The banks here were steep and barren, scoured periodically by floodwaters. In flat places, the family saw boneyards of silver logs and sandstone ledges. The only docks they saw were thirty feet in the air, perched like lonely tables above the wide and mighty flow. These high docks were needed in spring flood waters. At occasional curves in the river, fallen trees created shaded eddies and pockets of swirling debris.

Suddenly, there was a loud scraping sound. The passengers froze in shock, as the boat slowly leaned toward the center of the river. The three young women were tossed against the outside rail, where they all held on with white knuckles.

The riverboat had stopped. The whistle screamed five times, and everyone on the boat stood still. The captain walked down the main deck, wearing a white uniform with gold buttons and a white hat with a shiny black brim. He held a black megaphone with his right hand and twisted a jacket button with his left. His brow was furrowed as he began to speak into the megaphone.

"The *Sidney* has struck a submerged tree on a sandbar. This has caused the boat to list to the starboard side. Snags are common on the river—and dangerous! We are sending men into the water to assess the damage. Ladies and gentlemen, please stay calm, and listen for further messages."

When the boat stopped, the elder Robey family members and the Langs were still at their table, which slid out from under them. The frightened group now stood at the center of the bow on the main deck, above their table, holding the railing in front of the windows with one hand and their new hats with the other. The girls and Blanche made their way inside to the parents' tilted location.

"I don't know how to swim, Blanche!" wailed Alma, as she tugged at Blanche's hand.

"None of us do!" screamed Beth, her face as white as the side of the boat.

"Let's stay together and stay calm, girls. Our screaming and crying will not in any way help save this riverboat. The captain needs quiet to make his decisions."

Blanche spoke in a soothing, mature tone. She knew how to swim from her days in Rattlesnake Creek, and she thought she could hold onto the girls in the water, if necessary.

From the railing, the group could see men wading into the river. They carried shovels and started digging at a large log that was barely visible in the muddy water.

A sturdy tugboat appeared upstream. The men on the

tugboat deck seemed to be surveying the tilting riverboat. They began waving flags and sending some sort of signals with the toots of their boat whistle. Crewmen from the *Sidney*, carrying large coils of ropes, inched their way along the starboard deck outside the first floor. The tugboat moved in dangerously close to the *Sidney*, and the riverboat crew tossed their rope coils onto the tugboat deck. The sailors on both vessels quickly wound figure-eight lines around the heavy iron cleats on both the riverboat and the tugboat. The tugboat, now somewhat slowed down by the ropes, was drifting past the riverboat in the faster current.

Suddenly the ropes became taut and groaned at the cleats. The *Sidney* inched downstream, away from the sandbar, and slowly began to right itself. It rocked dramatically from side to side, tossing passengers about on the decks. Finally, with a swooning lurch that sent the tables skidding again, the boat righted itself.

Two of the sandbar diggers dove into the churning waters and began bobbing up and down near the site of the snag. One dove while the other, heaving for breath, held onto the riverboat's gunwale. The riverboat captain shouted directions from the promenade deck, listening to their replies. Finally, he rested his forehead on the deck's side rail in relief.

The Robeys could not see the captain from the main deck, but they could feel that the riverboat was free of the snag and floating in an upright position, although moving backwards down the fast-flowing river. The rescue was all so dizzying—the frantic whistles, the long, slow wobbles, the fast, backwards float!

Once again, the captain spoke into his black megaphone.

"Ladies and gentlemen, our boat appears to be undamaged. We will turn the boat and continue upstream to the St. Louis waterfront. Thank you for remaining calm. Thank you to our crew for a heroic rescue."

All eight members in the Robey group still clutched the window railing, as they breathed sighs of relief and talked to one another nervously.

"My goodness, what a scary trip!" said Beth. "I think I will do a school report on what happened!"

"I am so glad we did not have to swim to shore. I was very scared!" exclaimed Alma. "The muddy water would ruin my new sunbonnet!" She had already learned to tilt her head to the side, which best showed off the hat's cabbage rose.

"Well," said Mr. Robey, "I think we will all remember this trip for years. It all sounds glamorous in the ads, but the river really is more unpredictable than I realized. I think we should leave this river to the fish."

Blanche smiled to herself as she watched the muddy swirls of water, standing with the Robeys at the center of the riverboat. She had loved the thrill of the rescue effort, although she was glad the boat had avoided a serious mishap. Since she could swim, she had not been very frightened. In fact, this river trip had whetted her appetite for travel, for more adventure beyond St. Louis. She felt ready to see the world.

The *Sidney* drew up to the St. Louis waterfront at about five o'clock, apparently without leaks. The rattled crowd departed quickly, some passengers stopping to shake hands with the captain. The Robeys took a horse cab home, ate a cold supper, and retired early, glad to be safe and sound back home after their Mississippi River adventure.

Blanche's final St. Louis week was spent shopping with her very first wage money. She needed fabric to make new clothes for her new job. First, she bought navy serge for a second long skirt. Then she bought a pattern and navy fabric to make a double-breasted Eton-style jacket with a navy velvet collar. She also found a lovely tan fabric with a navy lantern print, brought this home, and made a pattern of her high-necked white blouse. She sewed the new blouse for fall and winter use.

On the Friday of Blanche's evening departure, Greta and Blanche took a trip to Soulard Market for weekend food shopping. Blanche wore her black and white working clothes and new white hat, and she carried her new purse. She looked very refined—stunning, actually. As the carriage stopped at the familiar corner, Greta turned and put both of her hands over Blanche's.

"Now, lass, I know you have a special friend to visit at the market," she started.

Blanche's eyes grew wide and her mouth opened as if she were about to bite into an apple.

"But, how?" was all Blanche could get out.

"I knew about Angus McGregor after the first month of our market trips. The people of this market, they watch

out for each other. Ye picked the most educated man at Soulard Market to be yer friend!" Greta squeezed her hands. "I
know you two became close and that this friendship meant a
lot to you. I will never tell yer secret, lass. I think this friend
and his books became family for you. Now, run along to Mr.
McGregor."

Her eyes glistening, Greta gave Blanche a warm hug,
then turned her head toward the book wagon. "Just get a
dozen peaches, and be back here in about an hour," she said,
laughing and shaking her head.

Blanche strolled toward the book wagon, smiling
sweetly. She was serene, a striking young woman in a fancy
white hat in the boisterous, dirty October market, where almost everyone else was in drab or dirty clothes.

Mr. McGregor had not seen Blanche in several months
because of the hat-making workshops. As she approached,
his mouth opened wide, his eyebrows went up, and he took
his hands out of his pockets, opening his arms to the well-
dressed lady with fine posture walking straight toward him.

"Goodness, look at you! The hat-making job has made
you grow up. And I suppose it's given you new St. Louis
friends and clothes. And you made this lovely hat yourself?"

"Yes, Mr. McGregor, everything you say is true! Tonight my company is sending me to Cobden, Illinois, to assist
a hat-store owner. I came to say goodbye. I will be my own
boss now, and I will write letters to tell you of my new adventures. I will never forget your kindness, your fatherly support,
and your books."

Mr. McGregor held both her hands and took a deep
breath.

"My dear, I told you that you were a strong lass the day
I met you. Now you have conquered St. Louis and found

a new career. You can steer your own life. I will miss you terribly. You have become my St. Louis daughter. We must not say goodbye. We must continue our friendship through correspondence."

With a twinkle in his eyes and a warm smile on his face, he tenderly took her chin into his right hand. His hand lingered for a moment, as they looked into each other's eyes, and both teared up.

"God bless you, and safe journey. And please write to me at my home address, which you know."

Blanche looked down, overcome with sadness. He really had been her steadfast friend for these many years. He was her hearth, the warm place she could visit for guidance and compassion. They had talked and laughed and cried together in pouring rain, in freezing sleet, and on hot muggy afternoons.

Mr. McGregor turned her shoulder away from him. "Don't you still have to get the peaches?" he said lightly. "Hurry on to Farmer Eckert's wagon, and don't forget me!"

Today's peaches looked extra delicious. Blanche purchased the usual dozen to put in her straw basket. Then she took the shortcut behind Eckert's wagon, walked across the street, and took the long route back to the Robey carriage, watching all of the bustle and dust and color of the wonderful market.

Greta had planned a special Friday night farewell dinner for Blanche, which included a chicken casserole, vegetables, warm rolls, and a blackberry cobbler for dessert. When Blanche came to the table, there was a large bag on her chair.

"This is your travel bag, Blanche, a present from our family," said Beth, who was sixteen, older than Blanche had been when she first arrived in St. Louis.

"We chose this one because it had maps!" said Alma. "The maps are for travel to Cobden, Illinois, so you won't get lost!" She giggled at her own joke. The large carpetbag was made of sturdy tan, blue-green, and black tapestry with pictures of foreign maps, compasses, and the names of exotic cities.

"How lovely!" said Blanche as she stood behind her chair, smiled at everyone in the room, and clasped her hands on the carpetbag straps. "Thank you very much!"

There was soft light at the dining room table and, as always, the sweet smell of warm rolls as the lively dinner progressed. Beth and Alma, on either side of Blanche, could barely look at their plates. They worshipped Blanche and wanted to remember everything about her. Across the table from Blanche, Lara Doyle smiled shyly, amazed with the transformation of the young frightened girl into this sophisticated woman. Happy with how the dinner was going, Mr. and Mrs. Robey locked eyes from opposite ends of the table.

"Well, my train leaves tonight from Union Station, and I should arrive late evening. The Rosenthal-Sloan Millinery Company has bought my ticket and found me a room in a boardinghouse. I will send details soon after I get settled. Beth and Alma, you must answer my letters! Around April or May I should be back here in St. Louis working at Rosenthal-Sloan, unless they send me on another assignment."

"Then I will not say goodbye," said Alma, shaking her head and putting her fists on her waist. "Will you read to us tonight?"

"Well, no. Beth do you consent to take over the reading chore?"

"Yes. You have been a good teacher, as well as a good reader." Beth sat very tall in her chair, as Blanche always did. She looked Blanche carefully in the eyes as she spoke.

"Here comes the best of St. Louis, blackberry cobbler!" said Greta, using hot pads to carry a large casserole dish to the dining room sideboard. "Does everyone want dessert?"

"Yes!" the girls exclaimed.

"Greta, can you join us?" Blanche added.

"Mercy no, not in me cookin' clothes. But I sure would like to hear sounds of delight as you try me farewell cobbler!"

Blanche smiled and took a bite, savoring the cobbler.

I've left a family once before, and I will do it again tonight. I am stronger now and older. I have made hat making my career, and I will survive on my own. I am eager to start a new life as a single adult with complete freedom. These new skills of mine seem to please women around me, which pleases me, too. I am ready to put my skills to work in Cobden, Illinois.

Cobden Color
Cobden, Illinois • Fall 1909

The train whistled as it crossed the Eads Bridge. Blanche settled in with a tight hold on her new purse. After a while she began to doze. Two hours later she awakened suddenly, as the train rounded a bend and slowed down. Blanche then found herself looking out at the two-story, red-brick depot of Murphysboro, Illinois, with its familiar yellow, blue, and white stained-glass windows. She remembered many years earlier, when she had sat for almost four hours in that empty building feeling empty herself, without a family, traveling alone to an unknown city.

Startled, she jerked her head back, feeling as if she had slammed into the brick wall of the station. She was here, in Murphysboro! At Union Station in St. Louis, when she had studied the Arrivals and Departures board in the Grand Hall, she had only looked for "Cobden" to find her departure track number. She had not looked at the other towns on the route. But here she was, exactly seven years later, back at the departure depot at Murphysboro. The memories of that day flooded her senses. Lamont with his swollen face. Her pa concerned about his sick son, leaving her at the depot by herself.

Blanche had closed her mind and heart to recollections of Oraville, but the stained-glass windows unlocked the memory of how small and alone she had felt in the depot. Tears cascaded down her face, as she frantically brushed her eyes with the long sleeve of her blouse.

I won't go back!

I can't see them now. Maybe never! This is blackberry season, and school has started! Would they even love me now if I returned? I know they are three hours away by wagon, and this is much too close!

Pa chose the wrong path for me and did not research what happened after the St. Louis train arrival. Then he abandoned me for the last seven years. His decision to send me away made me a live-in servant, someone who slept in a pantry and got no more education. He is an educated man! His decision about my life was careless. I will never let another man make careless decisions about my life! I must guard my own life and not let others box me into servile jobs and demeaning situations. I want to make hundreds of hats, learn about business, and meet new people. With this trip, I am taking charge of my life.

After leaving Murphysboro, the train stopped briefly in Carbondale, then traveled on.

Blanche was shocked when the train stopped in Marion, Illinois. She was supposed to be arriving in Cobden! She had been wrestling with her past and hadn't heard the conductor's call to get off at Carbondale, where she was supposed to catch the southbound train to Cobden.

Blanche was angry. On her first independent trip she had gotten so lost in self-righteous anger that she missed her train connection! She headed for the ticket master in the depot. He was kind enough to reissue her a return ticket to Carbondale at no cost, but he explained that the next train wasn't until the next morning. He suggested she spend the night in the small hotel across from the depot.

Blanche wearily crossed the street to a two-story brick building with a "Rooms" sign on its weathered front door. Luckily, Mr. Brenner had given her travel money from her first Cobden paycheck, which she could use to get a room. Setting her carpetbag down on a bench in the sparse lobby stale with cigar smoke, she stepped forward to rent her first room.

"Good evening, miss. May I help you?" asked a tall, dark-suited man with a large mustache.

"Yes, please. I need to rent a room for one night. Do you have any available?" Blanche asked politely.

"Only one room left, miss, first floor near the back of the building, with a bathroom out the back door. The cost is two dollars."

"That will be fine," she commented, relieved to find *any* hotel room in a strange town. The manager turned around a ledger for her to sign, as he wrote her a receipt.

"This way, miss. I will show you the room."

Blanche followed the man down a hall to the back of the building.

The room was next to an exit to the rear alley. Blanche took the key, thanked the manager, and hurried into the room, locking the door behind her. Her relief turned to disappointment when she saw the room had threadbare everything and a ragged carpet on the floor.

Blanche collapsed onto a wire-frame bed, feeling almost as though she were back in the pantry. Even the pantry smelled better than this. This room smelled of musty cloth and cigars.

Blanche heard a scuffle outside the window. Men from next door were yelling.

I hope I can endure this for one night, she thought. *I must not even leave to find food!*

Blanche dug through the carpetbag. She located a bread roll from Greta that had come unwrapped and partially crumbled, but she was grateful for any food at all. She sat back against the bed's scratched headboard and held the roll tenderly in both hands.

This is it, the first meal of my independent life, she thought, as she gnawed on the crumbled roll. *I am locked in this room, hopefully safe, with stale bread for dinner.*

Several hours later, when things outside had quieted down, Blanche unlocked her door, relocked it after she stepped out, and cautiously walked out the back door to the alley. When she looked inside the privy, she could not bear to enter. She hurried back to her room, where she found a chamber pot under the bed.

Blanche had a long and uneasy night. There were more scuffles in the alley, doors slamming down the hall, and—at one point—even someone rattling her doorknob! It was all so new and uncivilized and terrifying. She was coming from seven years of servitude with an overprotective family in a clean and refined flat. Now she was stuck in this downtown hotel room for one endless night. She wondered if all her freedom would be this scary. She longed for a quiet and loving home, the kind she remembered from her childhood.

Blanche awoke at dawn, stretched over the musty bedspread and still dressed in her working-girl clothes. She assembled her belongings, left the room, and returned the key to the front-desk clerk.

"Is there a café nearby?" she asked.

"Two doors down, past the bar. Opens in about half an hour," said the clerk.

Blanche sat in the hotel lobby and watched a rosy dawn unfold through the wavy glass window. When the café opened, she ate quickly, then hurried to the depot. Her train was an early one, and she did not want to miss it. She would never again miss a travel destination, she vowed.

Once on the train, Blanche sat in a trance, watching miles of cornfields pass by. This time she easily made the transfer in Carbondale to the train for Cobden.

After a short ride, the conductor announced they were arriving in Cobden. The train passed through a hillside cut, and the Cobden town center unfolded on both sides of the tracks.

The train stopped in a district of warehouses and loading docks. Blanche held her carpetbag tightly as she descended the train. Once it departed, she glanced up- and downhill, discovering that the town extended for about three blocks. She politely stopped a strolling couple and inquired about directions to Phillips House on North Front Street. She was directed uphill one block. She smiled her thanks and set off.

Bigger than Oraville, she thought, *but nothing compared to St. Louis.*

She walked through a portion of the business district, focused on her housing before turning her thoughts to work.

She arrived at a two-story clapboard house on North Front Street, the largest house at the end of the commercial block. The house was a magnificent rambling structure that extended far back on the lot. It was painted soft white and had many windows. An inviting porch shaded the house, and there were several chimneys visible on the roof.

Blanche tucked down her chin, smoothed her hair

back, and knocked politely on the front door.

A reserved middle-aged woman with a gray braid coiled on top of her head opened the door.

"Good morning," she said. "May I help you?"

PHILLIPS HOUSE,
East Side of the Railroad,
COBDEN, ILLINOIS.
Mrs. N. E. Phillips, Proprietress.
Good Sample Rooms for Traveling Salesmen,
Accommodations First-Class. Guests will be Called for Trains.

"Why, yes, my name is Blanche Spencer, and I—"

"Miss Spencer, I am the proprietor, Mrs. Allie Miller, and I have been expecting you. You must be exhausted! Come right in!" Mrs. Miller had a cheerful smile and wore a flowered apron. She wiped her hands on it.

Mrs. Miller showed Blanche into a large, dark-paneled front hall with a hanging chandelier and tall windows.

"This is a very large family home, with several rented rooms on the first floor. My family sleeps on the second floor. Let me show you the room."

Mrs. Miller walked to the rear of the house. When she and Blanche got to the last door on the left side of the hall, she opened it. Blanche saw a lovely pastel-green room with soft, golden sunlight glowing through sheer curtains.

"This is your room. It was once my daughter's, and it has a view to the backyard. I hope you like hollyhocks and clotheslines!"

Blanche thanked Mrs. Miller, closed the door, and sat for a few minutes on the bed, which was covered in a chenille bedspread.

My own room, she thought, *my very first own room.*

She looked around. She saw light-green striped wallpaper with alternating rows of pink roses, rolled-up shades and sheer curtains over the windows, and a dark chest in the corner, where there was also a closet.

Lots of storage and natural light! Clean and so lovely.

She stretched out on the bed and relaxed in the comfort of the safe room, so different from the nightmare of the night before.

"Miss Spencer, come join us for dinner!" came a call at the door.

Blanche had slept all afternoon. She jumped up, smoothed her clothes, and combed her hair. Then she headed for the large dining room table, just to the left off the entry of the house.

"Friends and family, this is Miss Blanche Spencer," said Mrs. Miller, carrying in a large platter of fried chicken and cooked vegetables. "This is Liza Spoon and my son Herbert, who is studying law." She nodded to the right. "And my two nephews, Sylvester and Raymond." They were on her left.

Liza wore a conservative navy calico dress, her hair in a modified pompadour. She had freckles and bright, smiling eyes. Herbert, looking dapper next to her, stared at Blanche.

"Good evening," Blanche said with a friendly smile, as she took the chair farthest from the kitchen door. "Very nice to make your acquaintance."

"Miss Spencer is a professional milliner and was sent from a St. Louis hat company to work in Candace Moraine's millinery store," said Mrs. Miller, carrying in a bowl of mashed potatoes and a pitcher of water.

"Hello, I am the assistant teacher at the town school," said Liza, tucking a curl behind her ear, as she looked across the table at Blanche. "Welcome!"

As they passed around the platters of food, the two young women began to converse. The two nephews, busy eating, said nothing. Blanche could not decide what she thought about the young man named Herbert. He was somewhat handsome, with a square jaw, jaunty mustache, and friendly smile. At the end of the table, Mrs. Miller smiled, happy to be hosting a family dinner and to have filled her empty bedroom with a new renter.

After Saturday dinner, Blanche returned to her room, unpacked, and stowed her carpetbag. Then she went out the back door to find the outhouse. She was back in the countryside, where she knew indoor plumbing did not yet exist.

Perhaps, she thought, *the primitive plumbing would distress my Sweet Sisters from St. Louis. But not me! A privy is just a minor issue in my overall plan for independence and success!*

Later, she returned to the dining room to watch Mrs. Miller show off her wooden music box, which played a lively tune. Music boxes were rare, so most of the guests had stayed in the dining room to listen.

Blanche then returned to her room and sat on the bed, looking at the rosebuds on the wallpaper. She could faintly hear the sounds of children playing off in the distance. She felt very tired, very safe, and blissfully independent. She decided to stretch out and listen to Cobden's ordinary evening small-town sounds. She put her head on the pillow and was asleep in a minute. She did not wake up until the next morning, when she heard the crow of a rooster at dawn.

My goodness, I slept a second night in my business clothes! thought Blanche with a start. *I must organize this day with purpose!*

Blanche washed in her basin, changed clothes, and sat on a chair to think about what to do with her first free Sunday.

I don't believe I have ever had a Sunday to plan for myself!

She stretched her arms, yawned, and tilted her head to one side. Then she closed her eyes and smiled.

"Miss Spencer," said a voice, accompanied by a knock at the door. "No need to open. I wanted to let you know your rent includes breakfast, but not lunch. There are coffee, eggs, and toast in the kitchen. You can help yourself when you are ready. Enjoy your Sunday! I am off to church."

Blanche appreciated that Mrs. Miller did not come barging in.

Blanche ate in blissful solitude, enjoying warm food, a meal she did not have to serve, and the peaceful surroundings of the large, neat house. The dining room sideboard and the table both had crocheted doilies of pastel thread, and the table itself had a small bowl of late red roses.

After breakfast, Blanche decided to explore Cobden. She donned her old sunbonnet and walked for two hours, up one street and down the next, until she came to the sparse eastern edge of town. The houses were all set back from the streets, in many styles and heights, all shaded by magnificent old elm trees. Beyond the houses were rolling hills with neat rows of fruit trees, their late-October branches full of colorful leaves.

Fruit crops are the currency and commerce of this bustling community, she thought, *and the reason for the loading docks and warehouses next to the train tracks.*

She walked back on South Front Street, crossed the tracks, and headed uphill to the boardinghouse. She had seen well-dressed families lingering in front of several churches, children on bicycles, and ponies followed by barking dogs. She had also seen many folks visiting on front porches. Her overall impression was of a quiet but prosperous town, one that was safe and easy to get around on foot.

A nice place to unfold my wings as a young adult. However, I am seeing many more sunbonnets than fancy hats in this town. This is not St. Louis with big-city buildings and sophisticated fashion. I think this town is just right for me personally, like my rosebud room! But I definitely wonder if Cobden needs my big-city skills and fancy hats.

On Monday, Blanche dressed in her black skirt and white blouse. With anticipation, she walked to the store in a single-story building on South Front Street. The storefront, which faced the train tracks, had drab white paint and was not impressive from the outside. Blanche hoped it would be nicer inside.

A tall woman about her age was fastening her long white apron, while standing in the doorway. She had curly, light-brown hair, which was parted on the side and drawn into a bun at the back of her neck. Blanche politely inquired if the woman was Miss Moraine. When she got a smile in response, she extended her hand and introduced herself.

"Welcome, Miss Spencer! How lovely to have you arrive in Cobden!" She took Blanche's elbow and escorted her inside. "I very much need a helpmate."

The two women stood in the middle of the hat store, which was twenty feet wide and forty feet deep, with a single gaslight hanging from the ceiling. Blanche thought the store seemed oppressive and stagnant, with its low ceiling and gray walls.

"How can I be most useful, Miss Moraine?" she inquired.

"Well, by coming to work promptly, opening and closing the store on time—even if I have to leave—making some winter hats to bolster the hat inventory, and developing ideas to make the store more friendly to customers."

Miss Moraine took Blanche's left hand into her own hands.

"Blanche, please call me Candace. Any of these tasks would be helpful. Doing all of these things just might allow me to stay in business during these difficult times when my health is unpredictable."

"I am ready to start right now, if you will show where to set up a hat-making station," said Blanche, rolling up the sleeves of her white blouse.

Candace took Blanche to the back of the store, to a storage area behind a curtain. She turned on another gaslight. The space was piled high with boxes and crates. It was quite cluttered and dusty.

"This is the only extra space I have," Candace explained.

"Well, what about the alterations table we just passed?" Blanche asked hopefully.

"Yes, you could use that table. Actually, there are not many hat changes, so you could use that table almost full-time." Candace's voice brightened.

"Well then, it's settled! May I look through the boxes back here, so I can take inventory of what you have and put together a list of two months of hat-making supplies?"

"Oh Blanche, I am so glad you are here. You are a much-needed source of fresh energy and creativity—just what this store needs," said Candace.

Blanche spent the day organizing existing hat-making supplies, writing down a list of supplies she needed, and cleaning and consolidating boxes in the back room. She also thought about how to make the store inviting for customers.

At dinner on the second evening in the house, Herbert Miller sat next to Blanche, seemingly staring more at her than at his plate. After the meal, he invited her to go on a walk in the twilight. Flattered to be invited by a professional man, Blanche accepted. Herbert wore a dark, worn suit and had penetrating eyes.

Herbert opened the door for Blanche, and she stepped outside. She was nervous, but she also wanted to learn about the town.

"Shall we walk downtown? I can point out businesses to you," Herbert said.

"I have just been here a day," she said, glancing at his face, then looking straight ahead as she tied her sunbonnet strings.

"I know. I will show you the town," he said.

Blanche blushed. She did not dare speak or look at him again. This was all so new to her. He was the sort of man she wanted to meet, but she should not have agreed to go out with him after just two days.

As they walked downhill by the storefronts on North Front Street, Herbert mentioned each business and its owner as they passed the storefronts. This continued down the block in the evening dusk. At the bottom end of the second block, they stopped at a corner, where a brick stairway led down to the street.

"Shall we proceed to the other side of the street?" Herbert asked, hopeful. He gently took Blanche's left arm and put her hand into the crook of his elbow. Holding his hand over hers, he looked at her for guidance on how to proceed.

Blanche looked up at him, shocked he would be so forward with his hand gestures. She tightened her shoulders, as fear crept into her.

"These stairs are steep," he cautioned, as an excuse for taking her arm.

"Yes, I see," she murmured.

"Let us proceed," he said, making a sweeping gesture with his left arm.

"I beg your pardon, but I am really exhausted and need to go back to my room," Blanche stammered, as she withdrew her arm. She turned on her heels and started back up the street.

"Please wait," he called after her.

Blanche kept walking, looking straight ahead, focused on the white house at the top of the hill. She did not look back. She rushed through the door and down to her own room, quickly went inside, and locked the door.

Confused, Blanche sat on her bed for a few moments. Yes, it was nice to turn heads, but she needed to be careful. Mr. Robey had told her not to look directly at strange men. She had looked at Herbert a couple of times while passing plates of food and that must have encouraged him, she thought. Additionally, his personality did not seem interesting to her. This was Blanche's first experience in the scary world of men suitors, and she wanted to be cautious.

She spent the rest of the evening drawing sketches for new

ideas for the store. The Millinery Shop was somewhat dark. Blanche had watched an earlier transformation of the Rosenthal-Sloan showroom, and she remembered the main tricks they used. This millinery shop needed white walls, mirrors to bounce light around the room, and some rich upholstery fabric to add a touch of elegance. And she wanted to add a small oval mirror next to the front door, at head height, so a woman could see herself when she left the store wearing a new hat.

The next morning, Blanche seated Candace on the entry bench and showed her the shop sketches. Candace put her hands over her face, almost crying with relief.

"You bring such lovely ideas from St. Louis! With your ideas, the shop will be in good hands! I am so grateful," Candace said.

That same day, Blanche wrote a letter to Mr. Brenner. She received a quick answer. Hat supplies, a crate of cast-off mirrors, and several tapestry samples would be shipped by train straightaway. He wished them both good luck and new customers!

Candace then authorized the store to be painted per Blanche's suggestion and put up a "Temporarily Closed for Remodeling" sign on the door. Blanche spent her second week in the store boxing up supplies and supervising the painter. She also worked with a carpenter, sending him home with bench and tapestry fabric, so he could create a more elegant bench.

At the boardinghouse, Blanche continued to love the solitude of her room and the conversations with her housemates. Every night after dinner, Allie Miller set the lovely music box on the dining room table, and folks gathered to sit and listen to the music. Herbert managed to sit next to

Blanche every evening and pressed for another walk into town, but she always declined, saying the store renovations were exhausting, and she needed her rest.

In late October, Liza, her schoolteacher housemate, invited Blanche to a Sunday afternoon pie supper at the local Presbyterian church. Blanche happily accepted, thinking it would be a chance to meet other young people.

Late afternoon on Friday before the pie supper, Blanche heard a knock on the shop's front door. She opened the door to find a strikingly handsome man. Behind him she saw another man.

"I'm sorry, we're in the middle of renovations," she said.

"Yes, but we'd like to talk to the owner. I'm Charles Menees, and this is Benjamin Storm. Our boss, Mr. Johnson, owns the A.S. Johnson Clothing Store in Carbondale. He feels the two stores would complement one another, and he wants to work on a fashion show with your store and a women's clothing store in Cobden."

"I am Miss Blanche Spencer, the shop's hatmaker. We are remodeling this week, and the owner is not here. May I give her a message?"

Mr. Charles Menees stepped forward, standing very close to Blanche. He had a chiseled jaw and sharp green eyes. He was a striking figure in his three-piece suit. Blanche, with her lack of experience, did not know how to interpret his manner, but her heart fluttered with him so close.

"Here's my business card, with the name and address of our store." As he handed her the card, his hand lingered over hers for a fraction of a second.

"Thank you for stopping by. I will write to you with the date of the store reopening."

As she closed the door, Blanche felt an unexpected shiver.

Liza had said to be ready at 2:30 on Sunday. They would walk to the church for the three o'clock event. Blanche decided to wear her new tan blouse, which nicely complemented her long navy-blue skirt. She had never been to a social event with her peers, and she was looking forward to meeting other young working women and men in a non-threatening setting.

Will that handsome salesman be at this event? she wondered to herself. *He seemed dashing yesterday, but a bit bold for my taste.*

The brick and white clapboard church with a bell tower sat at the top of a hill on the block behind North Front Street. About thirty young professionals were congregated at the far end of an assembly room, where there was a stage with chairs arranged in front. A church committee had set up two tables for pies. One also had a coffee pot. Trays of sandwiches were set out on the stage, and the young people were starting to help themselves.

A group of musicians wearing straw hats had gathered on the stage steps. The three handsome young men took off their jackets, revealing matching red and black suspenders and red garters on their sleeves. They bowed their heads together as they tuned their banjo, accordion, and ukulele.

Liza and Blanche got sandwiches and pulled up chairs next to three young women. Liza introduced Blanche to them, and they began to get acquainted. One of the young women mentioned that a women's choral club was being formed in Cobden and invited Blanche to join.

How nice, thought Blanche, *to find friendly young women just like me in Cobden.*

The musicians stood up and started playing old favorites, including "Sunbonnet Sue" and "My Gal Sal." Next they sang "My Bonnie Lies Over the Ocean." The musicians were lively, and two of them waved their arms occasionally to encourage the crowd to join in on the chorus. Soon everyone was singing and even clapping to the music.

"Announcement everyone!" someone cried, as the third song ended. "The pies are ready to serve, five cents a slice. Come and get a piece!"

The young people rushed to the pie tables. Liza and Blanche went back to their seats with pumpkin pie. One young woman was giving out her mincemeat pie recipe as the rest ate.

"Miss Spencer?" One of the young men in gaudy suspenders stood next to Blanche's chair. "I am Charles Menees. I met you Friday at the millinery store. Call me Charlie. May I escort you to a second serving of pie?"

Blanche looked up with a smile. He was quite handsome, his curly hair in a smooth wave above his forehead. Since he was wearing suspenders, she knew he was one of the musicians, although she had not recognized him earlier.

"Yes, I remember you from Friday. Do you live in Cobden?" she questioned.

"No, I currently live in Carbondale, but my friends asked me to perform with them at this event. Ready for another serving?" Charlie leaned in and offered his hand to encourage Blanche to stand up.

She accepted, stood up graciously, then quickly caught her fork as it tipped off her plate.

"Yes, and maybe coffee!" Blanche joked. "Liza, want to join us?"

"No thanks, Blanche," said Liza, who knew more about social interactions than Blanche.

"Then let's head for the fresh pies!" said Charlie.

Blanche stepped forward, looking toward the table and ignoring his offered arm.

As Blanche and Charlie stood in line, Charlie explained that his family was from Cobden and that he had moved to Carbondale to work at the A.S. Johnson Store. Blanche shared that she had been sent by her St. Louis boss to help the Cobden hat-store owner upgrade her fall hat inventory and help generate more business. Afraid of this stranger, Blanche kept a safe distance, but Charlie casually clicked his plate into hers every so often. What's more, he would step closer, and she would step back a step. This continued until they reached the pie table.

The two took their pie and sat on the stage steps. They talked further about the town of Cobden. When Blanche finished her pie, she stood up, thanked Charlie, and started to walk back toward Liza.

Charlie quickly put down his plate and picked up his ukulele.

"Miss Spencer, one moment," he called eagerly. Blanche turned back toward the steps. Then he stood up and, to the tune of "My Bonnie," began to sing:

> I know that your name is not Bonnie,
> I know that it really is Blanche,
> But come and just sit here beside me,
> And give me your sweet smiling glance!

Charlie's melodic tenor silenced the room. He looked straight into Blanche's blue eyes with his penetrating greenish-gray ones. At the end of the verse, everyone burst into applause.

Blanche stared back, blushing, mesmerized. No one had ever sung her a personalized song, let alone in front of thirty people!

The two other musicians appeared by Charlie and picked up their instruments. Then the trio sang several verses of the traditional "My Bonnie" song.

Liza and the three other girls ran over to Blanche.

"What did you do to get your own song, Blanche?" blurted Liza, stunned. "Things like this don't often happen in Cobden!"

"I have no idea!" Blanche's eyes went wide in wonder.

The room buzzed while the musicians continued strumming away. Other young women rushed to the steps to ask for personal songs for themselves, but Charlie and the other musicians strummed on without responding to the ladies' requests. Even though Charlie had made a bold move, he did not seek Blanche out again that evening.

Liza and Blanche left before the music was finished. Blanche could hardly process what had happened. She was perspiring, embarrassed, flattered—all of these things. She could hardly even walk straight. A very handsome young man had just made up a song for her, calling her Bonnie instead of Blanche, and letting the whole room of people know who she was. She was new in town, and she was dizzy with the thought of the impropriety of the outburst.

The two young women left the church and walked downhill in the twilight.

"I don't know what to think of this," Blanche stammered.

"Well, that Charlie is a charmer and a man of rhymes. He set out to capture your heart. Better be careful!" warned Liza, half laughing as she spoke.

"What do I do now?" asked Blanche.

"Well, continue to be a lady, do everything correct to keep your new job, and do not encourage his advances. And decide if you like him. That's my advice!"

Blanche undressed and lay across her bed for a long time before falling to sleep that evening. Her life had been so terribly sheltered. In the safe environment of the church social, she had looked into those green eyes, and now there was trouble! What had happened? Well, she had definitely turned the head of a handsome young man! But what an introduction to Cobden! How would she explain this to people who asked? It was all so upsetting, even on the edge of being improper. She fell asleep thinking random thoughts about the new man with the romantic tenor voice and the charming song that suggested she change her name.

The last week in October, Candace declared the following Friday—the beginning of the Cobden Harvest Festival—as the official reopening of The Millinery Shop. The festival was centered at the depot, and Candace felt the crowds would bring new people to her store. She asked Blanche to send an invitation to the owner of the Carbondale store. Blanche sent it, requesting that the owner and staff drop by for the weekend opening.

Blanche realized she needed more new hats! She had somehow forgotten about hat production, with the interesting and time-consuming store remodeling and the distraction of male suitors. Working straight through the weekend and continuing through Thursday of the following week, she made fifteen hats. In addition to black, she concentrated on fall colors—tan, rust, and dark green—and brought her white straw hat from home to add one last summer hat to the collection. She decided not to make her hats too fancy—nothing like the World's Fair fashions! Since she had not observed fashionable dress on North Front Street these past three weeks, she felt that conservative designs would sell better in this country town.

On Friday Blanche got to The Millinery Shop at eight o'clock, before Candace arrived. Everything was freshly painted and ready for the open house. On a whim, Blanche tried on one of the newly made hats, then walked slowly between the newly placed front and back mirrors. Her head held high and her hands at her side, she walked as she had seen a model walk at Rosenthal-Sloan. She studied a view of herself in the new mirrors on the back wall. She was amazed at her own elegant carriage and personal beauty. She stopped at the back mirrors, smiled, and tilted her head down slightly to show off the hat at a different angle. Then she turned and walked gracefully to the front mirror, which had a small oval frame set into a larger oval frame encased with rich tapestry fabric. The first rays of the morning sun shone through the rippled-glass front window and highlighted Blanche's peachy complexion, as well as the lovely browns and rusts of the hat. Looking in the mirror, Blanche had an overwhelming sense of both professional pride and feminine allure. With her hands clasped below her chin, she smiled into the mirror and purred, "What's next, Miss Spencer?"

The sound of Candace's key in the lock brought Blanche out of her reverie. Candace walked in, her mouth and eyes suddenly wide open in response to how good Blanche looked in the hat she was modeling.

"My goodness Blanche! You could certainly sell merchandise just by wearing it!" she said. "Leave the hat on until you *do* sell it."

It was almost ten o'clock. A new sign hung over the door, and the door itself was framed in red, white, and blue bunting. Blanche could see the harvest festival from the doorway. It looked like an expanded farmers market, and it included a pony ride and pumpkin patch. Looking uphill across the street, the reds, golds, and oranges of fall leaves were predominant, and crowds of shoppers were beginning to walk in and out of this lower area near the railroad tracks.

A few customers wandered into the store around eleven o'clock. Soon after, Mr. Johnson, the proprietor of the Carbondale men's store, Charlie Menees, and Benjamin Storm walked in the door, too. Charlie looked very handsome and businesslike in his three-piece suit.

Blanche scooted to the back room to retrieve a hat, waiting there until the men were ready to leave. As they did, she looked out through the curtains. Charlie turned, saw her framed in the curtains, and, lifting his hat, he bowed. He then turned to follow the other men out of the store.

The Millinery Shop had a steady stream of guests on Friday and Saturday, and hat sales were good. Midafternoon on Saturday, as Blanche was about to sit and rest her legs, two women and a young girl came into the store. Both women wore pale calico house dresses and shawls and sunbonnets. The child wore similar clothes. The shorter woman had brown hair pulled back into a roll at the base of her neck, as well as an oval face and very plump cheeks.

They received a welcome tour from Candace, who summoned Blanche. The shorter woman asked Blanche a question about alternate ribbon colors, as Candace turned to another customer. Blanche gave a somewhat technical answer but could tell that the woman wasn't really listening. Suddenly the woman uttered a faint cry and firmly put her hand on Blanche's arm.

"Pardon me, miss, may I inquire what your name is?" she said, a puzzled expression on her face.

"Yes, my name is Blanche Estelle Spencer."

"Blanche, I am your older sister, Bertha, Bertha Modglin!" Bertha whispered in total shock, still holding Blanche's arm. "We have not seen you since you were fourteen years old!" Her eyes opened wide, even as they teared up.

"Oh my!" choked Blanche. She grabbed her sister's other arm, so that the two women were locked together. For a moment they just stared into each other's eyes. Then Blanche freed her arms and stooped down to face the young girl, who looked just like her younger brother Lamont. "And who is this?" Blanche took the girl's hand.

192

"This is your niece, Vivian, just seven years old in May!"

Little Vivian buried her head in her mother's skirt but turned slightly with a shy smile to look at Blanche again.

The sisters moved to the front door, away from Candace and another customer. Bertha talked of her marriage, her child, and her farm near Makanda, Illinois, north of Cobden. She talked about how the family had missed Blanche after she left.

Blanche had not had a close relationship with either Lelia or Bertha because of their differences in age. Bertha had domestic leanings, taking almost all responsibility for care of Blanche's two brothers and baby sister Grace and babysitting other children in the neighborhood. Blanche, with her more intellectual nature, poetry recitations, and book reading, had not shared many interests with Bertha. But Bertha had taught her to crochet! And Bertha was the tie to her long-lost family, her bittersweet bond with her past life, which was again coming into focus.

Bertha explained that Lamont had had an allergic reaction to strawberries on the day Blanche had left town, and he quickly recovered. Blanche's chest rose and fell with mighty sighs, and tears ran down her cheeks as she listened to her sister talk.

Candace walked up to announce closing time, wondering why Blanche was not trying to sell hats. After telling Candace of her long-lost sister, Blanche introduced Candace to Bertha. Candace suggested they all leave together, then she would lock up. Blanche, Bertha, and Vivian all departed together and settled on a shady bench across the street. The other woman, Margaret Brown, took Vivian for a walk while the two sisters chatted further. Their conversation became very serious.

"You know, Blanche, Pa has never recovered from your departure. Just after you left, he talked about his hopes for your new life. Then, after a few weeks, he rarely mentioned you at all. When we asked, he gave vague answers and said he knew nothing. His face was always sad. We did not know where you lived in St. Louis. We waited years for you to return! What happened?"

Blanche's face went through a series of contortions as she answered.

"It was a sad beginning for me in St. Louis. I was taken in by a family from Austria. I became nursemaid to their two daughters and never again went to school. It was only recently, when I attended the Rosenthal-Sloan hat-making workshops, that I had further education. And now I have this travel assignment. I had a secret friend who sent letters to Pa, but Pa only answered about twice a year. I gave up completely, thinking the Spencer family was gone from my life. Because I received no information about any of you, I thought the family did not want to count me among their relations and did not love me anymore!"

Bertha wrapped her arms around Blanche. They put their warm faces together, cheek to cheek. The working girl and the farmer's wife went back to being sisters.

"Well, now we can be family again and begin to recover the lost years. Oraville is about ten hours away by buggy, slightly less if you use both train and buggy. So maybe you do not make that trip right away. Our farm is near Carbondale, only three hours away. *We* certainly can keep in touch! I will speak to my husband. Maybe we could ride in to pick you up, and you could spend a weekend with us at the farm. Would you like that?"

"Oh yes, that would be lovely! And it would give me a

chance to get to know Vivian!" The little girl's resemblance to her memories of young Lamont tugged at her heart.

Margaret and Vivian walked up.

"Blanche, we have to leave now to get back to our farms before dark. I can write to you at the store about what sorts of plans we can make. Margaret's husband was meeting with fruit packers about upcoming deliveries."

"Yes, I look forward to further visits," said Blanche, standing up and smoothing her skirt. "May I ask a favor? If you write of my appearance to the family, please do not mention a visit to Oraville. I need to think things through. Can you wait?"

"Certainly, we have our own catching up to do! I will write a letter soon."

Blanche and Bertha shared a long and loving hug, then Bertha, Margaret, and Vivian turned and left. Blanche watched with soft eyes as the trio descended to a wagon at the end of the packing yard below. She then gathered her purse and walked slowly across the tracks and uphill to Phillips House. She maintained her professional demeanor, but then for a moment her shoulders sagged, and she choked. Was her long-lost family coming back to her?

Sunbonnets
Cobden, Illinois • April 1910

It was early April, sunny again after a dark winter with gray skies and bone-chilling weather, though only a few snow-storms.

The store now had a particular smell, which Blanche could not easily put into words. She breathed it in as she stepped through the door. Old floorboards, new paint, new starched fabric, hat-making glue. Combined, it created a more personal smell than in the Rosenthal-Sloan building.

Blanche arrived at eight thirty to put her work space in order. Candace arrived at nine forty-five, for the ten o'clock opening. She had just shut the door, when someone started pounding frantically on it.

"I have a small emergency!" exclaimed a distressed woman with flyaway hair and a large frown.

"Please, come in and explain," said Candace.

"Well, it's about sunbonnets. Do you sell sunbonnets? My name is Becky Case. Last week I visited my sister's farm near Carbondale with my two daughters, five and ten years old. Somehow the canvas bag with all three of our sunbonnets was left at the farmhouse. Since it was cloudy, we did not notice it at the time. But tomorrow we are driving south to visit my husband's ailing mother. I burned myself badly yesterday boiling water," she said, as she raised her bandaged right arm, "and I cannot sew. My ten-year-old girl cannot sew well enough to make sunbonnets. We cannot ride all day in that hot sun without them! Do you carry sunbonnets, or could you make them overnight for me as a special request?"

"Mrs. Case, we do not have any sunbonnets in stock. But, Blanche, can you make a sunbonnet—or three sunbonnets—by tomorrow morning?"

Blanche stepped forward.

"Yes, Mrs. Case, I can make the sunbonnets you need," she said confidently. "I have two questions for you. What color do you want them? And could you bring both of your daughters in after school today so I can measure them?"

"Oh, what a big relief," sighed Becky Case, cradling her burned arm. "Well, mine would be best in brown or tan. And the girls, they always fight. So use the same fabric for both, a pastel calico would be fine. And what would these cost me?" she asked with a frown.

"Mrs. Case, I will give you one of the hats for free, if you will pass the word along to your friends that we carry sunbonnets. It will be two dollars for the others. How does that sound?" offered Candace, thinking on her feet.

Mrs. Case agreed to the price, said she would bring her girls back later, and requested the sunbonnets for ten o'clock the next morning.

"Now Blanche, how do you want to start? I am hoping you can handle this."

"I will go home right now and get my own sunbonnet to make a pattern. Then I will start sewing the first one. I might be able to finish it by the time Mrs. Case comes back.

When the girls come, I can measure them and create smaller patterns based on the adult one. If I work all evening, I think I can have all three done by morning. How does that sound?"

"I am glad you *have* a sunbonnet—and also glad you can do this!" Candace sighed with relief.

Blanche loved the challenge of a busy day of creative sewing. Her heart quickened. She would be at the *back of the stage*, making creative and useful hats for individual customers.

She hurried home and back, then quickly took her sunbonnet apart and made a pattern using white muslin. She purchased a soft tan fabric with a tiny dark-brown vine pattern from the general store and worked through her lunch break. Blanche did initial pleats and basting by hand, then put the sunbonnet together with final stitching on Candace's Singer sewing machine. She was just finishing up when Mrs. Case arrived with her two daughters. Blanche went to the front of the store with the first sunbonnet and took Mrs. Case over to a side mirror for a fitting.

"It is perfect, Miss Spencer! I love the wide brim. I hope you can do as well on the next two hats!"

Blanche smiled brightly at Mrs. Case, took a deep

breath, then turned to the two girls. She carefully took their measurements, then sent them off.

Blanche went back to the general store and chose a soft blue calico with tiny white flowers for the girls' hats, to match their blue eyes.

By eight o'clock, she had finished both of the blue sunbonnets. She spread them neatly across her worktable. *These are not fancy big-city hats,* she thought, *but they just might start bringing in more customers! All the women of Cobden are a hat challenge for me!* She hugged herself with a contented sigh.

She locked up the store just as dusk was settling over Cobden.

The rest of April brought a steady stream of customers into The Millinery Shop, thanks partially to Mrs. Case's recommendations. Most women were shopping for a new sunbonnet, but they also tried on Blanche's new dressy summer hats.

With Candace's permission, Blanche spent the last two weeks of April making only sunbonnets. They were selling almost as fast as Blanche could make them! She added lace fringe or alternate-color brims on some, and she put alternate-color straps on others. Using different combinations of bright colors and pastels for further variety, the new sunbonnets were more stylish than the homemade styles common in Cobden—and they were starting to fill the streets!

Candace was thrilled with both the success of the sunbonnets and the dressy hats. Some customers were now coming back a second time to discuss hat orders for summer weddings and anniversary parties.

The first week of May, Charles Menees walked into The Millinery Shop with a letter from his boss. After delivering it, he requested Candace's permission to take Blanche to tea, explaining he had met her at a church social event. He stood quietly, holding his hat with both hands. He looked more like a church-choir member than an ardent suitor.

"Well, she *is* working nonstop and could probably use a break. Keep her out for an entire hour, and make sure she relaxes and enjoys herself."

"Blanche," Candace called to the back, "A Mr. Menees has arrived on a business errand, and would like to take you to tea!"

"Good day, Miss Spencer," said Charles, as she walked toward the front of the store. "Shall we go to the café up the street?" He was polite and cheerful; this was their first meeting since the pie supper.

"Good day, Mr. Menees," said Blanche demurely. "How thoughtful of you to offer a tea break. I am very busy and cannot be gone long."

As they both turned to exit, Charlie offered his arm. Blanche accepted this time, and they walked together to the café.

How strange, thought Blanche, *holding a man's arm for a walk to tea!*

Blanche smiled to herself, shivering in the cold. She had not had time to make her navy-blue jacket yet, and she no longer had her blue shawl.

"Cold, Miss Spencer?" asked Charlie.

"I'll be fine inside," she said. They were almost to the café.

Charlie delicately touched her left elbow as they were

directed to a table against the wall. The small café was painted pale green, and its windows were partially fogged by con-
densation. Each table was covered with flowered oilcloth
and flatware. Charlie and Blanche's eyes met briefly over the
menu, and both he and she smiled self-consciously. They ordered hot tea and slices of pie.

"Well, Miss Bonnie, why are you in need of a break
from work?" asked Charlie, with a grin.

"I'm not sure about the name, sir. Though it does have
a certain ring." She tried to keep her face solemn, but her lips
rose up at the edges.

"'Bonnie with the blue eyes'—it totally suits you, Miss
Spencer!" He looked at her with friendly, smiling eyes.

She laughed, relaxing.

"There have already been two people come into the
store asking for Bonnie Spencer. I guess gossip and songs
travel quickly in this town!"

"Why are you working so hard?" he asked, as the pie
was being served.

"Please, start your pie. We have had a run on sunbonnets, so I have been sewing every working moment! I am
thrilled to be bringing customers into the store, and also
thrilled that some of these customers are now returning. I
cannot let up my pace. Summer is coming, and I will be departing in a few weeks."

"You're leaving so soon?"

"Yes, this was an eight-month assignment to help get
the store revitalized. I travel back to the St. Louis main office
around the middle of May," she said between bites.

"My goodness, Blanche—I mean Bonnie—I will hardly get to know you. I just spent four months in Chicago at
a large department store, learning shoes and the dry-goods

trade. And now I've come to renew our acquaintance, and you are about to leave!" Charlie exclaimed with a bewildered face, his fork in midair.

"Well, business is business. I believe Mr. Brenner, my St. Louis boss, already has another job for me."

And I must move on, Blanche thought, as she wiped her mouth with a paper napkin.

"My Carbondale boss is proposing a joint fashion show with several Cobden stores, sometime next fall. That would also bring business. Could we convince you to stay for that?" asked Charlie with a charming smile. He reached across the table to touch the back of her hand.

"I am afraid not. I am already committed to my next assignment, in Oklahoma!" she said.

Blanche had recently received a letter with this proposal. She was confident she would go, and she definitely felt the need to put distance between herself and this handsome suitor. She was quite flattered by his attention, but she was just beginning her career. She had no interest in getting entangled with a young man in Cobden, Illinois.

After tea they walked back to the store, talking part business, part pleasure. Blanche turned down Charlie's request to get together again, explaining that she was visiting her sister the following weekend and departing a week after that. As they got back to the shop, Charlie leaned against the door frame, trying to draw out the conversation.

"Must you get back to work so soon?" he questioned, raising his eyebrows.

"Yes, yes. Duty calls," she answered. She smiled, reached out to shake his hand, and politely excused herself.

Blanche hummed all afternoon, thinking about the talk and the pie but engrossed in her sewing, unaware she was making sounds at all. But Candace certainly noticed.

Blanche had been looking forward to the visit with her sister ever since their chance meeting in the fall. Unfortunately, circumstances prevented their getting together. Both Vivian and Leonard were ill over the Christmas holiday. Their illnesses and the winter weather made a visit impossible.

During winter months in Cobden, Blanche continued her self-education program by learning about the local fruit crops and fruit-shipping industries. She read the local newspaper, the *Cobden Sentinel,* and always asked her friends about things she read. She looked at fruit-shipping statistics, which might indicate economic prosperity that would lead to more hat sales. She also started a habit of posting articles on the wall of her room with hatpins. She put the collection at the edge of her closet door, where the hatpins would not damage the wallpaper.

Blanche also spent winter evenings in Cobden remembering the Oraville book readings in front of the fire. That was one of her strongest childhood memories—family members watching Pa's face as he took them through Robinson Crusoe's adventures of shipwreck, earthquakes, pirates, and cannibals. She remembered a warm hearth, where the family's well-being glowed like the embers of the fire. But she also recalled more recent memories of nights alone in the vinegar-scented St. Louis pantry and her anger about not going to school. She also remembered the anger she felt toward her father for sending her away.

The glowing Oraville hearth, the dark loneliness and anger in the St. Louis pantry. Blanche was unable to reconcile these two images in her heart. Now that she was a young woman with a successful career, she was hoping a visit with Bertha would give her new insight on how to view the Oraville family.

Finally, Bertha sent a letter inviting Blanche to visit the farm the second weekend in May, once the crops were in the ground.

Blanche decided to make a spring hat as a present for little Vivian. She found a blank pink-felt pattern hat in a child's size, which seemed perfect. She checked in her Bonnet Book for the three pages of notes on children's hats. The first sketch in the book would work, a pink hat accented with white chiffon.

With the book open for guidance, she covered the crown in a deep-pink cotton and glued it in place. Then she banded the crown in a belt of crushed white chiffon. Next she made a rosette with pale-pink chiffon and glued it on at the left front corner.

Charming! The perfect spring hat for a pretty young girl.

The Modglin family was due to arrive around lunch on Saturday. Blanche had directed them to the store, since Bertha already knew its location. Blanche was dressed in her navy-blue skirt and tan blouse, and she had her own sunbonnet reassembled and ready with her purse. The three Modglins pulled up in their wagon. Blanche saw them arrive and met Bertha at the door, then all four went across the street to the depot, where they ate on a bench. Bertha brought sandwiches and apples for lunch. Leonard, Bertha's husband, who was tall, sandy-haired, and quiet, passed out the sandwiches.

After they ate, Blanche presented the hat to Vivian.

The little girl broke into a smile and insisted on wearing the hat immediately.

A bright and saucy hat, thought Blanche, *and sweet Vivian loves it. This could be a holiday hat in red—and also a promotion for the store! I must order a dozen children's pattern hats in red.*

The group departed after lunch and began sharing their lives, as Blanche told them of her recent sunbonnet marathon, and the Modglins described their spring planting and vegetable-garden projects. The adults' conversations were interrupted by Vivian, who was talkative and wanted to tell her version of farm life.

Near Makanda, just before turning into the farm, the Modglins drew up to another wagon. Both stopped. The Modglins introduced Blanche to their neighbors, the Silas Brown family. It was this couple who had brought Bertha and Vivian to Cobden on the fall trip. Blanche nodded in recognition to Margaret Brown.

The Modglins and Blanche arrived midafternoon at the farm, which was flat as far as the eye could see. There was one acre of orchards near the house. The rest of the land was cornfields.

Bertha's kitchen brought back memories and smells from Blanche's childhood. Bertha used the same stew spices her mother used, and their scent wafted up from the stove. The biscuits and apple pie in the oven also had a familiar smell. There was even a towel on a kitchen rack with clumsy embroidery by a young Blanche. The sight of it took Blanche's breath away.

"When did you last go to Oraville, Bertha?" Blanche asked.

"Let's see, we went back for Thanksgiving two years ago—that was the last time. We all gathered in Vergennes, hosted by several families. Lamont is now fifteen and Merwin eighteen, and they are both handsome and respectful boys. Ma enjoyed the visit with her sisters. Pa talked to everyone at the table, but I caught moments when he had a pensive look. Vivian loves Vergennes and fits right in with her cousins!" Bertha seemed eager to give an accurate report.

"It is so *hard* for me to understand why I was sent away, what I did wrong." Blanche's voice trailed off.

"Well, I don't think we should speculate on the family situation from eight years ago. I personally have no idea of Pa's motives for sending you away," Bertha said, crossing the room and encircling Blanche in a warm hug. "Let's just enjoy this time together and not worry about things we cannot resolve. By the way, your pompadour hairdo is very flattering!"

"And Blanche," added Bertha slowly, "I have gotten a brief letter from Pa that I want to share with you." She pulled a white sheet from her apron.

The letter was in Pa's writing style, addressed to both Bertha and Blanche and telling them both to enjoy their weekend family reunion. One sentence in particular caught Blanche's attention: "I am so pleased you two have reunited. It was such a hard decision to send you away, Blanche, and now you can begin to mend the family ties."

"Well, it is relief to hear from Pa. Maybe I *can* visit Oraville in the future. It is so lovely here now, and so welcoming in your sweet kitchen." Blanche tried to put on a smile, but her mind and heart had never been able to forget being abandoned.

Vivian was a three-foot whirlwind, darting in and out of the kitchen, sometimes wearing the pink hat, sometimes not, apparently involved with doll business in her bedroom.

The small family group enjoyed a comfortable Saturday

night dinner and talked into the evening. A glowing candle on the table softened the plain room. Leonard and Bertha seemed warm and loving with one another. They occasionally touched and sometimes put an arm around Vivian. The dinner filled Blanche with rich savory tastes and smells and low-key family conversations and left her feeling included in the family again. Blanche hummed as she helped Bertha with cleanup, while Leonard put Vivian to bed.

Later, in the spare bedroom, Blanche pondered what she should do with her own Oraville family, now that she had heard from Pa. She ached to see the family again, but her thoughts were still confused, and the idea of a strained visit was heavy in her heart.

Bertha had suggested Blanche make a summer visit to Oraville. Blanche decided to let her write her pa about this first visit. She would depart the following week to return to St. Louis and would not even consider a visit to her Oraville family at this time. Her business travel was a convenient reason not to make the return to Oraville and not to risk any sort of rejection.

Sunday morning included a tour of the farm. Vivian stomped among the vegetables, waving her arms and putting on a comical show. She reviewed the names and personalities of the two mules and two cows, shared how many eggs a week the chickens produced, and explained how many piglets had been born that spring.

After lunch, Vivian disappeared while the adults cleaned the kitchen, laughing easily together. The day seemed almost like Christmas, full of blessings and good food.

Suddenly, the tranquil setting was shattered by a loud crash. All three adults rushed into Vivian's room. The eight-year-old was on the floor, partially covered by a large dollhouse that Leonard had made for her. As Leonard lifted the dollhouse off Vivian, a more serious problem became apparent. Vivian had one blade of a pair of scissors lodged into her right thigh. She screamed in pain and terror. Keeping calm, Bertha took off her apron, kneeled next to Vivian, and pulled the blade out of her leg. Then she tied the leg up with the apron.

"Leonard, we will need to take her to the doctor in Carbondale right away," Bertha said firmly. "Please get the wagon ready. Blanche, I think you should come with us. We might have to put you on the train at Carbondale for the return trip to Cobden."

Bertha sat holding Vivian while Blanche gathered her belongings. Leonard raced to the barn. With Vivian still whimpering in her mother's arms and the mules in a brisk trot, the group headed to Carbondale.

When they arrived, the whole family hurried into a white clapboard house whose front rooms had been converted into a doctor's office. Blanche sat alone near the entry, wringing her hands, while both parents went into the room with Vivian to see the doctor. A stranger came limping into the waiting room with a bandage on his right knee.

"Hello, ma'am. I'm Silas Brown Junior. We met yesterday. Are you waiting for someone, or are you next to see the doctor?"

"The Modglins are with the doctor. Vivian hurt her leg."

"My cousin Charlie Menees was out for dinner last night and heard about your visit from my parents. He was surprised that you were in the neighborhood. He said he hoped to see you this weekend."

"Well, I am waiting to be sure my niece is taken care

of. Then I am hoping to catch the train back to Cobden this afternoon."

"Miss, there is only one train on Sunday, at 10:00 a.m. It has already been through Carbondale today."

Then, without warning, he added "Pardon me for a moment," and limped out of the building.

How curious, I wonder what scared him off, thought Blanche.

Ten minutes later, Silas returned, along with his cousin, Charlie Menees.

"Well, Miss Spencer! What a pleasure to see you in Carbondale," said Charlie, with a grin, as he took off his hat. He was in his Sunday church clothes and looked quite dapper. "I understand you may need a ride to Cobden this afternoon?"

"It seems I have missed the train," Blanche said with some obvious frustration.

"Yes, it *has* left." Charlie, self-assured, stepped closer to Blanche. "But I have come to offer you a ride to Cobden with our family's wagon. Would this be suitable?"

"Perhaps." Blanche spoke cautiously, looking down, since she thought it inappropriate to look into those green eyes again. "Let's discuss it with my sister when they are finished."

It wasn't long before the Modglin family came back out. Bertha looked tired but relieved. Leonard followed, carrying tear-stained Vivian. She had a bandage on her leg and a red sucker in her hand.

"Mr. and Mrs. Modglin, I am Charles Menees, your neighbor Silas Brown's cousin. I have made the acquaintance of your sister, Miss Spencer, on two previous business meetings in Cobden. I am free this afternoon and, since the train has left, I have offered to escort Bonnie—I mean Blanche—back to Carbondale in our family wagon."

Blanche blushed at Charlie's use of "Bonnie."

"Mr. Menees, you would be the answer to our prayers. We need to stay with Vivian. We trust you will deliver Blanche safely. And may I ask what the 'Bonnie' name is about?" asked Bertha.

"Mrs. Modglin, Blanche and I met in October at a pie supper at the Cobden Presbyterian Church. Everyone was singing 'My Bonnie Lies Over the Ocean,' and I made up a comical verse for Blanche, using the name Bonnie. That's all!" Charlie raised one hand in the air as if to dismiss his action.

"Well, 'Bonnie' is sort of cute! You with your blue eyes," giggled Bertha, turning to wink at Blanche. "Seriously, can your family spare their wagon?"

"Yes, ma'am. I'm happy to make the trip. I will just drive one way today, spend the night with my musician friends in Cobden, and then drive back early tomorrow before work."

"Well, Blanche. How do you feel about all of this? I do not know how else to get you back to Cobden. What a relief to us!" All eyes turned to Blanche, who hesitated for a moment before saying, "Thank you, Mr. Menees."

Bertha grabbed Blanche's arm, and they walked outside. Touching their heads together, they then shared a long hug.

Leonard lifted his daughter into the wagon, helped his wife in, then turned their wagon around. The family waved as they headed out of town. There was even a limp wave from Vivian, who was buried in her mother's arms.

"Come, you two, I can give you a ride to Charlie's house to get the other wagon. Climb in! After I drop you off, I will come back to see the doctor," said Silas.

A short time later, Blanche and Charlie began the wagon ride south to Cobden. The afternoon sun was strong, so Blanche donned her sunbonnet, which she felt also shielded her somewhat from Charlie's attentions. They tried to stay on neutral conversation topics. They talked about jobs, farms, crops, children, and, finally, about the surrounding countryside. The spring color was lovely and reminded Blanche of why the countryside offered spiritual renewal not found in the city. There were red blushes of new growth on the sumac along the road, and yellow mustard bloomed at the edge of the cornfields. Young cedars grouped at the tops of limestone bluffs lined up like fat pigeons on a windmill blade. Blanche soaked in the sights of spring, trying not to think too much about the man next to her. Charlie was gracious and proper and handled his mule team and wagon with consummate skill.

As they neared Cobden, Charlie turned to Blanche and exclaimed, "Well, what do you know! By some quirk of fate, I have gotten you to sit beside me! Now, I just need your 'sweet smiling glance'!" He grinned, looked at her, and slapped his knee.

"My goodness, you continue to be a man of rhymes, Mr. Menees," Blanche said, grabbing the brim of her sunbonnet with both hands and smiling to herself between them. "Please follow this road down across the railroad tracks, then go left uphill, and stop at 210 North Front Street. You've been a perfect gentleman."

Charlie followed her directions. When they arrived at the white house, he stopped the mules and tied the lead to a fencepost. He then came around to help Blanche descend and offered his arm to escort her to the door.

"No need for an escort, Mr. Menees," she bowed her head, trying to hide her smile. "But you *can* walk with me to the door."

"My pleasure, Miss Spencer. I hope we meet again! Who knows, maybe in Oklahoma!"

She laughed and put out her hand when they reached the door. He put his hand on top of hers for a lingering touch. Then he walked briskly to the wagon.

Blanche turned to go inside, her hand quivering as she opened the door. She turned again, smiled at Charlie in the wagon, and quickly went in. Once inside, she leaned against the door and took a deep breath, waiting for her flushed face and racing heartbeat to subside.

Heading to Oklahoma
St. Louis, Missouri • Early May 1910

Blanche had already said her goodbyes at the boarding-house. She stopped at The Millinery Shop to say goodbye to Candace, who was sorry to see her leave, especially since business had picked up considerably during Blanche's time there. During her last week, Blanche had made dozens more fancy hats and sunbonnets for Candace.

The two women stood in the middle of the store. With Blanche's decorating touches, the store had become reminiscent of a fancy doll house. Mirrors sparkled everywhere and gave off twinkles of semi-colored light. The upholstered bench and frame added rich fabric at the entrance. White walls made the hat colors stand out and encouraged customers to take a closer look.

"Blanche, you have been a wonderful friend to me. You have been very helpful in making this store more visible in town. Remember, if Oklahoma does not suit you, I would love to have you come back for another eight-month session to make hats. Keep that in mind."

"Well, I must be going. I will write you with my Oklahoma address. Thank you again for everything. Goodbye!" Blanche reached out to shake hands with Candace but got an unexpected hug instead.

Carrying her leather purse and carpetbag, Blanche walked across Front Street to the railroad depot and farmers market plaza. The northbound train arrived soon after. Blanche made the twenty-five-minute ride to Carbondale, waited a half hour, and then caught the next train north to Murphysboro, before continuing to St. Louis.

This time Blanche did not get upset in Carbondale or Murphysboro. Because she had written a loving thank-you to Bertha, Leonard, and Vivian and said goodbye in the note, she now felt somewhat connected to her birth family again.

Blanche had also written to the Robeys, letting them know she was arriving on Friday evening. Both she and the Robeys still considered their home hers as well.

While working in Cobden, she had spent little money except for food, and she had left most of her savings in the Cobden bank. She would transfer it when she got to Oklahoma. For now, she had adequate travel money.

The train arrived at St. Louis' Union Station in the late afternoon. As she took the Grand Staircase down to the street, Blanche glanced up at the blue and yellow stained-glass angels. She smiled, remembering her first train ride and the first time she had seen the angels.

Blanche signaled a horse cab—another first for her—and gave the McPherson Street address. Twenty minutes later, she arrived at the Robey flat and knocked on the front door.

"Yes?" Beth called, before opening the door. "Blanche! Alma, come to the door! Blanche is here!"

Beth had a broad smile on her normally serious face. She pulled Blanche inside and took the carpetbag from her. With happy tears running down her cheeks, Alma ran into Blanche's arms.

"You're back in St. Louis! Did you come to read to us?" grinned Alma, now fourteen.

"Hello, Blanche. We did not know exactly when to expect your arrival," said Mrs. Robey, her hands clasped together at her waist. "Well, you look the same as always, a young businesswoman with lovely clothes!"

"Thank you. It is good to see everyone again!" she said cheerfully, as she glanced around at the familiar somber furnishings. "I do not expect to be here more than a week or two. Rosenthal-Sloan has another traveling assignment for me!"

"Let's save that for supper. I know Mr. Robey will want to hear the details. He is not home yet. Girls, take Blanche to your bedroom to store her belongings. I expect we will have our meal in about half an hour."

The evening meal was one of Greta's best: beef brisket with vegetables, fresh rolls, and oatmeal cookies. Sitting on either side of Blanche, both girls spoke at once. Mr. Robey cut them off.

"Now girls, let's let Blanche tell us about her adventures and plans, shall we?"

"Well, the hat store in Cobden was a quiet and ordinary place when I arrived. But I was asked to help with remodeling it, as well as making hats to restock the inventory," explained Blanche. "Miss Candace Moraine, the owner, gave me a fond farewell and invited me back anytime if my assignments elsewhere proved unsuitable. I have sewing work to do this weekend, and I want to spend time with the girls. Also, I

215

have received a proposal from Mr. Brenner to work in Oklahoma. I meet with him on Monday to discuss the details."

The Robeys sat still, forks suspended in midair, listening to Blanche's every word, very curious about her next assignment.

"Did you do any social activities in Cobden?" asked Mrs. Robey, changing the subject.

"Just one pie supper at the Presbyterian church when I was invited by a housemate. Otherwise, all of my activities centered around the store. My lovely boardinghouse was just two blocks away."

After dinner, Blanche spent a happy hour reading and talking with Beth and Alma. The three of them snuggled up on Alma's bed in their usual way. Later, Blanche took a long, hot bath, something she had missed in Cobden. She retired early.

Blanche began sewing on Saturday after breakfast, setting up a sewing center on the dining room table, after asking Mrs. Robey if she could use the table. She got out the pattern for her jacket, lay it on the navy-blue broadcloth fabric, and cut pieces for the jacket and lining. She spent the rest of Saturday and all of Sunday finishing it.

She moved off the eating table and worked at the parlor sofa, with strong afternoon light at her back to help her see the navy thread against the dark fabric. First she basted the jacket and lining together, then she went to the girls' bedroom mirror to try on the garment. Making a few adjustments, she carefully completed the finished stitchwork, which, without a sewing machine, took several hours.

Her mind wandered as she sewed. At twenty-one, she felt too old for the trundle bed. Now that she had lived on her own in Cobden, she felt she had outgrown the living situation in the Robey's house. She was ready to travel again and began to focus on her upcoming adventures in Oklahoma.

Blanche woke up on Monday full of purpose and immediately dressed in her new clothes. She chatted with the family and Greta at breakfast, then left.

Her new form-fitted Eton jacket was a very elegant addition to her wardrobe. It looked smart with her navy skirt. As she headed out of the flat, the morning sun caught the sparkle of the velvet collar. On the streetcar ride, Blanche was the most stylish rider, even without a fancy hat.

Blanche arrived at Mr. Brenner's office just before eleven o'clock and was promptly ushered in. He was standing behind his desk, pinning notes on a map of Missouri that was hanging on the wall. He turned and gave Blanche a warm handshake, signaling for her to sit down.

"I'm happy to welcome you back, Miss Spencer. I have heard from Miss Moraine, and I want to thank you for your hard work and entrepreneurial spirit in helping her improve her store and expand her hat inventory," he said, with a twinkle in his eyes.

"Mr. Brenner, I loved the assignment," Blanche replied. "It was quite an experience to help remodel a store in a prosperous town and to watch the store become a more successful part of the community."

"Miss Spencer, I have recently gotten word from Oklahoma City that hatmakers are needed for the upcoming state fair in October. I thought I might send you to Oklahoma, where you'd have the chance to work in another big city. How does that sound?"

"I would love to go to Oklahoma. And, frankly, I am happy to leave as soon as possible!" Blanche said brightly.

"There is one thing you might want to do before you

go. On Thursday morning there is a half-day seminar about new hat styles and designs from Paris and London. I think you should attend. Could you wait and leave on Friday, after the seminar?"

"Oh yes, Mr. Brenner. The seminar sounds very interesting, and I would be happy to depart on Friday." Blanche's face lit up with the news of both the seminar and her upcoming travel.

At Monday dinner, Beth and Alma talked about school field trips and upcoming summer events. After, Blanche asked Mr. Robey if she might talk with him in his office.

"Blanche, tell me how things went at Rosenthal-Sloan today," he said.

"I had a nice meeting with Mr. Brenner. Thursday he is sending me to a half-day seminar, and on Friday I'm going to Oklahoma City! I will ride a train called the KATY."

"Oklahoma just became a state! That is *Indian* territory, and those savages roam the plains with horses and guns. It would be an overnight train ride with dim lights for several hours! Mrs. Robey and I think it is a very bad idea. Perhaps I should pay a visit to Mr. Brenner and get further details before we agree to let you go to Oklahoma," said Mr. Robey, turning red. "I really think it is far too dangerous to send you to Oklahoma by yourself!"

"The train is called the KATY Texas Special, which goes from St. Louis all the way to Texas, through Kansas and Oklahoma," said Blanche.

Blanche sat up straight and put both arms on the leather armrests. Leaning forward, she calmly announced, "I have already agreed to go, and the travel is being arranged. I do not feel I need anyone's permission to go." She looked directly at Mr. Robey.

"Well, we have not agreed to this trip, young lady," Mr. Robey spoke firmly, raising his voice slightly.

"I intend to go to Oklahoma City on Friday with or without your permission," Blanche said again, with more conviction. "I am pursuing my profession now. I am a grown woman."

Silence overtook the room. Blanche glared at Mr. Robey as he looked at his desktop, trying to figure out what to say next.

"Let's postpone this decision until I meet with Mr. Brenner," announced Mr. Robey, regaining his composure. "I will stop by his office tomorrow and try to get an appointment right away."

Blanche left the room with clenched jaws and fists. She was handling the big things now on her own—her education, her heart, her future. It was all on her shoulders now. She had the practical tools to chart her own destiny, and she was deeply committed to going to Oklahoma. Even if going to Oklahoma was a little dangerous, she had to do it. She felt it was the next move for her career.

Tuesday Blanche ran errands in town all day. She took the streetcar to the downtown library to read up on Oklahoma City. After, she took a horse cab to Soulard Market. As she approached his wagon, she found Mr. McGregor calmly watching the market scene. As he saw her, his face lit up in a broad smile.

"My goodness, I did not expect to see you again this

year!" said Mr. McGregor, as he put his hand on her shoulder.

"Mr. McGregor, I am only here for a week. I leave for Oklahoma City on Friday and have just been at the library researching Oklahoma. I am in the middle of a busy week of travel preparation."

"Research? You must be a scholar as well as a hatmaker! Are you with Mrs. O'Malley? If not, can I take you to lunch or out for a cup of coffee?" Mr. McGregor looked hopeful, his bushy eyebrows raised.

"Yes, I was hoping we could talk."

Mr. McGregor led Blanche to a nearby tavern. They sat at a small table in back and ordered hot tea and cheese sandwiches.

"Cobden was certainly educational," Blanche began. She explained the month of store remodeling and several months of making dress hats and sunbonnets. Her eyes sparkled as she talked about her business strategies and successes.

Mr. McGregor sat back in his chair as she talked, studying her intently.

"Blanche, I must tell you that for the first time you are speaking like a businesswoman. This trip has opened your eyes to the business world, and you have approached this assignment with an eye for business, not just hat making. I think you have creative skills in business that you barely recognize. You must keep this in mind!" Mr. McGregor said warmly.

"Thank you, Mr. McGregor, I hope you are right. I kept looking for more ways to improve how the store operated—I did not just make hats. And when I go to Oklahoma, I will have to further expand my business skills." Blanche took a sip of tea then changed the subject. "I have another question on a different subject. What do you know about a train called the KATY Texas Special?"

"Well, that train goes to Texas. It has been around almost twenty years. I have known several professors who traveled on it to get to universities in Texas. It is a very clean and convenient way to make a very long trip. It is perhaps twenty-four hours or more from St. Louis to Dallas, slightly less to Oklahoma. But I believe it would be safe for you to take the train, as long as you follow common-sense rules of modest behavior."

"Thank you for the advice," Blanche laughed. They continued to talk about the train to Oklahoma as she finished her cup of tea.

"Let's get back to my wagon," Mr. McGregor said, leaving money on the table and getting up to leave.

As they exited the building, Mr. McGregor offered Blanche his arm. They crossed the street to Soulard Market, and she continued to hold his arm all the way back to his book wagon. His arm felt warm through her jacket.

At the book wagon, they shared a long hug.

"Keep your eyes open in Oklahoma, Blanche. And write to me about your thoughts and inspirations. I know you will have a successful trip."

"Thank you for your friendship and wisdom. I will keep in touch." She looked into his intelligent eyes, then turned to leave the market and get a horse cab back to McPherson Street.

As Blanche rode to the Robey flat, she tingled with excitement about her upcoming trip. It seemed like a bigger sort of adventure compared to her small adventures in Cobden, Illinois. So far she had not met with any problem she could not handle. She had new clothes and luggage and no sense of fear. She was ready to help another millinery company.

Late Tuesday afternoon Mr. Robey met with Mr. Brenner. Mr. Brenner slapped his friend on the shoulder and told him his fears were groundless. He sent people and supplies to Texas all the time. The KATY train was fast and reliable, and the Indians allowed the train through their territory without incident. Yes, Blanche was young, but she had proven herself in Cobden. Mr. Brenner felt she could easily handle the assignment.

On Thursday Blanche attended the morning seminar. The first part of the lecture was about the growing concerns among upper-class women and a society called the "Audubon Movement" about using bird feathers on hats, because of the destruction of rare bird species to supply the feather market. The second part of the lecture was about the construction of bigger and more complex hats without feathers, which include the twisting and construction of large, artful bows, new and bigger ribbons, and bigger artificial flowers. When it was over, Blanche headed to Mr. Brenner's office.

"Miss Spencer, I understand you have been making the rounds here, getting all of the latest information on supplies before you leave. You are an industrious young woman. Here are your travel papers, the train ticket for tomorrow, and a voucher for the hotel. Also included is another twenty dollars in travel cash to help with your trip. Goodbye, good luck, and enjoy the new challenge!"

Blanche arrived home in time for supper. She was slightly worried.

"Well, Blanche," said Mr. Robey, as he began cutting into his roast beef, "Mr. Brenner has done careful research concerning your Oklahoma assignment, and he has convinced me that you can make this trip. However, Mrs. Robey and I still feel the journey is very unsafe."

222

"Thank you for your concern, Mr. Robey. I understand you just want me to be safe, on the trip and in Oklahoma. The company found me a hotel in Oklahoma City that I expect will be fine. I am packed and ready, and I will depart tomorrow!" Blanche spoke with self-confidence. The rest of dinner continued somewhat quietly. Mrs. Robey smiled through tight lips but made no comment.

Mr. Robey and Blanche departed for Union Station at nine o'clock the next evening. Blanche insisted on stopping at the street in front of Union Station, rather than parking the carriage and walking with Mr. Robey to the station. When he got out of the carriage to help her down, she took her carpetbag from him and shook his hand.

"I will make this work, Mr. Robey. I will do a good job, and I will make you proud of me. Thank you for your concern. Thank you for everything. Goodbye!"

He barely looked at her and did not wish her well.

Blanche hurried up the front steps of Union Station, holding her head high and her back straight, thinking only of her trip to Oklahoma.

She boarded the KATY Texas Special at midnight.

KATY Texas Special
Oklahoma City • Mid-May 1910

The Missouri-Kansas-Texas train, the KATY Texas Special, in existence since 1865, tooted its whistle just before midnight. Casting eerie shadows on the steel trellis, it slowly rolled out of the St. Louis Union Station train shed.

Blanche was on a passenger coach halfway down the train. She had chosen a window seat, so she could tuck her purse between her body and the wall of the coach. Blanche studied the coach interior as the train picked up speed. It was trimmed in dark mahogany, with brass knobs and luggage racks, and it was lit by small lights with glass shades that looked like upside-down tulips. Each seat had dark upholstery with a removable white-cloth head panel. Blanche had hoped to study vocabulary words, but the tulip lights soon dimmed, which made her begin to feel drowsy. Under a starless sky, the KATY Texas Special crawled west through the hills of Missouri, stopping at many sleepy towns.

Though she didn't think anyone would trouble her on such a well-appointed train, mindful of Mr. Robey's warnings, Blanche had placed her carpetbag at her feet and wound the straps around her ankles. Mr. Robey was always giving her tips like this, which seemed so overprotective. During the night, she dreamt that a rope was pulling her legs, that her legs were actually being moved. The dream continued until she realized she *did* feel a tug on her legs. One ankle burned with irritation.

Blanche opened her eyes and discovered arms trying to untangle the straps from her feet! She kicked violently and heard a man yelp and curse. He had hold of her right leg and continued pulling—hard! She kicked and kicked, holding onto the seat armrest, screaming. A conductor wearing a gun holster came to her rescue, pulling the struggling man out from under the seats.

The would-be thief stood scowling in his dirty clothes. He smelled of alcohol, moved restlessly, and looked at the floor as the conductor held him with one hand and pointed the gun at him with the other. The conductor assured Blanche that the thief would be expelled from the train at the next stop, then led the angry man away.

Blanche was rattled and could not fall back to sleep. She rationalized that the alcohol had probably muddled the thief's brain and given him the courage to attempt to steal her luggage. She thought about the Temperance poem, its words and meaning suddenly more real, now that she had seen firsthand the horrible effects of alcohol. From that moment on, the Temperance campaign would be a life crusade for her.

Through the large window on her right, Blanche watched a late-night thunderstorm push dark clouds across the horizon, lit by flashes of mile-high lightning bolts. The violent storm only unsettled her even more. Though she was wearing her navy-blue Eton jacket, the storm gave her chills. She covered herself with her cape for comfort and warmth, but it was a long time before she fell back asleep.

At dawn, Blanche began to see the wide, flat plains of early-spring grass in Kansas. Here and there, she also saw a few solitary trees. She thought about her week in St. Louis. Though this trip was proving to be more dangerous than she had expected, she still felt she had made the right decision to go to Oklahoma. She *was* grown up now, and she needed to be on her own, making her own decisions and guiding her own future. She had left the Robeys in a defiant mood, but she now understood their concerns. And yet she still felt excitement about her trip.

Blanche also reviewed what her library research had taught her about Oklahoma. The brand-new state had large Indian populations, recent discoveries of oil and new oil refineries, and a large influx of business entrepreneurs looking for frontier opportunities. She hoped the new commerce also meant more demand for hats. She was very proud and confident to be bringing her hat-making talent to this new state.

Blanche studied the scenery for the rest of the day. The Kansas landscape was a flat mosaic of green: the bright green of the grassy plains stretching for miles, the spring wheat coming up in a softer green.

The scenery is picturesque, but I have seen few people, she thought.

She ate a lunch of bread, cheese, and an apple. After

lunch, she dozed. The sound of a harmonica awakened her. The musician was a man sitting near the front of the car. He wore a buckskin jacket and a ten-gallon hat, and he was softly playing "My Bonnie Lies Over the Ocean."

My goodness, I thought I was leaving that man behind, but his song is coming with me to Oklahoma!

The late-afternoon sky presented a vivid pink sunset over the cornfields of southern Kansas. Just after stopping at Oswego, the train slid across the border into Oklahoma. Suddenly the grass looked taller, the rolling hills seemed higher, and—as she already had seen—the cowboy hats appeared bigger. *Big country and big unknowns,* she mused. *Big challenges for a single woman.*

The KATY Texas Special pulled into Muskogee, Oklahoma late in the evening, past infrequent pools of light at the depot roof overhang. Blanche disembarked. She had to wait for another train going west to Oklahoma City.

She spent a miserable two hours in the dim depot. When she stepped outside for some fresh air, she almost stumbled into a cowboy leading a horse carrying a dead deer. At eleven-fifteen, almost twenty-four hours since her departure from St. Louis, she boarded another KATY train, this one bound for Oklahoma City. She quickly fell into a second night of restless sleep, a second storm pounding the train window.

At dawn the next day, Blanche began to see different vegetation. Through the morning haze, she occasionally caught glimpses of drifts of stubby trees with deep-pink flowers. The trees lined the gullies snaking through the countryside.

Blanche decided the train had avoided the Indians Mrs. Robey had worried about, and she figured she was now probably almost to her destination.

When the train neared the city, Blanche began to watch more closely. The colored mosaic of the prairie changed to the geometric blur of farmhouses and barns, followed by one-story white clapboard buildings and red-brick storefronts. Finally, she saw three- to five-story buildings. She also observed that the young city still struggled with muddy roads and dust.

As the KATY pulled into the Oklahoma City depot at seven o'clock, Blanche excitedly gathered her carpetbag and purse and hurried down the train steps. St. Louis had a big-city train station; this western city barely had one at all. Wearing her tall black boots, she stepped carefully around the muddy puddles, thinking the storm last night must have also passed through Oklahoma City.

As she walked outside the depot, a buckboard wagon lurched around the corner, splashing the puddles in every direction. The driver, a woman with curly red hair and a wide-brimmed leather hat, stood up, tugging on the reins. The wagon came to a halt a few feet from Blanche, who was startled by not only the commotion but the horse's loud snorts.

Off jumped the redhead, her wild hair flying behind her. She wore a long, dark skirt, a tailored pale-blue blouse with long sleeves and a white collar, and a dark-blue scarf. It was casually draped around her neck and knotted across her chest.

"Pardon me. Might you be Miss Blanche Spencer?" asked the redhead.

"Why, yes! Who are you?" The woman reminded her of Annie Oakley. She was square-shouldered and square-jawed, with an athletic body.

"I'm Mrs. Ruby Keyes, wife of Willis Keyes. Mr. Robey

of St. Louis, a former customer of my husband's, sent us a telegram asking that we meet your train. I am relieved that you arrived at the time listed in the telegram. Some trains get delayed by Indians, collapsed bridges, or stranded cattle on the tracks." Blanche's eyes grew wide with Ruby's list of predicaments her train had been lucky to avoid. "Let's get you in the wagon."

Ruby held out her hand for Blanche to give her the carpetbag, which she stowed behind the wagon seat.

"Mrs. Keyes, thank you for meeting me at the depot after my very long trip. Please call me Bonnie."

Blanche hadn't even realized she had decided to make the name switch, until she heard herself say the words.

"My formal name is Blanche, but I have decided I want to be called Bonnie for this next chapter of my life."

Bonnie was surprised at the strong feeling she had about adopting the new name on her first steps in Oklahoma. *This is* not *about Charlie,* she thought, *this is about the professional woman I want to be.*

"Well, Miss Bonnie, welcome to Oklahoma City. What a lovely concept, changing your name when you arrive at a new city. I like you, Bonnie. You seem forward-thinking. I'm going to take you to our home for a night, until we visit proposed lodgings close to your new job."

Mrs. Keyes cracked her whip over the head of a black gelding, held the reins tightly, and steered the horse onto the muddy street. Bonnie, utterly exhausted, placed one hand on her head, as if to hold an imaginary hat in place.

The wagon raced across town. They passed over roads that were paved with bricks and others that weren't paved at all—the horseshoes especially loud on the paved ones. The wagon bounced and rattled, unlike any civilized carriage ride she had taken in St. Louis or Cobden. And this wild woman, a little older than she, certainly fit Bonnie's image of a Wild West cowgirl! All she needed was a buckskin skirt!

The wagon careened nine blocks south on Broadway, the ride too wild and noisy for conversation. Blanche's first impressions were of buildings in many types and sizes, unlike the tidy red-brick buildings in St. Louis.

Ruby pulled up in front of a modest bungalow with a wide roof and a welcoming porch. There were no plantings around the house, though stubby grass grew between the house and the unpaved road. A line of tall trees separated the bungalow from a two-story house next door.

"I have made that trip myself, and I know it is exhausting. I want to give you a wholesome breakfast before you take a hot bath and have a nap. Then we will talk further."

Ruby spoke warmly as she grabbed the carpetbag and took Bonnie by the elbow, leading her to the front of the bungalow and unlocking the door. Bonnie, weary with exhaustion, followed Ruby into the cozy house.

"Why don't you wash up while I make coffee and scrambled eggs," Ruby said. "The bathroom is down the hall."

Ruby pulled off her leather hat and hung it on a peg on the kitchen wall. After she started a fire in the wood-burning stove, she put water in a kettle, and got out her cast-iron skillet.

Bonnie walked down the wallpapered hall to the bathroom. When she returned to the kitchen, she sank wearily into a wooden chair at a table opposite the stove. She watched as Ruby poured water into a metal coffeepot, scrambled eggs in the skillet, and flipped thick slices of bread on a griddle. Blanche looked around the kitchen, which had a low ceiling, white beadboard walls, oak counters, and cupboards with natural oak trim.

Ruby set down two metal cups of coffee, two tin plates of food, and a jar of berry jam.

"Welcome to breakfast in Oklahoma City!" She smiled and lifted her cup.

Bonnie smiled back and gratefully spread jam on a piece of toast. She then began eating the warm eggs with bites of toast. After her first sip of coffee, she breathed deeply, dropped her shoulders, and began to settle into her first Oklahoma meal.

"So, Miss Bonnie, what is your job? And who sent you to Oklahoma all by yourself?" asked Ruby.

"I am trained as a milliner—a hatmaker—and I love my work! Apparently Oklahoma City is looking for hatmakers, so my St. Louis boss sent me. I was eager to travel, partly to distance myself from a certain beau. So, I enthusiastically accepted this assignment, and here I am!"

"Such a long trip to make by yourself! I came here two years ago—also from St. Louis—with my husband, Willis. He runs a new livery stable here in Oklahoma City. We also have a small ranch outside the city. I breed horses and train some of them for rental and sale at the livery stable."

Ruby sipped her coffee and continued.

"Oklahoma City is a boomtown in this new state, and our stable has almost more business than we can handle. Willis also races horses at the nearby racetrack at Wheeler Park, a few blocks from here. Most of our friends are horse people, and horses are pretty much the currency of our lives. Very different from hats!"

A tall, broad-shouldered, robust man walked into the room. Dressed in denim jeans, a tooled leather vest, and a belt with a turquoise buckle, he also wore leather boots. His thick white hair was combed to the right, and his full beard was carefully trimmed in the shape of his oval jawline. He had a gun in the holster at his waist.

"Mornin', darlin'." Willis Keyes' eyes twinkled as he stooped to kiss his wife on the cheek. "And is this our guest from St. Louis?"

"Yes, Willis. Bonnie Spencer, this is my husband Willis Keyes. Willis, please welcome Bonnie, who is exhausted but at least has now had a hot meal." Ruby grabbed her husband's hand and looked up at him adoringly.

Willis smiled and reached across the table to shake Bonnie's hand. His arm was muscular and his hand calloused.

"Willis, there are coffee, eggs, and toast for breakfast. I know this is a busy day for you. I will get Bonnie off to a warm bath." She stood and motioned with one hand. "Come, Bonnie. Time to soak off your travel dust. I have briefly visited the hotel listed in Mr. Robey's telegram. It seems a little threadbare, with only one bathroom per floor. That is why I brought you here for a hearty Oklahoma welcome!"

Bonnie followed Ruby to the bathroom, which had a porcelain claw-foot tub big enough to get lost in.

"We have one of the first bathrooms in Oklahoma City with hot water," Ruby proudly announced. "I will draw the water, then leave you to the luxury of a long soak."

Bonnie closed the door, took off her clothes, and settled into the warm water. Steam rose out of the tub and floated across her in a gold haze, as the morning sun filtered in through flowered curtains. She had some amazing things to ponder. She had never in her life seen a young woman married to a man as old as Methuselah. They obviously adored each other. He looked a little like Buffalo Bill Cody, whose picture she had seen in the newspaper. His face was wrinkled and tanned, with bushy white eyebrows. He seemed spry and fit, despite what his age might suggest. *What an exotic couple I have met on this wild prairie!*

Bonnie wearily pulled herself out as the water began to cool and toweled herself dry. Ruby knocked, opened the door a crack, and handed Bonnie a gown.

"You can wear this for your nap!" said Ruby in a sisterly voice.

As Bonnie exited the warm bathroom, Ruby locked arms with her and walked her down the hall. They entered a small bedroom with white wallpaper featuring green vines.

"Here you are! I have lowered the shades. You can take a nap for a couple of hours and also stay here tonight. We are having a warm day after that storm last night. I don't think you need the bed covers, but if you crawl under the blanket, you might fall asleep more quickly."

Bonnie did crawl under. Ruby sat on the edge of the bed for a brief moment.

"I've never had a girlfriend stay over in our new house. My horsewomen friends are all older than me and rarely come to visit. This frontier city is attracting many adventure-some men but few women. Your visit is like having a cousin or a sister! I am twenty-eight years old and an orphan. I was very lonely as a child. I got introduced to and fell in love with horses, and I married Willis so I could ride his horses!" said Ruby, blushing.

"Oh Ruby! I spent eight years of my childhood away from my family, living with a St. Louis family as a nursemaid. I had a brief apprenticeship in southern Illinois and, finally, on this trip, I am becoming really independent for the first time," said Bonnie, in a sleepy voice.

"Well, I have quickly learned to be independent, given our second home out at the ranch, which Willis has left me to manage. I am happy to have you as a new friend, and I will see to it that you learn to be self-reliant like me."

Ruby embraced Bonnie in a loving hug.

Bonnie smiled sleepily as Ruby shut the door. *A new prairie sister,* she thought, as she drifted off.

Ruby and Darling
Oklahoma City • May 24, 1910

Ruby the cowgirl and Bonnie the hatmaker spent the late afternoon laughing, drinking tea, and getting further acquainted in Ruby's bungalow kitchen. Neither Ruby nor Bonnie had a close girlfriend of similar age and spirit, and the two women—both orphans of a sort—quickly became friends.

"So, Bonnie, do you have a beau?" giggled Ruby.

Bonnie blushed deeply and grew serious.

"I was sent by the St. Louis hat company to Cobden, Illinois, for an eight-month apprenticeship. I met two men in the first month who both wanted to court me. First, I met Herbert Miller, a young lawyer, who lived in my boardinghouse and was the son of the landlady. Since I had never socialized with men before, I was overwhelmed by his attention and kept him at a distance." She shifted in the chair, and a slight smile played at the corners of her mouth. "Halfway through the apprenticeship, I attended a church pie supper with a girlfriend. There I met handsome Charlie Menees, who sang a clever song about my name to the church group. For the next few months, he continued to stop by the hat shop to take me to tea. He tried to get me to change my name from Blanche to Bonnie, but I resisted."

"So you spurned Charlie's advances, ran away to Oklahoma, and changed your name *yourself*? Is that correct?" Ruby doubled over in her chair, laughing and slapping her knee. "Do you really think you escaped that man?"

"Well, I've moved three states away! He would have to be very determined to try to find me. Besides, I want to establish myself as a hatmaker, learn to support myself, and enjoy being an independent young woman unattached to a man. I was hoping to make wonderful new women friends like you!"

"Bonnie, are you sure you want *this* name?" said Ruby, still laughing.

"'Bonnie' seems to be a much more modern and friendly name than 'Blanche.' The word *blanche* means 'white.' The name 'Bonnie' means 'beautiful' and seems to suit a hatmaker, since we use colorful flowers. Please continue to call me Bonnie, regardless of who originally thought of it! How will he ever know I took his suggestion?"

"When he comes to find you, you silly goose!" teased Ruby.

"Oh dear," Bonnie covered her flushed face with her hands. "Tell me about your ranch out on the prairie."

"You know, my husband is a very smart man. He sold his Keyes Marshall Livery in St. Louis, brought the money to Oklahoma, and immediately bought the National Livery property and a dozen horses. We lived for a while in a boardinghouse. He was clever and convinced me we should build a small house and use further profits to buy land for a ranch, where we could raise more horses. It would also give me a place to manage. The ranch is only about ten miles from here. Riding Black Diamond, I can get there in under two hours. We have a full-time manager who lives out at the ranch. I ride out several days a week to work with the horses. I am raising new horses and, when they are exceptional, I train them for racing. When they are ordinary, I train them for rentals. I love managing the ranch. It's just forty acres, and it suits me perfectly."

"So you have found your Oklahoma paradise?" said Bonnie, wide-eyed.

"Yes, it seems that way! My whole world is centered on Willis and the horses, and I am as happy as can be!"

Midmorning the following day, Ruby and Bonnie set out by wagon to visit the Prince Rupert Hotel on South Robinson. Ruby insisted Bonnie view the room before consenting to stay there. The single room, clean and sparse, was at the back of the building, away from street noise. The communal bathroom was down the hall. The room was painted soft gold, with a single bed, one wooden chair, a small dresser, a small closet, and a window looking out onto the alley. Ruby still had doubts, but Bonnie felt it was adequate. She was not yet making money in Oklahoma City, and she just needed a warm, safe space to sleep, with an indoor bathroom. She could move to better quarters later on.

The women returned to the lobby. Bonnie talked briefly to the landlady, Mrs. Mudd, who had gray hair pulled back in a bun and a long, thin face with the rugged creases and blotches of a person who has worked outdoors all her life.

The next stop was Paris Hats at 211 South Harvey, only three blocks from the Prince Rupert Hotel. *Another good reason to stay in that hotel,* thought Bonnie.

Mrs. Marie Calais, the proprietress, wearing an elaborate hairdo, her lips painted very red, met them at the front. She had a bit of a foreign look, perhaps inspired by Paris?

"May I help you?" asked Mrs. Calais.

She looks like a flawlessly dressed window mannequin, thought Bonnie.

"Yes, I am your new trimmer, Miss Spencer, sent by Rosenthal-Sloan in St. Louis."

"Welcome, Miss Spencer. Please call me Marie. I am glad you have arrived on the day stated by Rosenthal-Sloan. I run a well-organized shop. Obviously, you cannot start work today, since it is midafternoon, but shall I give you a tour? We get a lot of natural light thanks to the wide windows in front. We have four display cases filled with both trimmed and untrimmed hats and hand mirrors."

She walked to one of the counters and put her hand on a gray flannel hat with white ribbons, which was featured on a plaster head.

"Behind the display cases is production space, with worktables for ten trimmers. I do not have ten trimmers, of course, but I occasionally teach millinery classes here. I currently only have two trimmers, plus myself. So, you are welcome to any of the empty tables."

Bonnie walked behind the display cases, to an empty table on the left side of the production space. Natural light from the front windows reflected off the tall, white walls and onto the table.

"How about this one?"

Bonnie took a deep breath. New city, new shop, new table. She could make wonderful hats here.

"Excellent choice, with good natural light. I assume you can start work tomorrow? Say, nine o'clock?" said Marie firmly.

"Yes, of course. I am eager to get to work."

"Well, that is settled. I will see you tomorrow, Miss Spencer. Nice to meet you."

Bonnie and Ruby left the store.

"Bonnie, we must stop for tea and talk. Now that your housing and job are set up, I have some interesting news to share with you." Ruby was excited.

They settled into a small café with a red-rock exterior and log cabin décor. Ruby took a corner seat below a mounted bison head. As Bonnie sat, she noticed that other city customers looked similar to St. Louis and Cobden folks. It was the weather-beaten faces, like Mrs. Mudd's, she thought, and the large cowboy hats and ubiquitous cowboy boots that made the ranch people of Oklahoma stand out.

"I could hardly sleep last night, thinking about the exciting events in Oklahoma this coming fall. Actually, Oklahoma City is becoming the state capital this month. And October is the opening month of the Fourth Annual Oklahoma State Fair. Most of the fair events will take place at Wheeler Park, which is almost at our doorstep," Ruby said brightly. "And, this year, the women's horse events will be the highlight of the fair's opening night. Our racetrack event may attract ten thousand people!"

"Willis and I both have horse friends on the planning committee for the fair. My friend, who's slightly older than I am, is also wealthier and more influential than me. But she's not terribly creative, so I helped her with ideas for the opening night. She is very interested in fashion and wanted to have a fashion show. I talked her into a much more exciting concept: the First Annual Horse and Hat Show. Women riders will model fancy hats, and the audience will participate by wearing their own elegant dresses and elaborate hats. So, high fashion will be presented on the racetrack! I will help plan the event, and I'll also wear a fancy hat and riding habit, as well as compete in several horse events. I suspect the reason your new employer advertised for trimmers was because of this event, and Rosenthal-Sloan heard about the ad and sent you here. You will no doubt be making hundreds and hundreds of hats between now and October 4, opening night. It is good you arrived early—you will be very busy."

"Where did you say the women riders would come from?" asked Bonnie, as her entrepreneurial spirit clicked into gear.

"Actually, they could come from all over Oklahoma—and even from other states. I have a group of women horse friends who all live on nearby ranches. They rode in a parade for the first state fair a few years ago. The women are now eager to participate in a more active way, and they were actually the inspiration for the First Annual Horse and Hat Show I just mentioned."

"Is there any way I could visit these women and personally make their state-fair hats, as my own hat-making business? I made hats to order for women in both St. Louis and Cobden, and doing so is even more rewarding than making hats for sale in a shop. I would love to try this personalized approach!" Her heart quickened as she spoke.

"Yes, you could do that. And National Livery can sponsor you!" said Ruby, getting excited.

"How?" asked Bonnie, a quizzical expression on her face.

"Bonnie, this is just falling into place. National Livery has a Meadowbrook cart that is rarely used because it is small and requires a pony, not a horse. And, everyone in Oklahoma wants a big, fast horse, not a pony. In the last year, someone moving out of town sold a pony to Willis for a few dollars, saying it could not travel fast enough for their frontier journey. The pony is sweet-tempered and broken in, with big, loving eyes. She hardly gets any rentals. She would—no she *will*—be perfect for you! I must train you to handle the cart and pony soon because the days are marching by."

"Ruby, I am thrilled. I actually had a little experience with a pony, back when I was twelve years old. So, the pony part seems easy. And my traveling-hatmaker concept, this is the chance for me to use my hat skills along with my newly learned business skills. However, I think I should work through Paris Hats because the owner has an established reputation in town. Near the end of the week, I will present the traveling concept to Mrs. Calais. She can hardly refuse, since it will give her even more customers and more visibility. And, she does not have to pay for the cart or the pony. I will just have to carefully negotiate a schedule for my in-town days and my travel days."

The two excited women talked on and on into the afternoon, cooking up the new business venture. Finally, they stood, and Bonnie spontaneously gave Ruby a long, warm hug. They chattered happily about hat plans as they traveled to Prince Rupert Hotel.

Bonnie sat in bed for a long time, unable to sleep and jotting notes in her Bonnet Book. Her business mind was already developing the traveling hat-making business—supply lists, schedules, and ordering procedures.

Bonnie awoke the next morning full of energy. She dressed in her white blouse and black skirt, ready to start her new job. She picked up a cup of coffee in the lobby, before walking four blocks to work. Bonnie and Marie talked as Bonnie set up her table. Yes, indeed, Marie had already started to order more supplies to expand her hat-making services in anticipation of the October 4 Horse and Hat Show.

Bonnie picked up two blank felt-pattern hats from shelves in the rear of the shop, piled supplies in a straw basket, and took them to her table. She immediately set to work. Marie had suggested she start with a Horse Show guest hat.

Marie, in her Parisian outfit with a high neck ruffle, walked among her three trimmers on Blanche's second afternoon at work. She stopped at Bonnie's table, and her eyebrows went up.

"These will go right into my display cases, Miss Bonnie. The red hat with the backwards red feathers is stunning, and the brown hat with white chiffon and the white silk rose is also quite elegant. Both will sell by the end of the week. Keep up the good work!"

Bonnie had not yet mentioned her traveling hat-making service, but she dreamt about it, even as her fingers deftly fashioned two more elegant hats.

The next afternoon, Ruby stopped by to pick up Bonnie from work, stayed a few minutes to admire the hats, then took Bonnie to National Livery. A little, gray road cart and the gray Welsh pony were waiting in front of the livery. All they needed was a driver.

"Hello," Blanche purred, as she gently rubbed the pony's nose. Her eyelashes fluttered, her nose rose up, and she nickered, stepping toward Bonnie.

"You do have a touch," said Ruby, surprised by how comfortable Bonnie was with the pony.

"Willow—the pony in Illinois—was also medium-gray with a black mane. This pony looks like her twin!" Bonnie turned and gave Ruby a warm hug, with tears in her eyes.

"Don't thank me yet. Let's try the cart!"

Both women got into the Meadowbrook cart. Ruby took the reins, clicked, and the pony walked down the street with a measured step, her head bouncing. The seat was snug. Bonnie and Ruby both fit.

The two enormous cart wheels had more than a dozen wooden spokes and were higher than the seat. The cart's slatted floor curved up in front to protect passengers from mud, and there was room for luggage behind the seat. The size of the cart was manageable for a lady. It was a perfect hat-making wagon.

"This pony is a 'driving pony' and can take you ten miles a day. Can you take the reins?" Ruby transferred both reins to her left hand and passed them to Bonnie.

Bonnie calmly took the reins, snapped them confidently, and the cart continued down the street. The pace was a bit fast, and the pony's movement too choppy for the large wheels. Bonnie cooed to the pony and pulled gently on the reins. The pony and the cart settled into a more comfortable pace. Bonnie smiled, and Ruby leaned back on the seat.

"You are on your way, Bonnie. So far, you are doing fine," Ruby said, with a broad smile.

After their arrival back at National Livery, Ruby taught Bonnie to harness and hitch the pony so she would be attached to the cart. Ruby also showed Bonnie how to attach the breast-collar harness, which allowed the pony to pull the cart, and the breeching strap, which stopped the cart from running into the pony. Ruby was thorough and patient with her friend, serious as she showed Bonnie all she needed to know.

The next day, Bonnie finished two more stunning hats. She took two wide-brimmed, white felt hats and covered each with a colorful garden of artificial flowers—one with yellow flowers and ribbons, and one with blue. These two hats alone, she felt, would fill up an entire display case. Secretly, Bonnie felt her hats were even more elegant than those of her boss.

On Wednesday afternoon after work, Bonnie and Ruby went for another pony-cart ride.

"I want to give the pony a name. I actually want to

name her Darling," said Bonnie.

"Fine, we will list her that way in the business registry," said Ruby.

At the end of Thursday, Bonnie approached her new boss with the traveling concept. Bonnie told her about her friend Ruby's horse-show work, the women riders on nearby ranches, and her traveling-hatmaker concept, explaining that the hat sales would mean expanded business for the shop. Bonnie proposed that she travel each Thursday and Friday to people not able to get into the city and that she work in the shop on Mondays, Tuesdays, and Wednesdays.

Marie smiled politely with her red lips, then looked down at her work as she gathered her thoughts.

"I will have to think this through overnight," she said. "I am not sure it is a good idea."

On Friday morning Marie came in and said she could not give her consent to Bonnie, saying she did not feel comfortable with the idea because it would leave her short on staff.

That afternoon Willis sent Ruby and Bonnie off to the ranch for the weekend. Bonnie drove the Meadowbrook cart with Darling, and Ruby rode Black Diamond. Ruby felt they could easily make it to the ranch with almost four hours of daylight left.

Bonnie had never been to an actual ranch and was intrigued by the promise of horses and ranch hands, a real Wild West weekend. She was caught between anticipation of the adventure and fear that she would feel out of place.

As they rode northeast, the city structures gave way to gently rolling hills—with no cornstalks. There were many wagons on the road, traveling in both directions—some with two wheels, some with four—carrying loads of cotton, hides, and produce. The primitive, unpaved Oklahoma roads were the arteries carrying the state's first crops to Oklahoma City for processing and distribution. Bonnie felt disappointed that her traveling hat business would not be part of this Wild West commerce.

They battled fierce southwest winds on the first half of their journey. The plains of Oklahoma had few trees to buffer relentless, chafing winds coming all the way from the Gulf of Mexico. Darling walked slowly, with her head down. Ruby's hat had a stampede strap to keep it fastened in the high wind, and she produced a scarf for Bonnie to tie over her puffy sunbonnet to keep it in place.

In the second half of the trip, with less wind, Ruby walked her horse next to Bonnie's cart and pointed out the geography of the area: the locations of neighboring ranches, creeks to water the pony, and dangers like steep washboard slopes on which the cart could skid.

The sun was setting as they rounded a bend and saw the house. The modest ranch homestead was a white frame structure, sound but with peeling paint. It had two stories in the center, a one-story bedroom wing on each side, and three chimneys. A lovely, blooming red rose climbed a trellis at the end of the front porch. Bonnie had expected a log cabin; this seemed slightly more modern.

"Here is the ranch house. No indoor plumbing, but otherwise it is a comfortable place. Willis bought this forty-acre ranch from a friend in bankruptcy. He got a good price! He thought the creeks and wooded areas would provide nice riding trails for me. Then he built a simple horse barn and several corrals. Our manager lives in the other house, over by the grove of trees. Welcome to Redbud Ranch! Redbud is the native flowering tree you see in gullies throughout Oklahoma.

We have many on this property," Ruby proudly explained.

Bonnie remembered the pink flowering trees from the train ride.

They spent a quiet evening by the fire discussing Marie's rejection of the traveling hat-making program. Bonnie even entertained starting the project on her own and ordering supplies from Rosenthal-Sloan, but she had little money to rent a storage building or to pay for supplies.

"Are you ready to learn survival skills today?" asked Ruby the next morning, as she cut up leftover steak to fry with eggs. "I'm going to teach you to shoot a pistol. Every woman on the Oklahoma prairie needs to know how to shoot. I did not tell you this last evening because I thought I might scare you, but I myself was carrying a pistol in the waistband of my skirt. We are out on the Oklahoma prairie here, and occasionally there are snakes, coyotes, and wildcats. Luckily, we had no problems last night."

Bonnie's eyes widened, and she sat up straight in her chair.

"Ruby, I heard Annie Oakley speak at the 1904 World's Fair in St. Louis. She encouraged every American woman to learn to shoot for self-confidence, as well as for protection. But at that time, I never believed I would need a gun. Since I do need one, we can start shooting lessons right after breakfast."

"My goodness, Bonnie, there is more cowgirl in you than I could have imagined. First, you seduced sweet Darling, and now you want a pistol. There will never be another hat-maker like you in Oklahoma!"

After they finished breakfast, Ruby and Bonnie hiked about one mile through a luscious meadow of tall, waving grasses to a small, rocky hill above a gully. Here, behind a tree, Ruby retrieved two weathered boards that had been nailed together and were marked with a charcoal bull's-eye. Ruby propped it on the red-soil slope of a small hill. Facing it, their backs would be to the sun.

"Here is the gun I brought for you. This is a single-action revolver with six chambers. I also brought a box of twenty cartridges. When you load the gun, do not put a cartridge in the chamber under the hammer. See here." Ruby put brass cartridges into the five chambers, one at a time, rotating the cylinder as she went. Then Ruby handed Bonnie the dark metal pistol, which had a wooden handgrip.

It feels almost as heavy as a St. Louis brick! she thought, as she took the gun into her hand.

"Hold the gun like this, with your index finger *not* on the trigger. And hold the gun high in the web of your hand. Then wrap your other hand around the right in a sort of over-grip." She turned her body to show the gun more closely. "This is the hammer, this is the rear notch, and this is the front sight. For every shot, you must cock the hammer, then align the rear notch with the top of the front sight. Now, do not shoot. Hand me the gun."

"See the target, the center black circle on the wood? I will aim at that!"

Ruby faced the target and gripped the gun with one hand.

"Now, these are the two points you align," she said, pointing. "Here we go."

Pop! went the gun, with a slight jump in Ruby's hands and a faint, acrid smell of gunpowder. They could not see the bullet hole from where they stood.

"Now, you try," Ruby said, pointing the gun down and handing it to Bonnie.

Bonnie positioned her hands, sighted carefully, found the trigger, and—*pop!*

She felt the kickback through her body. Then she realized she had closed her eyes as she pulled the trigger.

"Good! Try one more!" encouraged Ruby.

Bonnie shot several more rounds, using up the cartridges. She also practiced loading. Then she and Ruby inspected the target boards, finding that more than half of the bullets hit the target.

Bonnie's right arm was beginning to tire. She realized while practicing that she had to maintain the utmost vigilance, for someday she might need to defend her life from a dangerous wild animal.

"I think this is enough for today. You've made great progress," said Ruby.

They walked downhill, the valley below them. Several creeks with dark-green necklaces of trees and scrub wandered across the green carpet of the valley floor.

"By the way, Bonnie, if you are feeling comfortable with the pistol, it is yours to use. We have a drawer full of pistols at National Livery. The stable business attracts many swindlers and drunks who want to steal our horses, so we always have at least one employee wearing a gun."

Bonnie jerked her head at talk of swindlers. Ruby pushed her cowgirl hat back on her head, with a matter-of-fact smile. She looked directly at Bonnie.

"When traveling in the cart, put your leather purse

strap around your neck. Since you are right-handed, carry the pistol on the right side in your open purse, like a saddlebag."

Yes, Bonnie thought this seemed preferable to carrying the gun in her waistband.

On Monday Bonnie returned to her job at Paris Hats, feeling dejected that she might not be able to do the traveling hat circuit. However, Marie approached her early in the day with good news. She said she now felt comfortable with the traveling concept because she had three more trimmers starting in the next two weeks. And she realized that sponsoring this service for the women riders of opening night was valuable advertising for other shop customers as well.

On Tuesday, May 24, Ruby picked up Bonnie after work and took her back to National Livery. Once again the pony and the Meadowbrook cart were stationed out front, ready for service. But today there was a small wooden trunk sitting on the seat of the cart, sporting a large bow fashioned from red calico cloth with yellow flowers.

"Happy Birthday, Bonnie," giggled Ruby. "I saw your birthdate on the boardinghouse registry."

"I had the trunk made for you last week. It will fit behind the seat of your pony cart. Now you can bring all the supplies you need for hats," laughed Ruby, hugging Bonnie.

Bonnie ran to the trunk with tears in her eyes. She picked up the floppy bow and held it to her chest, flashing a smile at Ruby. Then she ran her hand over the lovely warm-brown finish of the trunk and carefully undid the front latch. Lifting the arched lid, she looked inside. The entire interior of the trunk, including its upper tray, was lined with a dark-blue and yellow-flowered wallpaper.

"What a fine supply case this is," Bonnie murmured softly. "Ruby, how can I ever repay you?"

"You will repay the horsewomen of the state fair with your fine hats," beamed Ruby.

"Oh yes! I will make lovely hats for the next four months for every woman within a hundred miles to wear on opening night of the fair!"

The two women took a sunset ride around town in the little cart, the sturdy trunk stowed under the seat. On this day, her twenty-second birthday, Bonnie felt excited about setting up her first small business making hats for the ranch women. She would not exactly be on her own, since she would be under the umbrella of Paris Hats, but she would work just as hard to establish clients and make hats as if the business were hers.

With the reins firmly in both hands, Bonnie sat tall in the cart. A proud and determined smile spread across her lovely face.

Opening Night
Oklahoma City • June-October 1910

As Bonnie analyzed the details of the travel circuit, her giddy excitement turned into creeping fear. All her previous work experience was in a city workshop with good lighting and unlimited supplies. Could she travel with bad roads? In bad weather? Would she be able to carry adequate supplies on the cart? Would she have access to good lighting?

Her usual preparation for a new project was to make a work list, so she would tackle that first. For the State Fair project she would need the following:

1. Transportation and safety: pony, cart, and pistol ready to go

2. Food and shelter

3. Hat supplies

4. Customers: Ruby's horse friends would be the first

Ruby would help her with items one and two. She needed to organize the hat supplies herself.

She started making more lists in her little Bonnet Book.
The customer item intrigued her. She decided that during hat
meetings, she would take careful notes in the Bonnet Book,
in order to carefully manage the individual demands of each
customer.

Thursday afternoon, Bonnie and Ruby rode to Redbud
Ranch for a Friday afternoon meeting with the first hat client,
Sadie Friend. Ruby packed food and supplies, guns and am-
munition. Bonnie packed the basic sewing supplies she had
gathered, including ribbons, tassels, hatpins in three sizes,
hairpins, sewing pins, a hand mirror, pattern hats, and fabric.
Her supply preparation gave her confidence for the first visit.

Sadie and Albert Friend had homesteaded their ranch
in the Land Run of 1889, when about fifty thousand people
lined up to stake claims on two million acres of unassigned
lands that were formerly Indian territory. The Friends had
done relatively well with their ranch, raising cattle and horses
and establishing apple and walnut orchards. They now had a
well-furnished log cabin next to a gnarled cottonwood tree.
Additionally, there was a large barn behind the house. Sadie
was thin, with a sweet oval face, turned-up nose, and short
curly hair.

Sadie was hanging out laundry and watching for the
ladies' arrival when the two came over the hill. She motioned
them to a plank table by the cottonwood tree. Bonnie pro-

253

ceeded to lay out a tape measure, a mirror, hatpins, a note-book and pencil, her Bonnet Book, and a color wheel from the shop. She also laid out a few pattern hats and a sample completed one.

"Now, Sadie, please come over to my 'office'," Bonnie said pleasantly.

Sadie, almost breathless with excitement, stepped over to the table.

"Let's get started. First, I need to know what event you will be entering at the fair and what riding habit you will be wearing. Then we can discuss appropriate hat designs."

"Well, I will be entering the relay race. My husband is fixing up a used buggy we bought. We will be using black paint with yellow trim. So, I am thinking my riding habit might also be black with yellow trim."

"Fine! This is all very helpful. Let me take a few mea-surements," Bonnie said, picking up her tape measure. "By the way, what is the name of your ranch?"

"We are the Cottonwood Creek Ranch." Bonnie jotted down the name in the Bonnet Book.

Bonnie efficiently took measurements of Sadie's head: circumference, distance ear to nose, length of neck, height of forehead, and shape of face. Eager to help, Sadie held her head still, her neck stretched high. Bonnie carefully jotted down the measurements.

Satisfied, Bonnie thumbed through the Bonnet Book to her sketches of "automobile hat" designs. Running her finger across a few, she landed on the Touring Hat, which had flat decorations that could not be blown off in a fast car. She showed Sadie the sketch.

"Since you will be riding in a race, I am thinking you will want a close-fitting hat like this, which will not get caught in the racetrack breezes. How does this look to you? I could add some layered ribbons and bows, with tiny yellow accents to add more glamour."

"Oh, my," blushed Sadie, looking at the sketch. "I think it will be elegant and practical. And the yellow accents would be perfect!"

Ruby, sitting with her hands folded on the other side of the table, grinned as she watched her friends.

"Sadie, on my next visit I will have a hat fit to your head and hairdo," said Bonnie, concluding the meeting and beginning to pack up her supplies. She felt quite successful with how it had gone.

The travelers rode back to Redbud Ranch with the late sun on their backs. Their contrasting behavior was almost comical. Ruby was on guard duty. Her pistol tucked in her waistband, she glanced side to side along the road looking for snakes, which could scare the horses. Bonnie was smiling and dreaming away in her little cart with the trusty pony. *Perhaps a little more bulk on each side of the hat to flatter Sadie's oval face,* she thought.

Giddy after her first prairie office visit, almost floating off the seat of the cart, Bonnie dreamed on, barely conscious of the road and not at all conscious of Ruby's vigilance. Before reaching the ranch, Ruby held Bonnie back while she shot a rattlesnake. Bonnie had not even seen the camouflaged snake on the road. The encounter once again reminded her that she was in the Wild West. She dreamt of snakes that night.

The women left the ranch early Sunday because Ruby had arranged another hat visit on the way back to Oklahoma City. Miss Clara Alden lived with her family at Alden Trails Ranch, a short distance off the main road.

As she and Ruby arrived, Bonnie saw a large clapboard house set in the shade of a few large trees. In anticipation of the meeting, several women were sitting on a front-porch swing, although only Clara was getting a hat. In these rural areas, a visitor was uncommon, so all the women wanted to be there for the event.

Clara escorted Bonnie and Ruby into the dining room. Bonnie set up her prairie office on a large wooden table, then asked her usual questions and took Clara's measurements.

Clara was a more challenging customer than Sadie. Tall and willowy, with fair skin and dark-brown hair, she had been to finishing school and had more polish. Her nose in the air, she did not look at Bonnie and gave her requirements in a condescending tone. She wanted height on her hat, tall, stiff feathers, and some white elements, since her black riding habit had white trim. Bonnie made copious notes of these particular requests.

I must construct a hat that includes all of her ideas, in order to make her a satisfied customer, she thought.

The hat-making visits proceeded through June, July, and August. Ruby set up the appointments with her ranch friends, and she and Bonnie visited three to five ranches every weekend, all over the east and north end of Oklahoma City.

When they finished these ranch visits, Bonnie wanted to expand to the west of the city. Since ranches there were farther away, she asked Ruby if they could stay overnight with her friends.

The west end of the city was lush with rivers and lakes, and it had big birds that looked similar to the sandhill cranes of Bonnie's childhood. She was thrilled to visit new places and meet so many industrious ranch women. Most of the rugged horsewomen were like Sadie, flattered by the hatmaker's visit and excited about the cowgirl glamour she brought to their lonesome ranches. They almost always accepted her design suggestions.

One prairie-office meeting was in an earth dugout set into a hill on a treeless stretch of prairie. The dugout offered the only shade. Another ranch had longhorn cattle with gentle eyes, slobbery faces, bony rumps, and horn spreads of five to eight feet across.

Bonnie began to see similarities among the athletic women she met on the ranches. She also noticed the individual adaptations the women made to participate in the fair. For instance, the more educated women chose less risky events.

By the end of August, Bonnie had measured all of the local women who were entering the First Annual Horse and Hat Show, about forty in total.

Bonnie diligently turned out hats on Monday, Tuesday, and Wednesday each week for Paris Hats in Oklahoma City. Each week she also wrote new requisitions for supplies to be shipped to Marie's shop for her traveling trunk.

Evenings after work, Bonnie returned to her Hotel Prince Rupert and excitedly worked late hours making ranch hats. Some nights she only slept a few hours.

There was gossip in the Oklahoma City fashion world about this traveling hatmaker. Society ladies who visited the shop for state-fair hats reported that sisters and cousins on ranches were getting custom-made hats for opening night. Marie Calais took full credit for the program, and her profits from shop and ranch hats continued to increase as the date of the fair grew closer.

The hat business was at its peak in September. Supply shipments arrived almost daily, the shop was always crowded with customers, and the many trimmers at the back tables worked long hours with bloodshot eyes and bleeding fingers.

By late September, there was a crescendo of excitement among the ranch women as outfits and hats were being completed. Working at a feverish pace, Bonnie was not certain she would get all of the commissioned hats made by early October. Still, she considered the ranch hats her personal business, and she was giving every ounce of energy to completing them on time. In her mind she was designing hats in every spare moment, even while eating and sleeping.

Bonnie began to make solo trips to deliver finished hats to ranches located within five miles or less of Redbud Ranch, because Ruby was often busy with fair organizational tasks. Blanche took a solo trip to Clara Alden, arriving with *two* hats to show her, since Clara had given her such exacting requirements.

Bonnie had taken the biggest risk of the summer with these two hats. Both were tall riding hats, as Clara wanted. One was white with elegant black trim at the hat's narrow brim-edge. It featured a tall black tulle bow and a drape at the back. The other, a black hat, also had a flat crown and narrow brim but was decorated with a dramatic white feather and an elegant white silk and black tulle banding six inches high. It culminated in a large swirl at the back of the hat, then draped down the neck. Since Clara was not riding in a race, both hats could be elegant as well as stately.

The two hats in her arms, both wrapped in black tissue paper, Bonnie went to the dining room with Clara and her friends. She felt as though she were going before a jury at a trial. Clara frowned, nervously fingering the collar of her white blouse. Her friends fidgeted, too.

Bonnie slowly unwrapped the white hat and put it on the table. Then she unwrapped the black hat. Clara and the other women all gasped, putting their hands to their mouths in shock.

"I made two hats that meet your requirements, Clara,"

Bonnie spoke carefully. "Since they are so different, I thought you might like to see both and determine which one best complements your riding habit."

"Well, I—" Clara stopped herself and walked over to touch the white hat and finger the exquisite black trim. "I must apologize to you. I guess I was expecting you to bring straw farm hats. I think you are correct about trying both hats on. These two hats look like they are from...Paris. Wherever did you get this black trim on the white hat?"

"Like you said, from Paris," Bonnie stood tall as she said this, trying to keep the smile off her lips. "Many of my ribbons and trims come from New York and Paris."

Clara picked up the white hat, walked to a mirror, and put on the hat. Bonnie slightly adjusted the angle of the hat and fluffed the black tulle into a lovely cascade down Clara's back.

The other women all swooned.

"My goodness! Paris glamour right in our ranch house. Oh Clara, you must keep this one!" said Clara's mother.

Next Clara put on the black hat. Again, Bonnie adjusted the angle and fabric.

"Another piece of Paris, Clara! You cannot give *this* one back, either. You must take both hats. The one you do not wear to the fair, you can wear for your wedding next year!"

Clara lifted up the tall black hat, turned to Bonnie, and bowed.

"Madame," she said in a theatrical tone, "I shall be glad to take both of these extraordinary hats. You are creative and very gifted. May I extend my compliments and gratitude to you."

With opening night just a week away, Bonnie was still fever-ishly working at Paris Hats to create stunning hats for the fair. Keeping in mind the shoulder-wide hats at the 1904 World's Fair, she concentrated on making equally wide hats for *this* fair. Marie watched her from the rear of the shop, marveling at her talent and energy—and the money she was generating.

Oklahoma had just become a state in 1907, and its first two state fairs had been mediocre. Ruby's husband Willis had joined other businessmen in helping finance fairground up-grades to make this fair more spectacular—a new agriculture building, new arc lights, and a carbon-microphone public address system for the grandstand. He told Ruby about other attractions that were expected to draw big crowds, such as a roller coaster, a giant Ferris wheel, a carousel, and a "Canal of Venice" boat ride.

On their Thursday ride out of the city, Ruby passed on this fair news to Bonnie. Bonnie imagined how the rides would compare with ones she had seen at the 1904 World's Fair, assuming the Oklahoma rides could never be as grand.

The state-fair racetrack grandstand had more than thirty boxes and held about five thousand people. Another five thousand could easily stand in the center field. Ruby occasionally visited the half-mile track while coordinating various events and noticed new electricity, telephones, and bathrooms being installed. She made sure to reserve stalls in the nearby stables for Black Diamond and Willis' racehorses. Willis would be racing horses at the fair, but not on opening night, when he would be a spectator.

Ruby had deliberately organized the First Annual Horse and Hat Show so that it would feature both society *and* ranch women, and she was hoping the combination would be successful.

Bonnie and Ruby finalized their schedule a few days before opening night. They both planned to be at the racetrack by noon. Ruby needed to supervise event volunteers, and Bonnie had to set up a dressing room for hat adjustments. Months earlier Ruby had reserved a concrete-block room below the grandstand for Bonnie's use.

Some of the women participating in the more vigorous events would need Bonnie's help securing their hats. She arrived early with three sizes of hatpins. She hoped they would hold, as she had never before dressed anyone for a strenuous horseback ride. To help, she had sewn chin straps into all of the hats.

Once her little wooden trunk was set up on two chairs behind her table, Bonnie laid out a few key supplies. She was wearing her customary black skirt—the old one from St. Louis—and a new white blouse. She had even managed to make a new white bonnet for herself. She had banded the hat crown in black, found two pieces of wide, light-gray ribbon bordered in black, and sculpted these into an elaborate double-vertical ruffle. She had glued the ruffle down the back of the hat like a horse mane and added silver stars at the front. A celebratory hat for a hatmaker!

She closed her eyes and breathed deeply, the past weeks of tension starting to melt away. So many months of preparation had taken their toll, but she felt she had done her very best creative work. The Meadowbrook cart pulled by Darling had traveled hundreds of miles, and Bonnie herself had made about two hundred hats.

Am I ready? Have I forgotten anything? Will anyone forget their hat? Will anyone be too late for my help? She ticked off the supplies she needed, certain she had them all. Still, she felt uneasy.

At about two thirty, the first two women riders arrived, both smiling expectantly. Each was smartly dressed in her new riding habit, and each carried her new hat. Bonnie jumped up. She placed two cloth tape measures around her neck and tied a pincushion with sewing pins and three-inch hatpins to her wrist. Her heart beat a little faster than usual, but her hands were steady. She was about to start her own hat race at the horse race!

For the next three hours, Bonnie worked nonstop, helping nearly forty women. The room was crowded and, even though it was relatively cool, many women were hot in their tailored habits. Thank heavens for the jugs of water and tin cups!

Most of the ranch women were excited about their impending performances, including their fancy costumes and fancy hats, as well as being on an unpredictable large horse before a grandstand of screaming people. This was a daring, once-in-a-lifetime public event!

After working her way through the hat placements, Bonnie had many pricks in her fingers from jumpy heads and somersault pins, and she had broken two fingernails. Her right arm ached terribly, and her own new hat was comically askew. Her table was covered in snowflakes of ribbon trim.

Ruby slipped into Bonnie's room dressed in her smart black riding habit. Hers was the last hat placement. There were beads of perspiration on her forehead, and she gratefully drank two full cups of water. Bonnie and Ruby hugged like sisters and looked warmly into each other's eyes, too tired for words.

Bonnie smoothed out Ruby's hair and placed a small black-plumed hat over the mass of red curls. She adjusted the plumes at each side, then slid the chin strap into place. She pinned the hat down with the black-headed hatpins, sinking them deep into the mass of red curls for a secure anchor. Then she checked the hat for its angle and stability.

Bonnie smiled and, from behind, put her hands on Ruby's shoulders.

"You're ready, sweet Ruby. Good luck tonight," Bonnie said softly.

Ruby rose, gave Bonnie a gentle kiss on the cheek, then squeezed both of Bonnie's hands. Ruby looked clear-eyed and confident, polished in her black riding habit. Her elegant touring hat was rimmed in crushed black satin with black tulle, which was gathered at the back and hung down to her shoulders. Black ostrich feathers and a white silk rose sat in front, anchoring the two black plumes facing backwards like wings. She looked regal.

Summoning her energy, Ruby shouted, "I'm off to the races!" and burst out the door.

After Ruby left, Bonnie finally had a chance to sit down and rest, thinking back through the hats of her first business venture. Ruby looked superb! All of the horsewomen departed looking like celebrities. Bonnie felt every hat was a winner! She took a deep breath, closed her eyes, and stretched her neck back, as a soft smile spread from her contented soul to her face.

Now, using her own mirror, Bonnie carefully adjusted and pinned her own charming hat with the fanciful ruffle. Then she packed her supplies in her wooden trunk, exited the room, and locked the door. Above her in the grandstand, she could hear the din of a thousand footsteps. The building—and even her bones—seemed to vibrate along with them. She felt giddy.

Bonnie headed up the long, sloped ramp at the north end of the grandstand. Under an apricot evening sky, she walked slowly, her back straight and her head erect under her new ruffled hat. She had a glow and a slight smile, and she felt a deep sense of self-confidence.

Straight ahead, the horsewomen were getting exhibition numbers and lining up. They sat calmly, like crowned queens, as their grooms handled their horses. Bonnie felt as though all the bustle of the grandstand was beginning to boil over. Bonnie saw a sea of men's derby and panama hats topping off dark suits and hundreds of women in long gowns of pale Dresden colors and dramatic elbow-length gloves. Costumes glistened and jewels sparkled for this, the first big event of the social season. This opening night in the refurbished grandstand was like a coming-out party for three-year-old Oklahoma State.

The elaborate hats of the society ladies in the boxes were bigger and more conspicuous than those of the women riders. Wide, tall, ornately decorated hats that offered grand-stand glory would not survive on the racetrack!

Bonnie smiled as she saw her Yellow Garden hat a few rows away and more of her hats nearby.

This state fair has been the biggest business challenge of my life, she thought, *but I have loved every minute and every hat.*

The carbon-microphone public address system broad-casted pre-show instructions, the voice a bit nasal and crackly at times. Never having heard an amplified voice before, for Bonnie this was yet another exciting novelty at the fair. She had never seen anything like the racetrack either. She had seen crowds at the 1904 World's Fair, but not a grandstand packed with such elegantly dressed attendees. She stood transfixed at the top of the ramp, watching the drama unfold. Colorful families were finding their seats, and a line of uniformed field men was grooming the dirt track with wide metal rakes. Bon-nie wrapped her arm around the grandstand railing without taking a seat, for she did not have a ticket.

Bonnie was disappointed to continue hearing an-nouncements and see clowns on the track. Finally, a trumpet call announced the beginning of the women's horse events. The Horse and Hat Show judges were beginning to gather in their high box, an enclosed, raised platform. A horse show official gave a welcome address, then a vaudeville produc-tion called Midway Carnival performed the first stunts of the evening, with brightly costumed acrobats and jugglers. The hum of the crowd began to swell. Then, suddenly, gloved arms flew up, pinwheels fluttered, jewels glittered, and the roar dropped to a whisper.

The first competitive event was starting, signaled by

another trumpet call. It was not a race, but a parade. The Ladies Turn Out Parade, as it was called, featured well-groomed horses and riders and their buggies. The riders, all women sidesaddle on their horses or in buggies, were led by their grooms into a single-file line toward the high box. All of the women held their heads high, wore smart hats and colorful outfits, and walked their horses in controlled steps. Most women were wearing a hat made by Bonnie, and she was thrilled to see her forty hats on parade on the racetrack! Each rider had been coached by Ruby on the importance of the Ladies Turn Out, the initial judging of one's entire presentation: rider, buggy, horse, quiet self-confidence, and posture. A totally elegant picture.

The riders walked their horses and buggies around the track. Bonnie could hardly see the riders on the far side of the track because of dust clouds from the horses stirring up the loose soil. But as they came back around to the grandstand, all were clearly visible.

Bonnie watched with her fingers crossed, as each of her hats flowed by, still in their original positions on the riders' heads. She easily spotted Clara in her white hat, turning her head from side to side with a graceful, theatrical wave of her hand. To Bonnie's delight, she heard a nearby spectator comment on the "extraordinary hats."

At the conclusion of the parade, the announcer named the winner, a Mrs. J. J. Zachary, who wore a black broadcloth suit with a fitted jacket and a Persian turban hat. A race official carried her a blue ribbon and a flower garland, the audience showing their approval with thunderous applause. Then, as the brass band played another song, all of the parade entrants marched off the racetrack.

Mrs. Zachary was from out of state, and Bonnie had

not made her hat. It was, however, elegantly made and appeared to be worthy of the award. All the same, Bonnie was disappointed that the winner was not someone wearing one of her hats.

Next the women riders were grouped by horse breed and by buggy style, with various societies giving awards for the best entrant in several categories.

Other demonstration events followed, including a demonstration by Morris and Company of their six-horse Clydesdale team. When they appeared, the gentle giants elicited a loud cheer from the crowd. Then C. H. Clark appeared with twenty-four Shetland ponies that performed various racing tricks, including some stunts even performed to music! The crowd loved the shows, but Bonnie was eager to see the rest of her women riders and her *race hats*. She tapped her foot in impatience.

The relay race was next. At the end of the track, four teams assembled behind a chalk starting line. When the teams were assembled and ready, an official fired a starting pistol, and the horses of each buggy lunged forward. Each lady rode one lap of the track in her buggy, then handed off a long wooden baton to another teammate in her own buggy.

The next four buggies started out in a tight pack, each rider passing her baton to the next rider on her team.

In the third lap, in which Sadie raced, one of the buggies sideswiped another and crashed. In a whirlwind of dust, the buggy's wheel came off, disabling the other buggy. This left only two buggies in the race.

Bonnie squinted, looking for Sadie's yellow-trimmed buggy, excited and relieved to see Sadie's horse and buggy still in the race. Holding her breath, Bonnie wondered if she had used the longest hatpins? Had she triple-stitched the chin-strap anchors? She couldn't see the yellow trim or hat details when the buggy was on the far side of the track. Was Sadie's hat still on?

Two buggies came around the bend and into the home stretch. The announcer screamed into the microphone, and the thunderous crowd of thousands jumped to its feet, waving hats and flags. The racers kicked up clouds of dust. Sadie raced dangerously fast on the home stretch and, just as the two buggies fought to get to the finish line, Sadie streaked across, winning by just the length of her buggy! The crowd went crazy!

Sadie slowed her horse, turned the buggy around, and returned to the finish line below the high box. Still wearing her black hat with yellow trim, she proudly received the blue ribbon and a flower garland for her horse. Then she turned to face the grandstand, raising her fist with the blue ribbon and generating a wild roar from the crowd.

After the relay race, the Bedini family presented their Quintuple Vaulting Equestrian Act with an acrobatic troupe. Their riding team made human pyramids on galloping horses. The crowd roared as the riders piled three and four high on the horses. The acrobats, dressed in colorful costumes, even had a trick dog that did two-legged tricks on the back of a prancing horse. The dog rode the horse as it jumped a low fence and pushed a barrel. Since Bonnie had watched many of her hatted women make it safely through the judging and racing, she began to relax and was able to laugh and clap at the dog tricks.

The last riding event was Sidesaddle Show Jumping. Ruby and three other women had entered this daring event. Sidesaddle required both of the rider's feet to be on one side of the horse. It could be frightening for both the horse and the rider, and very few women or horses had the skills for this style of jumping. An inexperienced woman unable to stay on the horse could easily be thrown and injured.

Wooden rails were set up just below the judges' high box, which was at the finish line, centered on the grandstand itself. A trumpet call quieted the crowd.

In the first round, the rails were set at about three feet high. All four horses easily cleared.

The rails were raised to four feet. One horse knocked down the wooden rails while jumping, and a second horse rode to the rails but then swerved sideways, refusing to jump and almost unseating the rider. These two riders were now disqualified. The remaining two, including Ruby, both easily cleared the rails.

Now only two riders remained for the five-foot jump. The roar of the crowd had steadily increased as the wooden rails were moved higher. Onlookers were crowded ten deep in the center field, close to the high box. Children were mounted on their dads' shoulders, waving pinwheels and flags. Everyone elbowed for the best view.

The other rider, in a flashy green habit and hat (not created by Bonnie), raced toward the high rails. At the last moment her horse refused to jump, sending her somersaulting. The announcer gasped into the microphone, and the crowd lifted out of their seats, straining to see if the rider was hurt. After a hushed moment, the fallen woman got up, hatless, and waved. The crowd cheered, relieved she was safe.

Black Diamond, Ruby's horse, stood calmly at the white line. Bonnie had already witnessed the tall, muscular horse's skill and Ruby's close relationship with the magnificent animal. Ruby bent forward to stroke his neck and whisper in his ear, to which he nodded in response. A long moment of silence followed. An official then whipped down a white flag, and horse and rider rushed forward, first in a trot, then in a canter. At the rails, Black Diamond sprang up with his front legs bent underneath his belly and his rear legs flying out back behind his tail. As he rose, Ruby leaned forward to lower her center of gravity, her body anchored by the upper and lower pommels of her sidesaddle. The horse arched and sailed over the rails. Ruby again sat up and barely bounced as Black Diamond landed. Through it all, the black satin hat held its place!

The crowd screamed hysterically. Ruby rode Black Diamond down the track, waved at Bonnie, and then rode back toward the high box. She proceeded to perform a second high jump just for show, without rails, to please the crowd. Bonnie felt her body flood with emotion, watching the arc of the second jump. The crowd, too, loved the showmanship! They roared. They whistled. They threw their hats into the air. Even the brass band kicked in with a set of trumpet calls. Anyone in Oklahoma City who didn't know who Ruby Keyes was *before* tonight certainly knew who she was *now*!

Ruby and Black Diamond cantered down to the other end of the grandstand, waving victoriously to the crowd, then came back toward center front. The wooden rails had been removed, and all of the horse-show judges and officials had assembled below the high box. Ruby rode proudly to the center of the group, dismounted, and directed Black Diamond to bow. He bent his head to the ground, knelt on his left leg, and pointed his right front leg toward the judges. As Black Diamond rose, a judge walked forward, slid a white garland over the horse's neck, and presented a large blue ribbon to Ruby. A mighty roar erupted from the grandstand. Bonnie cheered too, just as she caught sight of Willis standing below the high box. He wildly waved his top hat with one hand and blew kisses to his wife with the other.

Bonnie watched all of the ceremony. Cheering at the top of her lungs and waving both arms above her head, she knocked her fluted hat to the side of her head.

The months of hard work were worth the effort, she thought, as she again straightened her hat. Working behind the scenes making creative hats was such a fine career for her, combining her love of fabrics and sewing with her interest in helping women. Her idea for the prairie campaign had contributed so much to this stunning event, though she felt exhausted, as if she had ridden every lap of the track with each of her hats. But she was also deeply satisfied.

The roar of the crowd diminished as the society folks rustled in their boxes, the ladies turning to show off their gowns, jewels, and hats to everyone departing. Tuxedoed men in white gloves ushered the ladies to the exits.

Slowly, the crowd thinned, and Bonnie began to stir. The blur of many hats, many riders, and the spectacular performance of her dear friend Ruby lingered in her mind as the arc lights blinked. She stepped forward and joined the grandstand crowd spilling down onto the dusty track.

Courtship
Oklahoma City • October 1910-March 1911

Bonnie awoke late the next morning. Marie had told her to take Tuesday off, for everyone's urgent hat-buying days were over.

Ruby picked up Bonnie around lunchtime, and they went to the log cabin café to celebrate the successful opening night. As they sat down, both women propped their heads on their hands. They were exhausted.

"Ruby, you and Black Diamond were magnificent last night! You must be very proud of your blue ribbon, and also proud of the entire horse show," Bonnie spoke through her tired smile.

"Yes, Bonnie. They were both wonderful, but, to me, an equally important part was the team of Oklahoma ranch women. Each and every woman did her best. And you played a major role! You should *also* be very proud!"

"You know, actually, I feel that the hats of the women riders were even more personal and challenging to make than the hats I made for the grandstand women. Perhaps they were not as flashy, but they had to withstand the challenges of the racetrack. There were no hat mishaps—everyone's hat stayed on for the entire show."

Over homemade soup and hot tea, they continued to talk about the night before.

"After this milestone, what's next?" asked Ruby, sipping her tea.

"Marie Calais has decided not to return to Oklahoma City this winter. She has asked me to manage the shop for a six-month period, which I have agreed to do," said Bonnie.

"That sounds lovely! This will give you a chance to learn new business skills, something you mentioned as a goal when you first arrived. You can still keep the Meadowbrook cart and Darling and perhaps interest the ranch women in holiday hats."

As the shop's new manager, Bonnie spent the rest of the week setting up a new system of supply inventory and requisition forms for wholesalers, as well as ordering supplies for holiday hats. Paris Hats was now back to a manageable staff of two trimmers plus Bonnie, and the fall promised to be successful, thanks to all of the publicity from state-fair customers.

That weekend Bonnie and Ruby rode to Redbud Ranch, where they exercised horses and recuperated, arriving back in Oklahoma City on Sunday evening with renewed energy.

At the Prince Rupert Hotel, stern-faced Mrs. Mudd handed Bonnie a telegram as she passed the front desk. Bonnie hurried to her room with it, wondering about possible news from Bertha, with whom she had occasionally corresponded. As she sat on the edge of the bed to open the telegram, she pulled out a few hairpins.

BLANCHE SPENCER   OCT 7 1910
PRINCE RUPERT HOTEL   OKLAHOMA CITY
OKLA

HAVE BEEN HIRED BY MARSHALL FIELD DRY GOODS OF CHICAGO AS SALESMAN FOR OKLAHOMA TERRITORY STOP ARRIVE IN MUSKOGEE OKLA SATURDAY OCT 15 TO SET UP TERRITORY STOP WILL CONTACT YOU SOON AFTER STOP

CHARLES MENEES
CARBONDALE ILL

Bonnie sat stunned, unable to move, her head bent and her hair tumbling down across her cheek. *How could this be happening?* she wondered.

Ruby had been correct! This man *had* found a way to follow her to Oklahoma!

What now? I'm going to take a horse cab to Ruby's bungalow early tomorrow morning and talk this over with my friend!

Bonnie stumbled to the washbasin, hair hanging in her face, her hand blindly reaching for the pitcher. She tipped toward the pitcher and poured water over her face, gasping at how cold it was. She blotted her face, undressed, and shivered as she slid on her nightgown. Her body seemed to feel flushed in spite of the icy water. She felt utterly con-

275

fused. Unable to think about anything else, she had a sleep-less night, the enduring tune of "My Bonnie Lies Over the Ocean" playing over and over again in her restless mind.

Bonnie knocked on Ruby's door at breakfast time the next morning. With a look of concerned surprise, Ruby opened the door and invited Bonnie into the cozy kitchen for coffee. Bonnie sat hunched over the table, holding her head in her hands.

"Why is this so upsetting, Bonnie?" Ruby queried, as she poured two cups of coffee. "I told you it might happen."

"I have my own life, my own developing business career. I have just had the exciting state-fair campaign, and now I am managing the hat shop. I have waited so long to become a skilled and independent woman. I wish—"

"You wish he wouldn't come?" interrupted Ruby.

"Well, I'd like to make a man's acquaintance when *I* am ready, not when the *man* is ready! Can you understand?" complained Bonnie.

"Yes, you want a glamorous and successful hat shop of your own before you let a man into your life. Is that right? And is it Charlie you want—or do you even know?"

"I certainly want to be successful at business first, then romance. Charlie? Maybe yes, maybe no. I have had so little experience with men."

"Well, I don't know, Bonnie. Life and a man may not follow your perfectly planned career path, especially here in the Wild West."

Charles Menees took the KATY out of St. Louis and arrived in Muskogee late Saturday night. He looked disheveled in his new three-piece suit, his hair dangling over his penetrating green eyes. Aged thirty, he was still handsome, and his commanding posture made him seem more business-like, more determined than the former singer from Cobden, Illinois. He took a room at the Depot Hotel, adjacent to the KATY tracks, and immediately went to sleep after what had been an exhausting trip.

Charlie stayed at the Depot Hotel for a few days, eating in the second-rate dining room and heading out to scout for the nearest livery. He carried the banner of the well-known Marshall Field and Company, and he felt this gave his clothing products superior quality.

The Depot Hotel was crowded with salesmen like Charlie, all coming to the bustling new state to make money selling cotton, automobiles, sewing machines, and other goods. Determined to become successful, he felt he needed to fill out his territory with sales and customers quickly.

Charlie immediately bought four sturdy trunks for his clothing samples. He planned to travel with two and have two more on reserve for emergencies.

He learned that cotton was the primary crop of Oklahoma and that Muskogee had become the hub for cotton-gin companies. He guessed that local garment stores would soon follow, which gave further urgency to developing his territory as soon as possible.

After Bonnie's initial shock about the telegram, weeks passed before she had any further information from Charlie. She fretted, asking herself if she did or did not want to see him.

Charlie sent Blanche—as he still called her—a second telegram, explaining that he must establish an immediate traveling circuit encompassing the entire state. He would contact her in another month.

Charlie spent his time from mid-October to mid-December taking trains to large cities and small towns, even to Oklahoma City—but without contacting Blanche. Everywhere he went, he stayed at depot hotels or rooming houses, establishing a route of new customers eager to buy supplies from Marshall Field Dry Goods of Chicago. His sales pitch was breezy and quick, relying on the famous company name to expand his sales. He was determined to visit Blanche once he had a glow of success. He wanted to show her he was one of Oklahoma's pioneer businessmen, pushing back the frontiers and helping to civilize the Wild West.

In early November Bonnie had begun developing an entire inventory of women's and girls' holiday hats. She made samples and directed the other two trimmers to copy them. The colors used in the hats were red, gold, green, white, and black—Christmas colors.

Fully confident in her management abilities, Bonnie had a wide shelf built below the storefront windows. She decorated the shelf in white felt and set up an artificial, decorated Christmas tree and a snow-covered deer, as well as a few shiny garlands, just as she had seen in St. Louis all those years ago. Among these holiday decorations, she displayed felt hats for girls. She took a gamble and made about fifty of the red and green girls' hats in two sizes. Each hat had a white chiffon band and a crushed-chiffon rosette and included a chin strap for the Oklahoma winds. She priced the hats at three dollars each. When they sold as fast as she could produce them, she made another set of fifty. Word had gotten around: Miss Bonnie Spencer could make much more than horse-show hats!

Bonnie immensely enjoyed this period, developing her skills at managing a shop and producing popular hats. She worked long, exhausting days and had little energy to think about Charlie. Still, sometimes she did wonder. She wondered if he got caught in the occasional icy storms. She could not visualize his travels. She was content in her cozy, dry shop and boarding house, as the freezing winter weather and icy winds moved into the young cities of Oklahoma.

When Ruby wasn't out at her ranch, the two friends met often to discuss business, horse developments at Redbud Ranch, and whether there was news from Charlie. They usually went to their favorite log cabin café.

"How is the holiday-hat campaign going, Bonnie?" asked Ruby.

"Well, I brought a clever girls' hat design from St. Louis, and we're selling them as fast as we can make them."

"Good! And Charlie, any news from him?"

"He's sending me boastful postcards of far-flung adventures, and I don't know whether to believe him or not! Charlie apparently wants to sell clothes to the entire state. How can he have such quick success when our hat-making circuit took months to accomplish?" said Bonnie, turning her head.

"Is he boasting, making up stories? You know, there is a saying in the West, 'Big hat, no cattle,'" Ruby added.

"Well, I will stay here in Oklahoma City, sell charming hats by the dozen, and watch Charlie's career unfold."

Monday afternoon a week later, Bonnie was on her knees decorating the display window with newly made hats. The doorbell rang as someone walked in. Bonnie turned, her arms full of hats, expecting another of the many mothers and anxious daughters who made up her clientele.

Bonnie looked up, gasped, and dropped the hats. Charlie Menees, handsome in a new pinstriped suit, a wool neck scarf, and a dark derby hat, stood inside the shop door. With a nervous smile, Bonnie rose to greet him. Charlie took off his hat and overcoat, made a gracious bow, and took Bonnie's hands into his own.

After a moment of silence, Bonnie pulled her hands away, embarrassed she had let him hold them. Her heart was racing.

"Welcome to Oklahoma City," she said softly, struggling to organize her thoughts. "Let me just quickly arrange these hats on the display shelf, then we can talk."

Conscious of his gaze, she artfully placed the holiday hats across the shelf, then stood up again, brushed her hands together, and faced him.

"My goodness, this is unexpected! How nice to finally

see you. Are you getting all of Oklahoma into your sales accounts?" Bonnie spoke with more composure now.

"Yes, indeed. I felt it important to get things set up before winter weather. I'd very much like to take you out this evening. Will you come? Can you leave early?" Charlie sounded businesslike and polite, but Bonnie thought there was a slight urgency to his request.

"Why, yes, I can do that. You can have a seat by the door or just look at hats for a few minutes, while I close up."

"I will just admire your handiwork!" Charlie said cheerfully, wandering back over to the window display shelf.

Bonnie dismissed the two trimmers and prepared to leave. She was wearing her navy skirt and the Eton jacket, but she had also brought the navy cape. She grabbed it, her purse, and the store key. Charlie appeared behind her, ready to help her put on the cape. He rested both hands on her shoulders. Bonnie trembled.

"I've waited a long time to see you, Blanche. I'm very much looking forward to this visit. I want to invite you out for an elegant dinner. We've never done that before. I asked at the train station, and I believe one of the best places is the Hotel Threadgill dining room."

"Oh my! Yes, that would be lovely! It is just three blocks from here, but I have never been there for dinner."

Bonnie stopped at the display-case mirror and put on her dark-red holiday hat with red and white accents. She set the angle, inserted the hatpins, and pushed back a low curl at the side of her neck. In the mirror, she saw Charlie grinning behind her. She felt a flush beginning in her face and nervously looked down at her key as he squeezed her shoulders again.

Charlie took Bonnie's elbow and escorted her out of

the shop. She stopped to lock the door, then jiggled the lock to make sure it was securely closed.

"I believe we go this way," Charlie said, as he put his arm around Bonnie's waist and guided her to the right.

They walked three blocks in a biting wind. Bonnie held onto her hat, using it to shield her eyes from Charlie's, and moving slightly out of his grasp as she tried to gather her thoughts.

They entered the Threadgill Hotel and checked their coats, before proceeding to the dining hall, a large and elegant room with marble columns, long, draping curtains over tall windows, and tables covered in white linen tablecloths. The walls were painted soft green, and there were brass accents everywhere, on wall sconces, candle holders, and the buttons of the waiters' jackets. Bonnie had rarely been in such an opulent room. The décor gave the room the feeling of a jewel box.

"Is there a window table for two?" Charlie politely inquired of the tuxedoed host.

"Yes, sir. This way."

When they were seated, they took a moment to look around. The large space, with its elegant carpet and subdued lighting, offered a very romantic setting. Was this a romantic dinner, Bonnie wondered.

"Tell me how the Marshall Field appointment came about," Bonnie said, taking off her gloves and setting them on the table.

"Well, I had returned to Cobden to help my mother after my uncle died, and I saw an ad in the local paper. The Marshall Field Company was looking for salesmen for challenging frontier assignments. Since I was looking for a job more exciting than selling shoes in Cobden, I took a train to

Chicago. I interviewed for two days, requested the Oklahoma Territory, and got the assignment! That was in September. The final contract came through in early October, and here I am, carving out a business career in the Wild West. And, of course, I chose this assignment so I could look *you* up! Your sister, Bertha, reluctantly gave me your hotel address, and the hotel proprietor pointed me to the shop."

"I had no idea," Bonnie said, nervously wiping her nose with her napkin. "I have been so busy here." She wondered to herself why her sister had done *that*.

"Go on."

Charlie reached across the table and put his hand over hers.

"Rosenthal-Sloan of St. Louis sent me to Oklahoma City in May to make hats for the Oklahoma State Fair. That just happened in October and was very exciting. Now I am managing the store for my boss, who went back to Alabama for the winter," Bonnie explained.

Bonnie took a sip of water. She wasn't sure how much to share with this friend. Looking down, she felt his eyes feasting on her face.

"I..." She blushed, unable to find more words.

"You're a success in Oklahoma City, that's what you are! Outfitting every woman in a splendid hat seems to be your version of taming the West. I always knew you could do more wonderful things than make hats in Cobden, Illinois. Congratulations!"

"Well, it seems we are both taming the West with our own special talents."

Bonnie withdrew her hand and smiled.

"I have been making lots of changes in my life. I am concentrating on learning business strategies, not just on making hats. And now I am managing an entire shop. This move has been good for me, in many ways."

Looked around the room, she gathered her thoughts.

"I have one thing more to tell you," she began. "I decided to change my name to Bonnie when I arrived in Oklahoma City. So, all of the hats I talked about were made by Miss Bonnie Spencer, not Blanche. I left Blanche back in St. Louis!"

Charlie reached across the table and took her hand again.

"That's my girl! The spunky gal I knew was inside the prim lady at the pie supper! My, my, so I am having dinner with a cowgirl named Bonnie!"

Bonnie felt another flush creeping up her neck.

A roast beef dinner followed, featuring many courses and a lovely baked-apple dessert. Charlie and Bonnie talked for another two hours in the soft light of the jewel-box dining room.

"It is probably time for me to get you back. I have checked into the Depot Hotel near the KATY station. Would you like to share Christmas with me and spend a few days showing me Oklahoma City through your eyes?"

Bonnie smiled. His hands were over hers again.

Bonnie started the new year with a flush of energy. The holiday visit with Charlie had been eye-opening. They had met every night for dinner, sharing the ups and downs of their working days. In Oklahoma, Charlie seemed focused, aggressive, unlike the carefree singer she had known in Cobden. She was watching this plucky young salesman and trying to sort out her feelings.

Charlie's schedule was dependent on when product shipments arrived by train. Marshall Field had dictated that Charlie use Muskogee as his home base because Muskogee was becoming the transportation center of the state. It had large shipping facilities accessible by both rail and river. So, Charlie had departed Oklahoma City soon after Christmas.

The Muskogee shipment arrivals required careful scheduling, and Charlie kept a detailed notebook of transactions, shipment dates, and train schedules. He jumped on and off trains in blizzards and freezing rain. He rented wagons in faraway towns to deliver his goods, and, during some weeks, he didn't spend even two consecutive nights in the same hotel room.

Bonnie received brief notes from Charlie, mostly hotel postcards from faraway towns, talking of hectic deadlines.

In late January Charlie was scheduled to deliver a large order to a store in Oklahoma City. He alerted Bonnie with a telegram a day in advance. They ordered a steak dinner at the Threadgill Hotel and spent a long evening talking about their work.

"I've gotten several postcards from you, and your work seems to be taking you to every corner of the state. Your experience here is so different from mine selling hats on South Harvey Street. Are you happy, and are you having success?" asked Bonnie.

"Juggling shipments and schedules and train rides is quite exhilarating, but not as easy as I expected," Charlie conceded. "My October arrival has left me little time with good weather to establish sales contacts. Plus, there are ever-changing railroad routes, bad weather that causes delays and damaged products, and unpredictable local circumstances, such as different store locations."

"I admire your perseverance," said Bonnie.

Charlie looked up from his food and smiled in acknowledgement of her compliment.

After dinner, they walked arm in arm back to the Prince Rupert Hotel. It was a cold, starry night. Charlie opened the door and pulled Bonnie out of the biting wind. He took her hand, raised it gently, and lowered his head to give it a tender kiss. Then he looked into Bonnie's eyes with a charming smile. After explaining that he had to leave for an early morning departure the next day, he was gone.

Oh my. This visit had been just one evening, but somehow Bonnie now had very different feelings. His ambition. His tenderness. He had left such a warm glow in her heart.

All through the cold Oklahoma winter, Bonnie happily made hats for Paris Hats. She even started on the spring and Easter inventory. She was able to dream a bit when her hands were busy.

Bonnie also began some research in the new Carnegie Library. After witnessing the state-fair crowds, Bonnie wanted to learn more about the local Indian population. She read the *Daily Oklahoman* when she could. She also read books about the Five Tribes land allocation and the Trail of Tears migration of tribes to eastern Oklahoma. Though Indians did not come into the hat shop, Bonnie did see them at the horse races she attended with Ruby.

Bonnie and Ruby continued having lunch. Sometimes Ruby invited her to the bungalow for dinner with her and Willis. He was a wise and seasoned businessman who had repeatedly been successful. Bonnie looked at him with renewed interest, imagining that Charlie would be similarly clever and successful in his own pursuits. Bonnie was starting to have fantasies about the two of them owning dry-goods stores spread throughout the city, like Willis' livery stables.

In late January Charlie sent Bonnie a postcard of the Threadgill dining room. The postcard had a serrated edge and appeared to have been torn off a dining room menu. He said he was back from a delivery, sitting in bed eating soup, and was cold and wet from a stormy trip. He hoped she was dry and warm, and he told her that his memories of their Threadgill dinners thoroughly warmed his heart. He signed the postcard, "Falling in love with you, my dearest, Charlie."

The postcard confirmed that Charlie shared the warm glow in Bonnie's heart. She was so thrilled with Charlie's words that she read them each night, before going to sleep with the postcard under her pillow.

Near the end of February, Charlie sent Bonnie another telegram. He had complicated business in Oklahoma City in the middle of March and would stay for about six days.

Bonnie carefully organized her hat making for short days in the shop, setting aside long evenings for dinners with Charlie.

Two days after Charlie arrived, Ruby invited the couple to dinner at her bungalow. Ruby had not yet met Charlie, and both women were eager for Willis and Charlie to meet.

Dinner was cozy and relaxed. Ruby had set the table with four red-bandana napkins. Overhead, a candle-lit glass lantern gave the room a nice glow. Ruby had baked delicious flaky biscuits and cooked a tasty beef stew, which she served from a cast-iron Dutch oven. The stew had cooked slowly for many hours on the wood-burning stove.

Over dinner the four talked of Oklahoma's rapid and successful development. Willis predicted automobiles and airplanes would be the vehicles of the future, knowing full well that his own business would be obsolete in a few years. Charlie predicted ready-to-wear clothes, fur coats, and divided skirts for women horse riders.

"The key to successful business ventures is to stay ahead of the growing trends," Willis said, looking at Charlie. "I have invested heavily in Oklahoma City real estate, and so far these investments are proving to be solid. Look ahead, Charlie. Always invest in land as soon as you have the money."

"By golly, you seem to have this figured out for Oklahoma City!" smiled Charlie, eating dessert, a tapioca pudding with walnuts. "Me, I am investing my heart and soul in the entire state of Oklahoma!"

At the conclusion of dinner, Willis suggested the three friends make a weekend trip to Redbud Ranch. The spring thaw had just occurred, and they could all enjoy the prairie and exercise the ranch horses.

Ruby, Bonnie, and Charlie headed out to Redbud Ranch on a chilly but sunny Friday afternoon. Willis suggested that they drive a larger-than-usual wagon for the visit, so they could transport extra clothes and enough food for the three of them.

Before they departed from National Livery, Bonnie showed Charlie her beloved Meadowbrook cart and the sweet pony, Darling. Charlie thought the cart and pony were charming and suitable for carrying hats, but he felt they would not be useful in his business, where large quantities of freight had to be delivered quickly.

Winter seemed to have melted away. The Oklahoma City streets were muddy as the trio drove out of town.

The temperature rose as the traveling party drove northeast and neared Redbud Ranch. Ruby, in her leather cowboy hat, riding Black Diamond, gave Charlie a geography lesson as they rode.

As they passed a thicket of willows, they encountered a flock of wild turkeys, heads down, picking at the gravel on the side of the road. Charlie, driving the wagon a bit too fast, pulled on the reins as the birds flapped their wings and scattered to the brush. The horses stopped suddenly, causing the wagon to skid on the gravel and spin sideways. Bonnie was holding onto the side of the wagon seat but jerked and fell sideways.

Ruby rushed to the pair of horses to calm them down, then turned to Charlie and Bonnie.

"Is everyone safe?" she called out.

Bonnie nodded and gritted her teeth, remembering Ruby's lesson about slopes and skidding gravel. Charlie laughed and said they were fine. The three regrouped and headed onto Redbud Ranch road.

"Oh lovely!" exclaimed Ruby, "Look there. You can see the Oklahoma redbud trees beginning to bloom."

Along the gully below, they could see trees in shades of dark, medium, and light pink and the dark-brown trunks highlighted against the green grass. Growing low and unbent by the winds, these native trees were the true pioneers of the Wild West of Oklahoma. The paintbrush effect of the pink trees along the creek bed provided a romantic and colorful contrast to the wide-open plains of green extending in every direction beyond the gully.

On Saturday the three friends got onto horses, and Ruby gave an informative tour of the ranch property, with a picnic lunch on the highest point. From the hilltop, Bonnie could see ranches squared off by fences. There were also open areas, rolling plains of patchwork green spreading as far as the eye could see.

That night, after a meal and some fireside conversation, Charlie again retired to an east-end bedroom. Ruby and Bonnie occupied their usual rooms on the west end of the farmhouse.

The next day Ruby was unable to ride. Goldie, one of the ranch mares, was about to foal, and Ruby needed to stay at the barn to assist with the birth. She suggested Charlie and Bonnie again take a picnic and go back to their favorite locations from the day before. They glanced at each other with shy smiles.

Bonnie and Charlie set out on two trusty and gentle mounts. The Sunday midmorning sky was scattered with lazy gray clouds. Bonnie, always interested in flowers, wanted to ride along the gully that crossed the property and wore the necklace of blooming redbud trees.

For their picnic, Bonnie and Charlie settled at the base of a gnarled redbud tree. Several trunks supported a wide canopy of wispy pink. Some of the trunks reached over the creek, a few leaned over the fresh spring grass in the meadow.

Bonnie tied her horse to a twiggy willow and walked to the picnic spot under the redbud tree canopy. Charlie stood beside her. He gently put his arms around her and leaned against the rough, scaly bark of the redbud tree. Cradling her head in his hand, he then ever so gently kissed her on the lips. The first kiss was short, awkward, seeking. Bonnie briefly looked into his piercing green eyes then closed her eyes. The second kiss was urgent, powerful, lingering. They were lost in the overhead crown of the pink blossoms, lost in their own spring celebration.

"Oh, Bonnie…marry me," Charlie whispered in her ear after several kisses.

"Ah, Charlie," she tossed her head back in a rapturous smile. "Yes, yes, with all my heart!"

Spooked!
Oklahoma City • April-May 1911

Bonnie and Charlie rode back to the ranch house, glowing in the excitement of their betrothal. They arrived at the homestead just as Ruby was walking out of the barn, putting on her leather hat.

"Well, I have good news! Goldie now has a handsome and frisky colt," she said.

"Oh, we have good news, too!" giggled Bonnie. "We spent the afternoon under those gorgeous, blooming redbud trees—and Charlie and I are now engaged!"

Ruby stopped in her tracks. "What a busy day at Redbud Ranch! I am thrilled for both of you!" She gave them each a warm hug. "In honor of your betrothal, I think I will name the colt Charlie."

"Miss Ruby, I am honored and very touched." Charlie removed his Derby hat and bowed.

"Well, that's enough celebratory gestures. We need to get back to National Livery before dark. Can you love birds be ready to leave in about fifteen minutes?" Ruby asked,

292

walking toward the ranch house.

"Of course!" Bonnie answered, as she and Charlie walked toward the house arm in arm.

As usual, Ruby rode Black Diamond on the trip back to the city. At first the horse galloped, then it doubled back; finally, when the horse tired, Ruby rode next to Charlie and Bonnie.

"Where will you two get married?" asked Ruby.

"Well, we both have business obligations and families back in Illinois and St. Louis. This is a jigsaw puzzle we will have to tackle," said Charlie cheerfully.

Oh my goodness, how will I handle this, thought Bonnie. *Two families, neither close!*

"And will you stay in the Wild West or move back to Illinois?" queried Ruby.

"Again a question we have not yet addressed, since our engagement took place only one hour ago," laughed Charlie. "Ruby, you are relentless!"

Ruby took off and reset her hat. "Well, I'm out of marriage questions. I will be interested in how your plans develop."

The next morning, as Bonnie left for the shop, Mrs. Mudd handed her a letter. The return address was in Alabama, so she assumed it was from Marie Calais, about her summer return to Oklahoma City.

When Bonnie got to the shop, she sat down to read the letter. Marie was staying in Alabama, due to domestic problems, and would no longer return to Oklahoma City. Bonnie was to finish the Easter bonnet campaign by April 14, then the trimmers would be dismissed. Marie had paid the rent for April and May. She directed Bonnie to close the shop at the end of April and sell the supplies and furniture and vacate by the end of May.

Bonnie sat at her table, stunned.

After May, my job will be gone! One fast year of a thousand hats, then nothing.

Would she look for another job in Oklahoma City? Should she go to Muskogee? What would she tell Charlie? Bonnie started tapping her fingers on the table.

Well, Mr. McGregor said to look for business lessons. I guess this shop closure will be a lesson I must teach myself. More self-education than I could have ever imagined.

She had several things to organize. The clients were the most important, so she first needed to concentrate on making Easter hats. And she would close with a big splash to leave the shop's reputation in good standing, so she needed to make some spectacular designs for Easter. She also needed signs for the discounts after Easter.

There was minimal furniture in the store—just a few tables and display cases—which should be easy to sell in May. The financial books? Well, she had made weekly entries all along, so the final entries would not be too difficult.

The hat supplies were her most complicated challenge. She was lucky because she had already been thinking about restarting her own summer-circuit work, and the supplies for that campaign had arrived! She would settle with Marie to apply a portion of her May salary to purchase these supplies. She also had money in an Oklahoma bank, so she was secure for a while.

Bonnie drew up a sketchy shop-closure plan and sat the trimmers down after work to explain it. The two girls were shaken, but all three women pledged to make magnificent Easter bonnets.

The Easter bonnet campaign was steady in the first two weeks of April. Bonnie created a spectacular cream-colored hat. Her design started with a tan, wide-brimmed straw hat banded at the edge with black ribbon. She then piled the hat high with tan and white silk roses, chiffon swirls, black bows, and long black feathers. She directed the trimmers to copy this hat in many colors and variations. The only unusual element was the addition of neck straps or wide tulle chin bows to most hats, for the winds of Oklahoma were strongest in the spring.

On Friday, April 14, the two trimmers shared tearful goodbyes with Bonnie and headed out the door. As the doorbell rang with their departure, Bonnie sat in the nearest chair feeling very alone. Tears sprang to her eyes. Paris Hats had been her Oklahoma City *home base*. It had not occurred to her until then how helpful it had been to arrive in a new city in a new state and have a job waiting for her. A place to start. She must never forget this, the importance of one's workplace and the need to keep from losing it.

That night, tired and lonely in the Prince Rupert Hotel, Bonnie wrote a long letter to Charlie. It was spring with good weather, and Charlie was dashing around the state, taking Marshall Field clothing to every little town on the prairie.

She had no idea where to reach him, but she did know that he kept the room at the Depot Hotel in Muskogee. So, she addressed the letter to that hotel.

Bonnie's letter was sad and wistful. She mentioned the busy Easter bonnet campaign but dwelled on the shop's quick closure and how lost she felt. In all of Oklahoma, her only "home" had been Paris Hats, for she could not call the Prince Rupert Hotel or Redbud Ranch her home. The shop has been the center of her compass in the new state, and now it was gone. Charlie was moving around too much, and the two distant families were just that: distant in space and not close emotionally. She asked Charlie to watch for hat shops in Muskogee, although she had no idea if he even wanted to stay in Oklahoma. They had not discussed further plans.

Charlie, busy with spring and summer shipments, sent back a quick telegram saying, "Sorry about closure! Good luck. Will visit soon." Bonnie was quite disappointed with this brief and unsympathetic response. She knew he was busy, though.

On April 17, Bonnie placed a large sign in the window announcing store-closure discounts. There were just a few customers on Monday, but they alerted their friends, and the rest of the week was very busy. Each final hat sale became a goodbye between Bonnie and clients. She summoned great poise, so that she could be gracious during those final transactions. At the end of each day she was emotionally exhausted and had a heavy heart.

Feeling melancholy, Bonnie scheduled a Thursday night dinner to talk over her plans with Ruby. Bonnie had been corresponding with Mr. Brenner at Rosenthal-Sloan. She had finished her obligations to that company with the State Fair assignment and was now working independently.

She would take a deep breath and start a traveling hat-making circuit of her own. She was going to establish a sunbonnet clientele from the ranch women she now knew. Before she did anything else, she needed to make hats to make enough money to repay Willis for the pony and cart rental. Meeting this financial obligation was very important to her. She would try a month of traveling hat making before she closed down Paris Hats, taking advantage of the shop for credit to order hat supplies.

"You will be fine, Bonnie! You can probably decorate humble sunbonnets to make every ranch woman feel she needs a new one. Plus, you can advertise to make hats for weddings, funerals, and anniversary celebrations. I bet you will have more business than you realize!"

Ruby projected total optimism for this spring campaign, although privately she feared Bonnie might saturate the close-by ranches, then have a harder time reaching far-away ranches.

"Well, I will start with the state-fair customers and go from there. Thank you for your offer to stay at Redbud Ranch. I have sent a note to Sadie Friend and Clara Alden and will visit both of them the day after tomorrow to see about sunbonnets. You are welcome to join me on any trips, but I fully expect to make most of these trips alone with trusty Darling and the Meadowbrook cart—and a pistol. So far, I haven't yet encountered anything I cannot handle."

In the week after the store closure, Bonnie, her pistol in her leather purse, rode out of town toward Redbud Ranch, where she would spend the night alone. On each ride from town she was amazed at the difference between the high-rise bustle of the busy city and the empty rolling plains of the nearby prairie, with its long stretches of rutted road.

The night alone in the ranch house was windy, and she drifted off into a warm but restless sleep.

Bonnie woke early the next day, eager to visit her potential clients. Her plan was to visit Sadie Friend and Clara Alden on the same day. Afterwards she would go back to Redbud Ranch for the night, then later head south to the Bates family's Sidewinder Ranch. The Bates family had contacted Paris Hats about hats for a late-May party and promised to be a lucrative client for Bonnie. Their ranch was almost two hours from Redbud Ranch, but Bonnie felt she had enough experience for the longer trip and had agreed to the assignment.

Sadie was ready for the late-morning visit, waiting again at the plank table by the cottonwood tree. Sadie greeted Bonnie with bright eyes and a warm smile.

"Bonnie, I love your hats! The state-fair hat you made for me," she looked down, kicking the dust with her boot, "I really think that hat gave me courage to win the race, and I give you full credit. Somehow you made me feel not only glamorous but more capable. I would love a new sunbonnet, exactly like the one you are wearing, but maybe in my favorite yellows. Maybe the sunbonnet can give me glamour and skill for my farm chores," she laughed. "If you could get it to me before June, when the sun gets really hot, what would it cost?"

"A sunbonnet like mine would be one dollar. And, Sadie, your skill in the state-fair race was spectacular. You won that race on your own!"

Sadie blushed. "Thank you. You can drop off the sunbonnet whenever your wagon is coming this way."

On her way to Alden Trails Ranch, Bonnie's cart dipped into a hole on the rutted road, loosening one of the wheels. Bonnie had to get out and walk Darling very slowly to prevent the wheel from falling off. As she walked through a familiar tree grove, Bonnie gratefully realized she was close to her destination. She proceeded to the large Alden barn. The ranch men welcomed her and said they could mend the wheel while she met with the ranch women.

There were many women who might need sunbonnets. Clara had ten-year-old twin sisters who were full of fidget and tickle and very difficult to measure, but Bonnie succeeded. Clara's mother and aunt both had very fair skin and insisted on the widest hat brims possible. Bonnie took pages of notes. With girls' hats priced two for one dollar, and three adult hats priced at one dollar, the total price to make all five hats was four dollars.

The Alden men had completely fixed the cart wheel. Bonnie did not know anything about cart maintenance, and hoped she never had another cart problem—ever! She returned to Redbud Ranch to make six sunbonnets.

Hmm, maybe Redbud Ranch will become my summer shop, she thought.

She sat for four days at the sunny kitchen table making sunbonnets, going slowly and loving every minute of the work. She also made a lovely new sunbonnet for herself, using pale-blue fabric with navy-blue ribbon accents. She had plenty of supplies to create lovely sunbonnets, loose deadlines, and sunny late-spring weather at Redbud Ranch. Heaven!

A week after her initial visits, Bonnie delivered the six hats to her clients and collected her money. After the deliveries, she headed back to Redbud Ranch to prepare for the next day's trip.

Lovely! Business is off to a good start. She was full of optimism and spring sunshine. She mentally earmarked the five

299

dollars as part of the money she owed Willis.

Tomorrow she would travel two hours south to Sidewinder Ranch, where she would spend a few days making ladies' hats for a thirtieth-anniversary party. The wheel was fixed, she had more pistol cartridges, and she had her beef jerky. This longer trip had a few hills, but Bonnie knew to be aware of hillside gravel skids. She felt that her cowgirl skills were expanding with each solo trip she made.

She departed midday the next day.

Bonnie's ride south to Sidewinder Ranch was through barren landscapes with no trees for shade or wind protection. She had a new gray parasol tucked under the seat and stopped on a flat, open stretch to retrieve it. She also gave water to Darling.

Bonnie started down a gentle slope that veered to the right. She kept the pony at a slow pace and watched for loose gravel on the dirt road as they descended off the plateau. At the bottom of the slope, the road crossed a dry creek bed. Beyond this, to the left, Bonnie noticed three prominent twenty-foot-tall rocky blocks. Red-colored and striated, the bluffs jutted out into the valley floor. Two had a shadowy space between them.

Bonnie was so curious about the rock formations that she barely noticed the sky darkening with large blackish clouds. She frowned as she looked up but proceeded south a few more minutes.

As the wind came up, Bonnie had to fold the parasol. When raindrops began to blow into her face, she realized she was in trouble. She was on a windy plain, unprotected. In her roofless cart, she was very vulnerable to rain and lightning.

Bonnie carefully turned Darling and the cart around and headed for the rocky bluffs she had seen before. By the time she reached them, the rain was coming down harder, and the sky had gotten darker. Bonnie drove the Meadow-brook cart up to the opening in the bluff. She blocked the rain with her body to check that the gun in her purse was loaded. Before leaving Redbud Ranch, she had remembered to load the gun—but she just wanted to double-check to re-assure herself. She felt the need to be vigilant, but she was not yet frightened.

She dismounted, tied Darling's reins to a low branch of a scrub oak, and walked cautiously toward the shadowy overhang, fearing there might be a large animal inside. It was fairly dark, but she could see the space had a sandy floor. There were a few animal droppings, but no animal.

Good, she thought, *the overhang is shallow, but we will be protected here.*

Bonnie nudged the cart farther under the scrub oak, unhitched Darling, and led her into the area under the rock overhang. There was just enough room for Bonnie to rest against a low boulder and position Darling outside of her own body but under the overhang. She held the pony's reins in her left hand, so she could access the gun with her right.

The wind and rain blew at the bluffs. Darling's flank protected Bonnie somewhat from the elements. Bonnie cooed to Darling and rubbed her nose. The pony took a step closer to the boulders and to her master. Both of them were wet but not yet soaked.

The storm's intensity picked up for the next hour. Bonnie and Darling scooted closer to the damp inner wall. Bonnie could hear a drip from the overhead ledge, but the falling water was not hitting her. The pony stood quietly, comforted occasionally by Bonnie's touch.

Eventually Bonnie began to get drowsy. The wind had

stopped, but there was a steady drizzle. She balanced uncomfortably on the boulder and leaned her head into Darling's neck. The soft drip and the mutual warmth comforted them both.

Suddenly Darling reared up her head, snorted, and flinched her neck muscles. Bonnie woke up. Darling began an agitated step with her front feet. Bonnie stood and looked into the darkness but could see nothing. She slowly withdrew the gun from the purse around her neck.

Darling reared again, this time with a high-pitched squeal. Bonnie stepped up on a ledge, still holding the pony's reins, and brought the gun into a blind position above the pony's head. Her finger was on the trigger, but she could see nothing.

Darling squealed again, shuffled her feet, and moved about, contained only by Bonnie's firm grip on the reins. Bonnie fired the gun into the darkness. The pony jerked. Bonnie's heart raced.

Darling stomped her front and back feet. Bonnie fired the gun again. This time, in response she heard a frightened snarl a few yards out.

Maybe I hit a coyote or a bobcat, she thought, as she tried to calm her wobbling gun hand.

Darling continued snorting and moving about anxiously. Another, louder snarl came from the darkness. Bonnie tucked her chin and looked into the darkness.

I will not be ambushed by a large, wet, angry beast, she thought. *I am on a business trip and nothing will stop me!*

She fired the gun a third time and heard a louder growl, followed by branches breaking in the bushes.

Bonnie did not fire a fourth shot, thinking it important to conserve the bullets. She and Darling shivered together in fear and cold for an hour. Finally, Bonnie slid the gun back into her purse, stepped off the ledge, crouched on the boulder, and put her arm around Darling. They huddled together, occasionally dozing, waiting for the dawn.

The morning was bright and sunny, but in the shaded overhang Bonnie did not awaken until Darling started to shuffle her feet. Bonnie led the pony out from the overhang, pulled the cart out from under the scrub oak, and reattached Darling. Bonnie chewed on a piece of beef jerky from her purse, and the pony munched on scrub vegetation.

Bonnie continued south on the rustic road and crossed a small creek whose water was red from the previous night's storm.

Ruby had said that the ranch had a gate with a large "S" made of wood pieces nailed to the overhead span. When the gate came into sight, Bonnie breathed a sigh of relief.

A young man wearing a cowboy hat and a blue neck bandana walked out to meet Bonnie as she approached the ranch compound. The house was sprawling, a tall log structure in the middle with clapboard additions on each end.

"Morning, miss. I'm Bradley Olson, one of the Bates' ranch hands. Let's get you out of this cart." He took the reins into his tanned hands and tied them to a hitching post. "Can I take the trunk into the house for you?"

"Miss Spencer, welcome," said Sally Bates, with a wide smile, rushing out from the ranch house. She was a tall, dark-haired, and willowy sixteen-year-old. "My mother told me to watch for you! You'll be sharing my room with me. We expected you yesterday. How did you handle the storm?"

"Hello! Darling and I spent the night under a bluff a few miles north. I scared off a coyote or bobcat with my pistol. We are happy to arrive at your ranch!"

As she talked, Bonnie shook hands with Sally. Bradley walked behind them carrying the trunk. As they entered the house, Bonnie felt the strong contrast from the bright prairie. For a moment she stood still until her eyes adjusted to the much dimmer light.

"Welcome, Miss Spencer!" said Barbara Bates, as she walked from the back of the great room. "What a delight to have you visit! We all talk fondly of your hats from the state fair." Barbara was tall, big-boned, and robust. She wore men's pants and a man's shirt, and she had a denim apron draped across her chest. Her face was as tan as leather, and her hair was tied up in a careless knot on top of her head.

"Mother, Miss Spencer waited out the storm last night at the bluff overhang. She scared off a coyote or bobcat. Can we start on hats soon?"

"No, darling, let's leave hats until after lunch. Miss Spencer can wash up now and have a cup of coffee. You can show her the vegetable garden before lunch. We have several days to work on hats," directed Mrs. Bates.

"Then, Miss Spencer, I will show you to my room, where there is a pitcher and a wash basin," said Sally cheerfully. "Oh Miss Spencer, I know we are not supposed to talk hats, but I think your sunbonnet is so beautiful. Could I have one just like that?"

"Well, before bed tonight, we can look at supplies for your hat. But let's not tell the others." Bonnie conspiratorially put her finger to her lips.

Supper that evening at the Bates ranch was a big family affair. Beside the house, two rustic tables were pushed together under a crude arbor with grape vines. The Bates family shared the table with another six ranch hands and a cook and, tonight, Miss Spencer. There was steak for all, baked potatoes, baked beans, homemade pickles, and also cold tea and gingerbread. There was singing and guitar playing after dinner, the festivities finally winding down as the sky darkened.

By candlelight, Bonnie and Sally spent an hour going through the hat supplies from the wooden trunk. Sally was shy and would not consider a sunbonnet with colors. But she loved textures, so Bonnie showed her several combinations of white ribbons and white eyelets that she liked.

The next day Bonnie got to know the elder Mrs. Bates, mother of Barbara's husband Bill, who lived with the family. She was also quite tanned and had hair pulled back in a bun at the base of her neck. Bonnie thought she was probably a former cowgirl. She was to have a hat also. Nothing too fancy—a flower or two on a straw hat with a wide brim. Maybe something a little unusual. Unlike her very direct daughter-in-law, she had a more laid-back personality and reminded Bonnie of many of the shop clients, who were not very hard to please. Bonnie knew just what to make for her.

Mrs. Bates was a bit more exacting. This thirtieth-anniversary party was the first party the family had ever given, after decades of hardscrabble prairie survival. It was a party to celebrate *themselves*, shared with neighbors and friends. Barbara had a navy dress with tan trim and wanted a wide-brimmed hat, tan, if possible. But she wanted something distinctive, since it was her anniversary. Bonnie had an idea.

Bonnie had two full days to work, not including the morning of the party. The first day she measured all three women, then had them try on their pattern hats for size and accent flower locations. Then she partially sewed and glued accessories on both large hats. Late in the afternoon, she started on Sally's sunbonnet. Unfortunately, she was only able to piece together the fabric before she lost the critical daylight needed for the fine stitch work.

The second day she worked on finishing all three hats, jumping back and forth between them. The ranch women kept trying to pop in for a peek, but Bonnie kept them away from the big table where she was working, until she finished.

That afternoon, Bonnie called in Sally, and all three curious women came for the fashion show that followed. Sally eagerly tried on her white sunbonnet. The white eyelet on the hat brim and the layers of several white ribbons banding the cap created a symphony of texture. It was bold in style, but subtle because it was all white.

"Oh, darling, this is so lovely against your dark hair," said Sally's mother.

"I think it is lovely myself," agreed Sally with a grin.

The elder Mrs. Bates stepped up. She had a dark-blue hat with one side curved up and a large, white, silk cabbage rose below the upsweep. The hat also had lovely medium-blue banding on top. She tried on the hat, walked to a mirror for a look, tilted her head to one side to better expose the rose, and broke into a wide smile.

"Perfect, Miss Spencer," she said. "I wanted something unusual, and this side sweep with the rose below is just perfect. Something to keep me saucy in my old age. You do have quite a touch! Now, Barbara it is your turn."

Somewhat skeptical, Mrs. Bates walked to the big table toward the remaining hat. She had worn a man's leather hat to wrestle cattle and dig the garden, and she really did not think a fancy hat would change her looks. But after the state fair, her husband Bill had insisted on the ladies' hats for the party. He was so proud of her and understood the fancy hat would be a special present. Bonnie helped Mrs. Bates place the new hat in the correct position. She walked slowly to the mirror. She stood for a moment with a furrowed brow and pursed lips. Then a large smile broke out across her face.

"Miss Spencer, the navy ribbon band and the top arrangement on this straw hat are stunning. I have never seen anything like this! I feel so very, well, elegant for a ranch lady. I can't wait to wear this tomorrow night!"

Ah, thought Bonnie, *my skill comes through even out on this sunbaked prairie. Finishing touches tomorrow morning, and I can be on the road after lunch.*

As Bonnie left Sidewinder Ranch, preparations for the party were underway. Several smoking barbecue pits were sending up tantalizing smells, and a group of women busily prepared food under the grape arbor. The three ranch women waved Bonnie off with smiles. They had asked her to stay, but she wouldn't know anyone at the party and did not want to mix business and pleasure. She smiled proudly to herself as she left under the "S" gate and rode out onto the road toward Redbud Ranch. As she began her journey, in her mind she reviewed the three lovely hats.

Without warning, Darling threw her head up high, her eyes wild and her mane flying up between her ears. Something had frightened her, and her only defense was flight.

The tall wheels clattered on the gravel as the cart raced forward. Bonnie pulled tight on both reins.

As Darling continued her mad dash forward, Bonnie tried to regain control of the pony. But the cart drifted to the edge of the road, where the rocks were as big as mixing bowls. In the next instant, the Meadowbrook cart wobbled onto the rocks, rocking to one side, then the other.

Bonnie adjusted her grip to get a better hold. The left rein seemed caught on the rein rail. Suddenly the left rein broke, leaving Bonnie holding just the broken end. With only one rein, she tightened her grip, as the broken leather rein bounced in wild loops on the slatted floor of the cart. Bonnie leaned forward to catch the flapping left rein, but just then the right wheel hit another very large rock. The cart wobbled and bounced, sending Bonnie tumbling onto the floor, her head bouncing off the mud dasher.

Bonnie was now in a heap on the floor of the cart, turned sideways, her clothes twisted and her left shoulder lodged against the mud dasher. The right rein was coiled dangerously around her right forearm and elbow, her teeth were clenched, and her mouth was gritty. Her head pounded and already had a bulging lump. She tasted metal. The wheels kicked up dust into her face and onto her clothes. Her arm flailing about, she could not find a handhold. The frantic pony continued to gallop down the road.

The cart totally out of control, Bonnie had wild flashes of terror as she continued casting about for the handhold. She imagined a busted cart, a pile of splinters, a broken body and broken legs. Her heart pounded. Death was spewing up along with the choking dust coming through the slatted floor!

Bonnie turned and reached for the cart seat with her right hand, which tightened the right rein. The pony veered right and tumbled down into a drainage ditch!

"Help!" Bonnie screamed, as she felt the cart become airborne. She was blinded by the twisted sunbonnet.

Darling bolted up the other side of the ditch and onto the open prairie, pulling the driverless cart. She was still in a frantic gallop! She still pulled helter-skelter with wild eyes! The cart, with Bonnie still helplessly crumpled on the floor, careened over rough ground and dangerous rocks. She could hear the leaf springs squeaking and the cart boards moaning with every lurch.

Just when she was sure this would be the death of her, Bonnie leaned forward and made a frantic skyward stretch with her left arm and caught the flyaway left rein. She wrapped it around her fingers, put both arms above her head, and bent both elbows, bringing them to her temples as she pulled the reins backwards.

Darling eased her pace.

She slowed to a trot, then a walk, and finally stopped. She stood still, wet with sweat, muscles twitching, and panting through flared nostrils.

In spite of the pony's panting, Bonnie heard thunderous hooves coming from behind. She raised her head and looked to the left between the mud dash and the rein rail. A cowboy hat. A rider grabbing the bit at Darling's mouth.

"Miss Spencer, it's Bradley Olson from Sidewinder Ranch. Are you all right, miss? Are you alive?" He spoke as he bent down from his horse with an outstretched arm.

Bonnie saw the calloused open hand, but she was breathless, almost blind with pain. She still felt as though she were pulsing on the phantom chase. She couldn't move or speak.

Slowly, she lifted her right arm to the cart seat and tried

to pull off the twisted rein. Her arm was numb, ringed with bleeding welts. She was exhausted, slumped, nearly blinded by the red dust on her face. She could not loosen the rein.

Brad came around the front of the pony and dismounted. Leaving his horse to block Darling, he walked to the right side of the cart to untangle the rein from Bonnie's bloody arm. He then tied the rein to his saddle horn.

"Can you move? Can you speak?"

"Yes," she whispered hoarsely, spitting out red dust.

Bonnie put both arms on the seat of the cart and pulled herself to her knees. Then she tried to stand. Her back felt twisted, but she did not think any of her bones were broken. She gasped as she stood up. She felt screaming pains in both arms and shoulders, her back, and her left hip. Her legs were cramped. Lastly, she pushed back the brim of her sunbonnet.

The sky was still blue.

The horse and pony were still panting. Darling's breast collar hung loose on her chest. Bonnie collapsed in a heap on the cart seat.

"Let's just stay here a few minutes," Brad said gently, touching her shoulder.

The wild chase had lasted just a few minutes, but to Bonnie it had seemed like an eternity.

The grasshoppers buzzed for quite a while before Bonnie could move again. While she rested, Brad fixed the broken left rein with the rein splice and hole punch from the cart's spares kit. Bonnie eventually shook the red dust off her clothes and face, shaking off her remaining fear along with it.

As her head cleared, she watched Brad finish the repair. At the ranch house he had been a friendly anonymous cowboy. Now he seemed like a sinewy, skillful giant.

Bonnie sat up and exhaled. She felt an overwhelming

sense of relief, and large tears began to carve channels down her dusty cheeks. She grabbed Brad's arm as he brushed by the side of the cart.

"You came at just the right moment. I am so, so grateful," she choked, tears still flowing.

"My pleasure, miss," he said, tipping his hat. "I was scouting for early arrivals, and I saw your runaway cart. I saw your arms outstretched in your desperate leap for that flyaway rein. I am so impressed with your bravery! I'll get you back to the ranch."

Brad mounted his horse with Darling's reins in his hand and slowly steered the skittish pony back to Sidewinder Ranch. Bonnie was limp, bruised, and speechless. Slumped against the wheel guard, she still held on for dear life.

The elder Mrs. Bates was heading into the house when she saw Brad leading Bonnie's pony and cart back to the ranch. She scurried to the pair as Bonnie slowly got down with Brad's help. Brad whispered to Mrs. Bates the details of what had happened, and she took Bonnie's arm to assist her inside.

"Bless you, Bonnie. I am so glad you are in one piece."

For almost an hour, Bonnie sat in a rocking chair gathering her wits. She was in a blind, dusty state of shock. She knew she had almost died, and she had a vague awareness that she had saved herself.

Eventually, overwhelmed with curiosity, Bonnie limped to the front window and watched the party outside.

The thirtieth-anniversary party was in full swing. The yellow sun was low in the afternoon sky and beginning to darken to a faint orange. Two sassy fiddlers were playing, and a long square dance was underway. The people who were not dancing stood around the circle, clapping and cheering. The caller, in his string tie and black ten-gallon hat, had a gravelly twang. He kept everyone moving round and round, twirling and whooping and kicking up a bit of red dust. Bonnie found herself bouncing her foot to the music, in spite of her pain and her weakness, which made it hard to stand at all.

Mrs. Bates was in her new hat and dress, looking very proud, walking a promenade on her husband's arm.

Sally wore her new elaborate sunbonnet, looking very much like a young woman, no longer a girl. She leaned against a fence post, hoping to be noticed. Because of the sunbonnet brim, she could not see the two handsome cowboys smiling and talking about her as they lingered at the main barbecue pit.

Mrs. Bates' mother-in-law quietly watched from the sidelines. She had a certain tilt to her head, showing off the cabbage rose on the side of her lovely blue bonnet.

Suddenly, Mrs. Bates burst into the room to wipe her brow and get a drink of water.

"Oh Bonnie, dear Bonnie! News of your runaway pony is sweeping through the party. Come join us, everyone will want to give you a hug and a blessing. Come celebrate with us, and you must stay the night."

She stopped to pour a drink of water from the pitcher on the table.

"You know, don't you, that you have given the Bates women an incredible gift for this party. We will never forget your hats, and your bravery out on the hostile prairie."

On Sunday, the Bates women drove Bonnie back to Redbud

Ranch in a large farm wagon, trailing the empty little cart and pony. Bonnie had saved herself and was extremely proud to have done so, but she was very bruised, exhausted, and disheartened by the frightening adventure. For the first time, she realized she might not be experienced enough to handle the traveling hat circuit in this dangerous and unforgiving country.

She was very happy to see her friend Ruby at Redbud Ranch. Ruby invited the Bates women to stay, but they declined.

Ruby, bless her heart, could tell how fatigued and hungry Bonnie was, even before she told her the tale. Ruby set up a picnic in the grass next to the house, which was just what Bonnie needed, comfort and horizontal relaxation. The women rested on quilts and old pillows, looking at the big sky, the rolling hills that stretched forever, their dragonfly companions, and, eventually, the sunset. From her quilt perch, Bonnie told Ruby of the runaway cart at Sidewinder Ranch.

"What's wrong, Ruby? Why are things so crazy? Snakes, broken wheels. My runaway cart. Last summer, when you and I did this, it was easy!" she sighed, lying on her back and gnawing on bread and cheese.

"Well, Bonnie, this is the pioneer life. Storms, runaways, dust, coyotes—they're are all part of the Wild West. None of it comes easily. This summer you are on your own, with little help from me. So you are facing the dangers and obstacles of prairie life by yourself. This is how the West is being conquered, one storm and one broken wagon wheel at a time." Ruby spoke softly and slowly, wanting to make sure Bonnie understood the seriousness of her warning.

"You know, Ruby, making hats for ranch women is very gratifying, but it all seems so complicated. I guess your support made those trips seem easy." Bonnie frowned, rubbing her aching shoulder.

"Well, don't blame yourself! You have worked hard for these first three ranches. It's just like the long hours a rancher must spend before he has a steak on his plate."

"In the last month I have made fourteen dollars. And I owe all of it to Willis for the cart and pony rental. If I did not have your friendship and Redbud Ranch, I would not have been able to sustain the first weeks of this business of mine," said Bonnie, looking gratefully at her friend.

"Ranch life in the Wild West is exhilarating, challenging, and full of dangers—and the rewards are slow in coming. Maybe, just maybe, hat making is not meant to be a prairie career," suggested Ruby.

"You might be right. But giving up is just not in my nature! Although, Ruby, I thought I might have *died* on that runaway cart. It was so difficult to rein in that frightened pony!" cried Bonnie.

"If you had traveled on more solo trips, you might have had a better idea of how challenging this campaign would be, how difficult it would be to be successful and profitable. What do you think?" Ruby leaned in toward Bonnie, with a very serious look on her face.

"I think you're right. I think the state-fair campaign was special, a wonderful team effort for the two of us. These second-year attempts have been so difficult. Maybe this is why there are not many traveling business*women* on the prairie." Bonnie had both hands on her forehead, as if her insights were causing a headache.

"Oh, my friend," said Ruby, as she threw her arms around Bonnie, "last fall we had a *grand scheme,* and it was totally successful for the state fair. And we must give ourselves credit for that. This traveling hat-making concept on the Oklahoma prairie just does not seem safe or practical or profitable long-term for a city girl with city skills!"

"Well, the runaway chase has ended my traveling hat business. I will continue my career in hat making because this is my contribution to the women in my world. I will just find a place for this work which is more suited to *all* of my skills. I think my next chapter is in Muskogee, since Charlie is there."

Muskogee Marriage
Muskogee, Oklahoma • June 1911

As Bonnie's twenty-third birthday approached, she was busy making yet another change in her life. She spent the last week of May 1911 selling furniture and supplies and closing the financial books for Paris Hats. It was disappointing to be ending her traveling circuit, but also a relief. She kept her traveling trunk of hat supplies, which she stored in her Prince Rupert Hotel room for possible use in Muskogee.

Ruby and Bonnie continued their lunches at the log cabin café when Ruby was in town.

Bonnie had made the acquaintance of another friend while in Oklahoma City, Minnie Wilson. A short, bubbly, curly-haired gal, Minnie was a seamstress who occasionally came into the shop.

Since Bonnie had already worked at the best hat shop in Oklahoma City, she saw no need to stay in this city and decided to explore Muskogee, where she could be nearer to Charlie. Minnie Wilson had suggested two Muskogee stores for her to contact, Sheldon Bliss and The Emporium, both of which employed trimmers. Bonnie planned to visit these stores soon after her arrival.

The evening of Bonnie's birthday, Ruby and Willis invited her over to the bungalow, where they shared a lovely dinner and heartfelt goodbyes. Bonnie had never before felt the closeness of a girlfriend with whom she could share hard-won triumphs, adventures, and moments of personal confusion, introspection, and resolve.

Bonnie gave all of her hat-circuit earnings to Willis, as payment for the pony and cart rental. She was embarrassed by how woefully inadequate she felt the sum was, but Willis graciously accepted her payment as full compensation.

"You did your part for the state fair, Prairie Rose," he said with admiration. "And I was glad to contribute to your endeavor."

Bonnie's departure was difficult for the two young women. Hugging fiercely, they lovingly brushed away each other's tears. They promised each other to write, and even visit, after Bonnie was settled in Muskogee.

Willis shook Bonnie's hand with a twinkle in his eye and said, "Good luck, little Prairie Rose!"

On Friday Bonnie took her carpetbag, the wooden trunk, and her leather purse and departed for Muskogee on the midmorning train. She was ready to get back to city life with a job in a safe and well-lighted shop. In spite of her business failure with the hat-making circuit outside Oklahoma City, Bonnie still had confidence in her hat-making skills and her ability to find another job. Her passion for this work was still strong. She relished her work at the back of the stage, creating beauty and contributing to a sense of personal pride in other women.

Still exhausted from the store closure, she slept briefly,

awakened suddenly when the conductor announced Musk-ogee.

Charlie met her at the depot and checked her into the Depot Hotel, where he had booked a separate room for her. Their first evening meal was in the hotel's crowded and noisy dining room. The tables were close together, waiters clanged the dishes, and diners came in right off the dusty trail.

"Well, Bonnie, except for the limp in your left leg, you look healthy, in spite of your tumultuous spring. It must feel like ten years—instead of one—since you arrived in this state!"

Charlie reached over to hold her hand, as they waited for the meal. He had picked up a tan already and looked quite handsome in his summer suit.

Bonnie was eager to resettle. "Tomorrow I have two shops to visit here in Muskogee. I have brought my well-supplied hat-making trunk with me, but I have no interest in setting up another prairie campaign. I will see if anyone needs a trimmer in this city. How is your sales work going?" She raised her eyebrows and took a sip of water.

"Carving out territory is hard for me also. It has not been impossible, but it has been eight months of long hours, countless train trips, wagon rentals, damaged goods, and disgruntled customers. I, too, am reconsidering what my next career move will be." Charlie had a faint smile, but he did not have the look of a man on top of his career. "I am thrilled you are here, and I feel we should put our heads together to make our next choices."

Bonnie felt a chill shoot up her spine. She had not heard departure thoughts in the postcards. She had just given up her home base in Oklahoma City, and now things seemed uncertain here.

The lobby of the Depot Hotel was dark mahogany with stately columns and threadbare oriental rugs. After dinner the couple found a secluded sofa there and continued their discussion.

"Frankly, I would just as soon quit this traveling circuit and take you back to Cobden for a lovely wedding. Maybe soon," he said, as he leaned in to caress her cheek.

"This is not easy for me, Charlie."

She sat upright, pushing his hand away, then rubbed her forehead as she closed her eyes. Turning to him with tears, she said, "I was a confined servant to the Robeys and abandoned by the Spencer family. I have two families back there, and I feel neither would want to help me with a wedding! We should just get married here in Muskogee."

Charlie was speechless, a blank look on his face.

The next morning Bonnie dressed in business clothes and set out for the two upscale stores with hat departments. Sheldon Bliss' hat department was ruled by a middle-aged seamstress and her two longtime trimmers. They appeared to have been together for decades and had no interest in hiring more staff. The Emporium had a similar permanent and well-established hat-making staff and no job opportunities. Without references or a hat sample she was turned away at both stores.

Bonnie walked several blocks back to the Depot Hotel, almost stomping, barely noticing the construction of eight- to ten-story "skyscrapers" on every corner of this growing city.

How foolish I am! I stupidly barged in without references and samples, and I have ruined my chances at the two best shops. What can I do now?

Lost in her thoughts, she opened the Depot Hotel door and, as she barged in, bumped into Minnie Wilson, who was on the arm of a tall, dark-haired man with a huge, wide neck.

"Excuse me, I'm terribly sorry—Minnie? What brings you here?"

"Bonnie Spencer, my goodness! I would like you to meet my husband, Walden Wilson. I call him Wally. Wally, Miss Spencer is the fabulous hatmaker from Oklahoma City. Did you visit the stores I recommended?"

"Mr. Wilson, nice to meet you," Bonnie extended her hand to shake his. Bonnie was about five feet tall, as was Minnie. He was a giant compared to the two women. His handshake was gentle, however, and his smile was warm. Bonnie turned to Minnie. "I visited both stores today, and neither needs a trimmer. I am sort of at a crossroads, wondering what to do next."

"Well, I just moved here myself, because Wally has a new job here. Want to spend a few days helping me set up a house?" bubbled Minnie. "Wally is an elder of the Methodist church. He was invited to come here to the Methodist Episcopalian Church South of Muskogee to stabilize things until a new pastor can be found."

"It might be fun to help you for a few days," said Bonnie.

"Wally has already rented a place. Want to join me on Wednesday to set up house?" She grabbed a scrap of paper from her purse, scribbled on it, and handed this to Bonnie. "Here is the address. Come after breakfast."

Bonnie and Charlie spent the next few days getting to know Muskogee. There was an entrepreneurial spirit and excitement in the town, with the railroads bringing in thousands of oil speculators and other colorful opportunists.

Monday Bonnie rode with Charlie in a rented wagon to make a summer-clothes delivery two hours south of Muskogee. On the road out of town, they passed a street packed with wagons bulging with burlap sacks. The wagons were driven by Indians carrying cotton from their lands north and east of Muskogee to a gin in town. The Indians, with their square jaws, black hair, and dark skin, never came into her shop in Oklahoma City, but she had seen them on the streets. There seemed to be more of them in Muskogee, with its many Indian schools and clinics.

The couple arrived back in Muskogee at just about dark, and Charlie announced that he had a special nighttime surprise. He took back streets to get to the corner of Main and Broadway, where he insisted Bonnie cover her eyes. They got out of the wagon, and she giggled with childlike excitement and kept her eyes tightly closed as he led her the last few feet. Then he told her she could open her eyes. Newly installed scaffolding spanned the entire street, displaying a tall sign, "Welcome to Muskogee," lit up by the newest tungsten lights. It was currently the most exciting attraction in this frontier town, the place where everyone brought their guests. In the dusk, the bright sign twinkled, a new beacon bringing the progress of electricity and industry to this community.

"Oh Charlie! How lovely and romantic! I will always

remember Muskogee by this sign!" Bonnie giggled again and clapped her hands in delight. "We should get married right here!"

"Still, I would like to interest you in a Cobden wedding with my mother's help," he nudged.

"No, you cannot! It is this or another suitable Muskogee spot. I will *not* change my mind!" Now that she was rested, her resolve not to marry in Illinois was even stronger. She just could not imagine trying to work with the two families.

"All right, sweetheart! I'm not sure this is the spot, but we will find someplace in Muskogee for a special wedding," sighed Charlie.

On Tuesday Bonnie studied the *Muskogee Daily Phoenix* newspaper to educate herself on this bustling frontier city. She familiarized herself with the geography of the three rivers and quickly realized they were the source of rapid commercial and industrial development. Once again she pinned up a few newspaper clippings on the wall of her hotel room.

Later that day Charlie announced that he would definitely stop working in Oklahoma and return to Illinois. He had already sent a telegram to Marshall Field asking for a transfer assignment in Illinois. He would spend the next few days trying to close out his deliveries and accounts. Bonnie was shocked at this sudden decision, which had not included her at all.

Bonnie spent three lovely days helping Minnie Wilson. Her house was a small bungalow on a shady street, not too different from the home of Willis and Ruby. Bonnie had never had a home in Oklahoma and loved the opportunity to help a woman friend with a new start. Wednesday they opened boxes and placed things around the house. Thursday they measured for curtains and walked into town to shop. Friday they sat in Minnie's sunny living room and embroidered designs on new muslin kitchen towels. Minnie also invited Charlie to join them for supper that night.

Minnie and Walden welcomed Charlie into their new home, eager to hear the tales of this busy frontier salesman. As the four sat at the round dining room table, they began to converse.

"It is lovely to share dinner in your new home, and I know Bonnie is happy to have a new friend here in Muskogee," said Charlie, tucking a napkin into the neck of his shirt. "We are going back to Illinois soon, but we may get married here first, although I am not sure where and when."

"Oh Charlie, I—" Bonnie interrupted, blushing.

Minnie reached over and put her hand over Bonnie's. "Wait a moment," she said firmly. "Wally, during our unpacking, I learned from Bonnie that she wants to get married in Muskogee—and soon. What is on your schedule, say, June 15, about two weeks from now?"

"Well, I'm free midday. I have early and late church meetings."

"Bonnie, Charlie, Wally is ordained to perform weddings. What about a Methodist wedding at noon on June 15?"

"What?" Both Charlie and Bonnie blurted out together.

"Yes, that's right! He could marry you two weeks from today. Would that suit you?" Minnie was once again doing her favorite thing, setting up social events related to her husband's ministry.

"Well, I...we hadn't discussed this," Bonnie said, blushing again.

"I know. I pulled this surprise on you, but it *would* solve the problem you mentioned." Minnie put both hands on the table and smiled at Charlie and Bonnie.

"Yes," Bonnie said tentatively.

"Of course, for my lovely bride, this sounds perfect! Getting married in the Methodist church by a friend—but without a family crowd!"

Charlie grinned as he got up, walked around to Bonnie's chair, and bent down to kiss her cheek.

"What about it, sweetheart?" he asked hopefully. Charlie was now thirty-one, and he knew a good offer when it appeared.

"Perfect," Bonnie purred. "Just perfect!"

Bonnie and Minnie went shopping the next day. Bonnie had dated little and had never attended a wedding, so she really did not have many notions about wedding rituals or gowns. She had always focused on sewing for others.

On an impulse, she decided she would make her own wedding dress. She had just under two weeks in which to do it. She found a Butterick pattern with a floor-length skirt, capped long sleeves, and an inserted crocheted bodice. She chose a white cotton lawn fabric to make this gossamer dress, which was the current fashion. Minnie offered to make the slip and chemise to go below the filmy fabric.

Minnie insisted on bringing everything to her house, so they could use her big table to cut fabric. They could also use her iron and sewing machine. Charlie was off delivering final shipments this week, so Bonnie spent all of her waking moments in fabric heaven with Minnie measuring, cutting, sewing, and crocheting.

With her creative crochet work, Bonnie planned her first garden since Oraville on the bodice of her wedding dress. Open sunflowers circled the standing collar of the bodice. They were blooming all over the Oklahoma State Fairgrounds on opening night. At the bottom of the bodice, a bed of daisies cradled the garden. And across each breast, she put a white embroidered redbud flower and nub to represent her betrothal under the redbud trees of Oklahoma.

Bonnie spent two days lost in the stitches of her matrimonial bodice, barely speaking to Minnie. She gratefully remembered learning to crochet from Bertha. Basking in the sunbeams of Minnie's living room, making crochet knots and rubbing smooth the knotted flowers, she stitched together her past life and future dreams. Sewing was the work she dearly loved, and it felt wonderfully comforting to be using her skills to make a flattering and exquisite wedding dress for *herself*.

Following a sketch in her Bonnet Book, Bonnie also crafted an elegant white wedding bonnet from her trunk supplies. As she lifted silk doves out of the wooden trunk, she caught sight of the postcard of the Threadgill dining room, where her romance with Charlie grew. She sighed and held the doves to her heart. Smiling, she proceeded to construct the bridal hat with billowing white satin bows serving as a nest for the silk doves.

The night before the wedding, Bonnie finished,

pressed, and tried on the dress ensemble in Minnie's spare bedroom, where she would spend the night. Wearing all her wedding garments for the first time, Bonnie looked in the mirror, spellbound and overwhelmed. She was so pleased with the delicate crocheted bodice.

The wedding took place at noon on a sunny Thursday, June 15, 1911, at the ME Church South, at "F" and East Okmulgee. Bonnie's exquisite ensemble created a billowing gossamer silhouette as she walked through the church's red-brick arches. Charlie stood in the vestibule waiting for her, handsome in a new, silver-gray three-piece suit with char-coal-gray tie and silver top hat.

Elder Walden Wilson stood in a black robe, ready to perform the ceremony. He had brought in two other church officials to serve as witnesses. Behind them rose a wide wall of religious paintings fronted by long tables with tall ceremonial candles.

Charlie and Bonnie walked arm in arm to the altar. As they passed a large stained-glass window, morning rays of the colored light flooded across their bodies in streams of yellow, pink, and blue. Bonnie stopped, pressed Charlie's arm, and turned him toward the stained-glass window. Then she smiled radiantly to Elder Wilson and gestured for him to come to them. Taking Bonnie's cue, with their backs to the glorious window, Elder Wilson and the two witnesses re-formed their officiate group.

Bathed in the colored rays from the window, Bonnie and Charlie exchanged gold wedding bands from a Musk-ogee jeweler. They held hands in the kaleidoscope of colors, recited sacred vows, and committed themselves to each other. The ceremony was a sunlit convergence of blessings, love, and union. They kissed, smiled broadly, and thanked the elder. Then they locked arms and exited the sanctuary.

Minnie Wilson had watched from the back. Now she stood in the vestibule to receive the happy couple and direct them to a side table to sign the marriage documents. In her arm she held a straw basket, its handle wrapped in white satin ribbon and a large bow.

"Congratulations to you both!" Minnie said, as she approached Bonnie and Charlie with the basket. "Take this, your wedding feast, and walk outside to catch the Hyde Street trolley. Take it to the end of the line and get off at Hyde Park. Stroll through the park to an overlook and share this wedding feast with each other. Enjoy the first day of your married life! Now, go celebrate."

Neither bride nor groom knew of Hyde Park, which was built at the north end of the city along the Arkansas River. They boarded the gold and green trolley in their wedding outfits and made their way back to an empty double seat, eliciting smiles from all of the trolley passengers. The newlyweds laughed as they realized that, for them, the clang of the trolley bell had replaced wedding chimes.

Bonnie and Charlie strolled for an hour through the park, a riverside wonderland—their wedding park! Lawn panels were bordered by beds of fragrant roses for much of the walk. They strolled past a large greenhouse, an indoor pool, and a roller coaster built on a hilly perch above the river—but they were only interested in each other.

The newlyweds settled into a small hilltop gazebo for their wedding feast, reveling in the scent of the red and yellow roses twined above them in the beams of the storybook structure.

They shared ham biscuits wrapped in embroidered handkerchiefs tied with ribbons. They had carrot sticks, wrapped in twos in white satin and tied with fragrant pink roses in pale-purple satin ribbons. Their apple crescents were wrapped in white lace threaded with delicate pink satin ribbons. Also tucked in the basket was a glass canning jar filled with homemade apple juice. The bridal couple fed each other slowly, sharing kisses between bites.

After their ribbon-wrapped feast, Charlie and Bonnie wandered to a dance pavilion inland from the river, where they heard music. A small group—an accordion, a fiddle, and a piano—was performing popular tunes. Charlie and Bonnie placed their wedding basket near a side railing, and Charlie swept Bonnie into his arms for a first dance to "By the Light of the Silvery Moon." They twirled in their wedding dance, smiling to one another—oblivious to the Thursday afternoon crowd that had stopped to watch them.

The song ended, and they wandered back to the railing. Suddenly Charlie heard the accordion play the opening chords of a very familiar song. He placed Bonnie on the edge of the railing, handed her a bunch of pink roses and ribbons from the basket, swept off his silver hat, and knelt in front of her. In his tenor voice full of tenderness, he began to sing:

> Let me call you sweetheart,
> I'm...in...love...with...you,
> Let me hear you whisper that
> you...love...me...true...
> Keep the love-light glowing
> in your...eyes...so...blue...
> Let me call you sweetheart,
> I'm...in...love...with...you.

Bonnie held the tumble of roses and ribbons to her

heart and smiled rapturously at her new husband. Charlie's voice was so pure and beguiling. Once again Charlie was on-stage singing to her with his whole heart and soul.

The song was only a year old, and everyone knew the words. The crowd, mostly dressed in street clothes, continued to watch the wedding couple. With his top hat in one hand, Charlie rose at the song's completion, slipped his arm around Bonnie's waist, and turned to the crowd as they clapped. She blushed deeply and looked at her tumbled rose bouquet.

Bonnie continued to lean against the rail, beautiful in her crocheted wedding dress and white hat with the doves, holding the roses and many-colored ribbons. Charlie put on his tall silver hat and smiled at her.

Oh my, she thought. *I am so loved by this handsome man. I have found my heart's dream.*

They headed to the Depot Hotel, the late-afternoon orange ball of sun chasing through the trees before them, as the trolley drove back into town. They disappeared into Charlie's room, locomotives periodically screaming their long, hoarse and shrill whistles into the black prairie sky.

Going Home
St. Louis, Missouri and Cobden, Illinois
July 1911

Charlie jumped out of bed the next morning, washed up, and quickly dressed. He told Bonnie to stay in bed. They glanced shyly at each other, Bonnie blushing at each glance. Charlie hurried down to the hotel dining room, ordered scrambled eggs, toast, canned peaches, and coffee, and brought a brimming tray back upstairs. He joined her in bed, propped by pillows, the tray at their feet.

As they touched each other's legs under the covers, they agreed to spend the day packing and sending telegrams. They would depart the next day for St. Louis. Charlie had four wooden trunks in the room; he would pack two and discard two.

Giggling, Charlie and Bonnie fed each other luscious peach slivers. They agreed to cancel her other room and bring her supply trunk to this one.

The Depot Hotel had a telegraph office, where the couple spent an hour composing two telegrams:

MRS BERTHA MODGLIN   JUNE 16 1911
WINCHESTER FARM   MAKANDA ILL

DEAR BERTHA STOP BLANCHE SPENCER
AND CHARLES MENEES MARRIED JUNE 15
1911 AT ME CHURCH SOUTH MUSKOGEE
OKLA STOP COMING HOME ON KATY WILL
FIRST STAY IN ST LOUIS STOP PLEASE SET
UP COBDEN RECEPTION WEEKEND JUNE
25 OR JULY 2 STOP INVITE SPENCER ME-
NEES FAMILIES PLUS OTHERS STOP
BLANCHE AND CHARLES MENEES
MUSKOGEE OKLA

MR MRS ADAM ROBEY   JUNE 16 1911
4926 MCPHERSON ST   SAINT LOUIS MO

DEAR ROBEY FAMILY STOP BLANCHE
SPENCER AND CHARLES MENEES MARRIED
JUNE 15 1911 MUSKOGEE OKLA STOP WILL
TAKE KATY TRAIN TO ST LOUIS JUNE 17
1911 STOP WILL STAY AND VISIT FEW DAYS
HOTEL OR OTHER STOP
BLANCHE AND CHARLES MENEES
MUSKOGEE OKLA

The next afternoon they took a horse cab and went
to Minnie and Wally's house to return the wedding basket.
Bonnie and Charlie gave heartfelt thanks to the couple for
the wedding ceremony and picnic. They also explained their

plans to depart that evening.

Bonnie and Charlie boarded the KATY Flier for St. Louis. Charlie stored their three wooden trunks behind the stove at the front of the car, since they were too big for the overhead racks. Bonnie carried her carpetbag and purse to their seats. She carefully checked that her vocabulary book, Bonnet Book, and the Threadgill postcard were in her purse.

Charlie and Bonnie held hands, watching the sunset over the rolling hills of the prairie. The grasses were still a pale green but took on golden hues as the sun sank into the western sky. Charlie was thrilled to be taking Bonnie home as his bride, for he had been in love with her since his first song to her at the pie supper. Bonnie explained that she felt relief to have the wedding completed, although it had not erased her concerns about how two families would participate in their lives. The couple soon slept, Bonnie cradled in Charlie's arm. In spite of occasional stops and the shrill train whistles, they rested peacefully most of the night.

Over the course of the next day, Charlie rushed off the train at stops to buy food—whatever was available. The rest of the time they held hands and watched the miles go by.

The tired couple arrived in St. Louis on Sunday night and checked into the Union Station Hotel. Earlier Bonnie had heard from Bertha that there was mail for them in St. Louis, so they felt compelled to stop there, rather than travel through to Cobden.

"This all feels a bit strange but exciting to me," said

Bonnie, eating cheese, bread, and apples in bed. "We will be going to a new house—the Robeys have moved—and they will meet my new husband. I will be returning as an adult now, not a nursemaid. It may be awkward."

"I am sure they will welcome us into their home," offered Charlie, patting her hand.

Charlie has never been a servant, Bonnie thought. *But I still so love Beth and Alma.*

The next morning they left their luggage at the hotel and took a horse cab to 4926 McPherson, a three-story, red-brick structure with bay windows and a grand covered entry framed by stone pillars. It was one of the homes built for the World's Fair.

Bonnie knocked. She felt uncertain as she stood at the threshold, wearing a hat from her trunk and holding her husband's arm. He wore his three-piece suit. Together they looked like a downtown couple on a Forest Park stroll.

Mr. Robey answered the door, his initial look of surprise turning to welcome as he recognized Blanche.

"Hello, Mr. Robey. I've come to visit your new house. I want to introduce to you my husband, Charles Menees. Call him Charlie."

"Welcome! Geneva, please come see Blanche!" Mr. Robey stepped aside and extended his arm to usher them inside.

Mrs. Robey, cool as always, entered the room with a slight smile. "How lovely to see you. And this must be your husband, Mr. Charles Menees. We received your telegram. When did you arrive?"

"We arrived last night and checked into the Union Station Hotel. And I changed my name to Bonnie in Oklahoma, so you can now call me Bonnie," she explained.

"Well, Bonnie, many things have changed since we last saw you fourteen months ago. Beth is eighteen—she will be going to college in the fall—and Alma is attending Central High on Grand Boulevard. We have also started a small restaurant with Greta as the cook! As a matter of fact, we were just about to leave to go open for lunch."

Mr. Robey turned to his wife. "Geneva, you should go ahead to the restaurant, then send the carriage back for me. I will take Mr. Menees to Union Station to retrieve their luggage."

Mrs. Robey departed, and Mr. Robey continued.

"We are renting this house but hope to buy it someday. We have a spare bedroom for your visit," he said, raising his eyes to the ceiling. "Geneva's parents, the Langs, and their maid, Lara Doyle, live on the first floor, and we have the second and third floors. Both girls wanted a room on the third floor and love their young-adult privacy. They insisted on setting up the third-floor spare bedroom for you."

The carriage was soon back out in front, ready for the next errand.

"Bonnie, I suggest we leave you here to review your mail. Charlie and I will return shortly. I know the girls will want to visit this afternoon."

Mr. Robey handed Bonnie three letters as he went out the door.

Bonnie looked at the three envelopes as she walked down the dark mahogany hallway and ascended the dim stairway. She glanced at the girls' bedrooms, spotting Alma's large hair-bow collection on a dresser and, in Beth's room, a world globe on a floor stand.

Bonnie found the spare bedroom at the back of the house. The room had a trundle bed and a chair—nothing else. She pulled the chair to the window for more light and looked at her mail. She had letters from Angus McGregor, her sister Bertha, and her pa. Dated January 22, 1911, the letter from her pa set her hand trembling. Bonnie had never written to her father, even after she left the Robeys' household. She had received the last letter from him four years ago.

January 22, 1911

Miss Blanche Spencer
4926 McPherson Ave.
St. Louis, Mo.

Dear Blanche,

We are all well and busy. We were all at Sunday School and had a splendid school. The house was nearly full and much interest was manifested—Inez was at the organ. The closing hymn was "I Shall Follow all they

335

say," sung while people stood. Can't you imagine how we all looked? Could you almost hear Merwin and Lamont's strong, clear voices as they sang the words of that dear song? We had to organize a new class for beginners, and a committee of teachers selected Ma for its teacher.

[Two more pages followed concerning the work of cousins and friends in Oraville and Murphysboro.]

I saw Leo at the Institute, and we have had a card from Bertha this week. They are all well. Leo sold his mules and bought another and better span for $375. We killed Harry yesterday, and he was fine (to eat). Don't you think we are getting along nicely? Next summer when you come home we will have a world of nice flowers and will have the house repaired some. Be a good girl, Blanche. Remember we all love you, and that those big tough boys of ours think there is no one like Blanche.

Lovingly, Pa

Bonnie's eyes flooded with tears; she could hardly read through them. At long last, this was the *real* letter about ordinary family events and people, the letter she had never received since leaving home on the train nine years ago. The letter was about Sunday school, chickens and mules, and people's everyday lives. Pa wrote to her as if she were still fourteen years old, ready to tussle on the living room floor with her brothers. The ordinariness of the letter was an overwhelming end to her nine years of abandonment.

Bonnie sat perfectly still, holding the letter with both hands. She had a flashing memory of sitting on the floor with her brothers during the *Robinson Crusoe* readings. She thought about the loss of family, love, contact, and togetherness. All of that loss for so many years, it smothered her, it overwhelmed her. She stumbled blindly to the bed and collapsed. Lying on her side, she held her head, deep sobs coming from her throat.

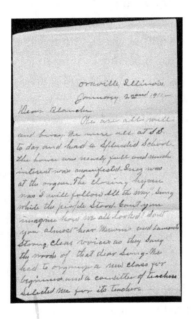

That was how Charlie found her when he returned. He put the trunk in a corner and sat on the side of the bed.

"What's happened dear?" he asked.

She limply pointed to the letter on the chair. He walked over, picked up the letter, and read it, leaning against the window frame. The letter seemed so ordinary that Charlie was perplexed by Bonnie's reaction. He knew she had lived with a second family, but her father talked about family gossip, a summer visit. Charlie again sat on the bed to comfort her. She was drowning in a swirl of emotions about lost love and lost years.

Beth and Alma came home from school, bounded up the stairs to the third floor, and burst through the door. Charlie got up, ushered them out, and introduced himself in a whisper. He explained that he and Bonnie were supposed to go with them to the restaurant for dinner, but that Bonnie had just received very bad news in a letter. He suggested they take the carriage without them, and maybe they could bring back some food for him and Bonnie to eat later. Beth, who was now very tall, seemed hurt and confused. She frowned. Alma's mouth was turned down. All the same, they agreed to go alone and visit with Blanche the next day.

Bonnie alternately cried and slept for several hours. Later, Alma quietly knocked at the door. She carried a box covered with a towel; inside was a plate piled high with warm food and fresh rolls. Charlie ate in the dark, sitting on the chair next to the bed. Bonnie would not eat. In the middle of the night, she drifted into a fitful sleep for several hours.

Bonnie roused on Tuesday, ate leftovers at midday, and came back to life. She took a bath and read the other two letters. Mr. McGregor sent her a list of books about business, and Bertha wanted to schedule the summer visit to Oraville.

I must think this family problem through, Bonnie reasoned. *Why has this letter totally overwhelmed me?*

That afternoon, Bonnie explained to Charlie the lack of contact with her family for nine years. Together they talked and talked about all aspects of Bonnie's personal nightmare. Charlie listened intently, touching Bonnie on the arm but not speaking. After much soul-searching, Bonnie came to realize several things.

Only *she* felt this overwhelming loss. She had been sent away from Oraville, while the family had continued their or- dinary lives. Perhaps they had felt no loss at all, and the family table had just felt less crowded. But maybe Pa felt something?

Only *she* could pull herself out of this depression. She must look for strength and comfort from *within* herself and from Charlie, not from either family. Could this dilemma use a work plan? Probably not. How could a work plan heal a broken heart?

She could not tell the Robeys any of this. It was simply too complicated and implicated them also. As such, it was better left unsaid. She had never described her Spencer fami- ly to the Robeys; they had never asked. They had only wanted an anonymous nursemaid.

In a stroke of clear vision, Bonnie decided to tell the Robeys that the news was about the death of her sister Lelia, which she had not told them about earlier. She felt slightly guilty about this white lie but thought this explanation sim- plest.

Bonnie and Charlie finally went to a family dinner on Tuesday night. She quietly explained the news about the death of her sister, and said she was now rested and well. The elder Robeys nodded respectfully, the sisters held hands tightly under the table. Greta poked her head in to say hello, ending the somber moment.

The newlyweds and the Robeys shared a modest din- ner in a back room of the restaurant, with wonderful food cooked by Greta. Beth and Alma wanted to talk about the move to the new house, which they both loved, especially given their third-floor privacy. And Bonnie began to brighten as she described the Oklahoma First Annual Horse and Hat

Show in detail for the girls. Both leaned toward Bonnie with bright eyes and smiles. Bonnie also mentioned her friendship with Ruby and Willis Keyes to Mr. Robey. He was pleased that his introduction had been a success. He offered Charlie and Bonnie the family carriage for their needs until their departure.

On Wednesday Bonnie and Charlie headed to Soulard Market to find Angus McGregor. Bonnie was eager to share her new husband with her wise teacher. She told Charlie all about the friendly book dealer and his little wagon, the Eckert peaches, and the afternoon with the Christmas carols. Charlie took Bonnie's elbow, barely able to listen to her as he concentrated on avoiding horse dung and the bloody rivulets in front of the butcher's booth. Mr. McGregor recognized Bonnie as she approached on the arm of the handsome man in a three-piece suit. He opened his arms and hugged her as he winked at Charlie.

"Mr. McGregor, this is Charlie Menees, my brand-new husband. I brought him to meet you! Can we take you to lunch?"

"Of course! Let me first pull a tarp over the books and ask the Eckerts to watch the wagon."

The three had lunch at a little German tavern near the market. It was a hot St. Louis summer day, so they chose a sidewalk table with an umbrella, where there was a slight breeze. Mr. McGregor watched Bonnie closely as he followed her tales of hat making for the state fair, managing and then closing the store, and adventures with the cart and pony. He looked at her with a father's pride and more than once reached over to pat her hand.

"Charlie, what are your plans now?" he inquired.

"I have applied to Marshall Field for a transfer to Illinois and hope to get a new assignment soon."

"I see," Mr. McGregor said, as he turned to smile at Bonnie again. "Good, so you both will be back somewhere in Illinois?"

"That's right!" said Bonnie. "So, St. Louis trips may happen now and then!"

"Then we needn't say goodbye!" Mr. McGregor smiled brightly, as they left the restaurant.

Back at the book wagon, Mr. McGregor shook Charlie's hand and gave Bonnie another warm hug. He held her tightly and whispered in her ear, "Remember, Bonnie, you put *yourself* together in these St. Louis and Oklahoma years. Hold on tightly to your self-respect, and do not forget me!"

On Thursday morning Bonnie and Charlie rose early, packed, and, taking Mr. Robey up on his generous offer, took the carriage into Forest Park for a tour before their train departure. St. Louis had been developing the park with permanent attractions after the 1904 fair. Bonnie enthusiastically showed Charlie the Bird Cage, the City Art Museum with scenic overlooks, and the ornate bridges among all of the fabulous fountains and waterfalls in the park.

They arrived at Union Station after lunch, summoned a porter, and headed for their Carbondale train. Bonnie was buoyed by the visit with Mr. McGregor and the exhilarating morning ride through Forest Park. She and Charlie were in a light mood, anticipating another adventure.

As Bonnie settled into her seat on the passenger coach,

her mood unexpectedly turned somber.

"No one knows when we will arrive in Cobden, correct?" she asked with a frown. "Maybe we should stay in a hotel for a day or two. And maybe we can send Bertha a telegram from Carbondale to get the date of the reception and the date of the Spencer family arrival, which is one or two weeks away. Then I can set up a schedule for the reception week."

"Let's see how we feel when we get there. Whatever you want to do to be comfortable is fine with me. We are *already* married, so everything else is secondary and easy to handle, Bonnie. It's not worth getting worried about." Charlie had his arm around Bonnie and put a soothing hand on hers.

"You're right, Charlie. I guess I am over the worst of it. I do not think anything will shock me the way that letter did. You are the constant in my life now, and that is a wonderful comfort to me." She snuggled into his shoulder, and they watched the cornfields fly by.

They arrived at Carbondale in the late afternoon and had just enough time before their train to Cobden to send a telegram to Bertha, alerting her of their imminent arrival. An hour later they were standing in the packing yard next to the Cobden depot.

"Well, we are back in a rural town, and there are no horse cabs," Charlie said, looking uphill at the shops. "I will walk to the hotel on North Front Street to inquire about both a room and a wagon."

Bonnie sat on a loading platform with her back to the sun, watching Charlie head up North Front Street. She noticed new paint and signs on a few storefronts.

I wonder if this town will be my permanent home? If I can just get past this family reunion, I can think about owning a store that sells hats, clothes, and supplies for the whole family. The next two weeks seem almost insurmountable. How can I face the Spencer family?

Charlie and his friend Mike Fuller pulled up with a farm wagon and a horse. The men loaded the trunks and carpetbag, and the three climbed into the front of the wagon.

"Where to?" asked Mike.

"Well, Bonnie, the hotel is full, and I don't think you want to try Phillips House, so let's head to my mother's house."

Bonnie smiled wanly, unsure what to expect from Charlie's mother, whom she had never met.

Mike drove his wagon to West Poplar Street, to the house of Isabelle Menees. Charlie hopped down and headed inside to talk to his mother. He had not sent her a telegram about the marriage.

Many minutes passed. What was Charlie doing? Bonnie tapped her foot and fanned herself, too involved in her own discomfort to talk to Charlie's friend. He seemed aware of the delicate circumstances and gave Bonnie her privacy.

Isabelle finally walked out on the arm of her son. A faint smile on her face, she was tall and lean, in a freshly starched day dress and with her gray hair in a tight bun at the back of her neck. Bonnie thought she held onto Charlie's arm very tightly.

"Welcome, Bonnie Spencer Menees. I understand you and Charles married last week in Oklahoma and came back to have a wedding reception. I did know about this, because your sister Bertha came to visit and explained all of it to me last week. It was a bit of a surprise, but I am happy for you both." She still held onto Charlie, a slight frown creasing her forehead. "I have Charlie's bedroom and two other spare bedrooms in the house. You two can certainly stay here. The reception is on Sunday afternoon, July 2, so everyone will be here next weekend. You sure do have an efficient sister. She is running around Cobden making church reservations and ordering food. Now you will be able to help her!"

Isabelle let go of Charlie's arm and stepped toward the wagon and looked up. "Let's bring you and the luggage inside. I am sure you are exhausted from travel. You will have several days to make plans and catch your breath before your family arrives. Charlie, help her down, and I will escort your new bride into my house!"

Bonnie descended from the wagon, glad she would feel at least somewhat welcome. With a warm smile, she took Isabelle's arm, and the two women walked toward the house. Isabelle hesitantly patted Bonnie's arm.

"It is lovely to get such a warm welcome, Mrs. Menees, and very nice to be back in Cobden!" Bonnie's voice was light, relieved.

"Why don't the two of you wash off the travel dirt while I fix you a light supper? How does that sound?"

A few minutes later they reconvened in the kitchen. Isabelle was humming and setting out plates as Charlie and Bonnie reappeared.

"What a lovely surprise! We really did not know when to expect you," Isabelle said with a genuine smile, as she put cold chicken legs, bread, butter, homemade pickles, and lemonade on the round table.

The three spent a quiet evening sharing Oklahoma stories. Charlie quickly brought up the runaway cart incident, and Bonnie enthusiastically described the whole scene, with Charlie adding details she omitted.

"This all seems so rough-and-tumble for a lovely hat-maker like you. My gracious, it is good Charlie brought you back to Illinois away from those dangers," Isabelle commented.

Bonnie and Charlie did nothing, really, on Friday, planting their feet back into the brown soil of southern Illinois, as they sat in the old two-seat swing in the backyard, listening to the cicadas. Bonnie thought about Mr. McGregor's parting message. Yes, the St. Louis years were lost family years. She had struggled through that pain, taken care of herself, and found a career. She was a much stronger person because of those years. She now had a St. Louis education, usable skills, and big-city sophistication, not to mention social and business savvy and a scrapbook of Wild West adventures. She was young and in good health, and she had a wonderful new husband. With a mighty sigh, she realized she actually *was* somewhat in control of her life!

She thought about the meeting with her pa. He still thought of her as fourteen years old! It might take him weeks or years to accept her as an adult. He would probably never admit that sending her away was a mistake. Would he be able to look her in the eyes? Would they be able to talk to one another? To love one another again? She had no answers to these questions.

Sunday afternoon, Bertha arrived alone in her family wagon. She had left her daughter and husband back at the farm. They would come the following week for the reception.

The sisters spent all afternoon in the rocking swing going over notes for the event, and, of course, catching up.

"It was me who pushed for getting married in Muskogee—I just couldn't imagine myself in an Oraville church, with Pa there giving me away *again*! But this is a secret only for you." Bonnie was firm.

"You absolutely did the right thing, Bonnie. Muskogee was by far the best choice. This reception does not have to be really formal—no wedding clothes—just lemonade and good wishes. There is no Methodist Church in Cobden, but there is the lovely Presbyterian Church up on the hill with a nice auditorium space that will work. I asked three people to make cookies, and the church ladies will provide lemonade. How does that sound?"

"Bertha, that room is where Charlie and I met!" Bonnie laughed and hugged Bertha.

"Now," Bertha frowned, "whom do we invite? Of course, I invited the Spencer family. But I also invited all of the relatives in Vergennes, knowing that since Cobden is about ten hours away, most of those folks will not come—but some might. Isabelle Menees has a few cousins near Carbondale, and we should invite these people. And I invited the Silas Brown family, our neighbors, whom you met. I think we should also invite some Cobden folks, since you both lived here."

"The hardest part, Blanche—I mean Bonnie—will be for you to meet family members you have not seen for nine years." She sighed and put her hands to her cheeks. "I have written for them to arrive on Wednesday, so you will have several days to get reacquainted with everyone. I think we should have a Thursday get-together to get all of the stories told before the reception."

"Fine," Bonnie covered her eyes with both hands. "I know this will happen. I just have no idea how difficult it will be."

Monday and Tuesday were taken up with laundry and local invitations. When Bertha left for the farm, Blanche lovingly spent many hours making hats for women for her own wedding reception. First she made hats for herself, Isabelle, and Bertha. She could barely remember her mother Lou, but she wanted to make her a hat suitable for the reception. Lelia was gone. And was Grace a little girl or a teenager now? Her wooden trunk was full of pattern hats and copious supplies. She could still assemble hats until the final day.

The frugal Spencer family had borrowed a wagon and mule for their trip and left at dawn on Wednesday, stopping briefly for lunch. Everyone wondered what Blanche and her new husband would look like. Lamont asked if they should kiss her or give her a hug or just shake hands.

They pulled up in front of Isabelle's house about four thirty. Bonnie, with Charlie by her side, watched in the shadows from the living room as the family alighted. She had carefully dressed in a black skirt and a long sleeve, tailored white blouse. Her hair was in the usual pompadour, but, whereas it had been golden in her youth, it was now almost brown. Her heart pounded, and her breathing was shallow. She squeezed Charlie's arm.

Merwin looked six feet tall, instead of just above Pa's belt line, which was how Bonnie remembered him. But she recognized him instantly from the shape of his nose. Lamont was not as tall as his older brother, but he had his same goofy smile, which made Bonnie's heart skip a beat. There was another girl, taller than Lamont—could that be Grace, Bonnie wondered. She didn't recognize that person at all. Next came her mother, who now had rounded shoulders and gray hair. Then Pa came into view. Once a tower of strength to her, he was now a bit stooped. He walked slowly, hardly looked up, and had white hair with hints of red.

Bonnie gasped. She choked and put her hand to her mouth. Tears filled her eyes and blurred her vision. Charlie held her firmly around the waist, supporting her as her knees threatened to give out.

She regrouped and instinctively held back as Charlie eased her out the front door. Standing on the porch, she clawed at the screen door behind her. She could not move. She could not go toward these people. She could not focus. A heart flutter made her light-headed.

All smiles, Merwin and Lamont rushed toward Bonnie, but she saw them as if in slow motion. Merwin tried to grab her from Charlie and pick her up, but she held firmly to Charlie. The boys instead enveloped Bonnie and Charlie in a friendly group hug. Her head buried in Charlie's shoulder, Bonnie wet his jacket with her copious tears. She only heard mewing sounds, like puppies, and felt the warmth of many arms.

The others stood by, as stunned to see brown-haired Bonnie as she was to see them. Grace did not recognize her at all and continued to hold onto the wagon.

Ever so slowly, Charlie turned Bonnie toward him, reaching over to brush away her tears as she was still weeping and sniffling. Pa and Ma came together as they approached Bonnie. Charlie released Bonnie's waist, and her parents engulfed her in an enormous hug. Ma's face was full of tears, Pa's was white, his mouth open but speechless. He was holding a beautiful and sophisticated weeping lady, not the fourteen-year-old he carried in his heart.

"Look at you!" Merwin burst into the group. "Fancy hair and fancy clothes, a big-city lady!"

"Well, I guess the blackberry picker is gone, and we have a librarian instead," giggled Lamont.

Everyone tried to smile at the feeble joke and looked sideways at each other. The tension gradually faded, and everyone wiped their tears, reaching in to touch Bonnie.

"This is Charles Menees, my husband. Call him Charlie," Bonnie said softly but proudly. Charlie stood up straight, flashed his winning smile, and looked at the many faces.

Just then the front door swung open.

"And this is *my* mother, Isabelle Menees. Mother, the Spencer family of Oraville just arrived!"

"Bless me!" Isabelle put a hand to her chest upon seeing all the tear-stained faces. "Welcome to Cobden, everyone. May I invite you inside to wash up, then share dinner with me and these smiling newlyweds."

Everyone crowded inside. Pa sent the boys and Grace for packages and luggage. She had light-brown hair and eyes that darted around the strange place.

The group of eight crowded around the kitchen table and passed around steaming bowls of ham and beans, which had been on the stove all day. And there was cornbread, too, mountains of cornbread!

Everyone reached for the hot cornbread as the conversation started. Bonnie felt warm skin touch both her elbows, and a warm arm when she reached for the cornbread. She heard someone gulp down a whole glass of water. She reveled in these ordinary experiences, brushing up against family at the table, listening to the sounds of sharing a meal. She could not have imagined what this moment would be like.

There were awkward silences as the Spencers, famished from their travels, slurped a bit on the beans and murmured on their bites of warm cornbread. Bonnie stared in awe at her reunited family noisily eating with her in a stranger's kitchen. Pa, across from Bonnie, could not even hold his spoon, which hung off his fingers. He kept trying to take a bite of his beans but could only look at Bonnie then down again.

Bonnie was watching Pa when, unexpectedly, Charlie tapped his spoon to his glass, looking around the table.

"I have a friendly family announcement," said Charlie. "We both have many stories to tell about our adventures the past year in Oklahoma. But the first thing that happened was that a shy girl named Blanche turned into a cowgirl and changed her name to Bonnie! She is still officially Blanche on our marriage license, but otherwise, she is Bonnie, the Prairie Rose of Oklahoma!"

"Oh my," said Pa and Ma together.

"Whoopee! Ride 'em cowgirl!" squealed Lamont "Did you ride horses and shoot critters?"

"Yes, I did both!" Bonnie welcomed the levity and lifted her hands in the air. "Let's save the rest of the Oklahoma tales for tomorrow."

Grace did not speak, instead just staring at the tall and

lovely lady, her so-called sister, with the dashing husband.

The Spencers ate all of the beans and cornbread, and the meal ended in record time. Isabelle, who was used to eating in a more leisurely fashion, stood up and wiped her hands on her apron as people pushed back their chairs. Nonetheless, she was proud to host and proud that her meal was so well received.

She showed the family to the two upstairs furnished bedrooms and set out a pallet of blankets and a pillow for Grace. By dark, the Spencers had all washed and were tucked into bed, exhausted and full, but happy and curious about the bride and groom. Isabelle returned to her kitchen and happily washed dishes for her new family.

Bonnie and Charlie lay awake a long time, processing the family arrival. It had been hard, but only initially. The brothers had bumbled forward and made things more loving and less tense. Bonnie was in a state of sensory overload with all the warm touching and slurping and even her parents' gray hair. She had not yet talked to her father, but she could sense his confusion, and she knew their talking would unfold slowly. The nine-year loss and everyone's changes would be so hard to get beyond.

Once she had spoken to Charlie about all her observations and hopes and wishes, she began to calm down. Charlie turned on his back, put her hand over his heart, and fell asleep. Bonnie took a very deep breath and felt her whole body relax.

There are not words to easily describe the blood bond shared with a family. This tie is a bond of survival and warmth and shelter and comfort, and it is comprised of smells, sounds, and tastes, and the deep caring we call love. There is no other bond quite like it.

Bonnie's tie to the Spencers had been broken by her pa when he sent her away on the train to St. Louis. His heart broke the minute she was gone. But now, almost nine years later, Bonnie and the Spencers had begun the process of mending their family bonds.

This awkward beginning was all Bonnie needed, except for talking to Pa.

The family reunited sharing meals and stories. On Sunday they came together for the wedding photographs and the reception.

Around noon the family gathered in Isabelle's living room. Lou, Bertha, Isabelle, and two Vergennes women all had new hats—each made by Bonnie—which they wore with pride, as if they were about to be in an Easter parade. Lamont had on a new suit with short pants, Merwin was in an Army uniform, and everyone else was dressed nicely for the reception.

Before it began, Charlie steered everyone down to the Cobden depot for a formal photograph. As Charlie and the photographer organized the wedding group around a cart in front of the Cobden train depot sign, Bonnie walked around to the far side of the cart. She put her left hand on the cart rail and grabbed her long black skirt with her right hand. From behind, someone grabbed her elbow to help her up into the cart. Bonnie steadied herself and turned to find her father's face just inches away. Pa looked into her eyes sweetly and softly kissed her right cheek, as he squeezed her elbow.

She looked squarely back into her father's smiling eyes and felt all of his love and support and fatherly concern. She pulled her hand up from her skirt and circled his neck in a loving embrace. Then, with his support again on her elbow, she climbed into the cart as Charlie ascended on the other side.

Bonnie and Charlie sat in the wooden cart behind a mule with white satin reins. A sign on the side of the cart said, "We're Married Now." Bonnie had redesigned her white wedding bonnet with lavish dark-blue bows and red and blue silk flowers. She had also added a net veil, based on a sketch in the Bonnet Book.

For the first photograph, Pa moved back with the photographer, brushing away the tears of joy on his cheek. At the moment the photograph was taken, Bonnie glanced over at her father, then impulsively grabbed the white satin reins of the mule, as she experienced a powerful upwelling of emotions in her chest.

I can *guide my life and my destiny, she thought. I have a useful profession helping women, an energetic husband, and now a loving father. Today is a special and sacred celebration of new and old family ties for me. I will, indeed, celebrate all of these. My life is surrounded with family love, and my heart is at peace.*

Author's Notes

During research for *The Bonnet Book*, I tapped many resources, including family heirlooms, journals, and photographs; Internet sources, field trips and interviews, and various historical city resources; and books, poems, and songs of the era. The timeline and the story twisted and turned as new information surfaced. The final story is the one you just read. I replaced a standard bibliography with the notes below in order to share the authentic details of the story development with readers of the book.

Chapter 1: Brush Arbor

One morning in Texas in March 2015, Mary Kay Menees, my mother, sat up in bed shouting, "Brush arbor, Nancy! Brush arbor! Blanche performed in a brush arbor, not a canvas tent!" And so it began, the search to uncover as much reality as possible for Blanche's story.

Further information about the Temperance Camp attendants and their behavior came from Mary Kay, who attended similar weeklong Chautauqua events as a child in and around Jacksonville, Illinois.

I found another research person in Illinois, Dr. Susan Whitemountain, who greatly assisted me in finding information about Blanche. Based on family journals, census and other legal documents, as well as newspaper articles and ads, I continuously revised the story timeline. Below is the final factual timeline of the book.

Aug. 1902	Robey family lives at 4362 West Belle Avenue, St. Louis.
	Blanche takes orphan train to St. Louis.
1903, 1907	Keyes Livery in St. Louis in three locations.
	(*St. Louis City Directory 1903*, ——— *1907*)
	(*St. Louis County Directory 1903*, ——— *1907*)
Summer 1904	1904 St. Louis World's Fair.
Summer 1906	Robey family moves to 5259A McPherson Street, St. Louis.
1908-09	Blanche Spencer probably at Rosenthal-Sloan workshops and apprenticeships in St. Louis.
July 1909	Keyes' new livery in Oklahoma City. (Newspaper advertisement)
1910	Maison Française French Millinery listed at 211 South Harvey Street. (*Oklahoma City Directory*)
Feb. 6, 1910	Newspaper advertisement: "First Ever Oklahoma City Horse Show and Hat Show."
Apr. 1910	Blanche in Cobden, Illinois, at Phillips House. (Census records)

May 1910	"Bony" Spencer registered in Prince Rupert Hotel in *Oklahoma City Directory 1822–1995*. She is not listed in 1911.
Oct. 4, 1910	First Annual Horse Show at Oklahoma State Fair in Oklahoma City.
Oct. 6, 1910	Newspaper article: "Marshall Field of Chicago announces new Oklahoma territory salesman Charles Menees."
Jan. 1911	Robey family moves to 4926 McPherson Street but is not listed as owner until 1913. (Census records)
Jan. 22, 1911	Austin Spencer's letter to Blanche at 4926 McPherson Street, St. Louis.
Jun. 15, 1911	Wedding of Charles Menees and Blanche Spencer in Muskogee Oklahoma. (Wedding certificate, W. M. Wilson, church official)
Summer 1911	Wedding reception photograph in Cobden, Illinois. Vivian Modglin (Parrish) not in photograph, reason unknown.

Chapter 2: Shoelaces

I visited Oraville, Illinois, in 2015. The town is even smaller today than it was in the time of Austin Spencer, Blanche's father. The same streets exist, and one road still goes out to Rattlesnake Creek. The Spencer home is gone. The house did face the railroad tracks, and there is a faint trace of the railroad right-of-way in town, as well as in Google Maps aerial photographs. Steven L. Grace of Ava, Illinois, served as my local railroad consultant for the book, sending me "The Mudline Railroad Report," an article in the *Jacksonian Ventilator* (new series 116, June 2004) and his own "Oraville Area Railroads" report (June 8, 2015).

The church that also served as the school was shared by four different religious groups, each having Sunday use once a month, as stated in the Curwen La Monte Hoover handout entitled "History of Oraville United Methodist Church" (October 2, 1977). It was furnished to me by Sandra Holliday at the Jackson County Historical Center in Murphysboro, Illinois.

Lead docent Cheryl Ranchino Trench gave me a guided tour of the Purdy One Room School at John A. Logan Community College in Carterville, Illinois, on March 26, 2015. The Purdy School layout became Austin Spencer's classroom at the back of the Oraville United Methodist Church.

Chapter 3: Hand Ballet

In 2015 I spent an afternoon in Murphysboro, Illinois. The old train depot was dilapidated but undergoing renovation. I photographed the actual colored-glass windows and just knew that Blanche had seen these and experienced their magic.

John Shontz, coordinator of the "Orphan Train Project Making A Difference" project, worked with me throughout book development to give me accurate train schedules. We worked together for two years on all train schedules in the book.

Chapter 4: Orphan Train

My mother, a teacher and a storyteller, figured out that Blanche Spencer was an orphan train child, because Blanche was sent to strangers in a strange city in 1902 during the height of the Charles Loring Brace program. At the time, these children were not called "orphan train children." This is a name given to them by history.

It is not known why Austin Spencer sent Blanche away, although his total salary as Oraville school principal in 1900 was sixteen dollars per month for a family of eight people, including six children, according to Vivian Parrish, quoted in Bonita Troutt's article, "One Room Schools," *Southern Illinoisan*, Southern Illinois section (Carbondale-Herrin-Murphysboro, June 4, 1973). Also, Austin was unemployed for eight months in 1900. In the story, I made my best guess about why Austin made the decision.

To research the trains, I rode historic ones, including the Iron Mountain Railway in Jackson, Missouri. I also visited the historic Kirkwood, Missouri, renovated train depot and visited the Museum of Transportation in St. Louis, Missouri to view the restored Wabash No. 573 engine. John Shontz confirmed that No. 573 traveled up and down the state of Illinois for many years.

Other orphan-train images came from Marilyn Irving Holt's *The Orphan Train: Placing Out of America* (University of Nebraska Press, 1992) and M. D. Patrick and E. C. Trickle's *Orphan Trains to Missouri* (University of Missouri Press, 1997). The other orphans and the placing-out agent and her orphanage are imagined.

The small second depot in Belleville is pictured in *Belleville Illustrated* ("Illinois Central Train Depot," Reid-Fitch

Publishing Co., St. Louis, Missouri, 1905; reprinted in Belleville, Illinois, for St. Clair County Historical Society, 1986).

Chapter 5: Union Station

One day of St. Louis research was spent exploring Union Station, which I visited many times as a child. The station is now a renovated tourist attraction with a hotel and many shops but few, if any, train tracks. The Grand Hall remains unchanged and was the largest train depot in the world when it opened in 1894. I walked up and down the stairways, finding the brass banisters, stained-glass windows, tiled ground-floor bathroom, and the theater space off the Grand Hall, all of which are mentioned in the book. The Union Station orphan event is imagined.

Chapters 6, 7, and 8

In 1910 Blanche was taken in by an Austrian family and lived with them from age fourteen to twenty-two. I gave the family the name Robey. I traced the original family through census records to the addresses listed in the Chapter 1 timeline. The first residence, gleaned from a 1900 census document, was at 4362 West Belle Place, which no longer exists. The names of Robey family members and servants have been changed. My mother recalled hearing that Blanche was given rags to wear and slept in a closet. The flat and the family routines are all imagined. My mother became close friends with the two daughters when they were adults, and their childhood personalities are based on their actual adult personalities. The names of my family members are all their actual names.

The St. Louis German population was forty-five thousand by 1860. The Germans brought with them their taste for lager, and they established local beer companies, storing their beer in caves below St. Louis before refrigeration was invented. This group of people is still a very strong and active civic influence in the city. Their taverns around the market still exist.

Eugene Field School at 4455 Olive Street was built in 1901 and converted to condominiums in 2016.

Chapter 9: Soulard Market

The factual information for Soulard Market came from my personal interview with Jerry Frandeka of Frandeka Butchers at Soulard Market on October 21, 2015. Jerry's grandfather founded the business, and Jerry described the market to me as his grandfather saw it. He also showed me antique photographs on the walls of the present building.

Eckert peaches are famous throughout the Midwest. I traveled to the Eckert's roadside stand in Belleville, Illinois as a child. The farm is still in existence, run by seventh-generation family members. I have no evidence that they had a booth at Soulard Market.

Chapter 10: Black Beauty

Book reading is the backbone of my family from many generations back, perhaps starting with Austin Spencer. Blanche's interest in books and in self-education through newspapers was the reality of her entire life. Blanche's young-adult struggle to bring books into her life is fictional, but perhaps not far from the truth. As a child, I saw newspaper clippings tacked on Blanche's dining room wall with hatpins, and Blanche often discussed what she learned about current events from these articles.

The oldest Robey daughter became a librarian in St. Louis, probably as a result of Blanche's tutelage.

Below is a list of children's books referenced in *The Bonnet Book*:

Alice's Adventures in Wonderland and Through the Looking Glass, Lewis Carroll (1865)

The Adventures of Robinson Crusoe, Daniel Defoe (1719)

Black Beauty, Anna Sewell (1877)

Heidi, Johanna Spyri (1881)

The Adventures of Huckleberry Finn, Mark Twain (1885)

The Adventures of Tom Sawyer, Mark Twain (1876)

Poetry was also a strong component of Blanche Spencer's education program, starting with "The Drunkard," which she could still recite in 1984, when she was ninety-six years old. The original tiny Bonnet Book diary contains pages and pages of poems and life-improvement quotes that Blanche wrote down as part of her self-education program. Blanche could recite many full-length poems all her life. I have listed below the major poems we remember. I did not attempt to weave them all into the story.

"The Drunkard," anonymous Temperance poem

"Kentucky Belle," Constance Fenimore Woolson

(1873)

"Maud Muller," John Greenleaf Whittier (1856)

"Presentiment," authorship unclear; attributions found to both Currer, Ellis, and Acton Bell, as well as to Charlotte, Emily, and Anne Bronte (1846). This poem is my addition in the book.

"Which Shall It Be," Ethel Lynn Eliot Beers (1827–79)

Chapter 11: 1904 St. Louis World's Fair

Mary Kay Menees is certain Blanche went to the 1904 World's Fair with the Robey family. My research uncovered that Rosenthal-Sloan Millinery Company had the only millinery booth at the fair. Blanche's encounter with this booth and the hats is speculation, but it is likely that it happened. My 1904 World's Fair information was obtained from the following sources:

www.mo.history.org/exhibit/FAIR/WF/HTML/Overview

www.1904World'sFairSociety.org

www.atthefair.homestead.com/1904.html

www.en.wikipedia.org/wiki/Saint+Louis+Art+Museum

www.washingtonmo.com/1904/is.htm

Additionally, I spent a morning at the Missouri History Museum of Jefferson Memorial, 1 Forest Park Road, reviewing the world's fair exhibits and photographs.

St. Louis's Forest Park was part of my own childhood, since our family lived across the street from the zoo in the park. The reflecting ponds and the fountains, the Palace of Art, the Bird Cage with its concrete tunnel—these are strong childhood memories for me.

I discovered that Annie Oakley attended the 1904 World's Fair, then took the liberty of speculating that Blanche saw and was inspired by her. Annie Oakley's quotes are from:

www.newsmax.com/girls-with-guns-quotes-annie-oakley/22015/04/16/id/638984/

www.clickamerica.com/media/newspapers/annie-oakley-why-women-should-shoot-1894' (para. 7)

Chapter 12: Sweet Sisters

Except for when they took her to the World's Fair, Mary Kay Menees believes the Robey family never let Blanche out of the flat for extended periods of time until the Rosenthal-Sloan hat workshops. I felt that her first seven years in the flat must have been very isolated. Greta O'Malley, Angus McGregor, and the Sweet Sisters are my inventions—men and women introduced into Blanche's isolated life to bring love and normality into her world. Mary Kay Menees named Angus McGregor, and I patterned him somewhat after my father, Charles Menees, Blanche's older son. (She had two sons. The younger was named Robert Menees.)

Blanche's historical records included the postcard of

the Rosenthal-Sloan Millinery Company building exterior, and it was common family knowledge that this was where she learned hat making. The interior lobby description is from a 1909 picture postcard captioned, "Flower Map and Writing Room Rosenthal-Sloan Millinery Company." The Rosenthal-Sloan employee names are fictionalized.

Todd Marshall is an invented brother of the Keyes Livery family.

Lelia's death actually occurred in 1905, not 1907, according to the *Belleville News Democrat*, volume 22, issue 246, page 7. All telegrams and letters in the book are my invention, except the January 22, 1911 letter from Austin to Blanche, which I have in my possession.

Chapter 13: The Bonnet Book

While I was doing research at Mary Kay Menees' condominium, she tossed me a tiny brown booklet, saying "I don't know if this is important, but maybe it is!" When I saw the book's pages of hat sketches and notes, I immediately named it "The Bonnet Book" and knew it would be the touchstone of the story. The actual sketches in that tiny book are the basis of almost all the hat descriptions in the story, including the girls' hat, which is also described in Vivian Modglin Parrish's November 1971 journal. Imagine my surprise when I found Vivian's description of her precious hat, then found the *actual design* in the Bonnet Book! I was equally astounded to find winning hats described in the Oklahoma State Fair newspaper articles that matched sketches in the Bonnet Book! The Pretty Miss hat was sketched in the tiny Bonnet Book. The hat history in the Bonnet Book diary enriched the book story over and over.

An interesting historical article about hat-making workshops was the basis of my descriptions for Blanche's workshops: "In the Millinery School," *Kansas City Star*, volume 27, issue 160, page 9 (Kansas City, Missouri, February 24, 1907).

Chapter 14: St. Louis Farewells

The *Sidney* riverboat trip is my inspired tale of Blanche's metamorphosis from nursemaid and servant to independent woman. I found the *Sidney* at www.steamboats.com/museum/jc.html. The *Sidney* was built in 1880 and was still in service in 1910. It was later rebuilt and renamed *Washington*. I took this Mississippi River trip on a boat named *Becky Thatcher*. The riverboat scenes were edited by retired US Navy Captain Norma Lee Hackney of Anna, Illinois.

Chapter 15: Cobden Color

The actual dates of the Cobden apprenticeship are derived from United States census data about both Blanche Spencer and Charles Menees. The exact store in which Blanche worked is unknown, but a hat-shop photo included in the book is the inspiration for the Cobden store.

In May 2017 I interviewed Mrs. Allie Jane Miller Davis, the granddaughter of Mrs. Allie Miller, the proprietor of Phillips House. We found Blanche listed in an April 1910 census document for Cobden's Phillips House. The lively details of this boardinghouse, the music box, and the personality of Henry Miller, Allie Jane's uncle, are derived from this interview. I spent an exciting morning in Allie Jane's living room hearing tales about Phillips House, and she suggested I photograph the rental sign on the table between our interview seats.

Since music was important to both Charlie and Bonnie when they were married, this must have also been the case when they met. The depiction of Charlie, his wonderful tenor voice, and his lifelong participation in singing groups came from Mary Kay Menees, his daughter-in-law. She and I conjured up the pie-supper introduction. The introductory song came to me in a dream. Below is the list of songs that appear in the book:

"Away in a Manger," William J. Kirkpatrick (music, 1895) and James R. Murray (lyrics, 1887)

"By the Light of the Silvery Moon," Gus Edwards (music) and Edward Madden (lyrics, 1909)

"Deck the Halls," Welsh New Year's Eve carol (music, 1794) and Thomas Oliphant (lyrics, 1862)

"Let Me Call You Sweetheart," Leo Friedman (music) and Beth Slater Whitson (lyrics, 1910)

"My Bonnie Lies Over the Ocean," Traditional Scottish folk song (1881)

"My Gal Sal," Paul Dresser (1905)

"O Tannenbaum," 16th century German folk song (music) and Ernst Anschutz (lyrics, 1824)

"Row, Row, Row Your Boat," English nursery rhyme (1852)

"Sunbonnet Sue," Gus Edwards (music) and Will D. Cobb (lyrics, 1908)

Chapter 16: Sunbonnets

The scissors incident regarding young Vivian is in her personal journal (November 19, 1971). However, the circumstances of the incident and the wagon rides are imagined.

Chapter 17: Heading to Oklahoma

The Eton jacket is from the following webpage: www.historymuseum.ca/cma/exhibitions/cpm.catalog.cat2502be.

The Audubon movement information regarding bird conservation and environmental education is from the Audubon movement section of the following webpage: www.americanhistory.si.edu/feather/ftam.htm.

Chapter 18: KATY Texas Special

The history of the K T Y railroad is about one hundred years old and quite convoluted. As best I can tell, the railroad was called KATY at the time of Blanche's journey.

In reality, the Keyes family had three livery stables in St. Louis, Missouri, according to the *St. Louis City and County Directories* for 1903 and 1907. The 5263 Delmar location was a relatively short distance from the Robeys' three residences, so it is probable that a carriage rental agreement existed between the two families.

The friendship between Ruby Keyes and Blanche is imagined, because of the closeness in their ages.

Our family never knew how Blanche obtained the pony

and cart, but we know they existed. Bonnie would never have been able to afford to rent them, so the relationship with the Keyes family seems like a probable way for her to have gotten access to them.

Chapter 19: Ruby and Darling

The name of Bonnie's pony, Darling, is referenced in Mary Kay's Elder Hostel Report "Angel" (October 23, 2001).

The small wooden trunk sits in Mary Kay's living room, next to the fireplace. It is the same size and as described in the story. Mary Kay kept the trunk for many years in a canvas bag. The trunk was in such poor condition that she referred to it as a "pile of sticks." Then she found Lucille (Lou) Findley of Jacksonville, Illinois, who loved to restore old trunks. Lou saved the wallpaper lining sample, felt the trunk had family significance, and encouraged Mary Kay to hold on to it.

In the 1910 *Oklahoma City Directory,* we found "Bony Spencer" registered at the Prince Rupert Hotel, 407 South Robinson, in *U.S. City Directories 1822–1995*. We found Maison Française French Millinery at 211 South Harvey in the *Daily Oklahoman,* volume 22, issue 19, page 11 (Oklahoma City, July 3, 1910), republished on genealogybank.com, copyright 2004 by the American Antiquarian Society. This address is just a few blocks from the hotel. I invented the hat-shop owner and environs and renamed the shop Paris Hats.

"Oklahoma City is to have a horse show. That means, also, of course, a hat show. The milliners and dress makers see business ahead." This was in the *Daily Oklahoman*, volume 21, issue 258, page 6 (Oklahoma City, February 25, 1910).

In March 2016 I visited Pat Morgan of Morgan Carriage Works in Oak View, California. Together we pulled out two small carriages that would have worked for a single person, and I instinctively gravitated to the Meadowbrook cart, which I used in the story. The Meadowbrook cart did exist in 1900, and I found several historical photographs of this exact cart. Pat Morgan was extremely helpful, providing me with carriage photos and vocabulary words, as well as stories of runaway carts. I am very grateful for the enriching hours we spent together at his compound.

Ruby's role in planning the first annual horse show at the state fair is imagined. Ruby and her husband's interest in horses and horse racing and their participation in the state fair are real, as shown in the *Daily Oklahoman,* volume 23, issue 12, page 10 article entitled "Hotly Contested Interest . . ." (Oklahoma City, October 5, 1911). Additional information was obtained from the "Gay Night" story referenced below.

Linda Baker of Circle G Carriages in Dallas, Texas, told me that any woman traveling on the prairie around 1900 would have carried a gun. Her advice prompted me to include Annie Oakley in the story and also include the gun-shooting lessons and adventures on the prairie. Karl Gross, member of the Sunnyvale Rod and Gun Club in Sunnyvale, California, showed me historical guns, taught me to shoot a gun, and edited the shooting lesson in the book.

Chapter 20: Opening Night

Blanche, my Grandma Bonnie, took me to several Illinois State Fairs when I was a child. Of course, I did not know then of her Oklahoma State Fair adventures. But this childhood exposure certainly inspired my colorful chapter "Opening Night." The chapter was reviewed by Mrs. Marilyn Meisenheimer in Jonesboro, Illinois, for its authenticity regarding how horses are represented.

Bonnie had pages of hat-supply lists in the Bonnet Book, and I am all but certain these are from the traveling hat-business days.

Dr. Susan Whitemountain found several articles about the entertainment and horse show events at the actual First Annual State Fair Opening Night on October 4, 1910. The following articles describe the horse entertainment events of Midway Carnival, Morris & Co., the Bedini family:

"Big Horse Show is New Feature for Oklahoma," *Daily Ardmoreite* 1st ed. (Ardmore, Okla., Tues., Aug. 16, 1910).

"Fun and Frolic is Part of Oklahoma State Fair," *Daily Ardmoreite* 1st ed. (Ardmore, Okla., Sun., Aug. 21, 1910).

This article describes women's riding outfits, winners, and society costumes and hats: "Society in Gay Night at Show," *Daily Oklahoman,* volume 22, issue III (Oklahoma City, Okla., Tues., Oct. 4, 1910): 10.

"Turn Out" information is from "Presenting A Winning Picture" (March 10, 2007) at: www.users.vermontel.net/~greenall/documents/PresentingaWinningPicture w.pdf.

Picture postcards of the state fair racetrack grandstand and sidesaddle jumping were additionally helpful.

Clara Alden's white hat is from www.thevictorianstore.com. Specifically, the hat is number 14020NB, "White Riding Hat with White Stripe."

Clara Alden's black hat is shown here: www.gothic_life/gothic-hats/image/6/.

The two hats listed above are the only hats in the story not found in the original Bonnet Book.

The millinery surprise of my life concerns the descriptions of Ruby Keyes' riding hat in the *Daily Oklahoman* "Gay Night" article listed above. I searched in the tiny Bonnet Book and found the *exact* design. This positive identification still gives me chills and proves that Bonnie made hats for opening night. I feel certain Bonnie would not have had a seat for the event, but she would have sewn her heart and soul into those many ranch women's hats!

Chapter 21: Courtship

The Marshall Field announcement about Oklahoma territory salesman Charles Menees is from the *Daily Free Press* (Carbondale, Ill., October 6, 1910), page 3. Charlie's routes and schedules and dilemmas were researched, but his actual events are fiction. The entry, "A Grip, A Sample Case, and a Train ticket. A brief history of the American Traveling Salesman," at www.arenastage.org/the-music-man-history-of-the-traveling-salesman.shtml was particularly helpful.

Penny postcards had just come into existence during the time of this story, and I made them an ongoing element of the courtship. Four books were very helpful:

Roger Bell, *Images of America: Muskogee,* (Arcadia Press, 2011): 25. Cotton as primary crop.

Roger Bell and Jerry Hoffman, *Postcard History Series: Muskogee,* (Acadia Publishers, 2014): 9, 10. Depot

Hotel.

Jim Edwards and Hal Ottaway, *The Vanished Splendor* (Abalache Book Shop Publishing Co., 1982).11, Grand Ave., 16 Good Old days.

Jim Edwards, Mitchell Oliphant, and Hal Ottaway, *The Vanished Splendor III*, (Abalache Book Shop Publishing Co., 1985).425, 100 West Main, 435 Old Missouri Depot, 520 Red Rock Motel.

Willis' predictions about the airplane are from James Johnson's article, "Early Heroes Taking Wing to Brave Oklahoma Skies" (April 27, 1997), which can be found at the following webpage: www.newsok.com/article/2575608/.

In Virginia, Illinois, where Bonnie lived from 1915 until her death in 1994, she and Charlie owned a large white clapboard house at the edge of the town. The backyard was a wide one-acre vegetable garden bordered by Job's Creek. The only tree in the yard, just outside the kitchen window, was a native Oklahoma redbud tree, which Bonnie planted soon after she moved into the house. I did not remember the tree when I wrote the betrothal scene but was reminded of it later by Mary Kay Menees. For information about the Oklahoma redbud tree and its description and range see the following webpage: www.en.wikipedia.org/wiki/Cercis.

Chapter 22: Spooked!

Bonnie's traveling hat-making business was alluded to in Mary Kay Menees' "Little Trunk" Elder Hostel Report (1996) but embellished by me in the text. As a child, I witnessed Bonnie's way of interacting with hat clients in the Menees' Cash

Store in Virginia, Illinois.

The winds of Oklahoma are described at: www.climate. ok.gov/index.php/site/page/climate_of_Oklahoma.

I had a lively 2015 interview with Bradley Daral Olson of Olson Ranch in Bemidji, Minnesota, when he worked for the summer at the stables at Yosemite National Park. He imparted to me his love of ponies, the behaviors of his specific ponies, and how a pony would behave on a runaway chase. Additional information for this scene was provided by Pat Morgan of Morgan Carriage Works, referenced earlier.

Chapter 23: Muskogee Marriage

I spent several days in Muskogee, Oklahoma doing field research, since this is the city named on the marriage license (Muskogee County, State of Oklahoma, Marriage License, June 15, 1911). The wedding ceremony and Hyde Park visit were imagined. I dreamt about a park, and Nancy Calhoun, Supervisor, and Nancy Lasater at Muskogee Public Library Genealogy and Local History led me to several sources for Hyde Park. The undated Hyde Street trolley photo, "Muskogee Electric Traction Car No. 51," by Chandler Allison and Stephan D. Maguire, and the Bell and Hoffman *Postcard History Series: Muskogee,* "Hyde Park Photos" (pages 90–93) and "ME Church South" (page 78), were very helpful. Unfortunately, Hyde Park was torn down around 1922 due to the Great Depression.

Many other colorful scenes from Muskogee are derived from Roger Bell's *Images of America: Muskogee,* showing Graham Sykes (page 75), skyscrapers (page 49), Spaulding gin (page 25), and the Welcome to Muskogee sign (page 50).

The crocheted wedding dress is from the St. Clair (Illinois) Historical Society, shown to me by Ann and John Glover.

When I was in college, with no explanation Bonnie sent me her Muskogee wedding ring folded in a tissue. Today I wear it as my own wedding ring.

Chapter 24: Going Home

When I first started research for this book, my mother and I visited many locations in St. Louis. She took me to lunch at Llywelyn's Irish Pub in the West End. While eating lunch, I suddenly remembered the *only* letter in Bonnie's file, the letter from her father, Austin Spencer. I called my husband in California and asked him to retrieve the letter. He called me back and said the address on the envelope was 4926 McPherson, St. Louis, Missouri. After lunch, my mother and I walked back to our car. We were parked at 4926 McPherson! The house had a "For Sale" sign, and my mother knew the real estate agent. We contacted her, but she was unable to get us into the house. The rooms I describe in the book are based on another historic brick house I visited in St. Louis.

The actual letter from Austin Spencer, dated January 22, 1911, and addressed to Bonnie Spencer at 4926 McPherson, is very precious to me. It is because of the letter that Bonnie returns to St. Louis before going to Cobden. I do believe she would have been shocked by the letter.

The Robey family did start a restaurant, according to *U.S. City Directories 1822–1995*.

My brother Hardesty Charles Menees has the original photo of the wedding reception taken at the Cobden railroad depot. I also found an unlabeled reproduction of the photo in *A Pictorial History of Cobden, Illinois, 1857–2007*, edited by Charles A. Swedlung (2007). I have since sent the names of people in the photograph to the Union County Historical Society in Cobden, whose volunteers Pat Meller, Patrick Brumleve, and Molly Beckley were extremely helpful to me. I wrote the ending of the book to this photo.

Nancy Menees Hardesty
January 18, 2020

Historic Timeline

1831-1877	Trail of Tears (North American Indian Relocation to west of Mississippi River, mainly Oklahoma)
1848-1855	Gold rush in California
1859-1929	Orphan train children across America
1861-1865	American Civil War
1869	Golden Spike (trains across America)
1888	Blanche Estelle Spencer born, Oraville, Illinois
1894	Union Station, St. Louis, Missouri, opened
1902	Blanche is orphan train passenger, Oraville, Illinois to St. Louis, Missouri
1902	Blanche receives two tiny books, Dec 24, 1902
1904	1904 World's Fair at St. Louis, Missouri
1910	Oklahoma State Fair Opening Night Horse Show and Hat Show, Oct. 4, 1910. (Statehood, 1907)
1910	Oct. 6, 1910, Marshall Field & Co. announces Charles Menees to become an Oklahoma salesman

1911	Bonnie Spencer marries Charles Menees, June 15, 1911. (Muskogee County Marriage Record)
1911	Bonnie and Charles wedding reception, Cobden, Ill., July 2, 1911 (Menees family photograph)
2020	*The Bonnet Book* publication (118 years after Blanche receives the tiny books)

Photo Credits

Preface
Young adult Blanche Estelle Spencer
Source: Blanche Spencer Menees Family Archives

Chapter 4: Orphan Train
Wabash No. 573
Source: Museum of Transportation, St. Louis, Missouri
Photo: Nancy Menees Hardesty

Chapter 5: Union Station
Union Station Grand Hall, St. Louis, Missouri
Photo: Nancy Menees Hardesty

Chapter 11: 1904 World's Fair
Flower Map and Writing Room
Rosenthal-Sloan Millinery Co., St. Louis, Missouri
Source: Private collection of Dr. Susan Whitemountain

Chapter 13: The Bonnet Book
Bonnet Book diary, original page with three hat sketches
Diary of Blanche Spencer
Source: Blanche Spencer Menees Family Archives

Photo: BMI Imaging Systems, Sunnyvale, CA

Chapter 15: Cobden Color
The Millinery Shop, Cobden, Illinois
Credit: Elizabeth Bigler (Cerny), Claudia Messamore, The Millinery Story
Permission of Elizabeth Cerny Gibbs
Source: Union County Historical Society
Photo: Nancy Menees Hardesty

Phillips House Cobden, Illinois (sign)
Source: Mrs. Allie Jane Miller Davis, Cobden, Illinois
Photo: Nancy Menees Hardesty

Chapter 19: Ruby and Darling
Meadowbrook cart, copy of lithograph
Artist: Edward Penfield
Country Carts Series, No. 1
Pub: R.H. Russell, New York, 1900
Courtesy: Jill M. Ryder, Executive Director, The Carriage Association of America

Wooden hat supply trunk
Source: Blanche Spencer Menees Family Archives
Photo: Nancy Menees Hardesty

Chapter 20: Opening Night
Oklahoma City State Fair Race Track Grandstands, 1912
Source: State Fair poster 2013.133.059c
Century Chest Collection, 1913
Oklahoma City County Historical Society
Oklahoma City, Oklahoma

Maison Française newspaper ad
Source: *Daily Oklahoman,* Volume 11, issue 19 (Oklahoma City, July 3, 1910), p. 11, from American Antiquarian Society (2004)

Chapter 24: Going Home
Letter Envelope: Miss Blanche Spencer, Jan 28, 1911
Blanche Spencer Menees Family Archives
Photo: BMI Imaging Systems, Sunnyvale, CA

Austin Spencer letter, Jan 22, 1911, page 1
Source: Blanche Spencer Menees Family Archives
Photo: BMI Imaging Systems, Sunnyvale, CA

Spencer Menees wedding reception photo
Cobden, Illinois, 1911
Blanche Spencer Menees Family Archives
Source: Hardesty Charles Menees Collection

Blanche Spencer Menees actual silhouette, about age 70
Source: Blanche Spencer Menees Family Archives

Acknowledgements

Family

Without family members and their life skills this book would not have materialized: Blanche Estelle Spencer Menees, Charlie Menees, Mary Kay Menees, Marcia Menees Kessel, Hardy Menees, Robert Menees, Bonnie Kessel Gregg (namesake), Sarah Kessel, Annie Menees Goff, Vivian Parrish, John W. Parker, Evan Spencer Hardesty Parker, Cailin Parker, Sandy Creighton, David Creighton, Stephanie Creighton.

Research

My research team found and focused the lovely details of Bonnie's story. I am deeply grateful for the research and support of Dr. Susan Whitemountain throughout the development of this book, as well as the following: Will Whitney, BMI Imaging Systems, Linda Baker, Allie Jane Miller Davis, Joan Deuschle at Kirkwood Public Library, Lucille Findley, Jerry Frandeka at Frandeka Meat Market, Judy Friedman, Steven Grace, Karl Gross, Norma Lee Hackney, Lauren Humphreys, Raymond Magyar, Marilyn Meisenheimer, Pat Morgan at Morgan Carriage Works, Julia Morrill, Brad Olson, John Shontz at orphantrainrail@outlook.com, Cheryl Ranchino Trench.

I am also grateful to the following institutions:

Jackson County Historical Society (Murphysboro and Oraville): Sandra Holliday, Kenneth Cochran

Missouri History Museum, Jefferson Memorial, St. Louis, Missouri

Muskogee Public Libary Genealogy and Local History: Nancy Calhoun, Nancy Lasater

Oklahoma City County Historical Society: Brian Basore, William Welge, Veronica Redding

St. Clair County Historical Society (Belleville): Ann and John Glover

The Carriage Association of America, Jill M. Ryder, Executive Director

Three Rivers Museum, Muskogee, Oklahoma

Union County Historical Society (Cobden): Molly Beckley, Patrick Brumleve, Pat Meller

Upper Musselshell Historical Society (Harlowton, Montana): John Shontz

Editors

My editors nudged and pulled the concise story from my DNA. I am forever grateful to my editor and publisher Matthew Félix for his talented and firm guidance in all aspects of assembling *The Bonnet Book* for publication. Peter Kline helped me start the book and gave me months of encouragement. The contributions of other editors were invaluable: Cheryl Cooper, Howard Franklin, Jeannine Hammersley, Christian Kiefer, Julie Langhorne, Diane LeBow, Jill Mosher.

Readers
This group offered to read the book during production and provided needed historical clarifications and theme refinements: Alan Austin, Amit Garg, Debra Diaz, Mary De Yoe, Marge Fleming, Marie Tagle, Norma Vance.

Support Team
These people were the cheerleaders who pushed me forward with new ideas, food, and kind support: Karen Bartholomew, Peter Schlenzka, Meret Aeppli, David Benevento, Anne Goldstone, Klemens Vogel, Emily Ma, Julie McDonald, Meg Milani, Helen Thawley.

Unlimited gratitude to anyone else whom I have forgotten.

About the Author

Nancy Menees Hardesty was born in Jacksonville, Illinois and spent her childhood in St. Louis, Missouri. She moved to San Francisco, California in 1969 and practiced landscape architecture for twenty-three years. Nancy lives with her husband and remains close with her son and two foster sons.

Nancy spent six years researching and writing *The Bonnet Book*. She had various family journals and artifacts and the extensive help of her mother, Mary Kay Menees, who was the daughter-in-law of Bonnie Spencer. The tiny "Bonnet Book" of hat sketches and the wooden hat-supply trunk are still in the author's possession.

www.nancymeneeshardesty.com

Book Club Questions

1. What did Blanche learn from memorizing poems?

2. Was Blanche close to her mother? Her father? Discuss the dynamics.

3. Why did Austin Spencer send Blanche away? Why was he upset after she left?

4. Do you think the orphan train program was an effective way to give opportunities to young people?

5. What did the St. Louis 1904 World's Fair offer to Blanche?

6. Discuss the significance of hats in the story.

7. Try to figure out which hat graphics represent actual hats in the story.

8. What is the meaning of the ongoing book thread about "on the stage" and "behind the stage"?

9. Discuss some of the ways in which Blanche was ahead

of her times with her self-confidence?

10. Was it helpful for Blanche to have an adult mentor?

11. Did Blanche like small towns or big cities better? Why?

12. What role did trains play in Blanche's life?

13. Why did Blanche change her name to Bonnie?

14. What role did Ruby play in Bonnie's life?

15. How and why was Bonnie able to rise to the challenge of the hat-making marathon for the Oklahoma State Fair?

16. How different was young adult Bonnie from the small-town girl? What caused the changes?

17. Why did Charlie and Bonnie travel back to Illinois for a wedding reception?

CPSIA information can be obtained
at www.ICGtesting.com
Printed in the USA
BVHW040246140920
588711BV00011B/674